Co

Crusader

Book 14
in the
Anarchy Series
By

Griff Hosker

Published by Sword Books Ltd 2017

A CIP catalogue record for this title is available from the British Library.
Thanks to Simon Walpole for the Artwork and Design for Writers for the cover and logo. Thanks to Dave, Kent and Julie, three of my New Zealand readers, for giving me such an enjoyable time in the Antipodes.

Dedicated to two future princes: my grandsons Samuel and Thomas!

Prologue

Part One
Aqua Bella

The Pillars of Hercules 1146

We had been at sea for more than a week now. I was at the stern of my father's ship, ***'Adela'***, with William of Kingston, the captain. My men had their sea legs and our horses were settled. They were the positive points. It was crowded and smelly aboard the ship. I was not the greatest of sailors. I took the discomfort and smell as part of my penance. I had given up the manor of Ouistreham and now I as William of Stockton once more. I was the son of the Earl of Cleveland, Warlord of the North and the Empress' Champion. None of that meant very much now. I had left the service of my father and my lord, Geoffrey, Count of Anjou. I had failed as a knight. I had sinned and failed to be true to the oath I had taken in the chapel in Stockton. God had seen fit to punish me by inflicting a plague upon my wife, children and retainers. They were all dead and I was going to the Holy Land in an attempt to atone for my sins and to do penance by serving the cross and reclaiming the Holy Land for God.

My men had tried to cheer me up during the first days of the voyage, but my mood was still black. My father had tried to tell me that I was not conducting myself as a knight should and I had ignored him. I had been seduced by the behaviour of the Count of Anjou and his court. He philandered and had a constant stream of women and I had not emulated my father but the Count. I had paid a heavy price. It was another reason why I had left Normandy and Anjou. My father was fighting to regain Normandy and England for the Empress Maud and her son, Henry. If I had been there then I would have had a constant reminder of my mistakes. It was better that I be forgotten. I would not spend my life in the Holy Land. I would seek a sign that God had forgiven me and then I would return to England. I was not Norman. I was English born of an

English father and an English mother. I was, like my father, an English knight.

I turned to look at my men who were gambling on the deck. It passed the time. Two were playing chess others were gambling and carving bone. I had ten men with me. My squire, Tom son of Aelric, was playing chess with Robert of Mont St. Michel. He was my captain and had served with me the longest. Henri, Louis, Guy and Phillippe were my men at arms. They were Norman. My four archers, Garth of Sheffield, Walther of Derby, William of Lincoln and Ralph of Ely were all English. They had been trained by my father's Captain, Dick. That meant they were not only archers but skilled swordsmen. It was not a large retinue but it was mine. They were all oathsworn and loyal beyond belief. Each had chosen to come with me and I took that as both a compliment and an honour.

William said, quietly, "Lord."

"Yes, William?"

"We have a decision to make. Do we sail directly for Cyprus and the Holy Land or do we head for Italy and keep close to the coast?"

"I take it there is a reason behind your question." Even as I said it, I knew that I was being unnecessarily prickly.

"The direct route is quicker but, apart from Malta, it is a sea filled with Arab Dhows and Moorish pirates. We have but twenty men aboard to fight them off. It is not enough."

I smiled, "Then the coast would seem a better choice."

He seemed relieved. "In which case, we will head towards Genoa. We can buy supplies there. To the west is the land of the Arabs. Sometimes they can be hospitable but it is never certain. The Genoese are different; they are Christian and they like money!"

"Take us there."

As he put the rudder over the wind seemed to make us fly. I took it as a sign and I smiled.

Chapter 1

My father had offered to give me money to aid me in my quest. I could not accept his offer. I had let him down enough. He had never chastised me. Whatever we did would be by our own efforts. We passed the island of Corsica and then a storm came out of nowhere. It drove us northwest. We were heading away from Genoa. My men were not ones to sit by while others toiled. All eleven of us helped the crew. It was fortunate that we did. I am not certain that we would have survived. When the storm was over the sails were in tatters and we were exhausted. Worse was to come. Two of our precious horses had died during the storm. We found them when Robert and Tom went below decks to check how they had fared in the storm. We had to have horses.

"Captain, head for shore. We need to repair your ship and to buy more horses."

He nodded, "Reluctantly I must agree. I am not entirely certain of our position but we will head north and see what we can find."

He put Henri the Breton on the rudder and he fetched his charts. "Genoa is here, to the east. There is Nissa; that is Genoese and is a big port."

"Are we close?"

William looked at the sun and shook his head, "The storm blew us off course. I could not say with any certainty where we actually are."

"Then we head north and trust to God."

A few hours later land hove into view and we saw a line of small islands. William smiled as Henri said, "Those are the Lérins. We are forty miles west of Nissa. There is a port on the landward side. It is small but they may have what we need." He pointed to the bow; the storm had damaged the bow spit. We could still sail but, as the captain had explained, not as quickly as he would like.

In the distance, I saw two ports to the east and the west of the line of islands. I could see ships' masts. "Which port will you use?"

"I know neither of them, lord." He pointed to the one which lay further east. "That one has no castle. We will try there."

"You fear a castle?"

"Lord we are in neither England nor Normandy. Your father is a benevolent lord and treats strangers well but here? Better we avoid a place where we can be imprisoned for being foreign."

I suddenly realised that he was right. I had left a world which I knew and where I was known. I was heading for a land where none knew me and all were, potentially, my enemies. I went to Robert and Tom. "Better have the men don their mail. We may be going ashore."

Tom asked, "Are we in danger, lord?"

"We may be but it will do no harm to put on our mail in any case. It will show us if the voyage has harmed it."

The archers had an easier task. They wore just leather vests for armour. They would not need their bows which were left wrapped in sheepskin. If we took care with our mail they took twice that with their bows. My archers would be a weapon which might well surprise the Seljuqs if they chose to attack us. My men could send an arrow further than any other weapon. They used the long war bow. Trained from childhood, the archers had powerful arms and chests. They could release a dozen arrows in the time it took horses to charge them. Sixty arrows could bring down horses and pierce mail. My men at arms watched over the archers. They knew the value of their presence.

"Do we wear our surcoats, lord?"

Our surcoats protected our mail and showed who we were. We had a wolf device on the right of the chest, like my father. Since I had left him I had felt guilty about disgracing his name and his device. Robert knew this, hence the question. I shook my head, "We will, when time allows, have new surcoats made. We will also have new devices on our shields. This is a new start and a new beginning."

"Aye lord."

As we drew closer I saw that it had a stone sea wall to narrow the entrance. That was its only defence. The more westerly port had a citadel on a high piece of ground overlooking the port. This was a more workaday port. There were no merchant vessels. We would be the largest. The rest of the vessels were fishing boats. There were only a few of them. I saw, on a high piece of ground perhaps five miles or so away, was another citadel. It was just a tower and a wall but it showed that this area suffered raids.

"Will you find what you need here, captain?"

"It is timber and a little rope. We have a spare yard and a mast. I am certain they will have what we need. And we can replenish our water."

"Should I try to buy supplies?"

"We have salted meat but fresh bread and some fruit might be in order."

It would be good to go ashore. "Tom, I will go ashore with you and Robert. Garth, you and the others guard the ship. Keep weapons handy and a good watch."

"Aye lord."

We tied up and I stepped ashore. I had coins. My father had also given William a small chest to give to me when we were at sea. I think he knew I would have refused to take his charity. That was below decks. I was not certain how we would earn coin in the Holy Land. I prayed that, as we were doing God's work, he would provide.

"What is the name of this land, lord?" Tom or as we called him when he had made a mistake, Thomas, was a curious youth.

"We are in the Holy Roman Empire. This is Lombardy and Genoa is the most powerful city on this coast. She is a city-state. Her sailors are renowned. They carry the red cross on a white background. Pirates fear them. Or so the captain told me."

Tom was English. His father served my own and this was all new to him. He was a keen squire but, being the son of an archer, he had much to learn about the outside world.

"What language will they speak?"

I laughed, "Not English, that is for sure. They will understand my Norman I have no doubt."

We stepped ashore. It was not a large place. There was no city wall. It was close enough to the other port for the people to take refuge in case of a Seljuq or Berber attack. We had swords but we had left our helmets on the ship. We followed our noses to the bakery which was just fifty paces from the port. To get to it we passed the fishermen's stalls. There was little fish left. The ones who had recently returned from sea had sold most of it. Henri the Breton caught fish for us from the ship. We needed no fish.

We bought a large quantity of bread. I gave the baker's boy a copper coin to carry it to the ship and we headed to the market. We had arrived late and the best had been sold but we managed to buy some fruit, onions, beans and carrots. Once again I paid for them to be taken to the ship and we continued our search. There was little meat to be had. I bought a large amphora of the local wine. It was a pale red, almost pink in colour. They did not have much choice.

As we neared the ship I heard the sound of hooves. Eight men galloped up from the west. They were between us and the ship. Three of them wore mail and all carried a shield. The shields had four red stars on a yellow background. I said, quietly, "This may be danger. Keep close."

They all wore helmets but they were the open helmet without a nasal. The Lombards had similar weapons and armour to us but there were differences. I did not hurry. We had not yet been seen.

Garth and the archers were standing by the stern. All had the bows strung but they had them by their side. My four men at arms flanked William of Kingston.

As we approached, unseen, we heard the conversation "I am Robert of Nissa and my father is the Count of Provence! You are trespassing on his land!"

I saw William bow, "I am sorry, lord, we meant no offence. Our ship was damaged. We came here to repair it."

"That is not good enough. You are Normans by your dress and accent."

"English lord."

The warrior whose back was to me laughed, "It matters not what kind of dog you are, the Franks whether English or Norman are all the same."

Garth had an arrow ready in a flash and he said, "Do not insult us lord, or you will die!"

"How dare you threaten me! I will have you all in chains!" He drew his sword.

I stepped close to him, "I would advise you to sheathe your weapons, Robert of Nissa. If my man sends his arrow your way I guarantee that you will die."

He glared down at me, "And who are you that I should heed your words?"

"Just a pilgrim in God's service on his way to the Holy Land. We mean no harm and your conduct is not seemly for a knight." I turned, "Tom, Robert go aboard."

Robert of Nissa's sword came across my chest. I looked up at the knight. He was younger than I was. His armour was the scale type favoured by Lombards but he did not look like an experienced warrior. I did not want his blood on my hands. Using the back of my mail mittens I moved it out of the way. "Have a care young Lombard. I am being patient with you but if you do not move the sword then I cannot answer for my men."

"I am not afraid of a few Englishmen."

I shook my head, "Garth, show him!"

The arrow was well aimed, as I knew it would be. It passed before my face and over the sword. It hit the cantle and went through. It scored a line on the rump of his horse. The horse reared and the rider barely kept his seat. He was forced to move his sword and I had mine out in an instant and, as he brought his mount under control, I put the tip to his throat.

"Now sheathe your weapon and tell your men to sheathe theirs. If not then this will be a bloodbath!"

His face was effused with rage but he could do nothing. "Very well but I will remember this meeting!" He sheathed his sword.

"Good." I walked towards the ship and said, over my shoulder, "And I hope you learn something from this."

As I stepped aboard William said, "Cast off!"

I said, quietly, "Did you get what you needed?"

"Aye lord and we can repair while we sail. I am sorry about this. I promised your father I would keep you safe."

I walked with him to the stern, "Whatever happens on this voyage, William of Kingston, you will tell my father that it was an uneventful voyage."

"But what if he asks me to swear?"

"He will not William. I have caused him enough distress without having him worry about me. He is the hope of the Empress and her son. That is responsibility enough. Swear to me."

He smiled, "Aye lord, you are right. I will so swear."

We sailed east and headed for the Norman kingdom of Sicily and Apulia. There we would be more likely to find a welcome. Amalfi was a strongly held port. I could see how the Normans who had travelled there with Robert Guiscard had managed to secure an Empire. There were other ships bound for the Holy Land. It meant we paid higher prices there than we might have wished. We did not stop again until we reached the city of Constantinople. It was an exciting journey and we sailed through azure blue waters and tiny islands. It was a different world to the grey of the German Sea.

When we reached the capital of the Empire William took us to the Langa Harbour. It was close to the Forum of Acradius and the Forum of Bovis. Both would allow us to buy what we needed for the Holy Land but, as my father had told us, it was a quieter harbour. The great and the good used the Golden Horn. This harbour was further away from the Palace. I did not need to be where powerful men gathered to plot and to plan. I wanted my life to be as simple as possible so that I could atone.

There were just two other ships in the harbour. One was a Genoese and the other was a Norman from Syracuse. I left Henry to watch the ship with two of William's crew. The rest of us would go ashore. We knew that the prices in the County of Tripoli would be higher than here. We intended to spend a few days buying what we needed. We had to find two good horses to replace the ones we had lost.

There was law in the great city but there was also a good deal of bad feeling about the Franks. The Byzantines had had a war against them. My grandfather had fought in that war. For that reason, we left our helmets and mail on the ship. My archers left their bows. We were less pale than when we had left Normandy. I hoped we might pass for warriors of the Empire. Guy and William of Lincoln accompanied the captain. I did not think we would have trouble but it paid to be careful.

All that we were needed were horses. If I could buy four I would but two were a minimum. I did not have a warhorse. He had been one of the ones who had died. A powerful horse, he had broken his leg. I had wept when we had to slit his throat. I knew that the Byzantines used heavy cavalry called Kataphractoi. That meant they had to have horses big enough to carry them. The problem would be the high price to buy them. I could not see the Byzantines being happy to sell such beasts cheaply. My father had lived in Constantinople. Before we had parted he had given me as much information and help as he could. His old house had been sold. I believe he had spent the proceeds on me. Most of his old friends had moved on or died. There was, however, one constant, the Varangian Guard. Erre, Olaf Leatherneck and Sven the Rus had all served the Emperor. They had told me that my grandfather, Ridley of Coxwold, was still held in high esteem by the English Varangians. None were left alive who had served with him but tales of his deeds and those of my father's namesake were still a legend.

We made our way to the Forum of Constantine. I had no doubt that we would find it. The Forum was close to the Hippodrome and the Imperial Palace. Erre and my father had told me that the Varangians spent their leisure hours there; gambling and drinking. They drank a lot. Constantinople was a well laid out and planned city. We were less than five hundred paces away and we soon found it. We had passed through the Forum of Theodosius. That was a place of relative calm compared with our destination. It was noisy and it was lively. Erre had told me that the Varangian guard units did not get on with each other. The Rus and the Danish elements kept to their own areas. The Forum of Constantine was filled with loud, beer-drinking Englishmen. They did not speak Greek but English. Garth smiled as he heard the swearing.

"Ah, lord, I have missed this. It is like being in England!"

"Remember our purpose. We are here to find horses. No more."

"Yes lord, but we can have a drink, can't we? The beer ran out weeks ago!"

I reluctantly nodded. We headed into the maelstrom that was what the locals termed, the English market. As soon as we entered I heard familiar words and accents. Garth was right, it was like being home once more.

This was neither England nor Normandy. The drinking was outside beneath the shade of trees. Here there were no rustic hewn logs for seats. There were stone benches and tables. Although it was busy and there were many warriors, there was some space and we made our way to it. As we entered the square the noise subsided and we were viewed with suspicion. My archers had beards but my men at arms, like Tom and I, were clean-shaven. The Varangians sported plaited beards and long hair. One huge warrior stepped before me and hurled some Greek at me.

I had not understood a word and so I smiled and said, in English, "We have just arrived from England. Can you tell us where we can get a decent drink?"

As soon as I spoke English his face broke into a grin. "Of course!" He spread an expansive arm. "You have found it! I am Ralph of Bowness. You and your friends are seeking employment perhaps?" He waved over one of the slaves. "Beer for these weary travellers."

I shook my head, "I am on my way to the Holy Land. I am on a pilgrimage. I am William of Stockton."

One of the three men who were stood with Ralph said, "Do you know Erre or Sven the Rus? They went to Stockton."

"They are the captains of the garrison there. They serve my father."

The speaker said, "This must be the grandson of Ridley Akolouthos." I nodded. "His name is revered here in Miklagård. You are among friends here."

The beer arrived and we were toasted. They plied us with questions about Erre and the others. I felt guilty for it had been some time since I had even seen them. I discovered that they had achieved what most of the Guard dreamed of. They had made it back to England.

Ralph of Bowness said, "This heat, it is unnatural. A man tires of it after a time. He yearns for green fields and rain!"

His companion held up his beaker, "This is as piss compared with ale made in Kent!"

That began a debate about beer. Garth and my archers joined in. Robert and my Norman men at arms looked bemused by it all.

We ordered more beer and Ralph said, "This is a strange coincidence. Not long after Erre and the others left, when I was still a young man and an older warrior came from the land of the Scots to join us. He was the grandson of Aelfraed Akolouthos."

I shook my head, "How can that be? My father said that Aelfraed left his family when he joined the Guard."

"It seems his grandson, Morgan, heard of his grandfather and wished to copy him. He became a Viking and raided. Then he came down the river and joined the Guard. He was older than we normally accept but we had lost men in a recent war with the Pechengs and he was accepted. He was a good warrior but very solitary. He died six years since when we fought the Seljuq Turks. His body is buried in Anatolia."

One of his companions said, "Aye, he had a warrior's death. He fought like a berserker of old. The Emperor does not like that. We are expensive men. He does not like them wasted."

"He took ten Turks with him. That is all an Emperor can ask."

Ralph shook his head, "I wonder what happened to his wife and son."

I remembered some of the things that I had been told about these legendary warriors, "Erre told us that you looked after the families of the dead Varangians."

Ralph downed his beaker and waved for another, "We do but Morgan was a solitary man. None of us knew of his family until afterwards. The Akolouthos told us that he had had a son and a wife. The son would be fourteen summers old now. By the time we discovered he had been married, they had both disappeared. It did not sit well with us."

The sad memory made a silence descend upon us.

My captain said, "Lord, do we ask them about horses?"

"In time."

Ralph had heard Robert, "You seek horses?"

"Aye, two of ours died on the voyage and a knight needs a horse."

Ralph grinned, "They are not cheap; especially not the monsters that a knight in mail must ride."

"We have money for the right horse."

"Leave it with us. We will return tomorrow before noon. Now we must go for it is time for our duty with the Emperor. Manuel Komnenos is a good Emperor but he is a warrior and we must be on time. We will tell our brothers of your presence. This is a dangerous city. There are many cutthroats and murderers here."

Garth looked surprised, "I thought this would have been policed."

"It is, by us and the Danes. Where is your ship?"

"In Langa harbour."

"That is good. It is on our patrol. We will tell those who watch it to keep an eye out for you." He put a huge arm around Garth's shoulders, not an easy feat. "While you are here you are as our family."

The Forum began to thin out as they left. We bought more ale and more Varangians arrived. They nodded and greeted us. Ralph had kept his word. His companions would watch out for us. "Come let us seek the other purchases we need to make."

Garth asked, "First, lord, could we not buy a barrel of the ale. It is not as good as in England but it will do. You know that we drink wine reluctantly."

"Aye, but you shall carry it!"

We left to buy bolts of light cloth. My father had told me that the finest cloth was to be had in these markets and he was right. As the market was frequented by the English Varangians we found one who spoke English. It made life easier. We explained what we wanted. He nodded and brought out a bolt of dark blue material, "The Moors and those who live in the hot lands always choose a dark material for their clothes. They say it keeps them cooler. I have this or I have black. Perhaps a dark red?"

I shook my head. As soon as I had seen the dark blue I had known it was the colour I wished. My father's banner and surcoat, like ours, were a light blue. This matched my purpose. "This will do. Do you know someone who could turn it into surcoats for us; perhaps with a design embroidered upon it.?"

"Yes lord. My wife and daughters are seamstresses but it would take six or seven days, depending upon the design."

I realised that I had not thought of the device I would use. This was a new start and that required thought. "How many surcoats could they make from this bolt?"

"Not more than twenty lord."

"Then we will have two bolts and we will need twenty-two surcoats. That way I will have spare material for repairs. I will return tomorrow with the design."

"I will get my wife to measure you, lord."

I smiled, "As you can see, my archers are a little wider than we are. Perhaps two measurements."

"Of course."

When we had been measured, we agreed on a price and I paid. We headed back to the ship. By the time we had returned it was getting on to evening and William of Kingston's crew had lit a fire on the harbour wall and were cooking. I had begun to realise that one did not dwell inside if one could help it. Outside, by the water, it was cooler with the breeze from the sea making it more bearable.

While his men cooked, I strolled along the wall with William. "We may need to be here for another week."

"That is not a problem. I am negotiating for a cargo. When we have dropped you off then we will return here and fill up our holds. Five days would be better but your father put me at your disposal."

As I sat with my men we stared up at the skies. They were filled with stars. William said, "The clear skies help us to navigate." He pointed. "These are our charts. Look there." He pointed at one star, brighter than the rest, "That is the North Star. That guides us home."

"Then that will be on my new surcoat. One bright yellow star."

"Will you have a wolf, like your father and as you used to wear?"

"No, I need something else."

My men began to suggest animals. I laughed out loud when Tom suggested a boar. "I think Tom, that you forget who we fight and where we go. There will be no pork in the Holy Land for neither the Jews nor the Muslims eat it. The sight of a pig might inflame the Seljuqs more than we might wish."

Robert said, "Then make it a mythical beast. They have many in this land. Did you not notice the statues we passed? There is the Medusa, the Basilisk. We could have a dragon, a Manticore. There are many."

"That is a good thought. I will sleep on it."

That night I dreamed of winged creatures. They swooped down and plucked Seljuqs from battlements with their talons. I saw it as a sign that my device would have a winged creature. There were many to choose. My father had told me that my grandfather and those who had fought for the Emperor were superstitious. They believe in the fates. He had used the word *wyrd* a great deal. I would trust that I would see such a sign.

We headed back to the Forum and I saw Ralph. He was already drinking. "Ah, my young knight. I have found you some horses. You will have to travel beyond the city walls but I have you a pass." He handed over a piece of parchment with the seal of the Emperor upon it.

"Thank you. How can I repay your kindness?"

"To hear English voices and see folks from home is payment enough. Your grandfather and, later, Erre, escaped here with great success. They enjoy a life in England. When we have money enough and when we tire of the wars we shall go home. Your visit is a sign that this will be so."

I told him of our search for a mythical creature for our new surcoats. He nodded, "There is but one for you."

"Really? You know of one?"

"Your grandfather had his own personal banner. It is still here in the barracks. We keep it as a good luck charm. Men touch it before we go to war. It is the Gryphon. The head and legs of an eagle and the body of a lion." He pointed to Garth. "Your archers have the body of a lion and you and your horsemen are as swift as the eagle. It is the Gryphon which is your sign. I would have thought your father would have told you that."

"*Wyrd.*"

He laughed, "Aye! You are, truly, descended from a housecarl! We have the day off tomorrow. I will take you to the horse trader. We will come to your ship." He smiled, "It is good to speak English again. It has made me want to go home sooner rather than later."

"Until tomorrow then."

The seamstress was happy to incorporate my design. The yellow thread she would use to pick it out would stand out well against the dark blue background.

Chapter 2

I just took Tom and Garth with me the next day. Robert and the others had a wish to explore the city. Garth was keen to talk with Ralph. They had much in common. Ralph's companion was Aethelward. He was a younger warrior. Like Garth, he had come from England and made his way to the last refuge of the housecarls.

"It will take an hour or so to reach the farm. It is up the Lycus valley." The huge city was the biggest I had ever visited and it seemed to take an age just to reach the huge walls which encircled and protected the Byzantine city. As we left the home of my grandfather I had a chance to admire the Theodosian walls. They were enormous. I had never seen the like. No enemy could ever force them. It was not just one wall, it was three. The second higher than the first and the third higher still. With a ditch around it and a rocky terrain, an enemy would find it hard to bring siege towers close to the walls. The city spread a little way out of the walls. They were meaner dwellings and the people who lived there just eked out a living. A mile or two down the road and we saw fewer dwellings. We could see, on the higher ground, farms with a protective wall around them. Here the people might be prone to raids and self-protection was important. It was pleasant talking with Ralph and Aethelward. We learned much about the land we were to visit, the Holy Land. The Crusaders had created four counties. One, Edessa, had been recently attacked and its major fortress captured. However, they remained strong. As Garth told us they were a buffer against the Kurds and Seljuq Turks.

"There is the farm, on the top of that ridge."

The farm was the largest we had so far seen. As we walked up the road I saw horses grazing on the valley sides. There were men on horses guarding them. We entered a courtyard and were greeted by the owner. The Greek who owned the farm was lean and wiry. He was not a warrior. "This is Basil. He was a Champion Charioteer for the Greens." Ralph spread his arm around the farm. "This is a measure of his success. He got out while he could and when he had made his money."

Basil smiled, “And I owe much to Ralph here. He and his brothers protected me from the other teams. I do not forget old friends. He says you need horses?”

“We lost two on the voyage. We go to the Holy Land. I need two large enough to carry a knight in mail.”

“That is not a problem. I breed for the Imperial stables. Kataphractoi wear even more mail than you Franks. But I would suggest that you have two smaller horses too. Out here you ride a small horse more than your warhorse. Save your warhorse for battle. The heat is as great an enemy as the Seljuqs, Egyptians and Mamluks.”

“I am a novice in this land and I will heed the advice of a horse master.”

“Come, my best horses are inside. The ones you see grazing are not for you. We need horses trained for war.” The stables were remarkably cool. They were scrupulously clean and each had their own manger with food. Stable boys scurried around cleaning as we entered. Basil turned to appraise me, “Will you trust my judgement or would you like to choose for yourself?”

“You know your horses the best.”

“Thank you for the trust. I will try not to abuse it. You are a big man and not yet fully grown. I think you will broaden out a little more and a man puts on more weight as he grows older. Alciades here is fast but he is also strong. To be honest I need a buyer for him.”

“Why is there aught wrong with him?”

“No, lord. But he is a stallion and he fights with the other stallions. If I keep him I will have to geld him and that is not right.” He handed me the halter. “Here lead him and watch him walk. This will test if he is the horse for you. If he baulks then I will choose another.”

I pulled on the halter. Alciades was magnificent. He was jet black with two white socks and a white blaze. He came with me. I was aware that he was watching me. I stroked him between his ears and then put my mouth close to his head, “Will you be mine, you black beauty? Shall we war together and fight the heathen in the desert?”

He stamped his foot. The gesture seemed to please Basil. “You are a match. You love horses and he approves of you. It is good.” I handed the halter to the stable boy who waited close by. “Now the second. This one is slightly smaller and he is gelded. He is older but he is Alciades’ uncle. This is Leonidas.” This one was also black and had three white socks. “I take it this is for your squire?”

“Perhaps.” I looked at Tom and saw that he was eager. “However, Tom, perhaps you should speak with Leonidas and see if he approves.”

Leonidas was a calm horse. Tom stroked his mane, "I will learn Greek, Leonidas, if it will help. I will make sure that you are fed and watered well. I will share when we are in the desert." The horses nodded.

"Good and that just leaves the two, what do you call them, palfreys?"

"Aye, workday horses."

We went out of the stables to a pen. The horses there were being groomed. "Those two, the chestnuts with the three white socks; they are twins. Romulus and Remus. They are gelded and they get on well. You could not ask for better horses. They can carry you and will be perfect for the desert. Their dam came from Arabia."

"It is good; we shall buy."

Basil laughed, "I can see you are no Greek for you do not haggle."

"I trusted you with the horses and I will trust you with the price. I do not know the prices here but I think my friend Ralph does."

"You have a good attitude, Norman." We agreed on a price and he even threw in some saddles. They would allow us to ride them back to the city.

Aethelward was happy to walk beside us. "I am no horseman, lord. I am happy to walk."

Ralph waved a hand around the land through which we would travel. "I will take us a different way back. I would like you to see the Gate of Christ. And the Golden Gate. They are my two favourite entrances to the city."

The land rose and fell in folds. We were afforded glimpses of the sea and then olive and lemon groves. It was beautiful. We were not far from the city when we heard an altercation. We were travelling through a stand of trees and, at first, we could see nothing. When we emerged there were half a dozen riders, a cart with a broken wheel and a boy who was being whipped. The leader of the men was a mailed warrior. He had an open helmet. He was a Lombard. This was not our country but I did not like to see the boy being whipped by the cart driver. I saw that the boy had paler skin than most of the other people we saw. He was a Frank or an Angle.

Suddenly Ralph threw himself from his horse. "Leave that boy alone!" he did not speak in Greek for the Lombards spoke either Italian or French. Instead, he used French.

I said, "Garth!" Garth nodded and quickly strung his bow.

"Who are you to tell me what to do with my property?" The Lombard had understood for he spoke French too. I recognised the accent. It was the same as that of Robert of Nissa. I saw that he also had a yellow shield but he had just three red stars. They were related.

"I am a member of the Varangian Guard and that boy is the son of a Varangian."

The Lombard laughed, "He is mine now. I bought him and the whore of a mother that spawned him. I wasted my money with her for she died. I will not do the same with him. Be off."

Ralph drew his sword as did Aethelward. None of us had shields but they did and there were seven of them. Six mounted men and a cart driver. I slipped from my horse and handed the reins to Tom. "Keep watch." I drew my sword.

The Lombard turned and, along with the other six drew his sword. "There are but four of you and a boy. Put up your weapons and you may live."

Ralph did not stop moving. He was swinging his left hand even as he approached the cart driver, "And you are threatening one of the Emperor's Guards. The punishment is severe. Put up your weapons." He smashed the cart driver backhanded and the man's head cracked against the cart rendering him unconscious. Years of wielding a shield in battle had given Ralph a left arm that was like an oak.

"You wretch. Get him!"

One of the Lombards had a spear and he galloped at Ralph with his lance couched. There was a whoosh and he was plucked from his saddle by Garth's arrow. Another was ready instantly. The Lombard knight seemed to have noticed Garth for the first time.

I spoke, "And now the odds are more even. However, if you wish to save all of your lives then sheath your weapons. Garth here is not only accurate, but he is also fast."

The Lombard pointed his sword at me before he sheathed it, "I will remember your face, Frank! Guy of Èze does not forget such injuries. What is your name?"

"I am William of Stockton and I do not fear a man who has others do his dirty work. I will meet you, sword to sword at any time you choose. However, I should warn you that I have won many a tourney with my lord, the Count of Anjou. Do not say I did not warn you."

Ralph held his sword towards the Lombard. "And do not even think of coming to Constantinople! I will spread the word. My brothers do not forget an injury either." Aethelward had gone to stand before the boy so that they could not do him injury. Ralph turned to me, "Mount, lord. I would not turn my back on a snake such as this."

Garth said, "I could end all their lives now if you wish. The mail might fetch a pretty penny!"

The Lombard hissed, "Put Michael on the horse."

Leaving their dead companion, they threw the cart driver on the horse and galloped off. Ralph shook his head, "They went quickly enough."

The boy spoke for the first time. He spoke in English. "We should go quickly. The Count of Provence is his uncle and he is camped up the road. He had twenty knights with him. Sir Guy is an evil and vindictive man but his uncle is worse. They will return."

I put my arm down, "Come ride double. Aethelward, ride behind Garth."

We galloped the last mile and a half to the walls of Constantinople. We had more on our minds than the beauty and strength of the gates and I was grateful when we galloped through them.

We stopped only when we reached the ship. While the horses had their saddles taken from them and Tom fed and watered them Ralph spoke with the boy, "You are Alf son of Morgan are you not?"

He nodded, "How did you know?"

"You have your father's complexion and his hair. I saw him in you. When your father died, we tried to find you and your mother. We had money for her."

"When word came that my father had died my mother was beside herself. Her cousin said he would care for us but, instead, he sold us to that Lombard. We spent the last four years in Italy. My mother died. She was used. I will kill that knight for what he did to her."

"First, we must keep you safe." Ralph, for the first time since I had known him, looked apprehensive, almost worried.

I waved over Garth, "He looks like he needs food and his clothes are in tatters. Take him aboard and feed him and change him."

Alf heard me and he snapped, "I am not a baby! I can fend for myself."

Ralph rounded on him, "Did you forget manners when you were taken from the Guard? Your father taught you better. Address this knight as lord or I shall finish what the cart driver began!"

Garth put his arm around the boy's shoulders, "Come young Alf. You can tell me about this Lombard. If you are English then you will appreciate ale and we have a fine barrel in the hold." Mollified, Alf went with Garth but not before giving Ralph a venomous look.

Ralph laughed ruefully as the boy was taken below decks. "That is because his mother was a Pecheng! They are a volatile people." He shrugged, "They are good in bed, or so I have heard. Now the boy, what do we do about him?"

"Is there a problem?"

"We could give him the money we intended for his father; save that we spent it celebrating his death, but that Lombard will be back. If he serves a Count then I cannot keep him from the city."

"What about you?"

"I will take my chances, but the boy." He turned to face me. "Lord, this is *wyrd*. You are the grandson of Ridley and this is the great-grandson of Aelfraed. He cannot stay here and you need someone who can speak Greek for you." I looked to the ship. "And I can tell that you are a good man. Many men travel on Crusade for gold but for others, there is a higher purpose. You are one of those I think. And I believe you are a good man." He shrugged, "However, if you cannot then we will take him into the city and I will find one who can bring him up as a Greek."

"I did not say that, Ralph. It is a great responsibility."

"It is. If you save a life then you owe him a life. I do not ask lightly. He will be difficult. I can see he has an attitude and life with him will not be easy. Your companions are like oathsworn. You know each other and I am asking you to put a piece of grit beneath your mail. It will irritate."

I laughed, "And you know that I will take him."

"I do lord. You come from good stock. Let us see if you can save this youth."

There had never been a doubt. This was my chance to atone. I had lost my own son. Perhaps God had sent this boy to give me an opportunity to save him. Tom returned. He was a year or two older than Alf. "Tom, I think we will ask Alf if he wishes to come with us. He can serve us in some capacity but I need you to watch over him." He nodded. "He may be difficult. You will need patience."

"My father taught me patience and I know that I tried his. He would I had been an archer. I will do penance with this boy for my father."

Ralph nodded approvingly as Tom went aboard. "You have good people around you, lord."

"Aye, I have."

"A word of advice. Beware those you find in the Holy Land. Not all the evil men are Muslims. You will need to exercise sound judgement."

"I know."

When Alf returned, I saw that Garth had not only dressed and fed him, he had attempted to tame his unruly locks. The youth looked a little happier. Garth was much older than I was and he knew how to deal with the young. He would have made him laugh.

"Alf, I have spoken with Ralph. If you stay here in Constantinople you may be in danger from the Lombard knight."

"I fear no knight!"

I saw Ralph roll his eyes. This would be a challenge, "I know but there is a time to face that which threatens us and there would be little to be gained by staying here. The Lombard has men who serve him. You would die. Your father would not like that nor would his comrades. I have not known you long but I would not either." I hesitated and then spoke openly, "We are linked, Alf son of Morgan. Your father's grandfather and my grandfather came here together as housecarls. They fought for the Emperor. They were brothers in arms. My grandfather would wish us to be together. Would you come with us to the Holy Land?"

"You are the grandson of Ridley?" I nodded. I saw him take in the information and to reflect on his situation. "I would like to visit the Holy Land but would I be your slave?"

"You are free. You can leave me whenever you choose or you can become as my other men, oathsworn."

"Oathsworn?"

"You would swear to be my mine and I would take care of you."

He pointed to Ralph, "He is not one of your men, is he? The Varangians abandoned my father on the battlefield."

Ralph started forward, "We did not you…"

I held out my hand. "Your mother told you that."

"How did you know?"

"Often when people, especially women, are hurt, they lash out in all directions. Your father died bravely and his comrades could not save him. Your mother had to blame someone. Believe me, Alf son of Morgan, your father's comrades would have saved him had they been able."

Ralph approached the youth. "The knight is right Alf. What we will do is to kit you out so that you go to the Holy Land with mail, sword and shield. How is that?" He nodded. "Then when you are kitted out you will swear an oath."

"Why?"

"Because that is what your father would have done." It was a statement as though there would be no argument. "I will return in two days' time. Then I will take you and Sir William and we will go to the baths. Garth has made a good effort with the comb but I think you should be shorn. Let us make a new start eh?"

He smiled, "Aye and I am sorry for my harsh words."

"I have endured worse." He turned to me, "And keep a good watch for that Lombard. They are a sly and sneaky race."

I told my men when they returned and we all agreed to keep a good watch. William of Kingston had finished his business. The ship was repaired and fully provisioned. We just had the surcoats to pick up. Ralph returned, as promised with the lamellar armour, helmet and shield. It was a smaller shield than we used. The sword and spear were also shorter. However, he had found a Norman helmet, complete with nasal. He had smiled as he gave it to him. "This is the last of the ones that old Ridley and Aelfraed took from the Normans they defeated. I knew not why we had kept until now. Come you can try them on when I have taken you and your lord to the baths. This will be my gift." As we headed for the baths he said, "I am to leave the Guard after the next winter. I have served my time. Speaking with you has fanned the flames of my desire to return home. Besides, there may be work for my axe there."

My father had extolled the virtues of the baths and, after this visit, I understood why. The barber there trimmed my hair and beard and shaved Alf's head. We had found wildlife there and it seemed for the best. I was not certain how either our horses or my men would take the sweet-smelling perfume with which we were doused but Ralph had assured me that even the Varangians enjoyed the aroma.

On the way back we called in at the seamstress. To my relief, she had finished them all. I paid her the last instalment and the merchant's slaves carried them back for us.

Garth admired the surcoats, "So, lord, you will be leaving?"

"My captain is keen to deliver us. It will be winter by the time he reaches England and we both know that the waters there are not benign like these."

We had reached my ship. "Then this will be farewell. I had hoped for another drink. I enjoy the company of your men."

"If you get to England then look up my father. He is keen to hire such as you and Erre would give you a good welcome."

"Then I may. Farewell."

We boarded and I saw him trudge back towards the Forum. We had been lucky to have met him. I wondered if our luck would last. When William found that we could leave he was delighted and he prepared for sea immediately. We had to load the horses first therefore it was late afternoon when we left. As we did and passed through the harbour I spied a ship arriving. We passed close enough for me to see her colours and her passengers. I saw a yellow swallowtail flag with two red stars. It was the Lombards from Provence. Robert of Nissa was at the prow. He saw me as I saw him. We just stared. Had we remained but an hour longer then we would have met ashore. Blood would have been spilt. My luck lasted still.

The Holy Land 1146

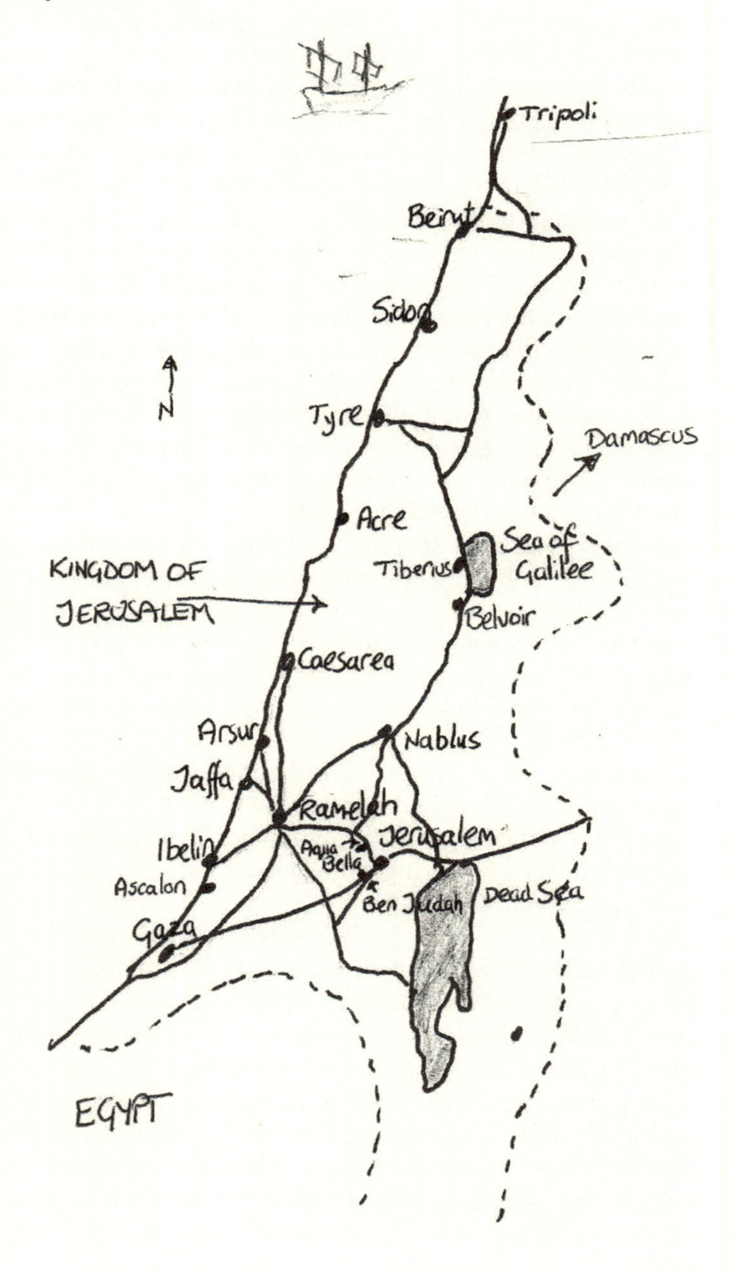

Chapter 3

While in Constantinople we had heard that the fortress of Edessa had finally fallen to Zangi. We had planned on landing close to Antioch. Now we decided to head for Tripoli. It was more secure. We sailed along the coast of Anatolia through the Greek islands. I took the opportunity to get to know Alf. It became apparent that when Alf and his mother had made their way in the world, he had been the strong one.

"Why did your mother take you away from the city? Your father's comrades would have helped you."

"I wanted to. I wished to be, like my father, a warrior. Mother thought that she would be enslaved again."

"She had been a slave?"

"Yes, lord. My father bought her and gave her freedom. She never liked the city. Her people were nomads who travelled the open lands. The city walls were like a prison for her."

"Then know that you may leave at any time you choose. I am here to do penance. I believe that I have begun to do so." He nodded. "Can you fight?"

"With a sword?"

"Yes."

"Not really. When the Lombards took me, they would not let me near a weapon. My father showed me how to hold a dagger for I was small when he went off to war." He took out a sling. "I can use this."

"Good. I will get my men to teach you how to use the sword and, perhaps the bow. You can ride?"

"A little." He sensed disappointment in my reaction. "I do not help you, do I lord?"

"We do not know yet. Your language skills are what I need most of all. You can speak Greek?"

"And Pecheng. I can understand some Arabic but I speak little of it. My Norman is good. But you speak it different to the Lombards."

"Tell me about them."

The Count is a cruel man. Guy of Èze is harmless in comparison. The Count would not have had me whipped. He would have had my hand taken instead."

"And what was he doing in Constantinople?"

"There is another crusade, lord. They plan to retake Edessa. That was what we were told. They are gathering the clan so that they can travel together. The Count intends to do as the Count of Anjou did. He wishes to steal himself a kingdom."

I clapped him on the back. "And already you have helped us. This knowledge is valuable. Now go and practice your sword work with Tom."

"But the deck is pitching so."

"If you can use a sword on a ship imagine how much easier it will be when you have solid earth beneath your feet."

The voyage passed quickly as we headed south. I spent more time talking with William of Kingston. "My father will worry. You must stop him doing so. I am a man grown and I can get myself out of any trouble that I find."

"I know, lord."

"I will not write. At least not for a while. I intend to become one of the knights who protect pilgrims. When I have done that I will decide what I must do."

"He is a lonely man."

"My father? Aye, he is. He misses mother. And he has dedicated his life to restoring the fortunes and title of the Empress. He had been the most loyal of subjects. I would that I had been as loyal. Know that I will return to England but I may come back as a white beard for I know not what God intends for me."

"Your father will miss you, lord."

Rather than brooding on my many mistakes, I organised the men to change the device on our shields. It occupied the time and stopped them from becoming bored. The changing of the colour was easy enough and once the dark blue was upon them all they matched our new surcoats. The star was easy too but it was the gryphon which proved more difficult. The seamstress had done a good job on the surcoats and none of us appeared to have the required skill to paint the Gryphon on the shield It was William's sailmaker who proved to have the skill. Nils of Bruges had had a mother who was a lacemaker. Although a sailmaker he had a good eye for detail. I paid him a silver piece for each shield and he did a good job. He painted the mythical beast and the yellow star upon them. What I did not have yet was a banner. I made do with a gonfanon. Nils made a swallow-tailed gonfanon for me from some of the spare cloth and we were ready to announce our arrival in the Holy Land.

When we passed Cyprus, I gathered my men in the well of the ship. We could all sit and both see and hear each other. "We are going to a new world. We have two purposes. First, we visit Jerusalem and visit Golgotha. We then seek a lord to serve and help to recover the Holy Land from the infidel."

Robert spoke, "When we explored Constantinople we heard that the leader of the Muslims is someone called Imad al-Din Ibn Qasim al-Dawla Zangi and his son is Nur al-Din. It is this Zangi who has captured the fortress of Edessa. He and his men attack from the northeast. The men we spoke to said that he was a cruel and clever man."

"Aye we do not yet know the identities of our enemies and I should warn you that not all the Christians that we meet will be trustworthy. This may well be like the war we have just left in Normandy and England."

Alf put up his hand. Garth smiled, "You do not need to put up your hand to speak, Alf. Our lord allows all men to speak."

"Thank you. The Lombards I served spoke of Edessa. I did not hear all of their talk but the Count seemed confident that he could gain power there."

Robert nodded, "We met many lords such as he when we fought for the Earl. They will lay with the enemy to get what they want. It is good that you have come into our midst, young Alf."

"It may be that the King of Jerusalem has need of us. We will see. That will be our first visit. Had we come three years ago then that might have been an easier task for the Count's father, Fulk, was king of Jerusalem. King Baldwin now rules with Fulk's Queen, Melisende."

Garth shook his head, "It appears we have left one melting pot only to fall into another. It seems strange to me that Count Fulk became king. Why did not his son come here to inherit his father's throne?"

"Because Queen Melisende was the daughter of the former king and it is Baldwin, her and Fulk's son, who is the heir. Count Geoffrey would have had to fight for his throne. Still, there may be some from Anjou who are still in the court. We will see."

We donned our new surcoats and the men had all polished both mail and helmets. When we arrived we wanted all to know that we were one company.

Tripoli had been captured over thirty-five years before and was a bastion of the Crusader counties. A massive citadel, as big as King William's huge donjon in London, dominated the hill which overlooked the port. The walls which encircled it were not as big as those of Constantinople but they were as big as any I had seen in England. The harbour itself was filled with ships. All were from the Christian countries. The lateen sailed ships were noticeable by their absence. It was as busy a port as I had seen.

William nudged us into a berth. Even as we were tying up a tanned sergeant with a maimed hand strode up and shouted to us, "Are you heading west?"

Henri the Breton recognised the French accent. He laughed, "Give us time to tie up, friend." He pointed to William, "This is the captain, William of Kingston. When we have unloaded our cargo then you may speak with him."

"Thank, you, I will return."

As we were secured to the dock William turned to me, "There may be even more profit in this."

"I hope so for you have performed a great service to me. I thank you."

"I serve your father, I serve you. Take care."

It took some time to bring up the horses and land them. They had been at sea for a long time. The time in Constantinople had helped but I knew we would not be able to leave until they had regained their legs. As well as our war horses and palfreys we had six sumpters to carry our armour, weapons and tents. Now that we had Alf we would need another. I still had coins left but soon it would run out. I needed the patronage of a lord or else we would starve. I would not turn to banditry as some had. I was here to do penance.

We had barely finished unloading when the sergeant returned with eight other warriors. All looked tanned. They were Crusaders. Their weapons showed signs of war. The sergeant spoke to me, "Is the captain a fair man, lord? None of us are rich but we would travel back home."

"He is a fair and honest man but I thought that all who returned from the Holy Land were rich men?"

"Perhaps the lords are, no offence, my lord but when your lord dies you seek employment where you can. Our masters were in Edessa and they fell. We are now no longer required. The good days here are gone and the Turks are on the rise. I have enough to return to France and, hopefully, find work there."

"Then God speed. The Captain sails to Constantinople to pick up cargo first. It will not be a swift voyage."

"It will be away from here and I will get to see green fields and feel a cool breeze. Thank you for your words, lord. You will not find many such as you here. This land changes a man. It does not just give him a dark skin, sometimes it gives him a dark heart."

The harbour was crowded and the animals were becoming skittish. "We will find somewhere quieter." I turned and shouted, "Farewell, William. Have a safe voyage."

"Take care, my lord. May God be with you."

We led our horses through the busy port until we found a road which was wider and easier to negotiate. I guessed that the middle of the city would be both busy and expensive. I turned to Alf. "We may need your language skills soon. Come with me. Robert, watch the horses."

There was an inn by the water. The fact that it was an inn told me that it was owned by Christians. I went inside. It was filled with a variety of men from sailors to warriors. I was the only lord and men nodded as I passed. From what the sergeant had told me I was their chance for employment. I went to the man who was pouring wine from a jar into beakers, "Tell me where a man may find stables and shelter for eleven men."

The man appraised my new surcoat and sword. He recognised me as a baron. "There is nothing inside the city, lord. Just beyond the walls, there are a couple. They will not be cheap but there will be stables. The merchants and their caravans use them. Head to the south gate and they are just beyond the walls."

I handed him a copper coin, "Thank you."

As we headed back Alf said, "Why did you give him the coin, lord? You had the information you needed."

"Who knows when we may need him again? We are in a strange country and I would have as many friends as I could get."

We did not get any strange looks as we led our horses through the streets. There were many armed Franks. This was the main port of entry to the Holy Land. Ascalon, which was closer to Jerusalem, was still held by the Egyptians. The first place we came to, once we were outside the walls, was full. There was a caravan of camels there but the second one, run by a one-armed Breton called Jean, had room for us. Despite the fact that he came from close to my home we were done no favours and the price was high.

"I am sorry, lord, but these are parlous times. I lost my arm when we took Jerusalem. My lord was generous and gave me enough money to buy this but the Turk is stronger now than he was. I have a wife and three children. I need to make enough money to take us back to Nantes."

"I understand. We will be here but two days to allow our horses to recover."

As we stabled them I noticed that there were five weary-looking horses. "To whom do these belong?"

"There are a group of sergeants. They leave tomorrow for home."

"Where are they now?"

"They sit in the shade of my lemon tree. It is a pleasant place to sit and the flies stay away."

I saw the six of them. Their surcoats had seen better days and the men were gaunt. Their weapons, however, were without rust. Two of them were sharpening them even as I approached. They saw that I was a lord and leapt to their feet.

I waved them down again, "I am William of Stockton and recently arrived from Normandy."

"I am Gilles of Valognes. I know Normandy. We go tomorrow to seek passage on a ship. We will have to work our passage."

"You are without coin?"

"Our lord died of the pestilence. It cost money to care for him. His squire died a day later. It has taken us a month to reach here."

I crossed myself for a disease had taken my family. I took out my purse, "I may be able to help you." I took out twelve silver coins. "Here are coins for your horses and here, "I took out a half gold piece, "is your passage back to Normandy. There is a ship in the harbour, the ***'Adela***'. She is captained by William of Kingston. He is a fair man and a friend of mine. He will take you home but you needs must hurry. He sails on the morrow."

The sergeant rose and said, "Lord, is there some trick? You pay us more than the horses are worth and you give us gold. Is this man a slaver and you would sell us into slavery?"

"You must have been ill-served in this land if you think so badly of me. Take the money anyway and find another ship. But you can trust William of Kingston. He carries some sergeants and men at arms already."

They looked at each other. One older man who looked thinner than the rest said, "I believe him, Gilles. He is new to this land and has yet to be tainted by it." He came and took the coins. "I thank you lord and beg that you look after the horses. They came from Normandy with us and have served us well."

"We will and God speed." I hesitated, "And Gilles of Valognes, if it gives you any more confidence in my word, I am the son of Alfraed the Earl of Cleveland and the Empress' Champion. I fought alongside King Henry and Geoffrey of Anjou."

All of them dropped to their knees. Gilles said, "Forgive me, lord! I would cut out my tongue for impugning your honour."

I smiled, "Perhaps I will not be tainted. Now hurry or you may miss the ship."

They all bowed as they passed. I wondered if I had made the right decision. Jean had watched me and heard my words. He said, "That was kindly done, lord. I will have my boy give the beasts some grain."

"Thank you, Jean." He was not as tainted by the land as he thought.

My men groomed the new horses. We would have to feed them up but they looked as though they had heart and that was what you needed in a horse. I did not want to leave our animals unguarded and so we arranged for five teams of two men to be on watch at all times. I put Alf with Garth as they seemed to get on. I went back into Tripoli with Robert and Tom to ascertain the position. We found an inn frequented by lords. There were even two Hospitallers there too. They kept to themselves. From the others, I learned that Pope Eugene III had urged European kings to come to the aid of the principality of Edessa. King Louis of France and King Conrad of Germany had heeded the call and were leading their armies even as we spoke. That explained the presence of the Count of Provence. The knights were waiting to seek positions in the armies. They were swords for hire. Each led, as I did, a small number of highly trained men.

As we walked back, in the late evening, Robert said, "How can we serve under King Louis when we were fighting him some weeks ago? Your father may be fighting him as we speak."

"It is something with which I shall have to wrestle. The decision can be delayed for a while. We have to travel to Jerusalem. Let us see what the King of Jerusalem has to offer."

The next morning, we groomed and attended to our horses. My men could act as a farrier if needs be. Surprisingly it was my archers who were the better at this skill. As Alciades and Leonidas had only had a short time on board the ship, Robert and I took them for a ride. I wanted to experience the conditions. After a mile of riding along the road, I realised that we could not travel as fast as we had in Normandy. It was too hot. Our horses were soon lathered in sweat. We were also hot but the surcoats helped us keep a little cooler. We took the horses along the scrubland. I found the going easier than I thought. The cobbled Roman Road was less forgiving than the soft sand and earth of the scrub. As we headed back I saw that we had learned a lesson.

That afternoon just after we had finished grooming our horses, a caravan approached through the gates of Tripoli. They had just reached us when they were overtaken by a column of Templars. I had heard of these. The Empress had granted them land in Essex and the Pope had recently passed his papal bull granting military privileges to the order. There were three knights and four sergeants. Their white surcoats just had a simple red cross over the heart. I waited for the caravan to pass for I wished to speak to these knights.

The leading knight slowed down as he approached the head of the caravan. The merchant spoke to the knight. I was close enough to hear them. They spoke in French. The old man took off the hood of his cloak in deference to the Templar, "Lord, I beg you to give us aid on our journey to the holy city of Jerusalem. Protect us from bandits!"

The knight was a young warrior. His helmet was hung on his cantle and he had a coif about his head. He laughed, "Help you, a Christ killer? Be thankful I do not slit your throats and take your goods. We protect Christian pilgrims and not Jews who murdered Christ. Out of my way!"

The rider spurred his horse and the seven of them galloped off. The old man put his hood back on his head. He saw me looking at him. I must have had a scowl on my face for he cowered a little as though expecting similar treatment from me. The scowl was for the Templar. I had been led to believe that they protected all travellers. Perhaps this was not so.

The old man said, "I meant no offence to the knights, lord."

I smiled, "I am sorry. I meant you no disrespect. Is there danger on the road to Jerusalem then?"

"Yes lord. There are Turks who would kill us. There are Franks who make a living preying on caravans and then there are the people who have always lived here and always attacked the caravans. Bandits have been here since before the time of Moses. Being a merchant is a hard job." I nodded and was about to turn when he said, "Lord, do you have men?"

"I do."

"If it would not cause offence, could we hire you and your men to accompany us to Jerusalem?"

"How do you know that I am not one of those Franks you fear?"

He smiled, "Your skin is still pale. You are new to this land and you speak to me with civility. It is a rare luxury."

I nodded, "As you say we are recently arrived and our horses need another day to recover. I would gladly escort you but not until tomorrow."

He nodded, happily, "To have you and your men escort me I will wait. We will camp yonder."

"Why not stay here? There is room."

"Lord you are new to this land. We are Jews. Everyone looks down on us. This might have been the land which God gave to my people but he has burdened us with Muslims and Christians who regard us as dirt beneath their feet. We will camp."

"Is it far we travel?"

"If you were a bird it is but two hundred miles. We are burdened with legs and it will be closer to over three hundred miles. It may take ten days."

I nodded, "I am William of Stockton."

"And I am David Ben Samuel. I am a merchant from Jerusalem."

Jean came over to speak with me when I returned to his mansio, "A word of advice, lord, the Jews are despised by all. Helping them will not bring you favour."

"I come to this land not to seek favour but penance."

"But it was the Jews who killed Christ."

I nodded, "I believe that Christ himself was a Jew." His face showed that he had not thought that argument through and he shrugged. I told my men of my decision. They were all happy with it.

William of Lincoln said, "At least we shall not get lost if we escort the old man home. And I have seen precious few trees. It will not be like travelling through Sherwood. We shall see our enemies!"

"I think, William, that this land may hold unpleasant surprises for us. Make sure you archers have a spare quiver on your horse."

"Aye lord."

My men were skilled fletchers but I was not certain if we would find the right fletch or the right arrow for them. What was certain was that we would need a blacksmith who could make the arrowheads we used. They were knight killers and could pierce mail. I had been told that the Seljuq Turks used mail.

We had to use the saddles which came with the new horses. In an ideal world, we would have used panniers but we improvised. We used them for the lightest things we had, the food and our spare clothes. The water and mail were put upon our own sumpters. Alciades and Leonidas were our only war horses. Louis would lead those by a halter. Before we went to bed I went over the arrangements for our caravan. "Garth and Ralph, you will be the scouts. William and Walter, you will be with the rear guard. Guy will lead the sumpters. Henri, you take the new horses."

Henri laughed, "I think new is too strong a word, lord."

The men all laughed too. "You are right but if we did not have them then think how much weight would need to be borne by our other horses. When we know the land and its people better we will hire servants to lead them. Robert, Tom, Philippe and Alf., we will flank the caravan."

They all nodded except for Alf who asked, "Could I not ride at the fore with Garth? We may meet Greeks with whom we have to speak."

I glanced at Garth who nodded. It would not hurt to have an extra pair of young eyes at the front. Alf was close to Garth. They seemed to get on well. "Very well but do not get into the habit of questioning my orders. Tom, we will unfurl the gonfanon tomorrow. We should let this new world know who we are."

As I prepared for bed that night I prayed to God for a sign that what I was doing met with his approval. I was in the Holy Land. I would soon be seeing the place where Christ died and where the most ancient of religions began. I did not sleep well and my sleep was haunted with dreams of my family. Once more they died in my arms and I was helpless. I could do nothing.

I was up early. I washed and broke fast. Jean's wife kept a good table and the freshly baked bread made me smile. As I stepped out it was still dark but I saw David Ben Samuel and his men already waiting for us. I could have struck myself. They would travel early while it was cool. They would rest during the heat of the noon sun and travel again after dark. He had been afraid to hurry us. He needed our protection.

I turned and went back to the inn. I roused my men, "Come. We work this day."

"But lord it is still dark!"

"Aye Walther and that means it is cool. Grab some food. We eat on the road."

I went and saddled Remus. He was a strong and placid horse. I had not ridden him yet but I was confident that he would be a good ride. Basil had been correct about the warhorses I knew he would be right about the other two. Once saddled I donned my mail and surcoat. Even though the sun had not risen I still felt the heat as I climbed upon my horse. Tom handed me my shield and I hung it from my cantle to drape over my left leg.

I rode over to the caravan, "You should have told us that you wished an early start."

He held his hands out apologetically, "This is our land and we know it. You and your men will need time to get used to it. It is coming to our winter now but the sun will still be too hot for you. We have learned to respect it."

I did not want us cosseting. "Do not change your schedule for us. We can ride as long and as far as you."

"Sadly, that is not true. We use camels and donkeys. They are slower than your horses but they can keep going longer than a horse."

"Let me be the judge of that."

"The sands are littered with the bones of Franks who thought they were back in France and tried to ride the same way."

My men began to arrive. I pointed them to their positions. "I have three men at the front. If you could send one of your men with them it would help."

"I will send my son, Saul, but he does not speak French. Nor does he speak English."

"Can he speak Greek?"

"Yes."

"Then Alf can converse with him."

I took off my helmet. I could now see why the Templar had not worn his. I hung it from my saddle and I lowered my coif. I saw that David Ben Samuel and the other men were all swathed in voluminous garments. They each had a hooded cloak. We had them too but they were in our bags. We only used those when we needed protection from the rain.

Seeing that they were ready I waved to Garth at the front and we set off. David Ben Samuel rode next to me. Already the light was grey and soon the sun would rise over the mountains to the east of us. "I would like to thank you again, lord, for this service. We did not agree on a price."

"No, we did not." I could see that I was not cut out for this. Basil's words came back to me. "Whatever you think is fair."

He laughed and I saw that while he was old, he had a grey beard, he had a twinkle in his eye and he had wit. "You are a strange Frank. I mean no offence but the ones I have met have been either greedy or arrogant or both and always cruel."

"Perhaps you have been unlucky."

"Perhaps but I think not." We rode in silence for a while, "I will pay you some of the price in advice, lord. You should use a hooded cloak to shield your head from the sun. The more layers a man has then the cooler he is. In this land, you respect the sun. We are lucky that we will be travelling, until Beirut, along the coastal road. It will be cooler. When we reach the Jordan valley you will feel heat like you have never felt before."

"Thank you. I know that we are novices but we will learn."

"You have a small number of men."

"Small in number but with the hearts of lions. I trust each one of them. They are good at what they do. And you, what is it that you do?"

"I am a merchant. I have ships and they sail to Constantinople. I use captains who are not Jews. It is easier for them to trade for me. The Franks who live in the Kingdom of Jerusalem still wish for many of the things they can only buy in the west. They may dislike me, curse me, kick me and spit on me but they need my services. I charge them a healthy fee and I smile."

"You live in Jerusalem?"

"I have a home just to the east of the city. It is close enough for us to be able to visit the bazaar and yet far enough away so that we are not disturbed when there is trouble. There are many of my tribe who live there. We are close enough to the castles that we have protection and yet we are not bothered by those who call us Christ Killers, like the Templar."

"Is there much trouble?"

"Occasionally a new Frank who has recently arrived will decide that Jews should be made an example of. It does not last long but I would keep my family safe."

"You have a family?"

His face darkened. "I have a wife, two daughters and three sons. God has been kind to me." He hesitated, as though he was going to say something and then thought better of it.

I smiled, "Speak, you will not offend me."

"I was curious about you and your story. We have a long journey. If you could I would like to hear your story."

The sun had now risen and already I could see a heat haze to the east. I sighed. This would be a long journey. I told him the story. I told of my father and grandfather. By the time I had finished, we had reached a village and we were ready to rest. I, for one, needed it. My head felt as though it was going to boil and, when I saw the others I saw that they had the red faces of freshly boiled crabs. After we had watered our horses and placed them in the shade of the trees which had been planted to give shade I said, "Tom, break out the cloaks. We will need them. It will stop us burning."

"Are you sure lord?"

"I am certain. When we reach Jerusalem, we shall buy the thinner ones such as the Jews wear."

David Ben Samuel handed me a gourd of water, "You are learning lord. There is hope for you."

Chapter 4

There were castles guarding the pilgrim route. The caravans had used the same route for hundreds of years already. David Ben Samuel apologized to us. He told us that we could have found shelter there because we were Franks. He, as a Jew, was barred. We camped. The cloaks helped us but we all suffered from the heat.

On the third night out of Tripoli, we camped by a spring and a stand of date trees. Sheep were grazing on the rocky slopes above us. It was our loneliest night yet. We had passed the mighty castle of Botron and the next one we would pass would be Gibelet, just north of Beirut. It was there we would turn east to head down the Jordan Valley. As usual, we camped after dark. We had a routine. My men hobbled the horses and then two of them would guard the caravan along with two of Ben Samuel's men. I would also do a duty. The caravan master was surprised at this but, as I explained to him if my men lost sleep then so would I.

I did not mind as it was difficult to sleep. The heat and the insects, not to mention the spiders and snakes made for an uncomfortable night at best. I shared a duty with Tom. Since the arrival of Alf, he had grown up a little more. He was older than Alf. Hitherto he had been the youngest of my men Now he had someone to teach and that changed him. Neither of us wore our helmets and our coifs hung down our backs. Tom had tried to talk with me but my mind was filled with the conversation I had had with David; I was distracted. The merchant had told me that in the next few days we would be passing close to the lands of the Seljuq Turk and the bandits. I was working out how best to defend against them. The land might not have trees as did Sherwood but the rocks and clefts afforded the perfect places to ambush us.

It was that reflective quiet which allowed me to hear the skitter of stones from the rocks above us. It could have been an animal but I knew that it was not. I slid my sword from my scabbard and turned so that my back faced the fire and I could peer into the dark. My dark blue cloak effectively hid me and I remained as still as could be. I smelled them. I had grown used to the smell of the men of the caravan, they smelled of camel. I knew the smell of my own men but this smell was the smell of sweat, stale beer and animal fat. These were Franks and they were unwashed. I saw two of them as they crept and slid down the rocks towards the horses. Now that I had spied them I could shout, "To arms! To arms!"

I was pulling back my arm as I strode towards the two of them. I had taken them by surprise and the slippery stone prevented them from stopping themselves. They had no mail and I swung my sword sideways. It hacked into the arm and then the side of one of them. The other found himself falling and he hurled himself at me. I stepped to my right and punched at him as he came towards me. My mail mitten knocked him to the ground and I pulled back my sword to stab him through the neck. Tom had managed to slay another. My men arrived as did David with torches. My archers sent their arrows towards the men who were seen in the light of the burning torches.

I turned, "Is anyone injured?"

No one answered.

"Garth, take your archers. Recover the arrows and check for any more enemies."

I turned to Tom. "You did well."

"How did you see them, lord? Until you shouted I had seen nothing and was dreaming of my bed." The merchant looked astounded.

"I smelled them and they made a noise. We were lucky. We must make a better camp next time."

David Ben Samuel smiled and gave a slight bow, "God sent you to us, lord. I will sleep easier at night from now on."

The men had little on them although we took their weapons and their few coins. My men covered their bodies with rocks and a better watch was kept for the rest of the night. "They look to have been soldiers once lord. They had the vestiges of surcoats but their weapons were neither sharp nor cared for. These were carrion."

Robert's voice was filled with disdain for these men who had fallen so far as to become bandits.

The road east led to Baalbek. This was a mighty fortress held by the Turks. It was less than thirty miles from our caravan route. In addition, there were many high places from which bandits and rogue Franks could attack. We had already met some and were now warier. Accordingly, I had us ride closer together. Here, where there was little rain, my archers could keep their bows strung and they carried them across their cantles. The attack the night before had made us all more alert. Even so, we were still surprised by attackers who appeared from nowhere.

A rider appeared from nowhere. He sat atop his horse two hundred paces from us on a rock which overlooked the road. He was a Seljuq horse archer. He had a horn bow. His armour was lamellar. His horse's tail was knotted and he carried a javelin. On his head, he wore no helmet but his long hair was held in a circlet of metal. He wore earrings and his horse furniture was ornate. This was the first Seljuq Turk I had seen and I wondered what it meant.

He shouted something in his own language. David turned to me, "He said if we hand over our horses and goods then we will all live."

I said, "Speak loudly so that my men can hear and understand." He nodded. "Garth, ready an arrow but do not aim it yet."

"Aye lord."

"Can you see others?"

"I can hear their horses. They are hidden behind him in the rocks."

I glanced to the right. There were no rocks there, just scrub and I could not see anyone. They were to our left. Robert led the men on the right. "Be ready to follow my lead, Robert and Tom."

The merchant was nervous, "What do I tell him? He waits."

"Tell him we wish no trouble but we will not give up our horses."

The Jew shouted something. Even as the Turk started to lift his bow Garth's arrow had hit him in the chest. At two hundred paces the Turk had thought himself safe. He was not.

"Ride! Robert and Tom, with me."

I held my spear overhand and I kicked Remus in the flanks. I hung my shield from my shoulder. My left side was safe from arrows. Remus scrambled up the slope. I saw more horse archers appear. Walther and William's arrows, sent over my head, struck two while Ralph and Garth hit another two. It bought time for us to close with them. The three of us knew the skill of our archers and we trusted them to miss us. The horse archers had miscalculated. They were used to crossbows and the poorer bows other Franks used. My men were from England. Only the Welsh came close to their skill and power. I rode Remus at the archer who pulled back his horn bow. I did not hesitate. I hurled the spear from ten feet. It impaled him and I drew my sword.

There had been twenty archers for I saw fourteen or so before me. Robert and Tom were as reckless as I was and they had both found flesh. When Garth and Ralph followed us and sent their arrows after them the horse archers turned and fled. Ralph was eager to get after them. I yelled, "Halt!" but it was too late. Three of them turned in their saddles and sent arrows towards Ralph. He was lucky although his horse was not. Two arrows hit it and Ralph was spilt from the saddle. Garth's last arrow managed to hit one of the Turkish horses in the rump but it did not stop.

I galloped to Ralph who rose unsteadily to his feet, "Sorry lord! How did they do that?"

Garth had arrived and he picked up a discarded bow from one of the dead. "It is shorter."

I remembered a conversation with the Varangians in the inn, "And they are trained to do so from childhood. Next time heed my words." The Turkish horses had fled. "Take your saddle and unload one of the sumpters. Robert, search the bodies. They look to have jewels about them."

One of the caravan guards had an arrow in his leg and was being tended to. "I am sorry about that, David Ben Samuel. We will keep a better watch next time."

He laughed, "Next time? You have driven off the deadliest horse archers in the land. I thought our time had come."

As I retrieved my spear I asked, "Will we see them again?"

He shook his head. "We have hurt them. They are here for profit. I fear that next time they will bring more men. We might have to use the coast route next time."

"Is it longer?"

"Just more expensive. The knights who guard that road with their castles demand payment for travel through their domains. The Templars do not pay but they escort only Christians. Those who are not Christian are forced to use this more hazardous route. We will need to move more swiftly."

"That suits us."

We left the Turks where they lay. My men butchered the dead horse. Archers were not squeamish about eating horsemeat. We ate well that night.

We were now used to travelling early. I was glad we had agreed to escort this caravan. We were leaning much about the land and the people. The horse archers had both shocked and surprised my men. Garth had gathered all the arrows, theirs and ours. Their arrows were longer. My archers could use them but they would need to be desperate to do so. The horse archers skills releasing backwards over a horse had unsettled them. Ralph, in particular, brooded about it.

"Lord, two out of three arrows hit my horse. They were riding away and uphill yet they hit my mount. Had they hit me then I would be dead too."

Walther looked on the brighter side, "They yielded treasure. They wear gold about them. I can see now why men stay here. It is not for the heat, it is for the riches."

"And yet, Walther, the men we have seen who were leaving were as poor as church mice. Think on that."

I nodded, "Aye, Robert, but the ones we did not see were the knights. If they charge a toll for the use of their roads then it is the lords who are rich. Their men, from what we have seen, pick up the crumbs."

We had one more run in with life-threatening danger before we reached Jerusalem. We had passed the Sea of Galilee. My men had been in awe of the tiny stretch of water. The priests at home had mentioned that as a place where Christ and his saints had fished. It was where Jesus had lived. When we halted there to rest they had all filled their water skins as though it was holy water. Alf had said, "Lord, Christ walked upon this water."

Perhaps it was the fact that they were all distracted that we almost fell foul of an ambush by bandits. The Jordan Valley was narrow and there were trees. It was almost verdant. Remus warned us of danger. Now that we rode closer together I was just five camel lengths from the front and Remus whinnied. I had learned from my father not to ignore animals. I hefted my shield and shouted, "Ware, danger!" A stone clanged off my shield. A heartbeat later and it would have struck my head. Then there was a rattle and cracks as stones hit metal and wood. It sounded like hailstone on a wooden roof. Horses, camels and men were hit.

Alf showed he had his wits about him. He saw whence the stone had come and kicked his horse on. Garth and Ralph had their bows ready too. I lowered my spear and kicked Remus towards the stand of olive trees to my left. Their twisting, tangled and ancient branches hid the bandits well but I spied a flash of white and I rode towards it. I aimed Remus between the thin and straggly branches. We battered our way through. I pulled back my arm and speared the bandit in his back as he turned to flee. Wheeling right, I saw the line of ten or so bandits. Arrows began to blossom from them as my four archers wreaked revenge.

Alf was clinging to his saddle but he managed to spear one of them before he lost his balance and fell to the ground. He had enough sense to hang on to his long reins. Two of the bandits saw their chance and they turned to finish off the youth. An arrow hit one in the shoulder and he turned to stumble away. The second whipped out a wickedly curved knife. He raised it to stab Alf when Tom' spear struck his chest. The blow was powerful and, aided by his galloping horse, the bandit was raised from his feet. He was dead. Tom reined in and lowered his spear. The bandit's body slipped to the ground, his blood staining the dried ground red.

The bandits had fled and I yelled, "Hold! Tom see to Alf." I did not need to tell my archers what to do. They recovered their arrows. Every head they recovered meant it would be longer before we needed a blacksmith. Robert checked the bandits to see that they were not feigning death.

I reined in next to Alf. "That was bravely done but Tom must teach you better skills. A horseman who cannot stay in his saddle will not last long on the battlefield."

"Aye lord."

Some of the camels and horses needed attention as the stones had wounded some of them. One of the camel drivers had lost an eye. David and the rest of his men seemed philosophical about it. "He can still work and had you not been with us then the bandits would have killed more of us and taken some of our camels and our goods. We regard this as an occupational hazard."

The rest of the journey was uneventful. I began to see the problems which lay in this land. There were few roads. The land through which these Roman Roads passed was rarely flat and afforded cover to an enemy who might wish to ambush. David told me that this was the greenest and most densely populated part of his land.

"Then why is it not better protected? I would have expected a castle." Belvoir, just south of the Sea of Galilee, had been enormous and imposing and Baysan had been imposing but, apart from Nablus we had not seen a defence for thirty miles. We had been within thirty miles of Jerusalem when we were attacked.

David pointed east. "There is a line of castles there but they defend against incursions. The King of Jerusalem and his knights fear the Turk more than bandits. We should be safe now, lord. We will go directly to my home. It is outside the city. When you have rested, I will take you to the city."

The next morning was our last on the road and we left the cobbled Roman Road to take a well-worn and more ancient caravan track to David's home. I saw Jerusalem in the distance. The heat haze made it difficult to pick out features but the wall which ran around it showed that it was imposing. It was a citadel. Just before noon, when we would normally have stopped, David pointed ahead. "There is my home. We are close enough now to ride in the heat. My home is cool."

I saw that he had a walled farm on a hill. It was not a castle. There were no towers but I saw that he had a wall and a solid gate. More than that I saw sunlight reflect upon the spears and helmets of the men guarding it. "You have armed guards?"

"Eight of them."

I turned and looked at the caravan. He only had four guards and the rest were camel and donkey drivers. "Then why do they not guard your caravan?"

He gave me a sad smile, "This represents money. I can replace it. The men I leave at home guard something more valuable than gold, my family."

He was right of course. As we neared his home I saw that the walls were mud walls. David pointed out salient features. "This has been here since the time of King David, my namesake. The mud walls follow a natural line of rocks. God has seen fit to give us a foundation on which to build. It means we cannot be undermined. We have a well which never runs dry. This is safe a place as a Jew can find in this land."

My warrior's eye took it in. "Why do you not have a ditch?"

"It is solid rock beneath. If the King of Jerusalem decided that he wanted me gone then a ditch would not stop Franks with their war machines. If Imad al-Din Ibn Qasim al- Dawla Zangi came south then he would take it as easily as a man brushes a fly from his cloak. This deters bandits and knights who think they can abuse my family." His voice was bitter.

Something in his voice told me that this was not a casual comment, "That has happened?"

He nodded. I saw him looking at my face to determine if he should speak. He sighed, "Two years since. In those days, I trusted to the King of Jerusalem to control his knights. The King was ill and the Queen had yet to exercise her power. I was away and an Angevin knight, Guillaume de Waller, came and attacked my home. I had just two old retainers in those days and they died. My sons were with me, else they might have died with the other men. My daughters and my wife were…" he shook his head. "I will not speak of it save to say that Rebekah, my eldest, she was just fourteen summers old, was left with a child. God was kind and it died. My daughter's heart was first broken and then, when she recovered, hardened. She lives in Caesarea with my sister. When I am away two of my sons guard our home. This will not happen again. If this Angevin comes again he will die. It may cost us our lives but we will not suffer at his hands again."

"That does not sound like the act of a knight. We are taught to respect women."

"Sadly, my lord, many of the knights who come here regard us as little better than animals and to be used as such. That is why you have been something of a revelation to me."

We passed through the gates and the mud walls. I was amazed by the beauty of the home which the merchant had built. It was made of faced stone and painted white. Olive and lemon trees gave shade and shelter from the sun. There was a cool pool of water which was fed from the spring. I could see why this had been chosen; it was blessed with both a well and a spring. Slaves and servants hurried from within to see to our needs.

David pointed to the eastern side of the house. "There are ample stables over there. Your horses need the shade more than the camels. Isaac, show these Franks the stables."

A wizened dwarf of a man knuckled his head and said, "Yes master."

I saw two strapping men emerge and embrace Saul. David beamed, "These are my other two sons, David and Benjamin." They both bowed although their faces showed a scowl. "This is Sir William of Stockton and he and his men were my protectors. They are to be treated as friends. They are not the de Wallers."

Their expressions changed.

"I do not blame you for your attitude towards Franks but, perhaps my men and I may change your opinion."

We were taken inside to a hall where it was cool. An older woman and one who looked to be little older than Alf bowed. "This is my wife, Ruth, and my youngest daughter, Mary. The girl looked terrified when she saw my helmet in my hand and my surcoat.

Saul said, "Mary, these are friends. They are not the ones who hurt you."

I looked at David, "But she is little more than a child!"

He nodded, sadly, "I know."

I knelt before her, "I apologise for what those who were supposed to be knights did to you. I can assure you that we will protect you and your mother with our lives. We are true warriors and not animals."

She smiled, "Thank you, lord."

Ruth said, "I will have a room made ready for you. There will be water for you." Her eyes went to my mail. "You will not need steel while you are in our home, lord."

A slave awaited me in my room and he helped me, in the absence of Tom to disrobe. The water was perfumed and the slave was a skilled man. He was Greek and he helped to wash and shave me. He oiled my hair and combed my beard. Without water on the road, I had allowed it to grow. I donned a tunic. I felt civilised for the first time since leaving Normandy.

"Your men said they would be happy in the guard's quarters. There is water there and they will be cared for."

"Good but I shall go and speak with them, if I may."

David shook his head, "For a lord, you seem to have an inordinate amount of thought for those who serve you."

"As I said on the road, they are oathsworn. They are more like brothers than followers." I shrugged. "I am like my father and I cannot change."

"It was not a criticism, lord."

He was right and my men were happy. They had got to know some of the men on the road and there was a bond. It was often thus. Men who had fought together liked to talk of their shared experiences.

The food was not what I expected but I had never eaten Jewish food. There was fish; a kind I had never seen and there was chicken but it was neither cooked nor flavoured in a familiar way. Finally, we had a lamb. I discovered that it was a celebration for a successful journey. It emerged, during the meal, that we had managed to help the merchant to bring more goods safely home than he normally did.

After the meal, we sat outside where a fire, fed with aromatic wood, kept the insects away and we drank cooled wine. "Your payment, lord. Do you still wish me to decide on the amount?"

"I have seen nothing to change my mind. You are a fair man."

He took out a purse of coins. "Then I give you a choice. This purse or a tenth of the profits from the trades tomorrow."

I saw his sons as they smiled at the offer. They knew the best choice to make. I knew he was testing me. "The tenth of the profits will be adequate."

"You are a wise man for they will far exceed the purse. And I will give you introductions to those in Jerusalem who can be trusted. I have, however, no influence at the palace. I am a Jew."

"That will suffice and if you need me or my men again then we are at your service."

"I may well do that. My daughter, Rebekah needs to be escorted from Caesarea. It will not be for a month or two and I will pay you handsomely."

"You do not go to Tripoli again?"

"My ships will spend the winter in the north. We have kin in Amalfi and Pisa as well as Venice. They will have our ships repaired and then begin to gather the trade goods. We make the journey twice a year."

It was a pleasant evening chatting with a hard-working family. It made me miss Stockton. I had been seduced by the life at the court of Geoffrey of Anjou. I had become one of his courtiers. Hunting, wenching and drinking; they were what had seemed important. I had turned my back on my father and England. It was only now, many thousands of miles from home, that I could see it clearly. Had I gone back to Stockton then my wife and family would still be alive. The disease would not have struck there. I could be fighting alongside my father. I knew he had the Earl of

Gloucester but I had served with the Earl and he was not as resolute or as honourable as my father.

"Could I ask a favour of you?"

"Of course."

"I have no doubt that stabling will be expensive in Jerusalem and our warhorses are a temptation. Could I leave our better horses here? I know they would be protected."

"Of course." He laughed, "For a moment I thought you were going to ask a real favour rather than a courtesy."

We also left our winter clothes, spare weapons and arrows. We would not need them. We escorted the caravan to the city of Jerusalem. If Constantinople was old then this was ancient. You could see layers of the city as we entered St. Stephen's gate. The walls through which we passed were new. They had been built by Fulk and his predecessors. Then we passed the Roman walls and finally, as we passed David's Tower and the citadel, we saw the Jewish walls built before Solomon. It was awe-inspiring. Like Constantinople, it was a maelstrom of humanity. All colours and creeds jostled and bumped shoulders. However, the only ones who were mounted on horses and wearing mail were the Franks.

We had been allowed through the gate firstly because we were Franks and secondly because we were with David. While we rode, within the walls, he walked and he and his men bowed their heads when they spied knights, sergeants or men at arms. I saw the three main holy orders: Templars, Hospitallers and Teutons. This was their city and it showed in the way they walked. He was heading to the main market or, as they termed it here, the bazaar. He had asked me to stay with him until he had sold his goods and I did not mind. It would allow us to see the people of the city and the centre itself. He was our guide.

His arrival had been anticipated and I smiled at what was, patently, a bidding war for his goods. I did not understand the words but I knew that they were bidding. He had told me that he had, at one time, sold his goods himself. However, that did not result in such great profits. There were robbers in the city not to mention those who lived on their wits and stole what they could find. This system allowed him to sleep easily at night and make much coin. I saw the piles of gold mounting up. Benjamin had come into the city with Saul and the two of them had swords at the ready. It was not needed for the sight of seven mailed men and four tough-looking archers was more than enough to deter any would-be thieves.

By noon, when the market quietened down, we had sold all of our goods. David sent his men and their animals back to his home. He, his sons and four of his guards remained. He divided the money and gave me a chest with my tenth. It was a fortune. "This is too much. We did little enough."

He smiled, "You would break your word? You said a tenth would suffice."

"You know what I mean."

"I am happy. My sons are happy and when you give money to your men, as I know you will then they shall be happy. My sons will take the money to our home and I will stay here with you. Jacob shall be my bodyguard. I will take you and introduce you to people. It will save you being robbed." He shrugged, "My people must live and it is the foreigners who now have all the money."

Rather than riding through the crowded streets, we walked. "You will want somewhere to stay. This will not be cheap but, until you have found a lord to sponsor you it will have to do."

He took us down a circuitous route through back streets and alleys. There was a double door. He knocked and a hatch opened so that he could be seen. When he was recognised the double doors opened and I was amazed. It was a huge courtyard and there were stables. From the outside, it had looked like a tenement. The owner came out. He too was of the tribe of Judah, David Ben Samuel's tribe. "This is my friend."

"A Frank?" There was surprise on his face and in his voice.

I smiled, "An Englishman but I can understand how you were confused."

"He needs rooms for the eleven of them and stables for their horses."

"I can accommodate them."

"At a fair price, Jacob."

The owner looked at David and he smiled. He nodded, "At a fair price. We shall starve but it will be fair." He waved over one of his slaves. He rattled something off and then said, "The boy will look after your horses for you. He is good with animals."

David Ben Samuel said, "I will take them around the city. We will return before dark."

"That would be wise. At night time the rats come from their holes. The unwary can fall victim to their knives."

He took us to all the people who might be useful, including a banker. It was not a concept with which I was familiar but the Jews had a system to move money around. I was assured by David that, if I deposited my money with his friend Simon he could arrange for me to be paid in York or indeed, anywhere in Europe. There was a fee but it seemed reasonable. I did not wish to carry the chest of money around with me, it was a temptation and so, after giving my men some coins for their purses, I kept enough for what I thought I would need. Two-thirds of the coins remained with Simon.

As we left I asked, "How does it work? I am not questioning the honesty of your friend but I cannot see how it works."

"When you leave Palestine then Simon will give you a piece of paper which has the amount you are owed. He will give you a list of our brothers in England, or Normandy. You present yourself and the paper to any one of them and you will receive your coins."

"Does that mean Simon will have to send that money to England then?"

"No for the system works both ways. There will be men who travel here and do not wish to carry money with them. This is a safer system."

This was a whole new world to me. He next took us to a man who would make cloaks for us, a bootmaker, a blacksmith and an armourer. Finally, he took us to somewhere we could buy food and wine. He looked up at the sky. "It is time we were getting home. It is not far but sunset comes soon and tomorrow is the Sabbath. Your horses will be safe at my home and if you find no sponsor and wish to have cheaper accommodation then my home is open to you. And I will need for you to fetch my daughter in four months if that arrangement is still agreeable."

"It is." I shook his hand, as was their way, and said, "Thank you, David Ben Samuel. We have helped each other and become, I hope, friends, may your god go with you."

He smiled sadly, "It is the same God but a different belief."

He turned and left. After ordering new dark blue hooded cloaks to be made we went to eat and then retired to our new accommodation We had heard the streets of Jerusalem could be dangerous for those who did not know its ways. When we reached our lodgings, we discovered that there was a roof garden. We had a jug of wine and we sat looking at the stars, discussing the day and planning our next move.

"Tomorrow I will go with Tom and Robert to see if we can visit with the King of Jerusalem. We need employment while we are here. I want the rest of you to find out how to get to Golgotha. We have come a long way. It will do our souls and our quest good to pray where our Lord died."

"Amen, lord."

Chapter 5

I made sure that we were all groomed and presentable. We mounted our horses and rode to the palace. There were, as I would have expected, guards at the gates. We halted and I waited for the inevitable questions.

"What business do you have at the palace?"

I had worked out my answer before he had asked it. "I am a knight of Anjou. My name is William of Stockton. My father is the Earl of Cleveland. I served as a captain of war to Geoffrey Count of Anjou. I would like an audience with his half-brother, King Baldwin." It was a tenuous introduction and I saw the man at arms frown. However, I had mentioned the name of the Count of Anjou and that could not be ignored. Leaving his three companions to watch us he hurried inside. Surprisingly we were not kept waiting for long. I had expected to be fried by the sun and for us to be left thinking our audience would be refused.

"You may enter. Leave your horses just inside the main gate. There is shade and there is water. I will show you the way."

We followed the guard. I noticed that he had a flat-topped helmet with a nasal. He did not wear mail but a padded gambeson which was studded with metal plates. It looked light but I was not sure if it would be effective in battle. Perhaps he was just a palace guard. He was there to stop the unwelcome rather than the dangerous. The road climbed through the palace. The whole edifice was higher than the city. Like David's home, the inside of the building was cool. We took off our helmets and carried them. I pushed the coif from my head. Pleasant aromas wafted through the courtyard. It had been cleverly designed so that the breezes passed through lemon and orange trees. As we walked we brushed by rosemary and lavender. There were fountains, the sound of which made you feel cool.

He led us through a court which was filled with the great and the good of Jerusalem. There were Templars and Hospitallers. There were merchants. Our guard said, "If you would leave your men here, lord. The King and Queen Melisende would see you alone."

Tom and Robert would enjoy waiting. Servants were serving sweetmeats and beakers of drinks. They would relish the luxury. I was led through a curtain into a small chamber. I saw King Baldwin III and his mother, Queen Melisende. She was a stunning woman. Her name was ranked along with Empress Maud. She was a powerful woman. She had been married to two kings of Jerusalem and was now Regent for her son Baldwin. Baldwin was just sixteen years old but, as I learned, he had inherited most of his skills and attributes from his mother. He was no one's fool. They were each seated on a Roman-style couch. There was a stool before the two of them. I bowed and Baldwin gestured to the stool. I sat and immediately felt foolish. I think that was the intent.

An older knight was there. He spoke first, "I am Theobald of Rheims. I served Count Fulk and fought against King Henry." I thought, for a moment, that I was unwelcome. He smiled, "Your father is an honourable knight. I never fought him but others that did so speak well of him. I look forward to speaking with you." He left.

Melisende spoke first. She had a deeper voice than I expected and her violet eyes seemed to penetrate through your skin and into your heart. I felt exposed as she spoke and yet her words and her face were both soft and gentle. "Theobald said that we ought to see you. We have heard of your father. Many say he is the greatest knight in Christendom."

It was phrased so that I would supply an answer. "He would not say so."

"Would you?"

I smiled, "He is my father and, in my view, the greatest man yet to be born. I expect his majesty feels the same way about his father."

The look they exchanged showed me that he did not. "You are both modest. You yourself, lord, are not without skills and abilities."

"It does not do for a knight to boast of his deeds. It is better to let his deeds do the speaking for him."

"And yours do," Baldwin spoke. Like his mother, he had a naturally deep voice. For some reason, I expected a piping high pitched one. "We may seem isolated up here on the hill but we hear much of what goes on in the bazaar. We are a small kingdom. You came to the aid of the merchant David Ben Samuel. You fought off Frankish brigands, bandits and Seljuq horse archers. You did all that and lost but one horse. Remarkable."

He was well informed! "I am served by good men."

"Ten I believe."

I looked at the Queen, "Yes your majesty." They were highly knowledgeable about us.

"This is a dangerous land. Many come here thinking that they can make a fortune and go home rich men. And what would you have of us?"

It was blunt and I was not quite ready for it. I had expected to be kept waiting for days. "I ... er."

She smiled, "You do not hesitate to charge up a hill and try to run down the most dangerous of enemies and yet you quail before a widow. Strange."

"I am sorry. I have come to the Holy Land to do penance. I wish to serve. I am here to ask King Baldwin if he has a quest I can be given."

"And if not?"

"Then I will help the pilgrims and travellers. I will protect them from all enemies."

"All?" The Queen's eyes bored into me.

"The bandits, the Turks," I hesitated, "And those Christians who also prey on the weak."

I expected censure but they both smiled, "A true knight. You must be like your father. As my mother said this is a dangerous land. There are many Christians who do not act as they should act."

Queen Melisende leaned forward, "You know that Imad al-Din Ibn Qasim al- Dawla Zangi has died?" I shook my head. "He was stabbed by one of his slaves, a Frank called Yarankash." She shook her head. It seems Imad al-Din Ibn Qasim al- Dawla Zangi was over fond of his servant. This means that there will be a new leader of the Turks. The fact that a Frank has killed their leader may well inflame them even more. We have lost the city of Edessa. It makes our position more dangerous."

"I am still uncertain what you wish of me."

"We wish you to serve us. When war comes, we would have you lead men to defend our borders. "

"You know that one day I will return home?"

Baldwin smiled and looked older than his years for it was a sad smile, "I do. And I understand." He looked at his mother. "We have more news we should tell you for it may well affect your decision. If you serve us then it would be until our lands are safer than they are now. When the port of Ascalon is in our hands then we would be happy for you to leave."

"I would do that."

"Then I should tell you that we have news that Robert, Earl of Gloucester has died. It was natural causes, so they say." I felt as though I had been slapped. My father's greatest ally was dead. He was alone and fighting for the Empress without me at his side.

The Queen said, "If you wish to return to your father we would understand. In the short time, you have been with us we have seen the love you bear for him and that is something precious."

I had had time to think. I shook my head, "I came here to do penance. I will stay. I will be your sword."

Baldwin rang a bell and an official came in with a box. "Thank you, Paul." He handed it to the king and left. King Baldwin opened it. He took out a chain from which hung a miniature shield. It had one large cross and four smaller ones engraved upon it.

"This is your seal of office. For the time being, we would have you protect the pilgrims who use the road from Jaffa to Jerusalem. Next month you will ride to Jaffa and escort an emissary from the Emperor Manuel Komnenos. You will bring him here secretly. You must reach Jaffa by the feast of Theophany and await the arrival of the Byzantine ship."

I nodded, "Your majesties, I am honoured and touched by your confidences but what if I were a spy? I could be a traitor."

The Queen shook her head, "You do not understand. We knew you were on your way before you arrived." She held up a piece of papyrus. "This came from the Emperor. You are named within it. If the Emperor trusts you then who are we to dispute it?"

"But I never met him."

There was a pause and Baldwin said, "But your father met and served his father. And you are your father's son. It is your name which precedes you and we were asked to look for the sign of the Gryphon. The mythical beast is well chosen; the heart of a lion and the speed of an eagle."

His mother smiled, "And a creature, which they say, lays golden eggs. That bodes well for you. Your manor, while you live here, is on the road to Jaffa. It is called Aqua Bella. You will be William of Aqua Bella."

I left in a daze. We were not to be quartered in the palace. We would not be wearing royal livery and no one outside the King and his mother would know of our connection. An estate on the road from Jerusalem was ours. There were servants there already. The lord and his wife had died childless and the King had inherited the estate. It had a tower we could defend and there was a curtain wall. Everything appeared to have been planned before we even arrived. Even as we had been travelling down the Jordan Valley we had been expected. While I had been wondering what we would do, it had been decided. My father had spoken of fighting for an Emperor. I shook my head. Were we all connected by a giant spider's web. I had with me a letter. It was a legal document to allow me to take over the manor of Aqua Bella. People might wonder why a young Angevin knight had been given such an estate but as I would not be visiting the palace again for a month or two it would soon become yesterday's news.

Robert and Tom knew me well enough not to disturb my silence. We rode back to the lodgings and I told Jacob that we would be leaving the next day. He accepted it without comment. While we waited for the others to return I gave Tom and Robert a shorter version of what I had been told. I left out the part about the Emperor's emissary. As far as my men were concerned we would just be keeping the road clear. The others returned in high spirits. They had enjoyed their day in Jerusalem. With money in their purses, they could enjoy life.

"Tomorrow we move outside of the city. And then we begin to watch out for pilgrims. The King of Jerusalem has asked us to guard all who use his road."

We called in at David's home to pick up our horses. I told him about our new home. He nodded, "That was the home of Odo and his wife Berthilde. We passed it on the way here. Odo was an olive grower. He made fine olive oil. He had good vines too. It is a good home. It is built into the rock of the valley. You will find it cosy." He smiled. "We are neighbours. It is but six miles from here. When my ships sail from Jaffa I use the port but Jaffa is smaller than Tripoli and…" Shaking his head he said, "It is not for me to say. If the King of Jerusalem has entrusted you with keeping the road clear then it may not be a problem."

"A problem?"

Sighing he led me into a small room filled with papers. It was his office. He closed the door. "There is a castle at Ramelah. It is the home of Guillaume de Waller. It is a mighty fortress and he taxes those who use the road. It is the crossroads. Not only the road from Jaffa to Jerusalem passes through it but the one from Nablus to Iblehin and Gaza. It is the most powerful castle outside of Jerusalem. The king only holds two domains: Nablus and Jerusalem. That is why the King needs you to watch the route. To avoid passing the castle most traders use an old caravan trail which passes through empty land. The section between Shilat and Ginaton; it is littered with the bones of traders who did not pay the de Wallers. Beware. This may be a poisoned chalice. It was the route we took. Do you not remember the wild track we took?" I nodded.

With that information in my head, we rode, laden towards Jaffa on the coast. I confided in Robert as we went. I did not tell him of the emissary but I did speak of the de Wallers.

"You have the king's seal. Surely that will afford us protection."

"I think that if the king's seal would make the road safe he would have done so before now. No, he has chosen me and since I have spoken with David Ben Samuel I have been wracking my brains. I have heard the name Waller before."

"I have never heard it."

"It was before your time with me. It was in a story my father told me as a child but I must have been inattentive or the story meant little. Whatever it was I have forgotten."

Eight miles from Jerusalem's walls, the manor of Aqua Bella was not on the road. A track led to what was, in effect, a fortified manor house. It was built into the cliff. The hillsides were covered in olive trees. I saw men and women at work as we approached. The curtain wall was not high but the gate looked substantial. There was an armed man at the gate and he looked up nervously as we approached. I saw him shout over his shoulder and a grey-bearded man hurried from the second gate which lay before the house.

By the time we reached the gate, he stood with the single guard. I dismounted. We no longer rode with either helmet or coif. We had learned that they were for war. I pushed back the hood and took out both the seal and the document.

"I am William of Stockton, now William of Aqua Bella. King Baldwin has given me this manor."

The old man bowed, "It is good that Aqua Bella will have a lord once more. I am Francis and I oversee the estate." He smiled, "We make good olive oil."

I shook my head, "I am not here to grow olives or to grow fat on them. The king has asked me to keep the road safe. We will be spending more time on the road than in this house."

"It will suit you, lord. Come."

He led us through the second gate and we found ourselves in a courtyard. My men dismounted and they looked for stables. We could see none. There were four large doors leading off from the courtyard. Francis pointed to the one furthest from us, "That one leads to the accommodation." He opened the middle of the other three, "Follow me." We stepped into a cool chamber. A slave hurried to Francis with a burning brand and when he lit the brand in the sconce on the wall he illuminated a huge barrel-vaulted chamber which had been hewn into the rock. I now saw where they had acquired the stone for the substantial house. "This is the stables. Slaves will remove the dung each day." He smiled, his teeth gleaming in the light of the brand. "So many horses will help us make the olive crop be even better."

"Robert, see to the horses."

"Aye lord."

I put my arm around the overseer and led him out in the courtyard. "How many men are there in the house? I need to know for our security."

"There are four guards. They take it in turn to watch the gate. There is Absalom, he commands those who press the olives. We have two men who are responsible for the storage and delivery of the oil. Then there are twenty slaves: eight men and twelve women."

"They are contented slaves?"

He knew what I meant. Many overseers abused the slaves making them dangerous.

He smiled, "The lord here was a kind man. We do not use the whip. Many of the slaves have lived here for twenty years. It is the only home they have known. We do not work them over hard and we feed them well. This is a rich manor."

"You have a family?"

"I have a wife and Absalom is my wife's brother. He has a wife and two children. Both girls."

We had reached the door to the house and when he opened it I saw that it was richly furnished. Tapestries hung from the walls. The wood of the furniture was cedar and there were oil lamps. There were no openings on the ground floor to allow in light. An attacker would struggle to take it.

"Do you have trouble from bandits and the like?"

"Occasionally we have a shipment of oil stolen. They do not raid every caravan." He looked nervously at me and I knew he was keeping something from me. I would find out what in due course. First I had to explore my new home.

"From now on you lose none. We have to patrol this road. When next you go to Jerusalem then the men of William of Aqua Bella will guard you." I had a sudden thought. "Are there any women here who can sew?"

He nodded, "Aye lord."

"Then I will get them cloth. I would have two banners made with my device upon them. One will fly from the roof. I want all to know that this manor is my home." I smiled at him. "There may only be eleven of us but, believe me, we are warriors all."

He nodded. I saw him take a deep breath. The secret he had kept from me was now about to be divulged, "Lord, it is not the bandits who cause us the most trouble. My lord Odo had to appeal to the old King to ask him to intervene when the Lord of Ramelah demanded half of our olive oil. Since my lord and his wife died we have had to give half of our oil to him."

"Guillaume de Waller."

"Aye lord."

"That stops now. You deal with the accounts?"

"I do, lord."

"When time allows, I would go through them with you." I saw his expression. "Do not fear. I am not here to bleed the manor dry. I will take coin for my men but I would have you make life better for those who live within these walls. I would have a contented manor. We will be on the road and I would wish this to be a safe and secure home for all of us."

"As you wish."

That evening we ate together with those who lived in the house. Odo had a large room, almost a hall, in which he could entertain. I did not think that either Francis or Absalom would wish to eat with my men and me every night but I wanted us to get to know each other. Absalom was a little older than me and he had two girls who were on the cusp of womanhood. It was a harmonious meal. There were six bedrooms for us. I had the old lord's and it was on the upper floor. Robert, Tom and Henri shared the room next to me.

Before we retired my men and I went to the roof. It had a single entrance and there was a small tower just the height of a man. Potted lemon trees and olive trees would give shade during the day. It looked a pleasant place. It would accommodate two men. Garth nodded his approval. "Archers in there would make this a hard place to take."

"This whole manor is perfect, Garth. Tomorrow we ride to Jaffa. It is thirty miles. We leave before dawn and we will return in the late afternoon. I would see if we can patrol it in one day. We rest for a day and then I will return to Jerusalem. I would hire more sergeants to guard this when we are gone. The four men who are here are watchmen and not guards."

Robert nodded, "What I do not understand, lord, is why we have been granted this manor?"

I smiled enigmatically, "All will be revealed in time, just trust me for now."

We were up before dawn. Francis' wife, Alice, prepared us a fine meal and we set off before the sun had risen so that we would be on the road as early as possible. As we headed first west and then north I had time to reflect on the harsh landscape and on the reasons we had been chosen. Were we sacrificial lambs? We had no allegiances to any in this land. If we all perished then King Baldwin would have lost nothing. The Emperor had suggested us because of my father; that I could understand but how did he know of me? The only reason I came up with was the Count of Provence and Robert of Nissa. Had they gone to the Emperor to complain that I had taken Alf? Ralph of Bowness had suggested that might be so. A fast Byzantine ship could easily have reached this land before our slow cog. What was certain was that I did not have enough men. I had been given a manor which would allow me to hire more men but would I choose wisely? Some of my decisions, in the past, had been less than wise. This was part of my penance.

When we reached Shilat I spied the trail which led through the scrubland. I remembered it from our journey south. I had thought it a mean little village then. It was dotted with both rocks and scrubby trees which would afford cover. We rode in a single file with Garth at the fore and Robert at the back. I rode behind Alf and Ralph who followed Garth. Tom carried my gonfanon. This first day was as much as about us marking our territory as anything else.

The sun had soon begun to burn. It was not as fierce as it had been on our journey south but it was still hotter even than Anjou. Although we wore dark cloaks I still felt the burning sun. I had my cloak spread around Remus' haunches to give him some shade but when I touched his head with my bare hand I felt the heat. He swished his head as we moved to create a draught with his mane. My mail mittens hung from my hands. I did not need the extra heat the hot metal would generate. Our time with David Ben Samuel had taught us how to eke out our water and yet keep ourselves alert. It worked for Garth held up his hand and made the sign for danger. I nudged Remus to join him.

"Lord, I hear the sound of metal on metal and the cries of battle."

I donned my coif and helmet and put my mittens on my hands. I turned as I picked up my shield, "Tom, bring the men forward." With Garth and Ralph behind us, Tom and I led my small column of men up the rise. When we reached the top, I saw a small caravan of ten camels and eight donkeys. They were being attacked by Seljuq bandits. I held my spear overhand as I spurred Remus. The sand and soil on the trail deadened the sound of our hooves and the bandits were too eager to slaughter the camel drivers and guards to keep a watch. The remaining guards were bravely defending their charges.

Garth and my archers had stopped and dismounted. They were a hundred and fifty paces from the fray on the top of the hill. I saw that Garth had Alf holding the horses. The four archers picked out four bandits and each was struck by a white fletched arrow. The ones who saw their comrades fall looked around. They saw us but by then I was less than fifty feet from the nearest bandit. He had a sword and a small shield. His metal vest showed him to be a leader. He yelled something and held his shield before him. I raised my spear. I whipped Remus' head around at the last moment as the man blindly swung his sword at where Remus' head had been. I plunged the spear above the edge of his shield and it tore through the mail links by his shoulder and entered his body. The angle and his dying body tore the spear from my hand and I drew my sword.

The bandits were fleeing. Garth and his archers had accounted for another five and the would-be robbers fled up the slope. "After them!"

I wanted the bandits to know that this trail was policed. I wanted them to fear us and I wanted as many dead as we could manage. It would make our task easier in the future. It was not glorious chasing down these bandits but it was necessary. As Remus scrambled up the stone covered scrub I leaned out and swept my sword. It bit through the head of the bandit. The top flew off and his body fell, lifeless to the ground. Two of them turned and put their shields together to face me. They were brave and obviously knew that a horse will not deliberately ride into a man. I reined back and stood in my stirrups, I had worked with Remus on this. His hooves flailed in the air. One struck the shield of the man on my right and he fell. The other was left isolated. Whipping Remus' head around I slashed at his face. My sword ripped across his cheeks and nose. I saw the bone through the wound. As Remus' hooves came down they crushed the skull of the bandit whose arm we had broken.

When I looked up there were none left to kill. Bodies lay on the hillside. I counted my men. They had all survived. "Search the bodies."

I turned Remus around and rode him down the hill. I stroked him between his ears, "Good boy!"

The camel drivers were tending to their wounded. Their leader strode over to me. I took off my helmet and slipped the coif from my head. I pulled up my hood to save me from the sun. When I reached the man, I dismounted, "I am in your debt lord. My name is Simeon Ben Levi."

He was younger than David Ben Samuel. "I am William of Aqua Bella. King Baldwin has charged me with keeping this road safe."

He gave me a wry smile. "I think, lord, that you have exceeded your orders for the road is some miles south of here."

"David Ben Samuel told me that this was where the bandits attacked." I smiled and tapped my nose. "Besides the lord at Ramelah protects that part of the road does he not?"

He laughed, "Then you do know David. I thank you, lord. Had you not come then I would have lost more men."

"I am sorry that you lost any but this road should become safer. When time allows, I will go into the hills and seek out the nests where these vipers skulk."

"Then you are a brave man."

It was after noon by the time we had buried the dead Jews. I decided to escort the caravan to Jerusalem. I would not have time to reach Jaffa and then return home. We adopted the same formation we had when we had ridden with Ben Samuel. I spoke with Simeon. I found that he was from a different tribe. He was a pleasant man. We had passed Shilat and rejoined the road when I heard a cry from William of Lincoln, "Lord, riders approaching from behind."

"Stockton, to me!"

My men galloped after me as we headed back down the column. This could be more bandits or it could be horse archers. When we reached William, I saw that they were Franks. They had a pale blue surcoat with two yellow stars. Two knights led ten sergeants in a column of two. The sergeants had spears.

I reined in next to William. Quietly I said, "Have your bows ready but smile. These are neighbours. Let us not upset them yet."

The leading rider reined in. He scowled at me. "Who are you? This is the domain of the Count of Ramelah. We are here to tax those Jews!"

I nodded, "I am William of Stockton. I am here to protect those who use this road and this is not under the rule of your leader. Guillaume de Waller has the manor of Ramelah; that is all."

"You have a handful of men and you are new here so I will be generous. Begone before I lose my temper and make an example of you."

I saw that he was in his early twenties. His slight build showed that he had not spent hours practising with sword, shield and spear. He played at being a knight. "You must do what you must do and I would avoid bloodshed if I could. We have already slain a number of bandits. We have yet to sharpen our blades. If we could perhaps have a whetstone we might put an edge to them."

Robert and my men at arms laughed. It was the wrong thing to do for the young knight coloured. He turned to his men, "I would have these men prisoners."

"Hold! Firstly, if your men move towards us then the four archers who are behind me will empty four saddles and then another four. They are English archers and you should know that they are deadly! Secondly," I took out the seal, "I am here as the representative of the King of Jerusalem. We are heading to Jerusalem. So, tell me, impetuous knight, what is your name so that I may tell him that you claim this road for the lord of Ramelah!"

The knight next to him put his hand to his sword, "Cuz, we have wasted enough time, let us kill them!" He drew his sword and Garth's arrow pierced his hand, knocking the sword to the ground.

"I did warn you. It is a shame that your companion did not heed my words. Now tell me your name!"

He had paled and he said, "I am Guy de Waller and this is Richard D'Aubigny. You are making a mistake. My uncle is the most powerful knight in this land."

"That will help then when I speak with the king."

One of the sergeants had brought a cloth and was binding the hand of the wounded knight. He took the arrow and flung it to the ground. Garth dismounted and went over to it. He picked it up and grinned at the wounded knight.

Guy de Waller said, “But these are Jews! Why do you protect them?”

“When the king tasked me with keeping this road safe he told me to do so for all travellers. He did not specify a people. You had best tell your uncle that for we are here to stay and the road twixt Jaffa and Jerusalem will now be safe for ***all*** travellers.” I emphasised the word ‘***all***’.

Garth mounted and held another arrow. We waited. The knight was confused but, as we were not moving, he did so and headed back towards his castle. They watched us over their shoulders. Garth said, “You have a way with you. Lord… it is a gift. We are here but one day and we already have a list of enemies.”

I laughed, “Aye Garth, now I know how my father feels!”

Chapter 6

We escorted Simeon to within a mile or two of the city. I sent my men back and then I went, with Simeon, into the city. I took just Alf and Tom with me. As we parted, at the market, Simeon thanked me profusely.

"It is what the king asked me to do."

"Nonetheless you have made an enemy of a very dangerous man, lord. I am grateful."

I intended speaking with the king. I felt he ought to know what I had done. He was not in the palace or, at least, that is what I was told. He could be avoiding me. Perhaps this was a poisoned chalice and I was a pawn in some kind of game I did not understand. We picked up the cloaks we had ordered and I took the opportunity to ask the merchant who had sold them to me if he knew where men were hired.

"Men, lord?"

"Soldiers. Those who seek to act as guards or warriors."

He smiled as though he was relieved. "That is simple lord. Go to the Temple of Solomon. The Knights Templar have their headquarters there. Many men wait close by for it is said that if you served the Templars then your fortune would be made. They are rich and powerful men."

We placed the cloaks on the back of Tom's horse and walked our mounts to the temple. It was like walking towards a sea of white and brown for it was filled with sergeants and knights. The knights wore white and the sergeants a brown mantle. The headquarters had been enlarged by taking over nearby buildings. The men I saw were mainly their sergeants but there were many of them. The ones who would be Templars gathered in the squares nearby. Their trade was obvious from their arms, shields and helmets. Some had mail but not all. There were some who looked to have a leather jerkin, old round helmet and just a sword while there were others who sported a full hauberk, masked helmet, shield, spear and sword. It begged the question of why they needed the Templars. The men we sought would not be those. While we rearranged the cloaks on the three horses I took the opportunity of observing the men. I would not hire any that afternoon. I would return with Garth and Robert. They were veterans. I had seen how my father had deferred to men such as Wulfric and Dick when it came to choosing men. I would do the same. I noted those who sat alone and those who were with comrades. I watched and saw those who were quiet and those who were loud. When I had seen enough we left and returned to Aqua Bella.

It was a reassuringly solid home to come back to. It was much smaller than Stockton and there was just one tiny tower but I guessed that it would be difficult to take. Francis had shown us the well which ensured that they could survive a long siege. The three vaulted chambers were enormous. One held horses. A second held amphorae of oil and wine and the third was used to store food. An army could have sheltered in those caves which had been hewn from the rock. The grapes produced enough grapes to supply wine for their cellars. We also discovered that this was the busy time of year. The olives and grapes had been picked and both wine and oil production were occupying all of the slaves.

As we ate, I told my men what I had discovered. "We will go tomorrow and try to hire men. The road patrol can wait until the next day."

Robert smiled, "You think that de Waller will be on the road and try to catch us?"

"I do. I am not afraid of a confrontation but he does not know where we live. He will come here soon enough."

"How do you know, lord?" Alf had a curious mind.

"Francis told us that de Waller came last year to take half of the oil which the estate produced. In a week, the oil will have all been put into jars. He will come then and I want to give him a shock. His knights will report eleven of us. I intend to have more when he does arrive. I have been over the accounts with Francis. We can afford more men. I suspect that the overseer was just being careful with the coin. I would rather spend the coin on men than expensive furniture and clothes."

Tom said, "We have the new cloaks. I will distribute them later."

I went, again, with Robert and Garth to the roof. Garth said, "Lord, we are doing well here but I still miss England."

"As do we all. The news of the Earl of Gloucester's death made me wish to return home." I shrugged. "It would do little good. My father will have already dealt with the problems the death created."

"It seems a different world, lord."

"Not so different, Robert. Here the domains are smaller but there is anarchy here too. If King Baldwin had real power then de Wallers could not operate as a robber baron. I wondered why I was given this rich manor. Now I know. It is a bribe to act as a buffer between de Waller and Jerusalem."

"A buffer?"

"Aye Garth. The king and his mother think I am my father." I shook my head, "I am a pale shadow but what they do know of my father is that he is tenacious. He is hard to budge. If we can slow the gains of de Waller then, even if we perish, we will have served the young king." I was almost tempted to tell them of the Byzantine emissary but I thought better of it. It was not fair on them.

"One thing is sure, lord, we will go home rich men."

I nodded.

Robert poured cold water on the archer's words, "Or dead men, Garth. It is a fine line between them."

Although the manor had good defensive qualities it could still be improved. I had my men clear away the scrub from close to the curtain wall. With our archers, we could make the approach to the gate a killing zone. I left for Jerusalem. Once again, King Baldwin and his mother were not at home. We went to the Temple of Solomon. The mailed warriors were no longer there. In fact, there were just a dozen men. Half of them were solitary. There was a wine seller. He had a table before his shop. I sent Tom to buy a large jug of wine and to fetch five beakers. We lowered our hoods. He returned with the wine, the beakers and some bread. He was resourceful.

"I would have us talk loudly, in English." Robert and Tom nodded. "It is not as warm here in the city as I thought it would be."

I winked at Robert, "Aye lord but this wine is welcome whether it be hot or cold." I sipped it and feigned drinking a draught.

We chatted as strangers to a new land would. Eventually one of the men who was across the square stood. He had just mail armour and an old leather helmet. His scabbard was not the best but the sword, from the hilt and pommel, looked to be a good one. He had a round shield. He looked thin, as though he needed a good meal. He approached and bowed, "Lord are you English?"

"I am. My name is William of Stockton and Aqua Bella although I had a manor in Normandy too. From your accent, you are English too."

"I am John of Chester."

"Would you care for a beaker of wine? And to break some bread with us. It is the least I can do for a fellow pilgrim from England."

I saw the gratitude on his face. "Aye lord."

"Sit. What brings you to this land?"

"I served the Earl of Chester. When he deserted the Empress some of my friends and I left his service to follow the Baron of Craven here. He died on the voyage. We sought service with lords. They do not like the English lord. Some of my friends were taken by lords but all perished within a month. They were used in the front line of the war against the

Turk. These Musselmen are fierce fighters. There was just me and my brother Peter left. He was knifed last month when we were in Ramelah. I appealed to the lord for justice and I was whipped. I walked here and have been seeking a lord ever since."

"Would you serve me?"

"I would serve the devil so long as his name was not de Waller."

"Then we have a common enemy." I held out my hand. "Welcome to my service." I took a silver coin from my purse. "Go and buy what you need. We leave in an hour."

He gave me a curious look, "I could leave and not return."

"For one silver coin? If that was true then what you have told me would be a lie and I do not think it was."

He nodded, "I will return."

After he had gone Tom said, "Strange that he served the Earl of Chester."

"I think we may find many here who fought in the civil war. Look around you, Tom. These few men at arms, sergeants and archers are the only ones who do not look as though they live off the fat of the land. The ones we saw returning home are the unusual ones. If you are willing to serve anyone then you will be rich."

I looked up for another man stood there. He was bigger than John of Chester. He had the red cheeks and nose of a drinker. He had a sword and a metal helmet. His shield had seen better days but he had one. He bowed, "I see you offered that other Englishman something, lord. I am English. What would you offer me?"

"That depends upon your story. I am William of Aqua Bella." His eyes widened. "You have heard of me?"

"I fought against your father at Lincoln."

"Robert give the man some wine for I like him already. He tells me he was an enemy of my father and expects me to take him on."

The man laughed but took the beaker, "I would kill for a beaker of wine but let me finish, lord." He downed the beaker in one and smacked his lips. "You may not give me another but I will speak the truth anyway." I nodded to Robert who poured him another. He drank half. "I thought the war was over. I had fought for Stephen and we had lost. When Stephen was incarcerated I thought it all over and I took ship for the Holy Land. When I reached here I heard that war was renewed and I cursed my ill luck. I could have still had a job."

"You care not who you fight for?"

"I lived in Kent. There, everyone fought for Stephen. I knew not the rights and wrongs. I was a soldier. I was paid and I followed orders.

When the war began, I was young and I fought for the King of England. Was I wrong, lord?"

"I can see how you thought you were right. Would you fight for me? And before you answer think on this. I am not here forever. I will return to England someday and I will fight alongside my father. Would you fight against King Stephen?"

"I will be honest with you, lord. I am a warrior and I fight because I enjoy fighting. I am good with a sword and with a dagger. I am not a clever man. I believe what the priests and my betters say. I will fight for you, lord and I will be as loyal a man as any. I would swear to this on a Bible… a stack of Bibles."

I laughed, "I like your honesty." I took a silver coin. "Do you need anything?"

He put the coin in his purse and sat next to Tom. "So long as there is wine in that jug then I am content to sit here."

Robert shook his head, "What is your name, villain!"

He was not put out by the insult. He smiled, "Henry son of Will of Dover, captain!"

John of Chester returned. He had a newly bought cloak wrapped around his other purchases. He sat next to Tom and Henry son of Will. I was contemplating leaving for we had hired two men when two other men rose. They had been sat together but not talking to each other. They spoke in French. Both had worn surcoats. They were so faded that I could not tell what colour they had once been or even if they had had a device upon them. Both had a sword. John and Henry had both been relatively young men. These two were of an age with Wulfric.

They looked at each other and the one without a beard spoke, "Lord, I am Gaston de Lyons. You have hired these two men. If you seek more then consider us."

"Are you friends?"

"He shook his head, "I had never met Gregor of Basle before yesterday but we have both served in campaigns across Europe. We are not young but we have skills."

"Know you, then, that I am English. My name is William of Aqua Bella. I am here to do penance and when that is done I will return to England. If that does not suit then tell me now. I demand total loyalty. If I have that then I will be behind you come what may."

Gregor of Basle spoke, "For myself, I care not who we serve. I would fill my belly. You have fine mail and a good sword. You are a lord who is successful. I would like to change my luck. Hitherto my lords have been unlucky."

"Then drink the last of the jug. Robert, go and see if you can find four animals for them. Sumpters, palfreys, donkeys or asses, I care not."

Henry downed the last of the wine, "Where do we go, lord?"

"Just a few miles down the road. You now serve me and I serve the King of Jerusalem!"

Robert bought four good horses. As he told me later he knew that we would need remounts. The four men might only be guards for Aqua Bella but good horses would not come amiss. When they saw the walls of their new home they were impressed. Once inside they were even more overawed.

Henry son of Will, as we soon learned spoke first and thought afterwards, "Well we have followed the muck cart and landed in a bed of roses and no mistake."

Robert shook his head. The English sense of humour had always been a mystery to him.

The next morning, I realised that I would need more surcoats. I needed my men to look the same. I would have to return to Jerusalem and have more made. Robert gave them the materials to make their own shields. I wanted us all to look alike. I would need a new helmet for John. The other three would suffice for the time being. I was about to ride into Jerusalem again when there was a cry from the gate. It was Joshua, the duty guard, "Lord! Knights and banners!"

We hurried to the gate. By the time we reached it, I saw a column of men riding up the road. They followed the de Waller banner. I turned to Francis, who had joined us. "Speak to them. Do not let them know we have a new lord here. I will speak when the time is right."

"Aye lord." I heard the nervousness in his voice.

"Everyone hide. I want you to appear when I rise!"

Apart from my new men, everyone smiled. They knew me and they knew why I did this. I had not explained the situation to my new men. This would be a good test of their nerve.

I had my back to the wall and I looked up at the pole which should have held my standard. It was not yet finished and there was a bare pole. I realised that this would help us. De Waller would have no idea that the manor had been given to me. I heard his voice.

"Why is your gate barred! Open it so that I may come and take what is due to me."

"Lord, I have been ordered not to allow entry to any."

"Ordered?"

"Yes lord, the King has given the manor to another!"

"I care not. This road is mine and I will take my tithe! The olive oil is the price you must pay for living on my road."

Francis glanced down at me. I shook my head. "I am sorry, lord. I cannot admit you!"

"Then we will take this pathetic little shit hole and I will have your back flayed and you and your brood sold into slavery!"

I had heard enough and I rose as did all my men. "I do not think my overseer would like that lord nor would I." I held up the king's seal, "Especially as King Baldwin has asked me to guard this road from all or did your nephew not tell you that when he skulked back to Ramelah?" I saw his nephew colour.

Guillaume de Waller was almost the same age as my father. He had a cruel look in his eyes exaggerated by a hawk's nose. He drew his sword and pointed it at me. "You are the wretch who maimed my knight! I will have your head on my gate!"

"Are you stupid or are you deaf? I am King Baldwin's lord of the manor. I am his sentinel of the Jaffa to Jerusalem road. I am a servant of the King of Jerusalem! Sheath your sword or you will suffer the same fate as your knight." I raised my sword and four war bows appeared over the walls.

He sheathed his sword, "You are the son of the Greek boy are you not? I have a blood feud with him. Your father killed my cousin, Guy Fitz Waller. I do not forget nor do I forgive. Your family cost my cousin his estates. You have the better of me today but you have but a handful of men. Watch your back, Englishman!"

"Aye, I had better for it is obvious that you are no knight and certainly have no honour. You would be a backstabber! I give you fair warning. I will use deadly force against any who try to hurt those who use the king's road. The next time my archers will not maim they will kill. You do not frighten me, de Waller. If you are so confident then fight me here and now before my walls!" It was a gamble for I had not seen him fight but my father had always taught me to beard bullies. There was a silence which seemed to echo off the cliffs above us. Every eye was on de Waller.

He broke the silence. "I will not soil my sword on you. The next time I see you then you die!"

I laughed, "But obviously not by your hand! You will have one of your lackeys do the job. No matter, I will fight any man you nominate as a champion! Do you have confidence in any of them?"

Once again it was a bluff. His men looked eagerly at their leader waiting for him to choose one. He did not and I saw the hearts ripped from them. He did not think he could defeat the son of King Henry's Champion by fair means. It was a victory!

We watched them turn away and ride back down the road. I saw that Francis was sweating. Garth and my men grinned. Henry son of Will shook his head, "I'll say this for you, lord. You have a pair of balls on you!"

Robert shook his head and Garth grinned and clapped Henry son of Will on the back, "You have it right there, brother!"

Leaving Gregor and Gaston to watch the gate, we headed indoors. "I take it we stay here tomorrow, lord?"

"No Robert, we patrol the road. We ride all the way to Jaffa if we have to for I think that he will attack a caravan, any caravan and we will punish him!"

Chapter 7

Gaston de Lyons had proved himself to be the natural leader. Henry son of Will spoke the most and was the loudest but many of his words were empty; they were harmless but had no substance. I left Gaston in charge.

"I know not if they might attack the manor. If they did then it would be a mistake but be on your guard. We still have people working in the field. Have John in the top tower. He will keep a good watch and he has reason to hate the de Wallers."

"Aye lord."

I rode Remus again. There was nothing wrong with Romulus but Remus seemed to understand every nudge of my knee or flick of my wrist. My father had had the same relationship with his horse Scout. He had never been the biggest of horses but he had been the cleverest.

We used a different formation. Garth and the archers were at the rear with Alf. If we came upon trouble then Alf would hold the horses while they rained arrows upon the enemy. The six of us would have to deal with whoever we came across. Unless the Lord of Ramelah used all of his knights and sergeants then we stood a chance. We had left before dawn. Our new cloaks were much lighter and I noticed the difference as soon as the sun came up. I was not as hot as I had been.

I used my eyes to search for danger. I had ridden the road a few times now and was getting to know it well. I could see something which was out of the ordinary. We did not take the trail after Shilat. We kept to the road. It was Tom's ears which picked up the noise of battle. The caravan which was being attacked must have camped north of Ramelah and had been heading up the road when it was stopped. Ramelah lay twelve miles to the south of us. The land through which we travelled was riven with ravines, gullies, twists and turns. We found the caravan in one such narrow valley. The men of de Waller had the camel drivers on their knees. The sergeants were not keeping watch and, as we came around the bend, we surprised them.

There were twelve sergeants and four knights. The knights were mounted while the sergeants appeared to be examining the cargo. All of them turned when they heard our hooves and saw the six of us. I recognised Guy de Waller. With him were three knights, all older than he was. The young knight pointed at me, "It is the knight my uncle spoke of! It is the Englishman!"

The knight to whom he spoke already had his sword out. He pulled his horse's head around. "This is no business of yours. Our lord's castle is close to here. We collect his taxes." I looked at him. He had a swarthy complexion and the blackest hair I have ever seen. His beard and moustache were oiled. His armour looked different too. I could not quite place its origin but it was not Norman.

I saw that some of the men who were on their knees had bloodied faces. One looked to be the merchant whose caravan this was. Ignoring the knight, I said to the man, "You should not have to pay a tithe for using the king's road. When I have dealt with this bandit then I will escort you hence."

The knight roared, "Bandit! I am Roderigo of Santiago! I will have your head for that."

I had my spear couched, "I warned you de Waller and now you pay the price."

The four knights galloped towards the six of us. They saw but one knight, a young squire and four men at arms. They did not know that my men at arms were armed as they were. Any of them could have been a knight. They chose to serve me instead. I rode at Roderigo. From his name, he was Spanish. I had never fought a Spaniard. I was not arrogant enough to believe that I would win just because I had won every tilt before now.

He cleverly used the road. It was narrow and I did not have the space to manoeuvre as I might have liked. I did, however, have the advantage that I held a spear and he only had his sword. I pulled back the spear and kept the head high. He did as I expected. He pulled his shield higher. At the last moment, I punched, not at his head but at his leg. He almost got the shield down in time but my spearhead scraped along his boot and into his horse's side. In pain, it reared and the knight fell to the ground.

A second knight clutched the arrow in his shoulder. I whipped Remus' head around and rode at the third knight. He did have a spear. The road was narrow and neither of us could use the speed of a galloping horse to knock the other from his saddle. The knight was older but I could see that he had not jousted as much as I had. The head of his spear wavered up and down. Mine rested on the cantle of my saddle. As he punched forward I concentrated on my strike. My left hand flicked up and the spear slid up the leather cover of my shield. I punched over his cantle, towards his middle with my own weapon. It is almost impossible to use your shield to protect there unless you know that is where the blow will come. My spearhead tore through mail and I felt it strike something soft. The knight's spear dropped and he turned his horse to gallop down the road.

I saw that Guy de Waller had yielded and that four sergeants clutched wounds. One lay dead. I turned Remus and had my spear at the throat of Roderigo of Santiago as he stood. "Yield or by God, I will have my archers slay every one of you!"

He looked around and realised that we now outnumbered him. Sheathing his sword he nodded. "This will not end today."

"I know but it is your men who bleed and it is you who will be walking back to Ramelah." Without turning I shouted, "Take their arms and their horses. Leave them two for their wounded." I saw that the wounded knight had stopped just beyond the last camel. He would need help. "Now walk back to Ramelah and tell your lord that your arms and horses are a fine for his banditry. If he objects then tell him to come to Jerusalem and put his case to King Baldwin."

Roderigo shook his head, "You know not the Lord of Ramelah! He has powerful allies."

"More powerful than the king?"

He gave me a strange smile, "Perhaps. You are a handy knight. You should join us. There is more profit fighting for the Lord of Ramelah than the king."

It was my turn to smile, "And I do not fight for money. That is the difference between us. You have a long walk. Take the water from your saddles, you will need it."

We watched them as they trudged down the road which was already becoming unbearably hot. They held their shields above them to afford some shade. I saw that Garth and my archers had scaled the sides of the valley and they watched them from their lofty perches.

The merchant approached me, "I am Phillipe of Jaffa. Thank you for your intervention. They are not normally so violent. Do we have to pay you now, lord?"

"No. As I told you, the king has tasked me with keeping this road clear for all merchants. Come, we have some way to go. I would reach Jerusalem today."

"Then lead on, Englishman."

"No, we will watch the rear. I left them some horses. They may come after us."

The camels and donkeys were whipped into line and they began to march up the road. I waved over Tom and Alf. Take the horses and the weapons to Aqua Bella. Warn Gaston that we may have company. You two wait for us there."

They nodded, “Aye lord.” Tom handed me the gonfanon.

Robert rode with me at the back. “This could escalate into a war, lord.”

“That is why I urged them to have their lord come to Jerusalem. When we reach Aqua Bella then you and I will ride to Jerusalem. I would speak with the king. If I have exceeded my orders then he needs to tell me.”

“You are like your father, lord. He is single-minded. You are both like terriers. Once you have locked your teeth on something then it is hard to shake you off.”

I laughed, “You could say that of many Englishmen, Robert.”

We reached my home in the middle of the afternoon. The merchant begged for the opportunity to rest his animals and I acquiesced. Robert and I took the opportunity of changing mounts. We rode Alciades and Leonidas. We had not ridden them much and Remus was tired after his exertions. Francis and my slaves fed and watered the merchant. He showed his gratitude by giving us some of the salted fish he was carrying. Francis’ reaction showed me that it was a welcome gift.

Phillipe of Jaffa said, “This is a gift and not a bribe, lord. I can see that you are a true knight. I wonder that you are not a Hospitaller.”

We set off for the last part of the journey and he rode with us. “I am not cut out to be a warrior priest. When I have done what I came here to do I will return to England. The Templars and the Hospitallers are here until their bones bleach by the roads.” He nodded as he took in my words. “Tell me why de Waller’s men waited until you had passed his castle.”

He shook his head, “I was tired of giving him a quarter of my trade goods. We passed it during the night. It almost cost us for Roderigo of Santiago demanded half. I would have been ruined. A quarter gives me barely enough profit to live. I had been tempted to take the old caravan trail like the Jews but I fear the bandits and the Turks.”

“We patrol there too. We left many bandits dead the last time. Tell your fellow merchants that the road twixt Shilat and Ginaton is not as dangerous as it might have been.”

“Thank you.”

When we reached the city, it was getting on towards late afternoon. I was bone weary but I knew I had to speak with the king. Leaving our horses inside the palace gates we strode into the hall. It was not as crowded as it had been but this time everyone looked at us. My name and device were known. The throne was empty. I went to his official who sat at a desk writing down requests from those in the chamber. It was the one who had brought the box to the king and was called Paul. He shook his head when I approached, “I told you, the king is not present.”

I leaned in and said quietly, "Then you had better get a message to him. I have three times bloodied the nose of Guillaume de Waller. I fear the Lord of Ramelah is less than happy with the king."

He looked up and I saw fear on his face, "You have hurt the Lord of Ramelah?" I nodded. He rose and scurried into the chamber at the rear. A few moments later he reappeared and his claw-like hand waved us towards it.

He closed the curtain behind the two of us. I saw that Queen Melisende was there. She smiled, "I hear you have, how did you put it, bloodied the nose of the Lord of Ramelah?"

I explained what had happened. "If I have exceeded my authority then I apologize. My orders were to protect all on the road. Without the use of force, I am not sure how I could have done that."

She held up a hand. "You have done nothing wrong. I expected that a few eggs might be broken. You did the right thing to suggest to the Lord of Ramelah that he ought to come here and speak with my son. There will be no need for you to patrol the road for the next few days in any case. Christmas is upon us and ships do not make as many voyages in the winter. The exception being…" she looked at Robert, "well you know of what I speak." I nodded. "My son is at Nablus. You need do nothing more other than he is aware of certain factions who wish to undermine us. We are biding our time. You came at a propitious moment. You were chosen, lord, because you were spoken of as someone who was not afraid of challenges. You have met the problems you faced head-on. That is good. Already we are hearing that our merchants are happier. The bazaars are already more prosperous. I have no doubt that when the caravans use the road in greater numbers that you will be called upon to scour the land of our foes. By then you will have more men. You have made a start with your first four."

I was about to ask her how she knew when I realised that, to have survived as long as she had there had to be a network of spies and informants in the city. "Then I will wait in my new home. I dare say the king will summon me when I am needed."

"We will summon you."

As we left Robert asked, "Does the king rule or his mother?"

"I think, at the moment, she is guiding her son with a heavy hand." We mounted our horses. "I had thought to hire more men but now that I have spoken with the Queen I will speak with the four that we have. They would seem to me to be the ones who would know where we should search."

It was dusk as we headed towards our home. I had forgotten that Christmas was so close. We had left Normandy in autumn. Winter here was as summer in England. It was dark when we passed beneath the gates. Henry and John were on the gate. They waved to us. "How goes it?"

"All quiet, lord. No one has passed up the road since you left for Jerusalem. A merchant and a caravan of camels headed south. You have just missed them."

I nodded. Caravans heading south held little for the bandits and de Waller. They were empty. The land around Jerusalem produced enough for the people of the area and no more. Once inside I walked Alciades to the stable. The slaves, we had learned, were good with horses. Even so, I supervised Atticus as he removed the saddle and began to groom Alciades. Satisfied I left and went to my chambers. The house slaves had hot water waiting for me and after helping me off with my mail they bathed me and combed and trimmed my beard. I could see now why so many lords liked the life here. With so many skilled slaves a lord could live a life of luxury. It was not the austere life my father led.

The original four guards who had been here when we came took over the watches at night. They had less to do now and did not have to endure a watch alone. The four of them worked in pairs and the twelve hours they watched were normally quiet. The new men watched during the day.

The salted cod had been cooked. It made a change from the diet of chicken and beans we had eaten thus far. Henry was more than happy with the wine which the estate produced. I had seen Robert having a word with him about the quantity he drank. My men enjoyed a drink but Henry seemed inordinately fond of it. So far it seemed he could handle it.

After the meal, I explained to them what the Queen had said.

Henri said, "The Lord of Ramelah did not seem the sort of man to accept our treatment of him. The Queen may say the king supports us but this appears to me to be more like England than Anjou. Nobles do as they choose."

Before I could speak Robert said, "And that is why, I believe, that we have been chosen for this task. We have not spoken of this before but when Tom and I waited for our lord the first time we visited the palace we listened to the conversation around us."

"And enjoyed wonderful sweetmeats!"

They all laughed at Tom's outburst. "Aye, that too. People were saying that King Baldwin was young and that some of his nobles were taking advantage of his youth. From what the Queen said and what I deduced, King Baldwin is securing his castles and he will deal with de Waller when the moment is right."

I wondered if I was a tool to deal with the renegade knight. "We have ten days here and then I will take some of you to Jaffa. There we are to meet someone and escort him to Jerusalem." I could see that I had surprised all of them. "Before then I would go back to Jerusalem to hire more men. We need guards for our walls but as we have the six horses we captured today then we can add men to my retinue. Gaston and John of Chester, you will come with me."

"Why not me, lord?"

"Henry, you like your wine too much. We will need discretion when we visit. I am not even sure you know what discretion is."

He shrugged, "Give me an enemy to fight lord. I need no discretion for that… whatever discretion is!"

The next morning Francis came to see me. "Lord we need to take our oil to the market to be sold."

"Then just do it."

He shifted uncomfortably. "Lord for the last few years it has been the Lord of Ramelah who took the oil to be sold. He gave us half. We have no animals any longer."

"No animals? Why not?"

"The Lord of Ramelah took them."

"I will get us animals. Francis, is there anything else that I should know?"

He shook his head and smiled, "That is all lord except that the servants, slaves and our families are all happier now. We feel safe and secure. I just worry about your leaving."

"That will not be for some time. I think I will be here for years but, before I go, I will make sure that Aqua Bella is safe."

Leaving him I shouted for Tom, "Have Romulus and Remus saddled, we ride!" Leaving Robert in command I rode to David Ben Samuel.

His sentries had spotted us and he and Saul came out to welcome us. "Have you come to celebrate Hanukah with us?"

I knew that was an important festival for Jews. "No David. I have need of your camels. We must take our oil to market. I will pay for their hire." I explained what had happened to the animals from the estate.

"Of course. If I might suggest?" I nodded, "We would take payment in oil. The oil of Aqua Bella is renowned for its taste."

"Then it is agreed. We will take the oil as soon as you and your men arrive."

"Of course. Simeon Ben Levi spoke with me. You have made quite an impact on this land. Yesterday you helped a Gentile. We have a wind in the desert. When it comes, it disrupts everything. Nothing is the same when it has passed. The land is different. You have a winged beast on your shields. You are like the wind."

"Perhaps but I am just doing that which I was ordered."

"Or what you were meant to do. We will bring the camels over in three days."

"Thank you."

Francis was happy. The delay would help him to have the slaves move the jars from where they were stored. While they worked, I helped Tom to train Alf. His hard life with the Lombards had given him a strong body. The good food he had had since joining us had helped him to fill out. He knew how to swing a sword but not use one as a swordsman should. Garth made two wooden swords for us to use. They were heavier than a real sword. It made using a sword seem easier. At first, it was I who worked with Alf. I quickly discovered that I had far too much skill. I was not cut out to train. I handed it over to Tom. My squire had recently undergone training with Robert and Louis. He was also better matched in terms of physique. The blows he struck hurt but not as much as mine did. When I was satisfied that he was making progress I went to the top of the house. The roof afforded a fine view down the valley and the road. John was on duty in the tower. I climbed up the ladder to join him.

"Anything?"

"A few riders but no caravans and no sign of the men from Ramelah."

There was venom in his voice. "Tell me more about this de Waller. How did it come about that your friend was knifed?"

"The knight you unhorsed is typical of the men he surrounds himself with. The same is true of the sergeants. They have no honour. Had you been unhorsed then I do not doubt that the knight would have slain you. Peter and I were in an inn. We were seeking work. Peter was strong. One of the sergeants started a fight with him. Peter felled him with one punch. As we tried to leave one of the other sergeants stabbed him in the back and then slit his throat. When I appealed to the lord, for it was murder, he told me I was lucky to be alive and he had me whipped and thrown into the street. Had the innkeeper not taken pity on me and fetched my sword and helmet I would have been defenceless."

"That does not tell me about the Lord of Ramelah," I said, gently.

"It does, Sir William, for you judge a lord by those whom he appoints and those who surround him. He has the sweepings of the streets. There is no sense of honour amongst any of them. I have not served you long but I have spoken with your men. You may not have many men but those you have are loyal and will back you in a fight."

"You are right."

Suddenly he shaded his eyes against the sun. "There, lord. I spy a banner. I think it is your enemy."

I had seen nothing but my young warrior had sharp eyes. A few moments later I saw the glint of sun on metal and then a breeze made the banner flutter. It was Guillaume de Waller.

"Keep watch, I will go down to my gate in case he means ill."

I descended to the ground level. "To arms. De Waller comes." Without being told Garth and William raced to join John at the tower. Tom fetched me my helmet which I donned. None were working in the field and so, when Henry and Gaston barred the gate, we were secure. The road was almost half a mile away. The scrub had been cleared from both sides of the trail which led to our gates. It seemed an age but, eventually, the column passed the end. They were not stopping. De Waller had not brought his full force. He had ten knights and twenty sergeants at arms. He was going to Jerusalem.

When it was obvious that they had passed, I told the men to return to what they were doing. "Robert, I think we will receive a message tomorrow to visit Jerusalem. Make sure that all our surcoats are cleaned and have the men sharpen their weapons and polish their helmets."

"Aye lord."

I went to do as I had ordered my men and I took my sword and dagger to the wheel to sharpen them. I did not think we would be fighting but a good knight was always prepared. As sparks flew from my sword's edge I wondered if my rule here would be short-lived. I had seen the importance of Ramelah. Could the king afford to alienate such a powerful lord?

We were eating when the messenger arrived from Jerusalem. It was a royal courier. When the courier was admitted, he said, "My lord, the King would like you to come to his court tomorrow. There you must answer charges made by the Lord of Ramelah."

I nodded, "Tell him that we will be there."

I was worried about a sneak attack while we were gone and so I left Gregor and Henry with the other sentries to guard the walls. The rest of us left before dawn. No time had been specified but I did not wish to offend the king. When we reached the city, I took Tom with me and sent Robert with the rest of my men to see if the banners were ready and to try to hire more men. I asked for more surcoats to be made. I asked him to buy more horses if the opportunity arose. The profits from the sale of the olive oil would enable us to be well equipped.

Tom dusted my cloak to remove as much sand as he could. With our helmets under our arms, we strode to the court. King Baldwin had not yet arrived but the two thrones were on a raised dais and the room was already filling up. I noticed that the Lord of Ramelah stood with four men who wore different liveries. They glared at the two of us as we entered. Their jabbing fingers left us in no doubt that they were talking about us.

A servant brought some sherbet for us and we stood to one side. A figure loomed up behind us. The black tunic with the small white cross over the heart told me that it was a Knight Hospitaller; the Order of St. John of the Hospital of Jerusalem. He was an older knight. Lean, almost gaunt he was taller than most men in the room. He reminded me of Theobald of Rheims.

"I am Raymond de Puy Provence, Master of the Knights Hospitaller. I apologize for forcing myself upon you but I have heard so much about you that I felt obliged to speak with you."

"I am honoured that you do so, sir. I admire your order. To care for the sick and the wounded as well as protecting pilgrims is noble work."

"Yet you have put us to shame for you extend the protection to Jews. I can see that you are a man to watch."

I laughed and gestured with my thumb at de Waller. "As you can see, Master, I am being watched already."

"That is an evil man. He is the antithesis of my order. He plunders and he wrecks. He has an unhealthy appetite for women. He likes virgins and when he has finished with them they are discarded. If he cannot buy slaves to serve his venal appetite, he takes them from the poor or anyone who does not guard their women. Surrounded by like-minded knights he can get away with this. The Pope should excommunicate him."

"Why does he not?"

"Did you not know? His cousin is the Count of Provence and he holds estates which are close to the papal summer home at Avignon. Few would cross the Count of Provence; not even the Pope. He is protected there by the Lombard Count."

My face must have shown my thoughts.

"Do you know the Count?"

"I have fallen foul of his family over the past few months. I thought that I was free from the threat. It seems that is not so."

"If the King supports you then you need not worry about either of those men although I would sleep with a knife beneath my blanket. They are both treacherous."

A knight emerged from the curtain, "Pray silence for their majesties."

We all dropped to a knee as the King and his mother entered. They sat upon their thrones. "You may rise. Where is Count Guillaume of Ramelah?"

De Waller stepped forward. He had the confident look of a man who knows the judgement which was to be made. He was convinced that I would be punished. "I am here, your majesty."

"What is it that you wish to bring to our attention?"
De Waller whipped his hand around and pointed it in my direction. "That knight maimed one of my knights, wounded three others, slew three sergeants and took horses and weapons from them."
"And what do you wish of me?"
"I wish him to be punished and for redress to be made."
"Step forward, William of Aqua Bella, guardian of the road and defender of the poor. What have you to say for yourself?"
I was almost too stunned to speak. I had just been given titles I did not know I possessed. I bowed. "Your majesties, I was charged with protecting all who used the road. I found knights in the service of the Count. They were preventing a caravan from using the road."
"That is a lie!"
I turned slowly, "My lord, I do not lie and I will not have my word doubted. Retract that statement else I will demand honour and we will settle the dispute before God. We will have a trial by combat."
King Baldwin just looked at the Count. Every eye was on the Count. I had challenged him before his men and he had backed down. Would he do so again?
He pointed at me again, "I will not fight with you. You had no right to stop my men. They were obeying my orders."
Queen Melisende said, "You ordered merchants to be robbed, Count?"
He blustered, "Your majesty it was not robbery. My men patrol the road and it was merely payment for using the road."
"Then you need not concern yourself any further. William of Aqua Bella will keep the road clear and he will not be making any charges on those who use it."
"You mean he gets to keep my horses?"
"Did you take his horses, lord?"
I smiled, "Your majesty my overseer told me that the Count confiscated every camel, horse and donkey from the estate when the last lord died. I was merely taking these until the Count could return those that he took."
The Queen said, "Ah, perfectly understandable. So, Count, I believe the matter is cleared up. As we can all see, it was a simple misunderstanding. Had you attended court more often, then you would have known that the King has become upset at the losses that the merchants of Jerusalem suffer on the Jaffa road. We have asked William of Aqua Bella to make it safe. We are pleased that he has done so and so speedily."
The Count was speechless. The King said, "If there is no further business then we will speak with Sir William privately." The knight

opened the curtain and I followed the King and his mother. I gestured for Tom to stay with the Master.

They waved me to a seat. King Baldwin smiled, “That went well.”

I knew that they had engineered this whole situation so that they could stop the Count’s privations. It had to be in public and it was obvious that the Count avoided Jerusalem. He preferred his fiefdom.

Queen Melisende said, “I wondered at the challenge, Sir William. Was it reckless or did you know what the answer would be?”

“I had challenged him once already. He is a bully and a coward. He would prefer for others to do his dirty work.” They both nodded at my appraisal of the knight. “Then my task is finished.”

“Finished?”

“The road will now be safe, will it not? My task was to goad him to have a confrontation. “

“I told you he was clever, mother. No, Sir William. You will still need to patrol the road and meet the Emperor’s emissary.”

“I have promised to escort the daughter of David Ben Samuel from Caesarea. That will be in a month or so. I gave my word.”

“Then, of course, you should keep it.” The Queen put her hand on mine. It was like a piece of white marble. It was flawless. “We cling on to Jerusalem, lord. I will not apologise for using you. You have been well paid and you came here to do penance. Already you have done good. Your work is Christian and God will forgive whatever sins you feel you have committed. Although for the life of me I cannot see what they were.”

I said nothing.

King Baldwin rose, “We will see you sometime late next month then. Remember that the emissary must be protected. Men will try to intercept him. That is why we are using you and not royal guards.”

“Surely that will put him in in even more danger? The Count will try to get at me some way.”

“Not yet. He will try to work out what we are up to. His spies are already asking questions.”

“Spies?”

“Of course. He has spies in the palace and we have spies watching his. It is a game out here. Do not worry about it. You just have to be yourself and all will be well.”

I left through the curtain. The Master was still speaking with my squire. He turned, “I will watch you closely, my young friend. You could be a member of our order but I suspect you are worldlier than my brothers.”

I nodded, "I will help those who need it but when I am ready I will return home."

"And that is good. If you need anything then just ask." He shrugged, "We are a poor order but we recognise a kindred spirit."

As we left Tom asked, "What happened there, lord? I thought we would have been punished."

"I think, Tom, son of Aelric, that we have wandered into a world where men's words mean nothing. We must watch out for each other."

We walked our horses to the Temple. There we saw Robert. He had men I did not recognise and he had horses. He also had two bundles. He beamed. I realised what he held, "They are our banners?"

"Aye, lord!" He suddenly looked apprehensive. "Is all well?"

I nodded. "We are like insects, Robert. The great, the good and the bad plot and plan. We just perform as they bid. The Count was put in his place and we return to Aqua Bella." I looked at the four men who were with him. "And who are these?"

Robert waved the four men forward. There were three men at arms and an archer. One had an axe and the other two were swordsmen and the last had a war bow. This is Jean de Les Monts. He is from Lombardy. Gurth son of Garth is an English warrior. He tried to enlist in the Varangian Guard. Harold Longsword is also English. He served with Walther of Buxton before he was killed at Ascalon. Lastly, we have Robin Hawkeye. He is an archer."

"An archer?"

He nodded, "I also came with Walther of Buxton. There were ten archers. The rest all died."

I sensed a story but now was not the time. "You know that if you serve with me I expect an oath?" They nodded. "And that I will return to England at some time?"

Robin said, "That is the reason that Harold and I have joined you. We want to go home rather than die here as our friends did."

"Even though you serve the son of a rebel who fights King Stephen?"

They laughed and Robin said, "Especially because we will serve the son of a rebel who fights King Stephen. Had not our lord come east we would have joined your father. His archers are the stuff of legends."

We headed back down the road. I made sure that we kept close together. The Count was still in Jerusalem and, despite what the King and Queen had said, I did not trust him. When my gate slammed behind us I felt safe. The new men were like John and the others we had hired. They had been without regular food and their clothes were in ill repair. When David and his camels arrived to take the oil to market I sent Francis and Robert with them to equip my new men.

I had decided to take Tom, Alf, Garth, William, Louis and John of Chester with me to escort the emissaries. I could have taken more but I felt that it would have attracted even more attention. I had planned on avoided Ramelah and taking the old caravan trail. When Francis and Robert returned, it was with all the equipment we needed as well as more gold than I had ever seen. I asked Robert to take it to Simon and deposit it. I left Robert in command. He was not happy for he wanted to be with me.

"Old friend when I am gone then I need our home protecting. Who else can I trust?"

"But lord you have two young boys and someone we do not know well."

"I need to find out about my men. This is a good opportunity. Watch the road. I know the Queen said that it would be quiet but I would rather we rode the trail."

"And how long will you be away?"

"We are meeting a ship. Answer the question yourself."

"Take care lord."

"I will."

Chapter 8

We left in plenty of time. I intended to take two days to get to Jaffa. It should only have needed one but the extra day gave me peace of mind. I took three of our horses with me for the emissary and his escort. The ones we had first bought when we first arrived had benefitted from both rest and good grazing. The soil at Aqua Bella produced not only fine olives and grapes but also enough grass to feed our small herd. John of Chester and Alf led our spare horses.

Like our mounts, Alf had grown since we had come to the Holy Land. In the short time we had been there he had become less abrasive and sensitive. I knew that was the result of being with Garth. Garth treated him like a little brother. He gave him a clip when he deserved it and he knew when to banter and jolly along the young orphan. Alf had been badly used. I suspected that he and John of Chester had much in common. Both had suffered at the hands of lords who misused the power that they had.

We took the old caravan trail from Shilat to Ginaton. It not only avoided Ramelah, but it was also faster. I had no doubt that eyes were upon us as we trekked south. The bandits would recognize our devices and would be wary. We had hurt and weakened them but their livelihood depended upon attacking travellers. They would rise again but not yet. We reached Jaffa just before they closed the gates.

The port was quieter than it would normally have been. Many ships spent these winter months undergoing repairs and maintenance. It meant we were able to find an inn with a stable. We had the coin to pay but my seal from the king meant that we were afforded a little more respect than otherwise.

"You are lucky, lord. Normally we are full but we have rooms and stables for you."

None knew of me here. My task had been to keep the road to Jaffa clear of problems but this was the first time we had managed to get to the port.

We did not need to walk around the town in mail. That was, in itself, a relief. Once we had established a good place to watch for the ship which would bring the emissary we explored the town. My men took it in turns to be the sentry at the mole who would watch for a Byzantine ship. Although not as large as Tripoli, Jaffa was the closest port to Jerusalem. There were merchants there who supplied the great city. I had learned enough, since I had been here, to know that what we did was important and I let the merchants I met know what we did. At first, they were wary. I could, after all, be a bandit seeking valuable information which might enable me to take their caravans more easily. Once I had shown them my seal and mentioned the names of David Ben Samuel, Philippe of Jaffa and Simeon Ben Levi they opened up.

That first evening, as we ate at the inn, I spoke of what I had discovered and what we had agreed with the merchants. "They are willing to gather together to make it easier for us to escort them. Philippe of Jaffa has left for Amalfi but he spoke to his friends. They are all fed up with paying de Waller. We have arranged for us to come to Jaffa and escort a number of caravans. We will not have to waste time riding up and down the road. Our time can be more productively spent."

Garth put the gnawed chicken bone on his platter, "What about David Ben Samuel's daughter, lord? Are you not supposed to be escorting her from Caesarea?"

"I am but that city is not far north of here. I will try to make it coincide with a caravan. If that is not possible then I will escort her with a few of you." I was intrigued by the continued absence of Ben Samuel's daughter. He had not said why she was in Caesarea. There was no real reason he should have told me but I was curious. Having seen Ben Samuel's home and his family I would have expected her to be there where she would have been safer.

The owner came over, "The food was good?"

Garth belched, "It was indeed."

"You came at the right time, lord. My last rooms have been taken. Some Frankish warriors took them. This will be a prosperous time for us."

"It is, indeed, lucky."

Over the next few days, we all spent some of our coins. I bought clothes which I could wear in Aqua Bella. I had war gear but this was a land where lords dressed comfortably. When the heat of summer returned, I wished to be cool. The merchants of Jaffa had some fine garments and I paid less than had I not been the guardian of the road. The new title now rolled off the tongue. William of Stockton meant nothing here but William, Lord of Aqua Bella, guardian of the road and defender of the poor did. As time went on it became associated with the gryphon on our chests. The fact that our dark cloaks looked similar to the black of the Hospitaller also helped.

John of Chester came running to the square where we sat beneath palm trees drinking chilled wine, "Lord, there is a Byzantine ship heading towards the port."

We finished our drinks and left. Other ships had come in the time we had been there but this was the first which was Byzantine. She was an Imperial ship. We had seen them when Ralph of Bowness had shown us Constantinople. They had all been moored in the Golden Horn. They had oars and slaves to row when the wind was not in their favour. William of Kingston had had to tack and turn with the wind on our voyage south. These ships took the most direct course and, as such, were swift. As it drew closer I saw that it was not one of the bigger ships. This one was still larger than the ***'Adela'***. I observed that it was under oars as it approached the harbour. It made it much easier for the captain to manoeuvre.

I shaded my eyes as I looked south, to the sun. It would be too late to return north. We would have to leave in the morning. I did not want to have to camp halfway to Jerusalem. That would place us too close to Ramelah. I hoped that the emissary could ride. If they had sent a clerk or diplomat then the journey might be difficult. I had brought good horses but they still needed someone who could ride. Although the Romans had built these roads they were not the roads of Normandy or England. Here the twisting roads climbed and descended. An unwary rider could be pitched from his saddle.

The marines by the stern were well-armed. The Emperor was taking no chances with his emissary. I turned to Tom, "Go and tell the innkeeper that we need another room for guests."

"Now then Englishman!"

I turned and saw a grinning Ralph of Bowness and Aethelward leaning over the side of the Byzantine as the crew tied her up.

"You are the emissary?"

The gangplank was lowered and he strode towards me, "And why should I not be an emissary? Do you think that because I am a warrior I cannot speak with a lord? He wrapped his huge arms around me, "It is good to see you William of Stockton and I am happy that young Alf now looks like a warrior. Come, Aethelward, we will get our gear and then we can talk."

He returned aboard the ship. Alf said, "But I thought they were Varangian Guards?"

"They are, Alf. There is a story here. Help them with their gear when they land. They are emissaries of the Emperor after all."

The two of them did not have much but I saw that they both had their axes. Ralph of Bowness also had a leather satchel which he wore across his body. My men took their chests and weapons. As we walked Ralph said, "The weapons are for the road. When we are close to Jerusalem then we will change, and become what is expected."

I nodded, "I was not expecting you, that is for certain."

Aethelward laughed, "Nor did I but Ralph here is full of surprises."

Ralph said, "This is not the place for such talk. We will speak out of the gaze of men."

When we reached the inn, Tom said, "We are in luck, lord. The two Franks who had the other room left but an hour since." He frowned, "They did not stay long."

"Have the bags taken in. I will speak with Ralph." The square was quiet and we would not be overheard. Even so, I said, "Garth, have two men watch. I want us to speak privately."

"It will be done as you wish."

We sat down and I said, "Perhaps you should begin with the time we were in Miklagård!"

He nodded, "I was not totally honest with you. For that, I apologize. A warrior should always speak the truth to a fellow warrior." I nodded. It was a good apology. "After I met you and your men the first time I mentioned it to the Emperor. He is a warrior. I helped to train him and ... well, he likes to talk to me. I am no politician and he gets honest words from me. He remembered your father and he asked me to keep an eye on you and help you in any way I could."

"Those horses were good horses, cheaply bought."

"The stables are Imperial stables. When he discovered you were going to the Holy Land he sent a message to the King of Jerusalem. He thought you might be useful."

"You knew, before I left, that you would be an emissary?"

"No. That was not known at the time. At the time, I had no idea why the Emperor had such an interest in you." He lowered his voice. "Now I know. There is pressure from Raymond, Prince of Antioch to have the Cilician lands returned to him. The Emperor needs King Baldwin to exert pressure on the prince. In return, the Emperor will allow the Crusader armies to cross through the Empire."

"And you? Why choose you?"

"Simple. I am known to you. It would not seem strange that I should visit with you, especially as, when I return to Miklagård, I will be released from service. Eventually, when I have made my fortune, I will be going home to England."

"Aethelward too?"

"No, he takes over from me and will command the English Varangians."

"I think that the King would have agreed to help the Emperor in any case."

Ralph laughed, "You do not know the politics of the east." He patted his satchel, "There is parchment here which will be signed. The Emperor wants this in writing."

"I do understand the politics," I told him of the Lord of Ramelah.

"Will he be a threat to us?"

"If King Baldwin signs the parchment then it becomes valuable. The answer is yes. We are not mailed yet but, when we leave on the morrow, then we will be."

"We do not leave today?"

"You are in my hands now. We rise early and we will try to reach Jerusalem in one day. I suspect that we will not manage that and so we will stay at my manor."

"You have a home?"

I nodded, "And a title: Lord of Aqua Bella, guardian of the road and defender of the poor."

"A grand title for one who came here as a penitent."

"The title is grander than the task. I escort caravans on the road and prevent bandits and robber barons from taking their wares. I guard shopkeepers!"

"Here, I brought you a present." He handed me a purse. I thought it was leather. But on closer inspection, I saw it was pigskin. "In the guard, we all have them. It stops these heathens stealing from us. They will not touch pigskin. It will keep your money safe. I meant to give it to you before you left."

"Thank you, Ralph of Bowness. It is a fine present."

"And now, sustenance. I am hungry, let us find food." We stood and he noticed Alf, seemingly for the first time. My young warrior was doing as I had asked and keeping watch. "And how is our headstrong young Angle?"

"Garth was wrought great changes in him. He is less likely to lose his temper but I am still unsure how he views you."

"I have a thick skin but I am pleased. It was *wyrd* that we found him. The Count of Provence tried to gain redress for the loss of his slave. He was less than happy."

"Where is he now?"

"He is on his way here. He is with the army of King Louis. They are waiting for permission from the Emperor to cross the Empire. So you see, speed is important. My ship will await my return."

"Then let us feed you and you can be reunited with my men."

I saw the wisdom of sending the two Varangian Guards. They did not look like diplomats. The fact that they spoke with my men and seemed at ease suggested that they had joined my retinue. It was only the arrival of the Byzantine ship which might have raised any suspicions. We left before dawn. We rode in a tight column. The two spare horses were now laden with the goods we had bought. Even though I knew that it was unlikely anyone would have guessed Ralph's purpose I still had Garth and Alf at the front. Alf had shown that he had good eyes and ears. We needed warning of danger.

When we neared Ginaton I took the caravan trail. "We leave the road?"

"We do. Although the Lord of Ramelah has been warned about his actions I think he is the kind of man who might choose to act and then wriggle his way out of consequences. I will not risk it. Besides this road is shorter. The only danger is bandits and I think that we can handle those."

He nodded. Although it was the middle of winter in the Kingdom of Jerusalem, it was still hotter than even Ralph was used to. We stopped frequently and took on water. It was as we had taken another stop, just three miles from Shilat that Garth wandered over. He took the water skin and, as he raised it to his mouth said, "Lord, Alf has spied men ahead. They are in the rocks."

I did not look but continued checking my girth.

"Have you seen them?"

"I saw a movement but I trust the boy."

"Bandits?"

"Your guess is as good as mine, lord. Men hiding does not bode well."

"Go around and warn the men."

"Aye lord."

I wandered over to Ralph and pretended to examine his horse's withers. He spat. "Trouble?"

"Men are hiding ahead. I intend to spring their trap. I will have Alf and Garth scout ahead. Men hiding will want us and not two scouts."

He laughed, "It has been a while since I exercised my sword arm."

As Garth passed me I said, "You and Alf ride fifty paces from us. I hope that they will let you pass and then attack us. You have your bow and Alf has his sling."

My men were all ready. I saw them surreptitiously sliding swords in and out of scabbards. We had no spears. We would be using swords. From Garth's words, I had worked out that the men were waiting where the trail went between two large rocks. It would hide them from our view. I waited until Garth had begun riding before I mounted. "Ralph when we near those rocks head left around it and I will head right. It may confuse them."

"This is your land and you are a horseman. I normally like fighting with the earth beneath my feet."

"Then today we teach you to become a horseman. Use your stirrups and do not overswing."

We began to move. I reached down to stroke Remus. As I did so I pulled up the long strap on my shield so that I held it, with my reins, in my left hand. My right hand was laid casually across the cantle of my saddle so that I could draw my sword quickly. Glancing ahead I saw that Garth and Alf had reached the ambush site. When they spurred their horses then I knew that the trap was sprung. A Seljuq archer, encased in robes suddenly rose from the rock and loosed an arrow. It struck Louis in the shoulder. Then the archer fell as Garth sent an arrow into his back. Another took his place but before he could strike Alf's stone had smacked into the back of his head and he had pitched from the rock.

"Go left and right!" Pulling my sword out, I rode right. A warrior leapt up at me. He was encased in voluminous garments. He jabbed up at me with his spear. I had my shield raised and I blocked it. Standing in my stirrups I brought my sword down on the side of his head. It grated along the bone and he fell. As he did so the cloth from his head fell and I saw that he was not a Turk. He was a Frank!

Garth and Alf had found a position some way from the ambush and they sent arrows and stones into the, as yet, unseen ambushers. Two warriors rose from my right. They had spears and they jabbed them at me. I deflected one but a second pierced my thigh. John of Chester was following me and he brought his sword across the back of one of them. The spear which I had deflected was pulled back for a second strike and I lunged down with my sword. I found the gap and my sword slid into his throat.

Another two archers rose ahead of us. An arrow from behind, sent by William of Lincoln, hit one in the chest. The other levelled his arrow at me. John of Chester had not stopped and he galloped towards the archer. The archer switched targets and released but John took the arrow on his shield. He did not stop and his horse trampled the archer to the ground. I heard shouts from the other side of the rock and knew that Ralph and Aethelward were laying into the ambushers with their axes which they used one-handed.

There was a shout, in French. "Fall back!" Ten riders broke from cover and rode south. William, Garth and Alf continued to send their missiles after them and were rewarded with two more men falling from their saddles.

"Tom, see to Louis!"

"Aye, lord!"

"Ralph!" I turned Remus to head towards the other side of the rocks.

"We are safe." As I turned I saw him. "I thought you said the Turks did not raid so far south?"

I shook my head, "These are not Turks. These are Franks." I sheathed my sword and dismounted. I walked to one of the so-called Turkish archers. I pulled his robes from him. He was wearing Frankish mail and he was white.

John of Chester reined in behind me and said, "I know him! He is the sergeant who stabbed Peter. These are de Waller's men."

Ralph said, "But how did they know we would be here?"

I shook my head. I had been a fool. I had been so confident that we had fooled our enemies that I ignored what we had been told. "The two men who left after your ship arrived. They were de Waller's men."

Garth and Alf rode up with four captured horses.

"Thank you. Had you not been so quick then it would have gone ill with us."

"As soon as we passed them I saw that they outnumbered us, lord. Did I hear you say that they were de Waller's men?"

"Aye. "

"But they used the Turkish bow."

Louis appeared, his horse led by Tom, "Aye but badly, Garth. The arrow barely penetrated my arm. It was used by someone who had not much experience of the horned bow."

Tom shouted, "Lord! You are wounded!"

I had forgotten the blow. I looked down and saw the trail of blood I had left. "It was a spear."

By the time I had been tended to and the weapons gathered I knew we would not make Jerusalem. "We will head for our home."

"What about the bodies? Do we take them as evidence?"

"What evidence Ralph? De Waller did not use his knights. He will deny it. He will say they were bandits. He is a clever opponent. We have thwarted him but he will try again on the way back."

"And how do we stop him then?"

"We will cross that bridge when we come to it."

Keeping a wary eye open we headed for Aqua Bella. We reached it after dark. I was pleased that my sentries spotted us long before we reached the gate. Our defences were intact. As the gate closed behind us I reflected that it could have been worse. Two of us were wounded but our charge and his missive were safe.

Alice tended to our wounds. Tom had been basic in his ministrations. He had bound the wounds. Alice cleansed them and then applied first vinegar and then a balm made with garlic and honey. When we were bandaged, we went to the hall for food. We ate well and both Ralph and Aethelward were impressed with my home.

"This King of Jerusalem has been generous in his gift."

"He has but we pay a price. We are tied to this road."

We talked long into the night. The wine was good and Garth and Robert got on well with the two Englishmen.

I awoke stiff for the wound was fresh but we left for Jerusalem when the sun was barely up. I took just Tom and Robert. If we were attacked on the short journey to Jerusalem then the world was awry.

"What is he like, this King of Jerusalem?"

I smiled, "Young but with an old head. His mother is the power behind the throne. He will agree to whatever you say. With Edessa captured Jerusalem is threatened from the north."

My seal gained us immediate access to the King. Paul, whom I had discovered was more than just a servant, whisked us through the curtain and into the presence of the King and Queen. Robert, Aethelward and Tom waited in the court with those who dreamed of an audience.

Ralph bowed, "Your majesty. I have a message from the Emperor. I am but a simple soldier and he did not trust the words to my mouth."

Queen Melisende smiled, "I do not believe that for one moment."

The two of them read the parchment. Queen Melisende asked, "Was there any difficulty in reaching us?"

Ralph looked at me. I answered. "We were attacked close to Shilat." I paused. "It was de Waller."

"You are certain?"

"Yes, your majesty. Could I prove it? No. You will have to take my word for it."

"And we do. We have known for some time that the Lord of Ramelah seeks to usurp me." The king smiled at Ralph. "We will need time to read this. Sir William, could you entertain the Emperor's man?"

"Of course."

"We will see you again this afternoon."

I saw the look of confusion on Ralph's face. When we were with the others I shrugged as I explained, "The king is young and he needs the advice of his mother. She has managed to hold on to power through two husbands. I have no doubt that they will confirm the treaty. We can go and visit the holy shrines. I have yet to do so. Come, Robert, lead on."

We spent the rest of the day visiting those places associated with Christ. Many of them were filled with those who sought to make money from pilgrims. Ralph displayed a temper and a fierce expression which enabled us to walk around without disturbance. The normal beggars and hawkers did not risk his ire. We ate well although Ralph and Aethelward were less than impressed with the wine that we were offered.

"Come it is time we returned. They will have debated long enough."

As I had expected they were more than ready for us. King Baldwin handed over the parchment. "You may tell your Emperor that we agree to this document."

Ralph bowed as he took it, "Thank you, your majesty."

Queen Melisende asked, "Will you need an escort, Sir William?"

I shook my head, "I intend to ride along the Ramelah road. If you could loan me a priest?"

"The Queen smiled, "We can do better. The Master of the Hospitallers is to take ship from Jaffa. He is to sail to Rhodes. The order has business there. He was waiting for permission to leave. This would seem a good opportunity to do so."

I saw Ralph frown and I wondered why.

"Should we wait for him?"

"He will meet you at Aqua Bella. You have a sharp mind, Sir William." The Queen held her hand out for me to kiss it.

"Thank you, your majesty, although I feel that I am in the company of the sharpest minds in Christendom."

As we left Ralph said, "Rhodes is Byzantine! What does this monk seek there?"

"As long as it gets us beyond Ramelah I care not."

In the end, we waited for two days for the master and his brothers to reach us. He apologized for the delay spouting the King and Queen as the reason. It was a large column which headed south. I had twelve men and with eight Hospitallers we would be noticed. As we passed Ramelah I saw the walls lined with de Waller's men. It was hard to gauge their mood but I suspected that we were flaunting our defiance in their faces and that did not sit well.

The journey allowed me to talk with the Master. I deduced that he was a serious man. He believed in what he was doing. He was not in the Holy Land to become rich. He genuinely wished to help pilgrims. I admired him but I could not do what he was doing. He had committed himself to a life of service. I was happy to be a penitent but when I had atoned for my sins I wanted a life. I wanted a family.

It was sad to say goodbye to Ralph. He would be returning, eventually, to England. I hoped I would see him when I returned but I had given my word to the king that I would not leave until Ascalon was captured. There appeared to be no sign of that. The rumour was that the king wished to take Damascus first. As the Crusaders were still in Anatolia that prospect was a lifetime away.

I clasped his arm at the dock. "You have your grandfather's blood coursing through your veins, William. If I was younger I would join your retinue but I fear I have seen too many of my friends die."

"And I am glad that I have met a serving Varangian. My father has spoken of them but until you meet one you cannot understand that the Varangians hearken back to a different time."

"You are right there. Your grandfather fought for Harold. He was with the housecarls who defeated Tostig and Hadrada. To those of us who now serve the Emperor, they are the ideal and we strive to match them." He smiled, "You would have made a good housecarl."

I shook my head, "I like being on the back of a horse too much. Farewell. Have a good life and a long life."

He nodded and they boarded the ship.

We rode back north feeling strangely downhearted. We had no reason to be. We had bested all of our enemies. We had completed all the tasks asked of us and we had yet to lose a warrior and yet, as I approached Aqua Bella I found myself yearning for England. I realised that neither Normandy nor Anjou would suffice. I had been seduced by the Count of Anjou and now, after barely half a year in the Holy Land, I realised that my father was right. I wanted to return to Stockton. I wanted to go back to my roots.

Chapter 9

David Ben Samuel came with Saul when the first shoots on the vines appeared. "Lord, it is time to fetch my daughter." He hesitated, "Unless, of course, your task prevents you from doing so."

I smiled, "I could be insulted by those words David Ben Samuel! I gave my word and I will keep it. Where do we find your daughter?"

"Saul will take you there. She does not know you and you are a Frank…."

"Of course. How inconsiderate of me."

"We have spare horses. I would not expect you to use your warhorses for such a task."

"Does your daughter require a carriage or a litter?"

"No, lord. She can ride as a man does. Before…" He closed his eyes. "She was a wonderful young woman and as a girl was full of life and laughter. That man…"

Saul put his hand on his father's arm, "Father we can do nothing about him. He is a Gentile and a Frank. He has power. If we try to do anything then it will end in the ruin of the family. Rebekah knows that."

David Ben Samuel shook his head, "I am sorry, lord, but I am a father. I know that you will understand that I would have endured any kind of pain or disfigurement to have prevented my daughter from suffering what she did."

"I know. One day this man will be brought to justice but until then your son is right. You must bide your time and bite your tongue. God has a way of punishing such wrongdoers. It is the same God we all worship. We have to believe that he will exact retribution."

We left the next day. I took Tom, Garth, Alf, John of Chester, Henry son of Will and Robin Hawkeye. The ones I left behind were less than happy. "Robert, I need you to carry on with the patrols. My duty is to the King but I owe David Ben Samuel. I will be away for seven days; that is all. This is not like bringing the Emperor's emissary. De Waller can have no interest in Rebekah. This will not put me in danger."

Despite my words, we went well-armed. Saul had brought four of his father's guards and they were all well-armed too. We took spare horses for Rebekah had servants and baggage. I was not arrogant enough to risk riding by Ramelah for a second time. I used the caravan road. The site of the ambush had been picked clean. Whatever bones had been there they had long since been picked over. We stayed in Jaffa. The port was busier than it had been during the Theophany. Ships were busy disgorging men and supplies. The Emperor had kept his word and the Crusaders were coming. I looked at their pale skin. That was us when we had arrived. We had changed both outside and inside.

Caesarea had been important when the Romans had ruled this land. Now it was something of a backwater. As we approached it I asked, "Saul, what was Rebekah doing here? Does your father have trading connections?"

He was evasive, "My father's sister lives here. She and Rebekah are close." And that was all that I could get out of him.

Judith, sister of David Ben Samuel, was a widow. She had four married daughters and no sons but she was a force of nature. When we reached her home, it was she who greeted us at the barred gate which led to her courtyard. She embraced Saul. Her smile and her twinkling eyes told of her fondness for him. I had not learned enough Hebrew to understand what they said. There was no need for all the people with whom I came into contact could speak my languages.

She glared at me and Saul said, apologetically, "I am afraid that my father's sister has a low opinion of all Gentiles and Franks in particular. She wants you and your men to sleep in the stables this night. I am sorry lord. She…"

I held up my hand, "It is her home and I respect her wishes. We will sleep in the stable. But we will need to leave early. I am reluctant to spend two nights on the road. We will have to stop once to sleep but that is all."

"You are right, lord. I will tell my sister and her women."

He turned and spoke to the woman. Her face cracked a little as Saul told her what I had said.

When they had gone, I spoke with my men, "Tonight we sleep in a stable."

Henry son of Will grumbled, "A stable? Where is the ale and the good food I expected?"

John of Chester chided him, "Our Good Lord was born in a stable not too far from here this will be a good thing."

In truth, we were all ready for our beds. They knew that it would be a hard ride the next day. Judith sent over plenty of food and wine. She was a generous hostess. Saul had told us, on the way over, that her husband had been a supplier of grain. She had continued somewhat more successfully than her husband. She was rich and, in Caesarea, an important woman. It explained why she had not moved closer to her brother.

We were up while it was still dark. I had my men prepare all of the horses. The sound of their hooves on the cobbles of the courtyard was an effective way of waking the house. There were, however, people already up for servants brought us out fresh bread with butter and cheese. The horses readied, we ate. Saul emerged with the servants and the baggage which were packed on the pack animals. The four female servants she brought came out next and we helped them to mount. As they did so I realised that they were no riders.

"Saul, you had better have one of your men assigned to each of these servants. If there is danger they will need to lead their horses. They can lead the horses with the baggage too."

"That means they will not be able to fight."

"And that is why you have my men. With respect Saul, I have seen little evidence that men who guard caravans are warriors like my men. All of my men have been trained since childhood to fight. We will fight better knowing that the servants are safe. I would like you to watch over your sister. If we find danger then your men guard the five women and we will do the rest."

He nodded, "You are right. I can fight but I have seen you and your men. You fight in a different way. You kill easily."

"Do not worry, Saul, if your sister is threatened you will fight as hard as we do. That is the difference, we fight as hard all the time."

Rebekah came out with her aunt. They embraced. I saw tears in Judith's eyes. Rebekah was encased in cloth. Only her eyes showed. She briefly glanced at me and all I saw were two dark pools then she mounted. I was relieved to see that she did so confidently. Saul had been right. She was a rider.

"Mount."

Judith came over to me and spoke. Saul translated, "She says that she has heard that you are an honourable man. Today is the chance for you to prove that her opinion of all Franks might be wrong." He smiled, "She orders you to take care of my sister."

"Tell her that your sister will be safe. She has my word on that."

He translated and Judith nodded.

"Garth, Alf, Robin, scout! John, Henry, rear guard."

My men were well trained. With the servants guarded on their left by Saul's men, Saul and I flanked Rebekah at the head of the column. We headed north. Rebekah kept her eyes on the rumps of my scout's horses. They were three hundred paces ahead of us. We really did not need scouts for the first part of the journey. We were travelling through houses and villages. I was heading for Ginaton. It would be a hard ride but it would bring us close to my patrol on the road. I intended to take the caravan trail.

Once we left the houses and headed towards Ramelah I became more alert. My eyes scanned the sides of the road and further ahead. We had been in this land for some time now and I was acclimatised to the land. In Normandy and England, I would have used the sound of birds to warn me of danger. Here there were fewer birds and fewer trees. It was your eyes which were of more use. You looked for movements. You searched for what should not be there. The rocks, gullies and scrubland were perfect country for ambush and that was why I had my two archers and Alf ahead. As they had shown when escorting Ralph of Bowness they had the hunter's instincts. If there was danger they would let me know.

We halted after two hours. We were not riding as hard as we would have had we not been slowed by the four servants but I knew they would be finding it hard. We all took on water. I made sure that Remus had water before I did. Here your horse was your life. I was under no illusions. If I was afoot then I would be dead.

We did not stop for long. It was just enough time for the women to relieve themselves and then we were on the road again. I say road but this Roman Road was not in the best of repair. Most traffic from Caesarea went to Jaffa and Asur. It would not hurt us but it showed that this was slightly less inhabited than the other road. It was, however, shorter. We had seventy miles to cover in two days. Had I just had my men I might have made it in one.

Rebekah and Saul chattered away as we rode along the road. It was understandable. Rebekah had lived away from the family for some time. As close as I could discover it had been more than two years since the attack and that was how long Rebekah had stayed with her aunt. I did not understand one word of their conversation. It helped me to concentrate on the road. Once we had passed Budrus the roads became ever more deserted. We had passed a few travellers heading west but after Budrus we were the only ones on the road, or so it seemed. The land to the south and west of us was fertile but to the north and east, it was barren. A few goats and sheep scrabbled for grazing but that was all. The shepherd boys were the only humans we saw. I knew that there would be other eyes upon us.

We were a little way from Ginaton when Rebekah spoke to me, "I am sorry that you have been left alone, lord. My brother and I were catching up. There is much to tell after so long apart."

She spoke with the slightest of accents. She was well educated. "You need not apologize, lady. I understand."

"My brother has told me how you helped my father. My aunt did not know. If she had she might have been more hospitable and courteous."

I laughed, "We are rough soldiers, lady. A night in a stable is a luxury compared with some of the beds we have had."

"Nonetheless I am grateful." Her eyes drifted south, "I am not certain that I could pass this close to that beast if I did not have your sword to guard me."

"It is not the Lord of Ramelah who worries me it is that." I waved my hand to the hills to the north and east. "There are bandits there. They will see five women. That is the danger. This time it is not my people who are the danger to you; it is your own people and, perhaps, the Turk."

"The Turks? Nablus and Jerusalem guard the roads!"

"Your father's caravan was attacked along this road by Seljuq archers on horses. We are just half a day of hard riding from the Emirate of Damascus."

She turned around. "And that is why you have my father's men watching my servants."

"If we are attacked then my priority is you, my lady. Once we are beyond Shilat then I will breathe easier."

We reached Ginaton without incident. It was a tiny place and there would be no accommodation for us but there was a wall with a gate. It was used by the caravans which plied their trade. We were lucky and it was empty. Henry and John of Chester made a crude barrier at the gateway. They would sleep there. Garth and Alf got a fire going while the rest of my men saw to the horses. I walked the perimeter seeking any weakness. The men who had built it had been camel drivers and they had made it as strong as they could. We would not be surprised. We would not be comfortable but we would be safe.

Saul and his sister ate with their men and servants. We watched while they ate and then we had our food. I had arranged for us to watch in pairs. It was not that I did not trust Saul's men but mine were warriors. Tom and I took the last watch. Garth shook me awake.

"All quiet?"

"Aye lord but…"

"But?"

"The hairs on my neck prickle. We are watched."

"We have been watched for the last ten miles, Garth. This is bandit country. Tomorrow we will need to be extra vigilant."

As we left the village I noticed that there was no one about. We had arrived late and we had not seen anyone but the fact that we saw none as we left made me wary. We were passing by the place the archers had attacked us. There were scrubby bushes and stunted groves of acacia.

Mainly there were rocks. The first that we knew of an attack was when one of Saul's men was hit in the back by an arrow. I drew my sword and wheeled around. They had waited until we had passed them.

"Saul, get the women to safety. Stockton! On me!" My three archers had their bows ready. Alf's slingshot whirled and the stone flew to hit the archer who had slain the Jew. Riders poured through the scrubby trees. They were not all archers but the ones they had were good. Another of Saul's men was hit in the arm and two arrows smacked into my shield. There were just four of us able to close with the attackers. They were Seljuq. They were after the women. Too many to count I led my men into the heart of them.

Remus was bigger than their horses and he barged between two of them. I took the blow from one Turk on my shield while sweeping my blade just above the other's horse's head. I almost hacked the rider in two. I wheeled Remus around and continued my sweep to slice through to the backbone of the other. A third Turk, on foot this time, rammed his spear towards my side. It tore along the mail and I backhanded blindly. I felt the blade hit something. When I looked, I had ripped open his face.

Henry son of Will might be a loud drunk but he was a mighty warrior. He was fearless and he plunged into the Turks using both his shield and his sword at the same time. John of Chester protected his back and side as Tom did with me. My archers and Alf were now dismounted and their arrows were plucking Turkish horse archers from their saddles. I saw that one of my men's horses lay dead. As I looked I saw a Seljuq Turk strike Saul and he fell from the saddle.

"Tom, follow me!" I wheeled Remus around and galloped towards Rebekah. The Turk who had wounded Saul was raising his spear to strike his back when Robin Hawkeye lived up to his name and sent an arrow into his head. Three more Seljuq Turks hastened towards Rebekah. She had dismounted and was kneeling by her brother. I did not slow down. I ploughed into the three Turks. Using my knees to guide my horse I slashed with my sword and punched with my shield. I saw a spear coming towards me from the third Turk and then Tom's sword appeared from his chest.

"Tom, see to Saul. Lady, mount. My squire will tend to your brother."

"I cannot leave him!"

"Nor will you! Now mount or more men will die and you would not wish that on your conscience, would you?"

"I would not." She rose and mounted.

We were outnumbered. We had to make a last stand. "Everyone fall back here! We make a last stand!"

Tom had managed to lay Saul over his saddle. His head was bleeding but I had no idea if he was alive or dead. Two of Saul's guards had survived and they brought the four screaming servants. The pack animals were gone. Alf rode double with Robin and they joined us. When Henry and John rode in, I saw that Henry had had his face laid open by one of the Turk's wickedly curved blades.

The Turks had also stopped. They were preparing to charge us. Garth and the others had slain their archers but the twenty who remained were ready to fall upon us.

"Rebekah, you and the women get in the middle. Isaac, you and Benjamin, guard the rear. Archers behind us. If they want the women then they will have to kill us to get to them!"

The leader of the Turks raised his sword and they hurtled down the slope towards us. They did not come in an ordered line as we would, they came as individuals. That suited me. I was in the centre and I had a trick ready. The leading rider made straight for me. Suddenly I stood in my stirrups and pulled back on the reins. Remus stood and flailed his hooves. The Turk's horse baulked and, as it turned, Remus' hoof smashed the rider's skull. The dying Turk pulled the horse to the ground and the others had to move left and right. Three archers can release arrows quickly and at such close range, they did not need much power. Even so, we would soon be surrounded and an unprotected back meant death.

Suddenly I heard the thunder of hooves. I looked to the east and saw Robert of Mont St. Michel leading my patrol to charge the Turks. The enemy did not stay but ran. Garth, William and Robin used the last of their quivers to pluck another five from their saddles as they fled. Leaving the reinforcements to chase them from the field I dismounted and went to look at Saul. He was lucky. The blow had damaged his helmet and knocked it from his head. The blow had rendered him unconscious. He was bleeding but he would live.

I turned to Rebekah. "There is vinegar in my saddlebag and a cloth. Clean his head and bind it."

She nodded, "Aye lord and thank you."

"I told your father I would get you home safe and I am a man of my word."

I went to Henry and saw that John was already binding his wound. Henry gave me a weary smile and then regretted it. "Well I was no flower before the fight but I reckon now I will have a scar to make me even uglier!"

John said, "Sarah is handy with a needle. She can stitch it. Just keep your mouth shut for a while eh? That would be something!"

By the time my men had returned with the baggage and captured horses, we had collected the dead guards and laid them across their horses. The last time we had left the Turks where they lay. Now I wanted a message leaving. "Take every Turk's head and plant them in two lines on the end of their spears. I want them to see the folly of attacking us."

Saul came to before we left. He looked around in fear as his eyes opened. Rebekah said, soothingly, "Fear not, Sir William and his men saved us. We are safe."

"My men?"

"David and Joshua are both dead. We have their bodies on their horses. We will take you home now."

It was a relief to see my banner fluttering above Aqua Bella. We did not all enter but Henry did for he needed to be tended to. We left our horses and baggage there and continued the last few miles to David Ben Samuel's. We stayed just long enough to see Ruth burst into tears as she embraced her daughter. When David saw his bandaged son, he came over to me and grasped my hands, "Once again, I am in your debt."

"I know not why. Your son is wounded and you have two dead men. Had I done a better job then I would expect thanks. I am sorry for your loss."

He shook his head. Rebekah turned. For the first time since meeting her, she had removed the silken scarf from around her face and hair. I saw that she was stunningly beautiful. Her long black hair flowed over her shoulders and shone like ebony. Her eyes were deep pools and her face was that of an angel.

"Sir William. I am sorry that I was not as friendly as I might have been. Forgive me. When I am settled again, I would like you to visit with us so that I may thank you by cooking a meal for you."

"You have no need but I will come. Thank you, lady."

She handed me the scarf. "Until then take this. Perhaps it will bring you good fortune."

"Thank you." I wheeled Remus and led my men back through the gates. When we were far enough from the walls to be hidden, I sniffed the scarf. I could smell her perfume upon it. I had seen an angel and my life would never be the same again.

My mail had been damaged by the spear and all of my men had wounds. We had come close to losing all. But for the timely arrival of my patrol, the women would be slaves and we would be lying dead in the wasteland. Alf was sad that he had lost his horse and so we gave him the choice of the ones we had captured. The Turks had yielded treasure and we shared that amongst the men. Henry's face looked red, painful and angry but Judith had done as John had suggested she might. They were neat stitches.

I led the patrol the next day. I took one of the workers from the estate with me. The heads were still there; the eyes pecked out by birds and the skulls filled with flies. They would not last long. I rode to Ginaton. We surprised the villagers who hid behind their doors as we rode through. I halted in the middle and then said to Sayeed who worked on the estate, "Translate my words as I speak."

"Aye lord."

"I am the Lord of Aqua Bella. I am the guardian of the road and protector of the poor. I give you fair warning. If any of you offer aid to the bandits or the Turks then I will raze this village to the ground and sell each one of you into slavery. My men will ride this valley. They are your friends unless you choose to side with the enemy. You are either our friend or our enemy. There is no halfway. Choose and choose wisely."

Sayeed translated. He turned after he had spoken. "I lived in a village like this, lord. I can tell you that they fear the bandits and the Turks more than you."

"Tell me, Sayeed, where do the Turks and the bandits hide?" I spread my hand around. Where are the places that they can live?"

He pointed to the high ground. "Up there are caves and there are springs."

"They must be close enough to see the trail."

"They are but they also use boys from the village. They send messages."

"Thank you, Sayeed. You have given me an idea of how to make their lives better and our lives safer."

When we reached Aqua Bella, I asked Francis if he or Absalom needed anything from Jerusalem. "Aye lord. Our wives need to make purchases. I was going to ask if we could visit."

"Then tomorrow we will escort you in. I have purchases to make. We will spend the day in Jerusalem."

"Thank you, lord."

"Robert, you, Tom and Alf will accompany me tomorrow. I have money to deposit with Simon. Ask the men if they need anything from the city. We will not be going again for a while."

King Baldwin had been generous with his gift but, as I rode in with Francis and Robert I realised that he had gained more from the arrangement. Francis had to take in the taxes for the King. Now that the Lord of Ramelah was no longer taking half he had more profits. More goods were reaching Jerusalem and so the taxes on the market meant more money for the king. I saw that he and his mother were astute. For the cost of an estate and a title, they had increased their profits.

"And I want to make our life easier."

"How will you do that, lord?"

"We will destroy the bandit and Turkish bases which lie to the north of us. We take this war to them. If we make the hills untenable then they will move elsewhere."

Absalom shook his head, "You would willingly go into a nest of vipers?"

"If you know where they are then you can be prepared. Sayeed said that they camp close to water. We find the water and we find their camps."

"You make it sound easy, lord."

"It will be anything but easy, Francis, but it can be done. My father found that the best way to deal with the Scots who raided was to attack their bases. They do not raid his valley. I will do the same here."

I intended to spend the whole day in Jerusalem. Alf and Tom purchased the items my men wanted and Robert and I visited Simon. His eyes lit up when he saw the chest. "You have been successful, lord."

His clerk began to tally up the amounts.

"And I hope to be more successful in the future." I lowered my voice. "How do the bandits move their money? Do they have a similar arrangement with you?"

He looked shocked, "No lord. It is against our religion however there are those in the city who deal with them. The city has quarters. Those who worship Islam live in their own quarter. They have men such as I with whom they can deal."

"Have you a name?"

"I could find out for you but why? What good would it do?"

"Just find the name and the address and leave the rest to me."

After we had left the money lender Robert said, "I confess I cannot see what we would gain from knowing where they sell their gold and jewels."

"It is not them that I am after. It is those who trade. I need someone who can pass amongst them. I would have those who trade followed. I need a local scout. We will keep our eyes and ears open."

We had plenty of time and so we wandered down to the temple to see if there were any men to hire. We had a jug of wine and looked but none seemed right. We were far from home. We could not risk hiring men whom we did not trust completely. I contemplated visiting the palace but I feared that the king would find more tasks for us to do. Instead, we wandered the streets. Sometimes your feet are guided not by your mind but by fate. We turned a corner and spied Roderigo de Santiago. He was with three other knights and two sergeants. I saw a new scar on his face. Had he been involved in the attack?

"The Englishman! You are still alive!"

"As are you. I put my resilience down to a clear conscience. That cannot be true of you."

He laughed, "I like you! You are like the young cockerel in the farmyard. You strut and you pose but when the time is right you will be crushed. You do not challenge the Lord of Ramelah. He is more powerful than you can possibly imagine."

"I have grown up around powerful men. Often the power is an illusion." I shrugged, "Just so long as your lord keeps away from me and my men then he is safe."

He coloured. I had provoked him, "He will be safe! You are one knight with a handful of brigands at your beck and call. If it suited my lord then he would crush you."

"I think that, if he could, he would and he hasn't so who is the cockerel now?"

He leaned in to me, "Beware my young friend. There will be a sea change soon. I would choose your friends more carefully!"

I nodded, "I thank you for the advice but you should know that I always choose my friends carefully" I smiled, "And that is why neither you nor your lord will ever be counted amongst them!"

My words had got to the Spaniard and he stormed off followed by the knights and sergeant.

"What do you think he meant about sea change, lord?"

"I think the Lord of Ramelah has a little treason running through his veins. It does not change what we do. We keep the road safe. This is neither Normandy nor England. I am here to do penance and, it seems to me, that I am doing so."

Robert smiled, "The Lady Rebekah is beautiful is she not, lord?"

For some reason, his words irritated me, "What on earth made you say that? Of course, she is beautiful. What has that to do with my penance?"

I could see that I had confused him, "Nothing lord save that saving her went a long way to atoning. I meant no harm, lord."

I realised that I had overreacted, "Of course not. Forgive me. The Lord Roderigo got to me." It was not true of course. Robert's words had. She was beautiful but I had come here to atone for the loss of my wife and family. It was not to get another! We walked in silence through Jerusalem's streets. I barely knew the woman and yet I could not get her eyes from my thoughts. Her scarf was still tucked close to my tunic.

We met up with the others and headed back to Aqua Bella. It was only as we were leaving the city that I wondered if Roderigo and his knights might try to wreak revenge. I dismissed the thought. We were too close to Aqua Bella and many others were leaving the city at the same time as us. It was a sobering thought, however, from now on we needed to travel the roads in greater numbers. We had been threatened and only a fool would ignore such a threat.

Chapter 10

Part Two
Damascus

A messenger came from Simon. I had the name of the money man the bandits dealt with and the place he frequented. I could now make firmer plans. For the next four weeks, we patrolled and we secured the safe arrival of ten caravans. One of them was that of David Ben Samuel. We met him south of Ginaton.

"It is good to see you again, lord. My daughter and my son have spoken often about you. Rebekah promised to cook for you. I think that she is offended that you have yet to take her up on the offer."

"I meant no offence but this is the caravan season. We have been busy. We have had to drive off bandits and Turks. They still try to disrupt your trade."

"They do."

"Tell me, have you any men who are good at tracking?"

"Good at tracking?"

"I need men with local knowledge. I will say no more for the work I have is dangerous but if you have someone who is willing to work for a Gentile, I have a plan to end the threat of the bandits for good."

"I will ask the other merchants. They may know of someone."

"How is Saul?"

"Recovered."

"If he is to be a warrior he needs mail and a helmet."

"He is a merchant. We trade."

"And when my men are gone? What then? You need to defend yourselves. Your men have courage and ability. The bandits are no real threat to men who are armed and prepared to fight them."

"It is the cost. Mail, helmets and swords are expensive."

"And how expensive is a man's life?"

He did not say much as we parted and I guessed that I had given him much to ponder upon.

We were now approaching the height of summer. The Crusaders who had journeyed from France, Germany and Austria were approaching

Antioch and soon could start to exert pressure on the Turks. I hoped for an attack on Ascalon for that would allow me to go home. Yet I knew that Edessa would be the first target. And so I was surprised when a messenger arrived summoning me to Jerusalem for the Crusaders were still far away. Once again there were many knights who thronged the court. There was no room for either Tom or Robert at the court and they waited with the horses.

There was no special treatment for me. I was one of the seventy or so knights who waited for the king to speak. I did not see the Master of the Hospitallers this time nor, for that matter, any of the Templars. It appeared to be a gathering of secular knights. The Lord of Ramelah and his knights formed a large block. There were knights who stood with them showing their allegiance. It was a large number of knights who appeared to support de Waller. I remembered Roderigo's words. They suddenly became more ominous.

Two knights preceded a very martial looking King Baldwin. He had grown in the time I had been in the Holy Land. He was now dressed for war. His mail was burnished and it shone. He had a good sword strapped to his belt. He looked as though he was ready to ride at the head of an army. Of course, that was an illusion. He was just going to tell us that we would be going to war. That much was obvious. This was ritual; this was a show. It told us that he was the King of Jerusalem and he was a warrior. The Queen, I noticed, kept to the background. Was this the start of the handover of power?

All eyes turned to him and he began to speak. "My lords I welcome you to this conclave. I bring great tidings. King Louis of France and King Conrad of Germany have brought many men to aid us in our struggle against the Seljuq Turk."

There was a great cheer from the assembled knights.

"I come here today to ask you all to prepare to join me when we march north to meet with the others who will attack Damascus."

If his first announcement brought cheers this one was greeted by silence. Men looked at each other. An attempt to retake Edessa was understandable. An attack on Ascalon, the last part of the principality held by the Turks was also a good idea but Damascus was not. A siege was never a good idea and Damascus was a hard city to take. I said nothing. I had but nineteen men. I knew that there were over six hundred and forty knights at the King's disposal and over five thousand sergeants. In addition, there were thousands of peasants who could be called up to the levy. They were men like Jean and Francis. I was a small fish in this pond. I kept my counsel. Others, however, did not.

"Who has decided this, your majesty?"

The '*your majesty'* was almost an afterthought from the silky mouth of Guillaume de Waller.

"I have! I am king!"

"Your majesty you are young and have not, as far as I know, taken part in a major campaign against the Turk. I have and Damascus is not an easy city to take."

He was not shouted down. I felt guilty. I should have defended the king and yet, although I did not like it, I agreed with de Waller. I suspect my motives were different to his. I did not see the point of bleeding on the walls of Damascus. After what Roderigo had said I thought that this was the start of de Waller's attempt to take the throne. The numbers of men who stood with him now seemed sinister.

"Lords I need your support in this."

It was the wrong word to use. He should have used the word command instead of need.

"Then perhaps you should have consulted with those of us who have experience in such matters."

The lack of respect was obvious and some of the knights who were not allied to de Waller now began grumbling.

The Queen spoke. "My son is doing so now, Lord de Waller. The attack is not imminent. Our allies have far to travel but we must be ready to fight when they get here. Remember your obligations. Each of you holds lands for the King. You owe him service. Are there any of you who wish to give up their lands and titles? Perhaps you are ready to return home with the riches you have accrued here?"

Although spoken by a woman there was a real threat in her words. For the first time, I saw Guillaume de Waller look less confident. He bobbed his head; he was accepting the obligation. "I for one am happy to give the king the fealty we owe. I would like, however, a council of elder knights to advise him. Is that too much to ask?"

"It is a reasonable request and I will give thought to the men who will make up the council." The Queen's words had given him confidence and King Baldwin sounded authoritative once more. "We will meet again in four weeks' time and I will have my council ready for the approval of this august body of knights. Until then carry on with your preparations. The siege will not be swift. We may well be in the field for the whole winter."

As men began to leave the Queen caught my eye and gave a subtle flick of her wrist summoning me to her side. I did not rush to join her. I allowed the majority of knights to leave and then followed her into her niche behind the curtain. The King was not there.

"Like de Waller, you do not like the idea of a siege, do you?"

"No, your majesty. I am a horseman and I prefer to ride to war. I have climbed siege towers and watched warriors die. I would have thought we could have taken Edessa more easily."

"Perhaps, except that Edessa lies beyond Damascus. If my son leaves that city to threaten our lines of communication it invites disaster."

I had not thought of that.

She smiled, "You are without guile, William of Aqua Bella. My son and I like you. You have done all that we have asked of you. Know this. When we go to war you and your men will be the scouts who ride ahead of the main army. You have shown yourself very resourceful. You will answer only to my son. Even if there is a council to offer guidance you will take orders from my son. You are the warriors who will protect him. There will be danger from within as well as from without."

"That is a great responsibility."

"And with it will come great reward. For now, carry on with your duties but when you return in four weeks' time be ready to ride. You will leave a minimum of men to guard your home. Your best men must be with you."

I found Robert and Tom waiting for me. "Well, lord?"

"It seems we have four weeks before we go to war or at least until we are summoned here again. I think we will visit with David Ben Samuel. I have less time than I thought."

Nestled as it was in a sheltered valley, David Ben Samuel's home felt even more welcoming than Aqua Bella which was tucked into a cliff. We were now recognized by our devices and welcomed as friends. I knew that when our horses were taken away they would be watered, fed and groomed. They would be kept in shade and they would be safe.

None of Saul's sons were to be seen and it was the merchant himself who greeted us. "Your sons are not at home?"

Shaking his head, he said, "They have gone to Jaffa. We have some ships coming there."

"Not Tripoli?"

"There are so many Crusader ships using the port that it is hard to get a berth and the roads south are clogged with lords and their retinue." He smiled, "Not all come as lightly burdened as you, lord. Did you want to see my sons?"

"No David. It was you I needed. Did you manage to find the man I sought?"

Before he could answer Rebekah appeared, "My lord. Have you come to taste my food?"

"I came to speak to your father." I saw her face fall and cursed myself for my words. I was used to speaking bluntly with soldiers. "However, as we are here and we have no plans then that would be most welcome."

Her face lit up. "Good. I shall tell my mother."

"That was kindly done, lord. She is still not the daughter she was. Before de Waller, she was happy, intelligent and full of curiosity. Now she is withdrawn and, seemingly, frightened of her own shadow. She flinches when men pass close by her. Even me. She does not eat. There is more flesh on a corpse than on my daughter. At night, we hear her crying. It is not every night, as it once was, but we hear her tears."

I had not seen her before but I had thought her thin, almost emaciated. "It will take time although, in truth, I do not think any man can understand what she is going through."

"You are right, lord. We must trust to God but I am certain that your presence can only help. Now, to the matter in hand. Come inside where it is cooler."

We entered the cool hall and took off our cloaks. We stamped our feet and shook our clothes to remove dust. We had learned the custom quickly. We even did it in Aqua Bella. A servant would sweep the hall regularly. It kept the rest of the house cleaner. The shaded courtyard with the bubbling water refreshed the moment we entered. Lemons scented the air.

The servant poured us the cooled wine and left us."

"I have a man. I would have brought him to see you but, with my sons away I did not wish to leave my family alone. You understand?"

"Of course. Who is he and where is he?"

"I will begin with his story. His name is Masood. He and his family lived north of here in the Beqaa valley. Turks came and raided his farm. His father was slain and he and his family made into slaves. On the way east he managed to escape in the wild lands north of Galilee. He learned to fend for himself. He became a solitary man. We found him some years ago not far from Ginaton. He had hurt his leg. We tended him and brought him here. He watches my flocks in the high pastures. He prefers that to the company of men. As for where he is," he pointed north. "Somewhere up there. Now, what do you need of him?"

"The bandits and the Turks who prey on caravans have to sell their goods somewhere. I believe it is in the Muslim quarter of Jerusalem. I have been given the name of a man who deals with the bandits and sells for them in Jerusalem. I need someone to watch him. When the bandits come to sell to him he can follow them to their lair. When we know where the nest lies then we will destroy them once and for all. At the moment, we are trying to swat flies when they come. So long as they have somewhere to hide, we will never rid ourselves of them. Destroy their home and the threat is gone."

"I will ask him but you must appreciate, my lord, that you cannot order a man to do that. He chooses to take the risk or he does not."

"I know."

"Then I will ask him and if he agrees I will send him to you."

We spoke of the caravans and I was told that all the merchants were now reaping the reward of our labours. "That may change, I am afraid. We go to war soon. The king wishes to use my men. It will be in your quiet time but even so…"

"When there is war that is the time the bandits come from their holes."

"And that is why I wish to destroy them before I go to war."

"And if Masood cannot do as you ask?"

"Then we will do it the hard way. We will go into the hills and seek them. I have men who are good scouts."

"But it would be easier if you knew you were looking in the right place." I nodded. "You have not given yourself an easy task and I admire the fact that it is not for you that you do this but for others."

"Penance, I wish to atone."

"And yet you have not visited a priest since you arrived here."

"How do you know that?"

"There is no priest at Aqua Bella and you have had no time during your visits to Jerusalem."

"I speak with God each night. I say my prayers and beg for forgiveness."

A servant came, "Lord, Lady Rebekah says to tell you that the meal is almost ready."

David Ben Samuel waved a hand and slaves appeared with water and towels. We were now used to this custom. We had copied it at Aqua Bella. Robert and Tom were summoned and they joined us.

We were taken into a large room. At home, in Normandy, we would have called it a hall. Here, however, it was light for three were openings to allow light and air through. Fine muslin stopped flies. It was pleasant. The smell of lamb cooked with herbs and spices drifted from the kitchen. It was an aromatic and enticing smell. We were honoured. Ruth, Mary and Rebekah came in and sat at the table.

David pointed to a seat between his daughter, Rebekah and himself. "Lord, sit here." I saw that there was a space between Rebekah and Mary and one between David Ben Samuel and Ruth. When we were seated, our host said, "It is our custom to thank God for our food before we eat. It will not offend you?"

"We do the same and we shall join you."

He smiled, "Always a gentleman. In my house, we have the custom of holding hands and making a circle." He gave me his hand and Rebekah held up hers. Her skin was so soft it felt like silk. I was afraid to hold it in case I crushed or damaged it. I did not hear David Ben Samuel's words. I was concentrating on not hurting the young woman to my right.

When David let go of my hand I released Rebekah. She said, quietly, "I will not break, lord. I am stronger than you might think."

I smiled at her. She was stunningly beautiful. "I am just a rough, clumsy knight. I treasure beautiful things and I do not break them."

"You think me beautiful?"

"There is no think about it. You are beautiful."

Her eyes went to the dish before her. "I am damaged and there is no beauty in me. The outside might be a well-painted vase but inside I can hold nothing. I am empty and dead." She looked so sad that it almost broke my heart. The servants brought in the food. The centrepiece was the lamb. We were served by the servants. Rebekah said, "Give the lord plenty. I want him to give me an honest opinion of my cooking." The sadness was gone and there was a smile but her eyes still showed the hurt.

I could see that it was important that I gave an honest opinion. I put the spoon into the stew. The lamb was so well cooked that it parted with the pressure of the spoon. It was unctuous. The taste was sublime. I could taste the lamb but there were undercurrents of other flavours. I took a second and a third. Each mouthful seemed different from the last. I tasted an apricot and I tasted mint and rosemary.

"You do not like it, lord?" She had a worried look on her face and I realised that I been concentrating so much on doing as she had asked that I was frowning.

I smiled widely, "It is delicious but I am enjoying the journey through the dish. It is like a beautiful lady such as you. There are layers hidden. Your find one taste and another lurks beneath ready to surprise you. I am enjoying discovering those layers."

She nodded, seemingly satisfied. As we ate we spoke. I had eyes for none but Rebekah. She reminded me of the Empress Matilda. She was clever and she was witty. She was well-read but through all of the conversation she held back from revealing anything about herself. In contrast, I told her about my wife and my children. I told her of my mother and her sacrifice. I laid bare my soul.

When the meal was over it was becoming dark. Robert said, "Lord, we should be getting home. The road is not safe at night and Francis will worry."

"You are right, Robert." I took Rebekah's hand and kissed the back of it. "Thank you for the evening, lady. The meal is the best I have ever eaten. You are a fine cook." I suddenly remembered that there had been others there. I turned and kissed Ruth's hand. "You have a most welcoming home."

She gave me a wry smile, "I am pleased that you noticed."

David Ben Samuel embraced me and said, in my ear, "Thank you, lord. My daughter looks happier already. I will speak with Masood."

As we rode home I was silent. I felt guilty. David Ben Samuel thought I had been kind to his daughter because I was a gentleman. The truth was that I was enamoured of her. I wanted her for my own.

The next day we went on the Shilat road to patrol and we met Saul and his caravan as they made their way through the parched landscape. We rode with them back up the Jerusalem road. He was happy, "There are many Franks in the land now. That is good for us. Prices will rise. We will make even more profit. Soon I will think about my own home."

"You would leave your father?"

"Not completely. He owns large parts of the land around our home. He has promised my brothers and I, our own plot for us to build. When I build, I intend to have a well-constructed home. One day war will come here again and we will have to be ready."

I nodded and told him of the coming war. "I do not think that it will be until after the winter but you should be ready."

"As you can see we have taken your advice. Some of us now wear mail beneath our garments and helmets on our heads. When time allows, we would like your men to teach us how to fight. A man should be able to defend his own home." I was pleased that my words had been heeded. We were like a thin layer of silk holding this land safe. One day we would be gone and they would be left alone.

We left them at Aqua Bella. The last section of the road was safe. Once inside I told Francis of the impending war. "I will leave men here but it will not be many."

"You have made our home stronger than it was. We will defend it for you, lord."

Three days later David Ben Samuel arrived with a small, thin man who was dressed as a shepherd. I guessed that it was Masood. I took them into my home.

David spoke, "Masood agrees to do as you have asked."

"And what is his price?"

"Price?"

"A man should be rewarded. Whatever he wishes he shall have."

David spoke to the shepherd. "He wishes for a horse."

"Then he shall have one." When he was told, Masood grinned and suddenly looked much younger than I had thought. I explained what I wanted. Masood did not seem worried by the prospect. "He needs to go to Jerusalem and wait by the Turkish merchants." I gave him the name and location of the contact. Masood nodded as did David. They both knew the place. "He should follow those whom he suspects of being bandits and find their home. That is all that I want him to do. He returns here and tells me."

Masood agreed and with that, the plan was hatched. David and I explained to him that he should blend in with the people who frequented that part of the city and that he should wait nearby and pretend to be a beggar. That done, David and Masood left. I spent the next day planning the expedition which would destroy our foes. Robert and Garth took it in turns to watch the road. Tom and I gathered what we would need to go into the high country and scour the bandits from their lairs. We now had some Turkish horses as well as horses which we had captured from the bandits. As much as I would have liked to use my own horses I knew that it would be better if we used horses used to that country. They would be less likely to alarm the other horses we might find there. We also gathered the curved bows we had captured. There were four of them. My new men had been practising with them. Although they would not be as effective as Garth and the other archers, the four of them would enable us to rain more arrows into their camp.

We then waited for Masood to return. I hoped he would return before the summons from the king. Ten days after I had sent him he returned with David Ben Samuel. I was eager for the news but I was patient enough to allow Masood to tell David and then for David to translate for me.

"There is a camp just two miles above Shilat."

"That close?"

"It surprised me too, lord. It explains why they are able to strike so quickly. Up on the ridge, there is a natural hollow with water. They have huts and they have families."

"Is he certain that they are families and not captives?"

After he had translated David said, "It is hard to determine that." Masood explained how we should get there. Then David said, "He is willing to lead you."

I realised that would be the best idea. I nodded. "Does he need a weapon?"

"He has his sling and a knife. They are all that he needs."

David taught me a few words so that I could speak with Masood and then he left. I took Masood and let him choose his own horse from the ones we had captured. He picked a hardy little one. I would not have used it for us. It was too small but it was perfect for him. I decided to strike immediately. I gathered my men and explained that we would travel overnight and attack the camp at dawn. We would attack from the west so that we were in darkness while the camp would be lit by dawn's early light. Masood had told us that there were up to forty men and young warriors in the camp. Although we would be outnumbered, we would have surprise on our side. I intended to destroy their home. Even if we did not slay them all we would make them find a new home and the caravans would be safe, for a while.

We muffled our horse's hooves with sacking and removed anything which would jangle. We did not need our shields. In fact, they would only get in the way. We left our helmets at home. We would just use our coifs and ventail. They would not be needed until we were much closer. We left just after dark. We had sixteen miles to travel and we would be in Masood's hands. He showed that he knew how to ride. I could not ask him how he had become so accomplished. He led us unerringly along trails and tracks which I did not know existed. We went steadily without stopping. As we climbed we moved more slowly. The last thing we needed was a shower of skittering stones to tumble down the hillsides.

Eventually, as we rose through a scrubby line of spikey bushes, he signalled for us to dismount. As we did so I sniffed the air and I could smell wood smoke. I could not see any glow. The fire was hidden. We hobbled our horses and I left Gurth on watch. We began to ascend the path which twisted and turned. Suddenly Masood held up his hand and we halted. He disappeared. I heard nothing. I hated waiting. Then he reappeared, wiping the blood from his knife. He was grinning. A few paces up the trail I saw the body of the sentry. His throat had been slit and his eyes removed. I remembered that to Masood, this was personal. His family had been taken and killed by people like this. In this land, it was an eye for an eye, quite literally.

As we moved higher up the slope I began to hear the noises of the camp. It was the sound of grunts and snores. It was the crackle of fires. It was the sound of animals. We had the whiff of smoke as it blew towards us. The wind was from the east. It took our smell away from the camp. Someone gave a cry but it was not the cry of danger. It was a cry of pain. Then there was a laugh. We carried on with our ascent. Masood waved us to the left and the right. We had arranged our positions while in Aqua Bella. Garth would secure one end of the line with Alf while William and Ralph of Ely would secure the other. The rest of us were spread out in the centre. With nine bows and two slings, we would kill or maim as many as we could before those of us with swords entered the camp to end their lives.

I looked to the east and saw that we had barely made it in time. There was the slightest hint of light from the east. I risked looking down into the camp and saw shadows huddled together in untidy groups. They were gathered around fires. I saw some shapes moving suggesting that they were awake or, active. I saw the heads of their tethered horses. The bandits did not risk them in a pen. Like ours, they were hobbled and tied to a line. Walter of Derby was next to me and it would be his arrow which would signal the attack. I saw that there was another sentry on the far side. When the light from the east became a pale grey, I saw his shadow. It would not be long now. I pulled up my coif and fastened my ventail. Only my eyes could be seen.

I saw one or two figures rise. When I heard the hiss and splash, I knew that they were making water. It would not be long now. I looked at the sentry on the far side. A shaft of sunlight lit him up. He had a spear in his hand. He was two hundred paces away. It was time.

"Now Walter."

Walter was almost as good an archer as Garth. He aimed at the sentry. He was a perfect target. The arrow flew straight and true. My men only used perfect arrows. Walter did not even watch its fall. He had another arrow in the air even as the sentry fell. Masood's stone struck one of the men who had been making water and then arrows flew from my archers. Even the ones using the Turkish bows found flesh. There was panic in the bandit camp. They could not see us for we were hidden in the dark. They would soon work out where we were but, for the moment they were confused. In the confusion, men died. I have no doubt that some women died too but it was dark and we had little option.

The sun, when it rose, broke like a wave over the tops of the ridge opposite. We were bathed in the cool sunlight of dawn. We were seen. I saw men hurrying up the slope towards us. I rose and drew my sword. Having left Gurth on guard I had just eight men. I slid down the slope towards the bandits. I had no shield but I had my dagger in my left hand. It had belonged to one of my grandfather's oathsworn. It was a seax and it was a wicked weapon. It could gut a man in one slice.

One bandit had outstripped the rest and he ran at me with a long, curved sword. I did not pause. I used speed and the quick hands my father had taught me to use. I blocked the sword with my own and tore my seax across his middle. It was though a nest of red writhing snakes fell from his stomach. As he fell I ran to meet the next warrior. Tom was next to me and his sword hacked across the neck of a bandit who came for me from the side. I swung my sword at another two who stood before me. My sword bit into the side of one as an arrow took the other.

I heard Robert of Mont St. Michel shout, "They are broken! Stop them getting to their horses."

The bandits had hobbled horses and an escape would not be quick. My five archers had moved from the ridge and each time a bandit tried to reach the horses they were slain. When four had fallen, the survivors, and there were not many of them, took to their heels and fled without horses. We moved through the camp slaying the wounded bandits. It was a kindness. We could not tend to them and most would have bled to death. There were, perhaps, a dozen women and twelve or so children. They cowered before us.

I waved Masood forward. I used, probably badly, one of the phrases David had taught me, "Tell them they will not be harmed. They come with us."

From his grin, I guessed I had made a mess of the words but he understood. He rattled words out and I saw that there was relief on their faces. I guessed that they had, in the main, been slaves or captives.

"Get the horses and search the bodies. Fetch any weapons you can find. I want to be away from here as soon as possible." He nodded, "Destroy any buildings. Let us make it hard for them to rebuild here."

I wiped my sword on the headdress of one of the dead bandits. Robert said, "What do we do with the women and children?"

"We will take them with us. I will ask Francis to question them. They may have families to go to."

"They will slow us down, lord."

I laughed, "And you have somewhere you wish to be? This means that we need not patrol for some days. I am content. We have made the road safer and it is good that we have freed these women and children." I knew that this was part of my atonement. My wife and children were dead but I had saved these. It was *wyrd.*

Chapter 11

My men put the older women and those who were not able to walk as quickly on the backs of the captured horses. I had already decided that I would give Masood a second horse, he had deserved it. Our journey home was both slower and more uncomfortable than the one to the camp. We had ascended in the cool of night and we descended in the heat of the day. We stopped more frequently to give the women and children, and our horses, water. Garth rode next to me, "Do you know, lord, I never thought I would miss England's rain but I do. There is not enough water in this land to wet a baby's head! How do people live here?"

"They are tough people, Garth."

Masood walked up and down the line of captives. He spoke to all of them at some point during the journey. When we reached Aqua Bella, I saw that David Ben Samuel and his son, Saul, were there.

He smiled. "I was curious to see how the venture went and I was not certain if you might need a translator."

"It went well, as you can see, but I am not certain if these are family or captives."

While the horses were taken into the stables Francis and his wife brought around bread and water for them. The high walls afforded some shade. Masood began to gabble at David Ben Samuel. He pointed to two women and said something. The two women suddenly ran out of the open gate. The two guards on the walls readied their bows, "Stay your hand! Let them run!"

Sometimes God moves in mysterious ways. They ran across the road towards the scrubland. It was rough and it was uneven. One of them turned to see if we were pursuing her. She tripped and hurtled through the air. When she landed, her head hit a large rock. The sound was like an axe hitting a log. Blood and brains spurted as her skull was cracked on the jagged rock. The other looked in horror at her companion and then carried on running through the scrub.

The other women and children were transfixed. David Ben Samuel went to speak with the captives. He returned to me as Garth carried the woman's body back inside the walls.

"The two of them were the sisters of the leader of the bandits. You slew him, lord. I would not shed any tears over the dead one. From what the captives told me the dead woman was as cruel as the chief. The women feared that they would slay you in your bed. The rest were afraid of the two of them."

"Nonetheless we will bury her. What do you suggest I do with the captives? Do they have homes to go to?"

He shook his head, "Masood spoke with them on the way here. They were all taken from two villages close by Nablus. Their men were butchered. They have lived with the bandits since the children were babies. It is all that they know."

"Then we will find a home for them here. Francis, these women and children will be staying here. Have one of the undercrofts given to them for a home."

He nodded, "You are a kind man, lord."

"They are women and children. A knight should care for those. Is there work enough for them?"

"There is always work, lord."

"Masood, take another horse. You deserve it." David Ben Samuel explained and Masood's face broke into a grin. "Will he go back to being a shepherd?"

"He will but he has a hut in the hills. I think the horse he requested was to give him freedom. He is a good shepherd and good with animals."

Masood tied his second horse to his first and mounted. Saul and David mounted also, "Do not be a stranger lord. My sister asks after you."

"I will but I fear that will be after we have campaigned for the king. Now that I have cleansed the bandits the road should be safer. I know not how long we will be away."

"The rumour amongst the merchants is that the Crusaders will attack Damascus. If that is true then it is a mistake. When you fight the Turk, you choose your battles. Nur al-Din is as good a general as his father was."

"I think King Baldwin is a young king and he needs to be seen as a leader. There are others who would take his throne from him."

"Like Guillaume de Waller?

"You know?"

"It is common knowledge. Take care, my young friend. You are moving in murky waters. As you know it is the pike which hides in such waters!"

Francis and his wife were good people and they procured better clothes for the women and children. They cut their hair and provided water for bathing. The estate needed labour. These were not slaves but they would have food and shelter. More importantly, they would have safety. That was not to be underestimated. This land was a dangerous one. When the Romans had ruled, it had been safe. Since then it had been anarchy.

The road patrols were event-free and I took that to be a good sign. Once we left to go to war the caravans would be safer for the Turks would be fighting us and the bandits were scattered to the winds. They would return but not this year.

A messenger came for me three days before the meeting was supposed to take place. I went with Tom and Robert to Jerusalem. The court was not filled with knights this time but lawyers and merchants. Everyone knew that the Turks would be attacked and everyone wished to have profits from it. This was not like my father's war. Here the main aim was to make money despite what the Pope might have said about claiming the Holy Land for the Church.

I left my men with the horses and strode into the court. I was now recognised. I saw Simeon and Phillipe of Jaffa. Both of them raised their hands in acknowledgement. Once again, I was swept into the chamber behind the main court. Queen Melisende awaited me. She poured us a goblet of wine each and I took one. She took the other. It was a sign that I could trust her. There would be no poison. The world in which I now moved was nothing like my father's court or even that of Geoffrey of Anjou. When King Henry had been poisoned it had been unusual.

"I spoke with David Ben Samuel. He tells me that you have destroyed the bandits." I nodded. "As you know they will return but you have done well. I asked you to come here because my son will need you and your men more than you can know. Have you heard of the Assassins?"

I shook my head.

"They are a sect, some would say religious. They live in the mountains north of Tripoli. They are killers. They are paid to murder leaders and important people. I have been told that my son may be a target for them."

"That would mean someone would pay for his death. The Seljuq Turks?"

She shook her head, "They also fear the assassins. I am not exactly sure but they may have been hired from within the ranks of the Christian knights." That was a hard piece of news to swallow. "We will have a better idea of who it might be when we select the council. We look for changes in opinion from the last meeting. If someone who wished us not to fight now does so then we have an idea. You need not worry yourself about identifying who it is. I have spies who will do that. But you and your men are the only ones I can totally trust to guard the King."

"From what you have told me the assassins could be anyone. There could be one or there could be twenty."

"They are expensive to hire and they rarely use more than one or two. They like to kill close. They use knives and poison. I am sending a food taster with my son but you must watch for the assassins. It will not be easy. They are invisible and they are fanatical. Death does not frighten them. That makes them the most dangerous of enemies."

"And I am guessing that there is little point in removing the ones who have paid for the kill."

She shook her head, "I have thought of that. Once the payment has been made it cannot be revoked."

"Then we have a problem. The king wants us to scout."

"Were you not listening? They will kill close up. It will be at night. Even if my son is surrounded by guards then the killer will find a way to get close."

I now understood. "You want us to hunt the hunter."

"Exactly. Do as you did with the bandits, although I am not naïve enough to think that the assassins will be as easy to deal with."

I sipped my wine. We could scout ahead and return to the camp each night. It would not seem unusual for me to report directly to the king. "The King knows of this?"

She shook her head.

"He must be told. How can I guard him if he knows not the reason?"

"I hoped to spare him the worry. This is a great venture he takes on."

"Then if you wish him to survive, tell him. It will be easier for us all that way."

"Very well, I will ponder your words for you appear to know your business."

"If I might suggest that you choose those who will serve him very carefully. If I was a killer I would try to suborn one of the servants. My father lost men when a killer ingratiated herself into his kitchen. A good priest died. We must know that all associated with the king are beyond reproach."

She smiled, "You have a mind like mine, young William. I have already done as you requested."

"And if, your majesty, the unthinkable happens and we lose this battle and this war what are my orders for the king?"

"That is simple. You bring him back here. He is the only one you need to save. He is the kingdom!"

"He has a brother does he not?"

"Amalric, he is eleven. He is kept safe but the nobles would not accept him as king. You are the protector of my son."

"And when Ascalon is his then my penance is over?"

"You tire of it already?"

"Let us just say that I am used to fighting but here the reasons are not as clear as at home. I am a simple knight."

She laughed, "No, Sir William, you are anything but that. When you return for the meeting keep your counsel and keep your eyes open. Your work begins when the army takes to the road."

I bade her farewell and went, once again, to see David Ben Samuel. I saw his men loading his camels. They would be heading to either Tripoli or Jaffa to trade again. Before I had come to this land I would have wondered at them leaving so late in the day. Now I knew the reason. It was to travel when it was cooler. The animals and their drivers could move further.

"A welcome surprise, my lord. Come I am ready for something chilled." We shook off our cloaks and laid them over our horses and then, after entering the hall swept the dust from us. Our host waved for a servant to bring us drinks and then we went to sit by his lemon and orange trees. I noticed that they were in fruit. He casually cupped one in his hand and smelled it. "I never tire of the smell."

The wine came and with it Rebekah, she looked radiant. She looked less thin and her face glowed. She sat on the arm of her father's chair with her arm draped around his shoulders. Ben Samuel nodded, "Each time I see you, lord, I wish to thank you for bringing me back my daughter. She has lightened our life once more."

She kissed him on the cheek. "It is I who should be grateful for having such a considerate father."

I sipped my wine and said nothing.

"You look troubled, lord. Share your burden." He hesitated, "Unless you do not trust us."

"Of course, I trust you but…I will ask you some questions and I hope that you can answer them."

Rebekah leaned forward, "You sound serious. If there is anything we can do to help."

I had not had the opportunity of speaking with my men. The news I was about to tell them would come as a surprise too. "The assassins."

I needed to say no more. David Ben Samuel drained his wine and poured another. "They are an evil. What have you to do with them?"

"I have information that they may try to kill one of the leaders of the crusade."

"Then whoever their target is, is dead already. They cannot be stopped."

I nodded, "And yet I have been charged with stopping them."

Rebekah's hand went to her mouth. David said, "They are killers. You are a knight and I have seen you fight but these are something different."

"I know what they are and how they kill. What I need to know is how to spot them."

"That is difficult." He sighed, "What do I know? They are skilled at hiding in plain sight. That means they are not big men. Masood would be a perfect assassin. They like to use poisoned blades so that the merest touch brings death. It is said that they use hashish, which is a potent drug. It makes them immune to pain."

Rebekah leaned forward, "But if they take it then they have wider, more open eyes than others and the black part is larger."

"My daughter is correct. It is said the drug helps them to see in the dark. They will wear anonymous clothes which help them to melt into the background. You did the same when you asked Masood to spy in the bandits. He was in plain view."

"So I should watch out for people who do not appear to be a threat? Harmless men, who look as though they have not the strength to kill?"

"That would make sense."

"I am glad I came here, David Ben Samuel. You and your daughter have given me valuable intelligence. I am in your debt."

Rebekah grabbed my hand in hers, "I beg you lord, do not put your life in danger. Surely there are others who can stop them?"

"The task has been appointed to me and you should know, Rebekah, that I am a knight who keeps his word. I will return and when I do I would speak with you again."

She smiled and squeezed my fingers, "Of course. I shall wait here for your safe return."

David Ben Samuel smiled. Then, standing his face became serious as he said, "But if you go to Damascus then I fear that it will not be for some time. Will your people be safe?"

"I am leaving guards. I will take enough to do the job but no more."

As we headed home I told my two men what Ben Samuel had said. "But how do we stop them, lord?"

"We now have an idea who to look for. He will be a Muslim. He will be neither large nor overweight. He will be muscular and he will have wide eyes. He will not carry a sword but he will have a dagger and he will keep to himself. I think that will eliminate many who are close to the king. Remember Masood would make a good assassin."

"And who do we leave at home?"

"We need the archers. You two go with as do Louis, Phillipe and Guy. I think Henry and John will be the others."

"Henry son of Will? He is loud and he is reckless."

"And he has the courage of a lion. Besides he stands out. We need that. If all eyes are on him then our eyes can spy out the danger."

I left Alciades and Leonidas at Aqua Bella. We would be scouts and I would not risk such fine horses. There would come a time when we would ride into battle on the back of our war horses but it would not be at the siege of Damascus. We now had enough horses to have a spare each as well as some mounts to carry our baggage. We took the curved bows. My men did not like them but I thought there might come a time when we might find them useful. We rode to Jerusalem for the gathering. The road to Jerusalem was filled with knights, sergeants, horses, servants and the feudal levy. Only the knights were admitted to the city. All the rest had to gather on the large open area to the north and west of the city. There a camp had been erected.

The court was packed. There were even more knights than before. Some had come from Nablus. I was pleased to see that they were on the opposite side of the room to Sir Guillame. I took it as a good sign. There were also Hospitallers and Templars. I recognized Raymond de Puy Provence and I guessed that the huge Templar was Robert de Craon, their master. The two orders kept apart. I was tempted to join the Hospitallers but something made me keep to myself. I had to become like the assassins themselves. I had to be invisible and unnoticed. With the Lord of Ramelah close by that would be hard.

The King emerged with his mother at his side. They were making a statement. Queen Melisende was the link between Fulk, her father, King Baldwin and her son. She was the surety of continuity and it was not lost on those waiting.

"When last we met I was asked by the Lord of Ramelah to appoint a council of nobles to advise me. Who would like to be chosen?"

I expected many men to put themselves forward but they did not. They were not reluctant they were being cautious and looking for alliances. The Queen showed her acumen. "I believe that the Master of the Knights Hospitallers should be on the council. They have protected pilgrims for many years and their knowledge of the land of Syria is well known."

"And I accept."

Robert de Craon pushed himself forward, "In that case, we need a Templar too. I nominate myself!" It was not the most modest of proposals but the Queen nodded.

The King said, "We need someone from the Kingdom of Jerusalem too." He looked at Sir Theobald of Rheims. He was the oldest of the knights who served the king. Roderigo of Santiago spoiled the moment for he said, "The third should be Guillaume de Waller, the Lord of Ramelah."

His knights and sergeants made such a clamour that Theobald stepped back. The King nodded and the Queen gave me a look. We knew who had paid the assassins. We could do little to prove it but we both knew who it was.

If I thought the creation of the council would mean we marched to war I was wrong. We did not move until February! We camped outside Jerusalem while the council of the king argued and bickered. Messengers arrived, almost daily, from the many kings and lords who were gathered in Tripoli and Antioch. I was not party to the letters and the messages but it seemed, from the rumour, that no one could agree where the blow ought to be struck.

Eventually, the huge beast that was our army began to move. We had over fifteen thousand men. The only saving grace for us was that we were at the fore. We did not have to ride through the dust of the army. The Hospitallers and Templars had sergeants who acted as scouts too. We were not the only force. As we rode I reflected that we had seen no sign of an assassin. Only Christians were allowed close to the camp. If that continued when we reached Syria then my task would be simple. I did not think for one moment that would be the case.

We made it to Nablus where we would be joined by many more men. We stayed for two days while the king and his council debated again. My men and I took the opportunity of riding north. We had travelled south on this road and I was anxious to spy out any dangers. The good news was that the road was in a good state of repair. The bad news was that there was little food to be had. I had made sure that we had plenty of grain for our horses and we had brought salted ham and beef with us.

We were just returning when Brother Günter, one of the Hospitaller knights who scouted and his sergeant rode up. “Lord, we have spied men watching the road.” He turned and gestured with his head. “They are on the other side of the valley. We were in Belvoir when one of the guards saw them.”

“Then we should go and discourage them.”

He grinned, “The Master said that you were game for anything. What is the plan?”

“If they are watching the road then they cannot be watching the approaches from the north. We cross the river and make our way up the tracks to reach them.”

“If they spy us they might flee.”

“They might but I suspect they think we will give up when it becomes dark.”

“And we will not?”

“We will not!”

I turned, “Garth take the archers. Work your way along the trail and cut them off.” He rode along the west bank of the Jordan. He would ford further north. These would be the scouts who would shadow us all the way to Damascus. It would not hurt them if they did not know when we would arrive but, as my father had taught me, if you could keep an enemy in the dark about your movements then you had an advantage. I wanted to keep the Turks off balance.

We forded the river. It was neither wide nor fast flowing. The irrigation scheme syphoned off a lot of the river’s flow to water the fields. The brother knight seemed surprised that we did so. “We normally just watch the enemy.”

“I was taught to find out as much as you can about the enemy’s positions and numbers. Even his scouts.”

The lush flat farmland on the east bank of the river was in direct contrast to the normal rocks and desert we were used to. It did not last long and soon we began to wend our way up the steep trails which crisscrossed the eastern side of the valley. We came to a fork in the trail. I turned to Robert, held up four fingers and pointed right. He nodded and led four men to the right. I was dividing my forces but that would make it harder for the enemy to ambush us.

They made the mistake of ambushing us when I had just turned one of the right-hand turns on the trail. My shield was up and the arrows thudded into the shield. I spurred Remus and he leapt forward. The cracks as the arrows hit my shield had given my men all the warning that they needed and their shields came up as did those of the Hospitallers. The ambush told me that they were less than two hundred paces from us. It was becoming dark. Perhaps they hoped to deter us before they could melt away in the night. I drew my sword and peered over my shield. Remus laboured up the slope. I would rest him when I could.

Suddenly the trail flattened out and I had reached the crest. I saw shadows running north and east. They were running for their horses. I followed them. Brother Gunther joined me. He spurred his horse to overtake me. One of the scouts, there were ten of them, turned and levelled his bow at me. I leaned forward to give Remus some protection. The arrow hit the shield and cracked off to the side. The attempt to kill me meant that Brother Günter reached him first. He swung back his arm and the sword cleaved him in two.

We twisted between rocks and I saw the Turks as they scrambled on to their horses’ backs. The flatter ground had allowed our horses to get their second wind. There was a delay as the Turks untied their horses and then tried to flee. They got in each other’s way. Three were still trying to mount their horses when we reached them. The setting sun actually helped us as it flared into the eyes of the Turks. They did not see our swords as they hacked into their bodies. We did not pause. This was a race now.

The trail ran north along the top of the valley sides. Our horses were tiring and I saw a lead begin to open. The trail was just wide enough for two horses and Brother Günter rode next to me. "We will not catch them, lord. Perhaps we should halt. We have hurt them already."

"We keep on. Save your breath."

It seemed a hopeless quest and then I heard the hiss of arrows ahead and three riders were pitched from their horses. The other three panicked and that was their undoing. Had they kept going they might have escaped. As it was they reined in to see where the danger lay and they died. Garth and his men had secured the horses and were searching the bodies when we reached them.

"They are warriors, lord and not bandits." He pulled back the headdress to reveal a helmet.

"Well done, Garth. Let us find Robert."

We retraced our steps to the ambush site. The other horses were gone but the bodies lay there and confirmed that these were Seljuq Turks.

"We will give Robert a little more time to reach us but I would descend before the light has totally gone."

"Then you had best be quick, lord."

I looked up and saw what Tom meant. We looked up as we heard hooves and Robert and his men rode up leading three horses. "There were four of them further south."

"Let us get back to camp although I suspect we will have missed supper."

It was pitch black when we reached the camp outside Nablus. We were fortunate that the Hospitallers had kept some food for their men and we shared their camp that night. We left for the rendezvous the next day. I rode one of the spare horses. I had taxed Remus and it would not do to injure him. Before we left I reported to Richard of Acre. He commanded the knights who guarded the King. The Queen had told him before we left, that I was to be afforded total access to the king. The old knight had been wary of me for I was young and I was new.

"We slew some of their scouts last evening. They were watching Belvoir from the east bank."

"I will tell the King."

"Will we be keeping this pace all the way to Damascus?"

He nodded, "It is the way we war here."

"Then it is no wonder that the Turk wins more than we do. He is swift. We move so slowly that there is no surprise."

"Sir William, I can tell you for I know that you have the Queen's confidence, that we have an army more than fifty thousand men strong. The Seljuq Turks can move as fast as they like, we will reach Damascus and we will take that city."

It took another five days to reach Merom Golam where we met up with the rest of the army. We were there first and I was pleased to see that a defended camp was set up. Then we waited for the huge metal snake that was the Army of the Second Crusade to join us. I saw the banners of France and Flanders leading the way. Behind them, I spied standards from every part of Europe.

I was with my men. We had our tents as close to the king's as we were allowed. I was sharpening my sword as the King of France and the Count of Flanders rode passed me to dismount and greet King Baldwin. More dukes, counts and other important nobles descended and entered the tent. Then I saw other banners as they peeled off to find a place to camp. I saw stars on a blue background. It was the men of the Count of Provence. Robert of Nissa had joined the Crusade. Our enemies within our army had now doubled.

Chapter 12

I went inside my tent. "Tom, fetch Alf and Robert."

It had been some time since we had had our confrontation with Robert of Nissa and his uncle. Perhaps they would have forgotten us. As Alf came in I wondered at the change in him. The scrawny youth had now filled out. He had worked hard to become a warrior who could wield a sword. He was still accurate with a sling but he could also use a bow. He was not as skilled as Garth but his talents meant that he was as valuable to me as any of my men.

"The Count of Provence has joined the army." I looked at Alf. He nodded. "He may have forgotten us. I hope so for I would not have trouble. He may not even recognise us. We have new surcoats and livery but I suspect he will know my name. I cannot avoid him for I will be as close to the king as will he. Alf, you know your former master better than I."

He nodded, "We had better walk in pairs. He is not above using treachery and he will not have forgotten us, lord. You bloodied his nose and that of his nephew. The insult may seem minor to us but the Count is a proud and arrogant man. He will seek vengeance."

"As I thought. Well, it looks as though we shall have an interesting time from now on."

The arrival of the main Crusader army also brought with it increased danger for the king. There were native servants with the army. Hitherto the only servants close to the king were his own and we knew them. Now the kings and lords from Europe had hired servants to keep them shaded from the sun. They had others who led their horses, fetched water and carried food. Now our work would begin.

The king held a meeting with the other leaders which went on long into the night. I used the meeting to walk around the camp to look for possible assassins. Each time I saw a huge brute of a Turk I was relieved. Every youth and wasted old man made me look at them to seek their knife and their eyes. I had no doubt that the assassin had joined the army. This was the perfect place to do so. There were now fifty thousand men. One small killer could pass unnoticed amongst so many. Where do you hide a valuable coin? In the middle of other coins. I could not stay awake all night and so we had a system. Robert, Garth and I took it in turns to watch with three others. It meant we all lost sleep but it was spread out between us all. None was exhausted.

I had hoped that with the army all together we would leave for Damascus. The weather was getting hotter by the day and the huge army needed a massive amount of fodder, food and most importantly, water. The Master of the Hospitallers came out of one meeting looking almost angry. He saw me, "Walk with me, Sir William, I would talk with someone who has both sense and honour."

"It is difficult in there?"

"The trouble is my young friend, that they lost many men when travelling through Anatolia. This is a shadow of the army which left France and Flanders. They met at Acre months ago and there decided to attack Damascus but none can agree who should lead. Each day brings more desertions and more deaths through disease. We should strike quickly!"

"I confess that I am surprised by this slow approach. There is nothing between us and the enemy. I have scouted."

"I know, Brother Günter was impressed by you and your men. He cannot believe that you have only been in this land for a relatively short time."

I would have carried on the conversation had not Theobald of Rheims approached me, "Lord, the king would speak with you, alone."

I entered the tent. King Louis of France and Thierry of Flanders were there. They had scowls upon their faces. I guessed that the king had told them the name of my father. He had been a thorn in both their sides for some time. King Baldwin smiled, "Your father's reputation, Sir William appears to have coloured the judgement of my fellow rulers. I have assured them that you only have the interest of the Crusade at heart."

"Of course, my lord, and if I offend any then I would happily take my men back to Aqua Bella so that I could continue to protect pilgrims and travellers."

King Louis shook his head, "Do not do that. King Baldwin has told us of your success. It is just that we are, quite naturally, wary of the son of the Warlord who has been our Nemesis for so long. We are just grateful that it is the Scots who are now bearing the brunt of his anger."

I bowed and waited. Count Thierry said nothing.

King Baldwin said, "We need you to scout out Damascus, lord. We are a large army and we need to find somewhere with food and water. We will move towards Damascus but you and your men can travel much faster. We would have you seek a campsite for us."

I worked out that as we were forty miles from Damascus it would take the army two more days to reach there. If we left now then we could be back not long after they had broken camp.

"Then I had better leave now, your majesty."

King Louis looked at me askance, "So quickly?"

It was my turn to smile, "Now you know one of my father's secrets your majesty, strike quickly!"

Even as I was striding out from the tent I shouted, "Robert! We ride!"

As I did so I saw that Robert of Nissa was there with some other knights. He did not recognize me immediately. I had a different surcoat and it had been some time since he had seen me but he had heard my voice. I put the Lombard from my mind. I had more important things to do.

Tom and Alf ran to me. They were already mailed, "Lord?"

"We need supplies for a day and a night. We are to do a long scout. I will take Remus."

A year ago and this would have seemed a daunting prospect. We had feared the warriors of this land and had been terrified by the land itself. We had fought both and knew how to win. We still respected both but we knew our own abilities. Brother Günter came over as I checked the girths on Remus, "You ride alone today?"

I leaned in, "We go to view Damascus. I would ask a favour of you, Brother Günter."

"Of course."

"We keep watch at night on his majesty. Tonight, we will be absent. I would appreciate you watch him."

"Any particular danger?"

"There are rumours that someone may try to kill him. Assassins. He has his own guards but…"

"But you trust only your own men. I understand and I am flattered that you hold me in such esteem. My sergeant and I will sleep in your camp this night. We spend many hours in prayer and it matters not where we pray."

Satisfied that I had done all that I could to protect the king we left and headed northeast through the mountainous trails which led to Damascus. Mount Hebron loomed to the north and we used our normal formation. Alf and Garth were an unlikely pairing and yet they got on well and seemed to have an understanding which was almost mystic. Dick and my father had a similar understanding. I did not. I wondered how such understanding came about. However, I used it. It meant I could watch the land around me knowing that the van was secure.

The road was empty for the first twenty miles. We saw neither traveller nor much in the way of houses. There were huts which I guessed housed shepherds but there was little else. Once we passed the col which led to the flatlands I saw Damascus far in the distance. It was indistinct for the sun would soon be setting but I saw the sprawl of huts and farms which spread out to the west. We halted while I sought a route which would avoid being spotted.

I waved my arm and we followed a track which led north. The main road went due east. We had not seen warriors upon it but I had no doubt that there would be guards of some sort. I was surprised that we had not seen any scouts. It would be easy to get close to Damascus in the dark. There would be the smell of smoke and the lights from homes to guide us. Getting back west would be more problematic. I turned to John of Chester. "I want you and Henry to mark our route. When we return, you will be leading and I want us to take the reverse of this route."

"Aye lord."

We rode in single file. I was third in line and I had my helmet hung over my cantle and my coif and ventail about my shoulders. I wanted to be able to see and hear easily. With our black cloaks, we were almost invisible. Our horses were moving through soft earth and sand. We made no sound. We were so silent that when Garth turned to take us due east we came upon an old man relieving himself. He looked around in surprise and shock. We said nothing and he did not raise the alarm. In the dark, we could just as easily have been Seljuq warriors.

Then the farms stopped and I saw trees. Below our horses' hooves, it was no longer bare soil and sand, it was grass. As we halted our horses greedily grazed. I reached up and discovered that it was an orchard. The trees were fruit trees. I plucked a peach from the tree and bit into it. It was not ripe but it was edible. We rode through the orchard. It was extensive. We were not challenged and we kept riding until we were less than four hundred paces from the walls. I estimated the distance from the height of the walls. The sun had long set behind us but there were torches shining from the walls and I saw guards patrolling. The wall had many towers. It would not be easy to assault. There was also a low wall with smaller towers between the orchard and the walls. That would slow up horsemen who tried to attack. I could not see it clearly but it looked to me as though there was a dry ditch before the walls. I knew that the River Barada flowed close to the city; perhaps that would be obstacle enough. So far the rivers had all seemed fordable to me.

One of the sentries must have had sharper eyes than the others for he gave a sudden shout. We had been seen. The worst thing we could have done would have been to run. I said, "Back slowly. We are still hard to see."

They turned their horses and did as I had commanded.

"John, take the lead. Garth and Alf, watch the rear. All of you, have weapons at the ready, they may try to follow us."

I could hear the sound of raised voices. The distance meant that they were muffled but there would be pursuit. I knew that once we were deeper in the orchard we would be hidden from view. As soon as I could no longer see the walls I said, "Now we can go a little faster." No one was pursuing us.

We could not gallop and that was our undoing. A column of horsemen had been sent to investigate the sighting from the walls. However, they had no idea where we were. They waited on the road and we almost bumped into them. Henry and John led us into the midst of the horsemen. Our approach had been quiet. We heard hooves on the road and then there was silence. John and Henry were not to know that the Seljuq horseman had stopped on the road to listen for us. We had advantages, as we struck them. We were moving and they were stationary. Our weapons were out and theirs were not and we knew who they were. All that their sentries had seen had been riders in the orchard and we could have been anyone.

The first that I knew, at the back, was the clash of steel and Henry's shout, "Die, you motherless heathen!"

I spurred Remus. He leapt forward. We were in a tightly packed column of twos and my men were laying about them with their swords. A spear rammed into my shield. I brought my sword down to slice it in two. I flicked it backhanded and it tore into the rider's throat. His hands went to his throat to stem the bleeding.

"Head east!"

It was confused but I could tell the enemy by their smell, their smaller horses and their distinctive helmets. This was not their kind of fight. They liked to use their bows from a distance or chase down fleeing men on foot. We were mailed and heavily armed. We had shields which covered most of our bodies and we were superior warriors.

"Go now!"

Garth, Robert and I turned to face the horsemen. I pulled back on Remus' reins as I stood in the stirrups. His hooves clattered down and struck a horse in the head. As it fell to earth, I lunged at the next rider and was rewarded by my sword sinking into something soft. A spear struck my shield and a second rapped my hand. I whipped Remus' head around to face west and, as I did so, I swung my sword in a wide arc. It takes courage to put your head or your body in the way of a Frankish sword and the Turks fell back.

Robert shouted, “Ride, lord, the rest are escaped.”

I slid my shield over my shoulder to drape along my back and I spurred Remus. We galloped down the road. Garth and Robert slowed down so that the three of us were the rear-guard. Something struck my back. I felt no pain and I ignored whatever it was. I risked a glance over my shoulder and saw that they were pursuing us and I saw arrows. They were releasing them blindly. An unlucky arrow could kill just as quickly as a well-aimed one. We rode hard and I kept looking behind. Gradually the pursuit slowed and then stopped. We had hurt them and they were letting us go. After another mile, I shouted, “Hold!”

Garth slowed and I felt my shield move. He held a Turkish arrow. “It is lucky you put your shield along your back. That arrow could have done for you.”

Robert nodded, “God was watching over you there, lord.”

Tom shouted, “Lord, we have wounded.”

As I reined in I saw that Alf clutched his leg. He shook his head, “It is a spear thrust I am…” He slumped into Garth’s arms.

“I will tend to him, lord.” As he fell he said. “He has a wound to his head too. There are others wounded, lord.”

I saw that Gaston had been wounded in the leg also but Jean de Les Monts had the most serious wound. His left shoulder was badly cut. Through gritted teeth, he said, “One of the bastards had an axe, lord.”

It was high on his arm but I saw that we could stem the bleeding. “Clean it with vinegar and apply a tourniquet. We need to stitch or burn it and we can do neither here. We have another twenty odd miles before we get home. Luckily it will soon be downhill. Gregor ride with Jean. Loosen the tourniquet every mile or so.”

As the men were being seen to Robert said, “It could have been worse.”

“It could and we have, at least, discovered a place we can both use to attack and to feed us. The farms and the orchard will give us shade, water, food and grazing. I think we now have a chance.”

As much as we wished to hurry I knew that we had to conserve our horses. The last thing we needed was for us to lose a horse. As we descended towards the Jordan valley I saw the lights from the fires. It looked like a sparkling carpet. This was a huge army and yet, from what I had been told, it was only a shadow of the number who had set forth. I glanced over my shoulder, dawn breaking we had made far better time than I might have hoped.

As we approached the sentries I shouted, "William of Aqua Bella returning with a patrol."

The voice which answered me was heavy with suspicion. "Walk into the light, my lord, so that we can make sure you speak true!"

There were eight men on guard. They were Templars. "What is amiss?"

"Treachery lord. A murderer was abroad in the camp this night."

My heart sank. Had I obeyed the king only to be the cause of his death? I spurred Remus towards his tent. I saw two bodies draped with cloaks. I dismounted and handed my reins to Tom. Raymond de Puy Provence stepped from the shadows. He put his hand on mine. "It is not the king. It is Brother Günter and his sergeant." He pointed to a brown form lying close by the tent. "It was an assassin. He tried to get to the king. The sergeant saw him but he was slain. When Brother Günter stopped and killed the assassin he was also killed. It was a poisoned blade. He lived long enough to tell me what you asked of him." He shook his head, "You should have told him you feared assassins. He would have been prepared."

It was a justly deserved rebuke. "I should have and for that I am sorry. I was sworn to secrecy by the Queen. Even her son does not know of the danger."

"And two brave men have died because of that oath." I hung my head. "I do not blame you but now that we know that assassins are abroad I will have my men keep watch. We know of them."

Robert said, "Lord, we have wounded men."

"Of course. "Could you have your men look at Jean and the others. They were wounded when we scouted Damascus."

The old master looked appalled, "And I have reproached you when you were doing your duty. I am sorry, lord, I did not know."

"You were right to rebuke me and I will make up for it. Now I must report to the king."

The sentry allowed me to enter. The king had been awakened by the noise and he was on one elbow, lying on his bed. "I heard a noise in the night. No one woke me. Is all well?"

"Someone tried to kill you, your majesty. Brother Günter killed the killer but paid with his life."

He stared at me, "You were supposed to be watching me and I sent you to scout!" I nodded. "I will pray for his soul."

"He was a good man, your majesty. He will be in heaven."

"And what did you discover?"

"There is nothing between us and Damascus. To the west of the city, the farms and the orchard will give us shade, water, food and grazing.

But the walls are high and they have a ditch. We will need to make siege engines; there are trees for timber."

"That is for someone else to worry about. Rest." He stood. "Did you lose any men?"

"Three men are wounded but they will fight again."

"Good."

Once outside I saw that the camp was coming to life. "Robert, have the men rest. They will break camp today. It will take them all day and part of tomorrow to set up the new camp. We will wait here until this evening. I want the men rested. Tonight, we will have no sleep. They have sent one assassin. There may be others."

"Aye lord."

Before I retired I went to look at the body of the killer. Although he was a man his body was that of a youth. There was not an ounce of fat on him. Beneath his headdress, his hair was oiled and tied back. His dagger lay where it had fallen. It was not as curved as most Turkish blades but I saw that it had a groove running its length and it was etched with a serpent. The handle itself was a coiled snake. It was distinctive. I sniffed the blade. Apart from the blood, I smelled something else, wolf's bane. The groove and the etching would hold the poison in place. I had learned much.

I took the man's headdress and wrapped it around the knife. I took it with me. I wanted to clean it and study it. Perhaps daylight would help me to see more.

My prayers, before I retired, were longer than usual. I had two more souls to pray for.

By the time we rose, the king and the other leaders had all left. It would not do for them to travel in the dust of lesser mortals. The tents were still in the process of being dismantled. Garth had organised food and we ate while our tents were taken down. John and Henry went to fetch the horses and we picked our way through the camp. I saw that the two Hospitallers' bodies had been taken away but the murdered killer's lay where it had fallen. In the daylight, the killer looked even more insubstantial. Brother Günter had paid dearly for the information but the body would help me to find another assassin should one attempt to kill the king.

We made our way through the slow-moving foot soldiers who moved inexorably east. Our horses did not need the road and so we rode on the rougher ground alongside the road. As we neared the front I saw that there was an unholy alliance ahead. The knights and sergeants of de Waller were marching with the Lombards of the Count of Provence. It filled me with apprehension. Nothing good could come of it. Alf had a heavily bandaged head and would not be recognised. The rest of us wore our new cloaks and were helmed. For some reason, I did not want my enemies to know I was with the army. They would bear watching.

We hurried through the ranks until we were with the Hospitallers who rode just behind the king. I joined the Master. "You buried your brothers?"

"We did. They are at peace now. Brother Günter was a good man. He had been a great knight before he joined the order. He had a true vocation. He admired you. He saw greatness in you. When you eliminated those scouts, he was amazed at such skill in one so young."

"I have been at war since I could ride. I was born into civil war and my father fights it still."

"And in your heart, you would rather fight for him than this desert and rock."

"I would. But I must do penance before I can go home. I have told the king that I will serve him until Ascalon is taken."

He nodded, "Now I see why you do not like this crusade. It attacks the wrong city."

"Do you think it is right?"

"I am unsure. This army has yet to fight together. When it does so I will know if this be right or not."

The city was harder to see because of the dust raised by the vanguard. Robert de Craon had insisted that the Templars lead the army. They made a magnificent sight with their white cloaks and red crosses but I think the Master of the Hospitallers thought it arrogant. His order were true warrior monks.

Our approach had been seen. I spied ranks of infantry and horsemen gather before the low wall.

When we reached the edge of the orchard Robert de Craon halted. Theobald rode from the side of King Baldwin. He smiled, "You did well, young William. Now we must chase these Turks from before the wall so that we may begin to take the walls themselves. Are your men able to fight alongside us? I could use your archers."

"Of course, lord. Will the Templars be alongside us?"

He shook his head, "Their master deems that they have done enough for the day by riding ahead of us." I looked at him and my mouth must have been open. Theobald nodded, "I agree with you but the Master has more knights and sergeants under his hand than any king or count here. He attacks when he chooses." Just then a rider galloped from the king. "Yes, Guy?"

"His majesty has just been told that King Conrad of Germany will support our attack."

Theobald looked at the dust heading from the west, "But he is the rear guard. It will take him some time to pick his way through the army."

Guy said, "I am sorry, lord, I am just the messenger."

Shaking his head Theobald said, "When we attack I intend to use both mounted and dismounted soldiers. I want you on the left flank. We will be attacking on a narrow front and you will prevent them from outflanking us on that side. Your archers should be able to hurt their horse archers. Our spies tell us that your encounters have taught them to respect your war bows."

I turned my horse. We had three wounded men and I left Jean in command of the horses and supplies. "Take them to the rear of the orchard. Find us a camp. When I find where the king will sleep we may move some of us closer."

"Lord, the wound is nothing. Let me fight."

"This battle we fight today will not decide the outcome of this siege. You will get your chance to fight."

We left our cloaks with Jean. The orchard would give us some shade and we needed to be unencumbered. We moved back to the line of men which was being assembled. I saw that de Waller's men were on the right flank. Was Theobald deliberately keeping us apart? Neither of us had made any attempt to disguise our animosity. The second rank was made up of Hospitallers and that gave me hope. I knew they would fight well. I had yet to see any of the other knights and sergeants who served Baldwin fight. Today would show me their mettle.

We were ready quickly but then we had been fighting for many years. It took the rest longer. Garth and his archers had left their horses with Jean. However, we had devised and practised a way of moving to battle quickly, they lay across the rumps of our horses and clung on to the cantle. It was neither elegant nor comfortable but it meant we would be in position first.

The horns sounded. Tom had my banner and when the other banners dipped forward he did so with mine. This was the first time we had gone into battle beneath its fluttering gryphon. As I had expected we moved more quickly than the knights to our right. The spearmen and the levy who walked beside the horses slowed them up. As we neared the enemy lines I saw that they had shields erected and archers prepared. Horsemen and horse archers were gathered behind the shields. They would allow us to attack and then make us bleed on their shields. When we were weak they would attack. Their arrows landing in front of us told us when we should halt. We stopped and the archers slid from the backs of the horses. We had plenty of arrows. Tom planted the standard in the ground in the middle of the arrow quivers.

The five of them chose their best arrow first. They would wait for Garth to release first. "Hit their archers Garth. Let us see if we can annoy them into attacking us before the rest arrive."

"Aye, lord!"

The advantage of the curved bow was that it could be used on horseback and, for a shorter bow, had greater strength than a similar size bow made from a single piece of wood. The long war bows my archers used were poor when used from a horse but had a better range when used on foot. Garth and his archers put that greater range to good effect. Garth's first arrow sailed high and true. The Turks had a leader parading up and down before his men obviously extolling them to acts of great valour. Garth's arrow threw him from the saddle. The effect was instantaneous. The shields were lowered to allow the Turkish archers to send their arrows back at us. My archers sent their arrows into the archers' ranks. While their arrows fell short my men's arrows found flesh. They kept sending arrow after arrow into them until the shields came up.

"Well done Garth. Rest while you may."

"Aye lord." My archers drank deeply from their skins.

I turned to Robert. "They have a choice. They can try to move the shields forward or they can try to dislodge us."

"There are but five archers, lord."

"And how many men did they slay? Archers take time to train. Keep a good watch. I think that they may send some arrow fodder here to shift us."

I looked to my right and saw that the Knights of Nablus had joined us. Their leader, Jocelyn of Tyre, waved a hand at me. "You have made a good start, Sir William, but it might have been polite to wait for us."

"I just thought to warm them up, lord."

He laughed and waved his men forward. We had been tasked with holding the left flank and so we let them move forward. The long shields would afford them protection but their slow advance, for they were on foot, would force them to endure long periods of attack from arrows. However, to use their bows they had to lower their shields and my archers were waiting. As soon as the sergeants of Nablus were in range then the shields were lowered to allow the Turkish archers to release. Garth and my four archers sent arrow after arrow into them. The Turkish arrows caused some casualties but not as many as we had feared.

"Lord, the enemy. They are moving!"

I dragged my eyes from the attack and saw that thirty horsemen had emerged from behind their shields. They were the lightly armed horsemen who fought with a spear, curved sword and small wooden shield. They rode fast, small horses. They would come for us.

"Form line. Garth, try to thin them out a little on the flanks, eh?"

"Aye lord."

There was no command, the line of horsemen just began to gallop. They rode loosely. We rode boot to boot as knights did. Robert was on the left flank and Gregor on the right. John and Henry flanked me. We had lances rather than spears. A forearm longer than a spear they had no metal point but a sharpened wooden one. They were perfect for the men we charged. We had the advantage that the trees of the orchard did not break up our line as much as the others. It was hard to maintain cohesion in the orchard.

Even as we closed I saw our arrows taking their toll on the men on the flanks. Horses and riders were struck. The enemy were moving quickly and their ragged line was spread out over a large area. I pulled back my arm. My weapon was much longer than the Turk's and I impaled him. I allowed my arm to drop so that his body slid from the end. I pulled back and punched at the second Turk who swerved his horse to avoid trampling his comrade. The spear smashed into his head. The lance was ruined but the rider fell dead. As I drew my sword I saw that we had broken their charge. "Back!"

As I turned I saw that Henry had also lost his lance in a Turk's body. He had drawn his sword and, even as he wheeled he leaned out to decapitate in one blow a rider who had fallen from his horse and was attempting to rise. An arrow smacked into my cantle and another hit my helmet. And then we had reached Garth and the archers. We were out of range. The survivors headed back to the walls of Damascus. There were seven of them.

The trees of the orchards had helped us. Some of the advancing men had been protected by the trunks and branches of the fruit trees. The men of Nablus had suffered casualties but they had reached the enemy line and a furious fight ensued. Garth and his archers hit any Turk that they could see but he did not want to risk hitting a crusader and we waited.

I had just stroked Remus when Tom shouted. "Lord, the lord of Ramelah and his men! They are withdrawing!"

His words made my heart sink into my boots. I looked to the right and saw that de Waller was leading his men away from the battle. Our right flank was exposed. We were betrayed!

Chapter 13

The effect was immediate. The Seljuqs poured into the gap and threatened the flank of the men of Nablus. Even as I watched I saw Raymond de Puy Provence lead the Hospitallers from the second rank to block their advance. It made the front line thinner and the enemy took advantage. They sent more horsemen from behind the defences to drive us from the field.

"We must stem them on this side to allow our men the opportunity to retreat in some sort of order." I turned Remus to face our front. Garth and the archers continued to pick off the leaders and archers amongst those who faced us. Already another line of horsemen was preparing to rid themselves of the insects who had annoyed them. This time I saw mailed men with them. My lance shattered I picked up a spear as did my other men. "Remember we make them recoil and then return here. I want no heroes. Henry son of Will!"

He laughed, "Of course, my lord."

We spurred our horses on. The enemy line charged too. The enemy had to negotiate their own dead and the trees of the orchard. There was little chance that they could maintain one line for long. We did not gallop. Our horses had made one charge. We would advance steadily and use the protection of our mail and our skill with swords. The advantage was that our line held firmly. We were a solid line of spears. I saw some Seljuqs decide to use their superior speed and charge around our unprotected left flank. Garth and my archers saw the threat. They aimed their arrows to the left. To the right, the men of Nablus were falling back but they were in some sort of order. I couched my spear. We were so close to each other that I felt John's boot touch mine. God must have been smiling on my retinue that day for an arrow struck a horse whose rider was attempting to flank us. It fell and two horses close by were brought down. It created a wall to our left and the men who were trying to get around us were halted. My archer's arrows found more targets for their horses were stopped.

And then we struck the line. Thanks to our close line ten spears struck five Seljuqs. They were thrown from their saddles and the four men following behind were also unhorsed. Their attack was in disarray. My archers, the trees of the orchard and our tight line of horsemen meant the Seljuqs would need time to reform. Had I had more men I would have charged the rest but we were isolated. The men of Nablus had been forced back. I saw the dead sergeants and knights mixed with Seljuqs. I saw one pinioned to a peach tree. His arms were folded across his chest by the spear which pinned him there. "Fall back!"

We whipped our horses to the right, holding our shields up. It was fortunate that we did so for a shower of arrows struck them. Guy's horse was struck and I saw blood spurt. The horse kept going but, as we neared our standard its legs began to give way. Guy threw away his spear and, kicking his feet from the stirrups was able to jump from his dying steed as it fell. He stood and had the presence of mind to grab his spear before running back. A Seljuq saw his chance and he galloped towards Guy's unprotected back. Tom whipped his horse's head around and rammed his spear into the side of the Seljuq who fell from the saddle. His horse continued towards our standard. Henry son of Will reached over to grab the reins. When we reached our standard, Henry held out the reins. "Here you are, Guy. It would not do to have you go afoot!"

"Thank you and thank you, Master Tom. I owe you a life."

"I think you have watched my back enough times before Guy."

"Turn and face." I envisaged us having to do this all the way back to our camp. I could not see us all surviving. We had, however, halted the attempt to outflank us. We were now an oblique line for the Hospitallers had been forced back.

Then I heard trumpets. Theobald was still alive and he shouted, "Open your lines, open your lines!"

I turned and saw King Conrad of Germany leading his knights. He had managed to make it through the army and his fresher men charged the Seljuqs. It was not the classical Frankish charge. They had to negotiate the dispirited and disorganized men of Nablus but once they were through King Conrad slowed them down until they could form a line and then they charged. Like the enemy, he found it hard to maintain a continuous line because of the trees. His men rode in conroi. That worked to their advantage for they were fighting for their lord who led them. The enemy were caught. They had thought we were defeated and had not expected to be attacked. They were not in a solid line. Their archers were still behind the shields and the horsemen they had sent were not as heavily armoured as the Germans.

With sharp lances and fresh horses, the Germans simply overran the Seljuqs. The horses of the dead Seljuqs barged through the shields and ran into the archers. The enemy began to flee across the river and into Damascus.

"Garth, mount your men, let us follow. Tom, the standard."

It was only when Guy mounted his captured horse that we realised how much bigger were our horses. His feet almost touched the ground but then he was a big man. This time our advance was slow. We walked. Remus was lathered. It was July and it was hot. We kept going, following the line of the Germans. They chased and harried the survivors all the way beyond the edge of the orchard and to the enemy shields and defences. There they began to take casualties. There were men on the walls and with their elevation were able to send their arrows into the Germans. Men and horses fell. They endured it for longer than was wise and then the order to fall back to the orchard was given.

The sun was setting as the fighting ended. We had done what was intended but it had cost us more than we had expected to pay. We were relieved by men from France. "Lord, we are here to relieve you. We will keep watch."

"Have you archers?"

The knight shook his head, "Crossbows."

"You will need them. Do not stray beyond the edge of the trees, my friend. These Turks have good bows and they know how to use them."

"Thank you for the advice. This is not what I expected when I left Dijon."

"It is not what any of us expected."

We did not ride our horses back, we walked them. We passed knots of bodies where men had fallen. Even as we trudged back to the camp we saw men coming for the bodies. Each contingent would care for their own. The Master of the Hospitallers had been relieved at the same time as we and we joined him and his men.

"Once again you did well, Sir William. You did not lose your head."

"Had it not been for you and your brave Hospitallers then it would have been a disaster."

He gave a rueful smile, "The problem with a council of war is that there are too many opinions. We will only defeat the Turk when we have one man's strong hands on the reins. I fear this will not end well." He lowered his voice, "Our brothers, the Templars, seem determined to have Damascus for their own and I have heard that Thierry of Flanders sees it as his kingdom in the making." He sighed, "We came here to free this land yet there are men now who just wish to claim it."

"For me, lord, I have not seen any that I would exchange for one acre of England."

"Amen to that William." He nodded to my archers. "They are a fearsome weapon. They have an effect beyond their numbers."

"They train longer to be an archer, lord, than a knight trains. If you have not begun training by the time you have seen seven summers then you will never be an archer. Garth."

My captain of archers walked over, "Lord?"

"Master put your hand around his upper arm."

The Hospitaller did so and his eyes widened, "It is like knotted oak."

"And that is why they can keep up a shower of arrows deep into the enemy lines for as long as they do. My father has thirty odd such men and more. It is the reason Stephen the Usurper has yet to claim the whole of England."

We went to Jean and my other men. They had made a camp in the shade of some fig trees. They had spent the day picking some and we ate them while Jean and the others took our saddles from our horses and watered them. I donned my cloak and placed my helmet on the ground. "Take charge, Robert. I will find the king."

I made my way through the camp. Tents were being erected in the orchard. I saw the standards of the kings, counts, dukes and other rulers as each claimed his own territory. As I approached the King's tent I heard raised voices. I recognised the king and the badgering tones of de Waller. I waited outside. The two sentries recognized me and nodded.

"You ran, lord! You fled! Had not the Hospitallers come to our aid then the men of Nablus would have been slaughtered."

"It was a poor choice of battlefield! The trees prevented us from attacking. I was losing too many men."

I heard Theobald of Rheims say, reasonably, "The men of Aqua Bella managed to do so."

The silence I heard was eloquent. Then the king spoke and I heard real authority in his voice. "If you do not follow my orders to the letter in the future, lord, then I will appoint another to be lord of Ramelah."

"It is not your castle!"

"No, but it is my kingdom. Tread carefully, my lord! You are perilously close to treason."

The flap of the tent was moved and de Waller stepped out. I was the last person he either expected or wished to see. He stepped close to me. "You keep getting in my way, boy. You are like an irritating insect which spoils a summer evening. Watch out that I do not squash you."

"I fear not a bully and blowhard like you, de Waller. I gave you the chance to fight me and you declined. You are nothing but a knife in the night!"

Suddenly his eyes showed fear and they flickered from side to side as though he was looking to see who might have overheard the words. He jabbed a finger in my chest, "Watch out, Englishman. I am not the only one who has a score to settle with you. The Count of Provence knows who you are. He has injuries at your hands. Beware. You and your tiny band of brigands are in the wrong place. Take my advice and go home."

"No, lord, we are Englishmen and we do not run when things become difficult. That is what you do!"

I saw the two sentries smile at my words and then the lord pushed past me and left. I saw that Theobald had been watching. "You care not whom you upset, Sir William."

"A knight must do what he believes is right. If he does not then he has no right to call himself a knight."

"Come inside, the king would speak with you."

I entered and saw a king who bore the weight of the world upon his shoulders. "Your majesty."

The young king looked sad and, somehow, ancient, "A bad day for Jerusalem. We were charged with making an attack and I have been let down by one of my most powerful lords."

I was searching for something positive to say, "The Germans did well."

"We all want different things, Sir William. I wish a secure border. The King of France wishes glory while King Conrad and Thierry wish their own kingdom here. Tomorrow we begin to build siege engines. I would have you and your men do what you did today and guard the left flank. The defenders may sally forth."

Theobald poured me a beaker of wine. "The trouble is we do not know what Nur -al-Din has planned."

"He will come to the aid of Damascus will he not?"

"It is not as simple as that, Sir William. Our divisions are reflected in our enemies. Mujir ad-Din Abaq rules the city. He is of the Burid dynasty. They do not wish to be ruled by Nur al-Din. The king had an agreement with Mujir ad-Din Abaq that they would be our allies. King Conrad of Germany has insisted that it should be a Christian city. His motives, as I said, are suspect."

"Then we will do as we have been ordered, lord. This crusade is not the venture I thought it would be."

"You are new to Outremer, Sir William, this is our way of life."

I nodded, "My men and I will watch this night."

"Thank you, Sir William. I will sleep easier."

I returned to my own camp. We now had a system of watchers. Garth, Robert and I split the watch with Tom, Henri, Louis and William. The rest of my men would have a better night's sleep but I could not risk the king's life.

The next day the army began to build the towers and machines which would lob stones at the walls. Our task was easier. We just sat in the shade of fig and peach trees and watched for sallies from the enemy. They tried one such attack in the late afternoon. The builders had felled trees from the western end of the orchard. The towers of Damascus meant that they could be seen from the city. As the first stone thrower began to be assembled a horde of horsemen with bows burst forth. They caught a conroi of French knights and sergeants by surprise. Releasing arrows at a prodigious rate from the backs of their horses the Seljuq archers slew many Frenchmen before they burst through the lines and headed for the stone thrower.

"To horse! Garth make sure fewer return than rode forth!"

"Aye lord." We had Alf returned to us and he took his sling to aid the archers as they hurried to the aid of the French knights.

We hurtled after the horsemen. They were fast and we had little chance of catching them. They would hurt our builders and there was nothing we could do. My only aim was to hurt them and reduce the numbers of these horse archers. We had little answer to them. Five archers and a slinger could not stop them. We had crossbowmen with the army but they were slow and they were vulnerable. They could do serious damage to an enemy but the Seljuqs were capable of sending arrows over the backs of their horses with such speed that crossbowmen would be slaughtered before they had a chance to kill enough of the enemy.

We rode steadily. Who knew how many times we would have to do this before the day was out? Other sergeants had mounted their horses and were riding towards the archers. They would be too late. The Turks rained arrows on the builders. Without armour, the men fell. We arrived at the rear before they had finished. I thrust my spear into the back of a surprised archer who was pulling back on his bow. I tossed his body to the side and pulled out my spear. The second archer I slew was turning when I thrust my spear into his neck. It did not kill him instantly and his dying hand grasped the spear and his body pulled it from my grasp. Drawing my sword, I was able to hack into the chest of a third archer who had turned to flee. My handful of men had carved a hole in the middle of the archers. Others had joined in from the side and the horde retreated. They had slaughtered all of the builders.

As we were amongst them it was hard for them to hit us with their arrows. Our mail and shields protected us against their swords and so we were able to kill all who approached us. We slew many but many times more escaped. By the time the men with crossbows had arrived the horse archers had fled. Garth and my archers slew more as the horse archers galloped back to their lines. We had hurt them but they had hurt us more. Our war machines would be delayed.

It went on like that for two more days. The work went on slowly but it was as though we were taking three paces forward and then one back. One late afternoon, we were just making our weary way back to our camp when we were stopped in our tracks. Dusk was almost upon us and we had repulsed four attacks. It was the Count of Provence who barred our way. He was with Robert de Nissa and Guillaume de Waller. There were twenty knights with them.

The Lombard jabbed a finger at Alf, "You have my property! Release him to me and no more will be said."

I did not answer him but stared at de Waller. "They say you judge a man by the company he keeps. I always thought you treacherous but now I know you for a snake." I turned back to the Count. "Out of my way. Unlike you and your men, we have been toiling to keep our builders safe."

"That is all that you are good for and I am not leaving without my slave."

I heard five bows being drawn behind me as Garth hissed, "Give me the word lord and these three will become hedgehogs!"

"A peasant dares to threaten a Count? I will have you on a gibbet!"

I shook my head and laughed, "That will be a fine trick for after they have released their arrows I will take your head." I whipped out my sword. "Come I have killed enough brave Seljuq's today. It is time I killed a cowardly Frank and a pair of cruel Lombards!"

I am not certain what would have happened then had not Raymond de Puy Provence appeared with eight brother Hospitallers. "Is there a problem Sir William?"

"The Count here thinks he can bar my passage to my camp. We were just pointing out the error of his ways. It is good that you stopped, Master, when we have finished with them your men may be able to aid some of those we do not kill."

The Master nodded, "We are here should you need us, lord and we can say a prayer for their souls too."

The Count's hand went to his sword. Garth's arrow landed so close to the Count's spur that it made it spin. The Count looked up in shock. Garth growled, "That was a warning, Count. The next one will give you a third eye."

The Count jabbed a finger at me. "This is not over."

"I know for you are still alive and that, in itself, is a miracle for which you should give prayers of thanks."

When they had gone, the Master said, "He is a dangerous man, William. He is not honourable."

"It is worse than that Master. I believe that de Waller conspires with our enemies. I have no evidence yet but his actions the other day just confirm my suspicions."

"Be careful."

"I will."

We ate and then I went with William of Lincoln to watch the tent of the king. To my surprise, he was outside his tent. All the other leaders were seated around him. The Count of Provence was there too. The Master gave me the slightest shakes of his head as I approached. I waved William to the rear of the tent and I squatted down behind the king's seat.

There was a debate in progress. King Conrad of Germany, obviously buoyed by his victory, held the floor. "I agree with the Count of Provence. It was a mistake to camp here. We are losing men each day. Last night they sallied forth and slew thirty sergeants and five knights. We cannot take such losses. The walls give them protection and they use the orchards for cover."

King Baldwin said, "But we have shade and have food and water here. What is the alternative?"

"The plain to the east is better for a camp. We can defend it."

Raymond de Puy Provence shook his head, "There we would be in the direct path of Nur al-Din. There is neither grazing for our horses nor food for our men. The heat of July will kill just as surely as a Seljuq arrow."

"I agree with King Conrad. Count Thierry and I are in agreement. We will move our men to the east on the morrow." King Louis appeared to cast the deciding vote.

I caught Theobald's eye. This was a conspiracy. King Baldwin was seen as the most junior of the kings and was being treated as such. His army represented the smallest portion of the enterprise. The King looked at the Master. "And the military orders?"

"We will stay with the King of Jerusalem."

All eyes went to the Master of the Templars. He smiled, "And we will support the majority. We will move to the east!"

The conclave broke up. I was left with King Louis, the Master and Theobald. "This is a disaster, Theobald."

The Master shook his head, "It is not yet the disaster but that is coming, believe me."

The King turned to me, "Did you scout the plain they speak of?"

"No, your majesty and I am interested to know how they managed to get that information. None of them seem the kind to risk their men scouting behind enemy lines."

"It is as William says. There is treachery afoot. I think it would be best if we all returned home. Nothing good can come of this." The master sounded sad and defeated. He was a pious man who believed that God was on our side. Our allies' loyalty was in doubt.

That night we neither saw nor heard anything. The locals who came close to the tent of the king were easily moved along by the king's guards and we were not needed. I knew that when the assassin struck the first to die would be the guards.

This time it was the Count of Provence and his Lombards who led the army. We must have taken the Turks by surprise for we were left alone. It took a day to move and to erect the camp. This time the initiative was taken from King Baldwin. It was King Louis, King Conrad and Count Thierry who made all the decisions. Theobald summoned me to the King's tent just before dark. He spoke quietly. "The King, I fear is dispirited. Tomorrow I would have you move your camp a little closer to the king. He seems brighter in spirits when you and your young warriors are close to hand. The Master and I are like two old relics. We have both lived here so long that we are as dry as the dust we breathe. We are a pair of desiccated old men."

"You do yourself a disservice but we will do all that we can. To be frank with you we prefer to be away from the rest of the army. The Hospitallers are the only ones with which we have something in common."

It was my turn, with Henri this time, to be on the middle watch. It was the most unpopular. The first watch and the last watch meant you had a short sleep but at least it was uninterrupted. We fell asleep only to be awoken from a pleasurable dream. In my case, it was the face of Rebekah which haunted me. I swear I could smell her skin in my dreams. So it was that I awoke grumpy and said little to Henri. We had a routine now. The sentries knew us and nodded as we approached. We did not speak for fear of disturbing the King. All around us was the sound of crackling fires and flatulent warriors. From the tent of the King of Germany, I heard the sound of bodies grinding together. The King had brought women he had purchased in Constantinople. From other tents came the sound of mumbled conversations. What was absent was the sound of silence.

With two sentries at the front of the tent, Henri and I took our places at the sides of the tent. That way we could cover both the back and the sides. I held my sword across my lap. I wore no helmet and my coif hung around my shoulders. I pulled my hood up. It was thin but it, and my cloak, would make me hard to see. I was certain that the assassin had come close before but our presence had put him off. After one watch I had seen the prints of a barefoot around the king's tent. Our men all wore boots or shoes. I sat and listened. I tried to filter out the other noises from around me. I closed my eyes for it was night and shadows were deceptive. I used my nose as much as my ears.

The noises diminished slightly. For some reason that seemed to heighten my sense of smell. A different odour came into my nostrils. It was not one I had smelled before. I could not place it but it was unnatural. Then I heard a soft sigh. It sounded like someone was disappointed with something. I would have ignored it if my nose was not suddenly assailed by the smell of blood. I leapt to my feet and ran to the front of the tent. The two guards lay in ever-widening pools of blood, their throats cut. I stepped into the tent. The king kept a candle burning and I saw the two assassins. They were so similar that they could have been brothers. One had just slit the throat of the guard who slept inside the tent and the other was closer to me and approaching the King. I swept my sword into the side of the nearest one. My sword cut through his ribs and was only stopped by his backbone. His back arched and the knife fell from his hand.

"Henri!"

The other picked up the king's mace which lay on the table with his left hand. He swung it at my sword. It was a powerful blow and the feeling went from my hand. He lunged at me with the dagger. The king awoke as Henri entered, "Your majesty the dagger is poisoned! Henri take him out."

I saw the blood dripping from the assassin's dagger but I also knew that it would be poisoned. One cut would render me dead. I blocked it with my mailed mitten. Pulling back my left hand I punched as hard as I could into his jaw. He reeled. Before he could recover I hit him again with my right fist. This time he was rendered unconscious. The noise brought in Theobald and the Master of the Hospitallers.

I knelt on the assassin's arms and sat on his chest. He was going nowhere and I would question him.

The Master said, "An assassin." It was not a question but a statement of fact. The snake handled dagger was proof enough.

I held the dagger at my side by the handle. "The other is dead. We need to question this one and discover who sent him."

Theobald said, "I think we know that well enough."

"We need proof. Is the King unhurt?"

"He is shaken but your man guards him like a tigress guards her cub. None will get close to the King."

The man's eyes opened. I saw the huge black pupils. He grinned at me and began to chant. I backhanded him across the mouth, "Silence until I order you to speak."

The Master said, "You will get nothing from him, even under torture."

"We must try. Ask him who sent him."

The Master asked him and the man just grinned. "Tell him he will die if does not tell us."

"That does not frighten him."

I suddenly remembered Ralph of Bowness' gift. "Master, on my belt is a purse, it is pigskin."

The Master chuckled, "That might work."

He held it before the assassin and said something. The man's eyes widened. I am a big man and I wore mail. I was heavy yet, even as the Master moved the purse towards the assassin's hand the killer head-butted the poisoned blade. I tried to move my hand back as he did so but it was too late. The dagger pierced his cheek. He smiled, closed his eyes and then his body went into spasm. A heartbeat later and he lay dead.

The Master shook his head as he handed me my purse, "I told you, Sir William. These men do not fear death. For them, this is no sin. He will go to heaven and be assailed by virgins. His life on this earth was as a preparation for a better life to come. That is why the true fanatic is hard to defeat. Do not reproach yourself. You have done all that could have been asked of you."

I held up the dagger. "We can stop these coming close. Every Muslim who comes into the camp should be stripped and searched. We allow them no weapons."

"The problem is they have an ally in the camp who is a Frank. They could come in without a weapon and we would be able to do nothing about it. We remain vigilant."

I went outside the tent where a crowd had gathered. I smiled at Henri, "You may relax your guard the two killers are dead."

King Baldwin grasped my hand, "I would have been dead but for you."

"I was just doing my duty." My eyes scanned the crowd and I fixed Guillaume de Waller with a stare, "We did not find the Frank who hired this killer but we are a little closer."

King Conrad said, "A Frank hired these savages? Are you mad?"

The master put his arm around my shoulder, "No, your majesty, I agree with Sir William. We have a traitor in this camp."

Chapter 14

That was the moment when all unity left the camp. Everyone viewed the other leaders with suspicion. Each king, count and duke had guards outside of their tents but the worst effect was the lack of direction. No one seemed willing to either take charge or let another command. King Baldwin was all for negotiating an alliance with Damascus as he had done before. Count Thierry refused to countenance it. Then we had the desertions. It was a trickle at first. One or two knights left the camp with their retinue. Everyone was a volunteer and so it could not be stopped. However, when whole contingents left, it became more serious. De Waller and the Count of Provence departed at the same time. We noticed their departure for they took over a hundred and fifty knights and sergeants not to mention their levy, peasants and servants.

The last straw was the news that Nur al-Din was coming. He had been summoned by the vizier of Damascus. The Turks had lost too many men to us and now they were resigned to the inevitable. They would follow Nur al-Din. This time it was neither a trickle nor a stream of men who left. It was a flood. There was little organization. We were luckier than most. The Master of the Hospitallers and Theobald were old friends. When we left we marched together. The baggage and those on foot were in the centre of our column and we, riders, were in a box around them.

The horse archers followed us. We were luckier than most. We still had some crossbowmen left and I had my five archers and Alf with his sling. Garth and the archers stopped and dismounted. Gaston held their horses. They were able to keep up a relentless rain of arrows to augment the slower crossbows.

Just before noon the Master and Theobald made the box halt. Water was distributed and the horses rested. The men of Nablus complained. Theobald shrugged, “Feel free to leave us and see how long you would last. We will not be camping until we reach Galilee.”

He was proved right. The horse archers came again and this time every knight and sergeant made a wall with our shields while the crossbows and bows thinned their ranks. The Master said, “They are trying to tempt us into a reckless charge. It is a foolish thing to do. When we move, we will walk our horses until the day is cooler.”

The King of France was behind us and they moved up the road and they passed us. The shouts from their sergeant left in no doubt that they thought we were madmen. Finally, the Count of Flanders passed our resting men. He was pursued by even more horse archers. I noticed that they did not bother with us. It was eerie. We were the last battle of warriors and the horse archers had left us.

"We march until late afternoon." Theobald looked at the king, "You too, your majesty." King Baldwin nodded and dismounted. Ahead of us, we heard the clash of arms and the screams of the dying. They were riding and we were walking. We would not catch them. After an hour, we found the bodies of thirty-foot soldiers. They were from Flanders and all lay dead. There were no dead Turks close by. The sergeants lay in concentric circles. They had been surrounded and the archers had ridden around them and picked them off.

As we marched towards the rise, a haze coloured and dusty mass of men, we passed more bodies. They were all Franks. Garth shook his head, "We can only hope that they run out of arrows, lord, for there is naught else to stop them. My five bows will do little. It is like spitting in the wind."

"And yet, Garth, they are not bothering us. There are easier targets up ahead."

"Aye, the Master and old Theobald know their business. It is a pity that they were not in charge of the siege."

The horse archers came thundering past us as some of them headed back to Damascus. A dozen or so were brought down by our archers and crossbows. "There you are, Garth, some have run out of arrows."

Garth pointed ahead, "There are still enough there. See they are attacking yet."

I nodded, "And when Nur al-Din reaches the city there will be even more."

We reached the top of the rise a few hours later and we were halted once more. A hundred and more bodies had been passed. The Hospitallers had found four wounded men and they were on the backs of horses with our own wounded. We had lost none killed but we had wounded with us. I was not certain that all would make it back to Jerusalem although at that moment all I wanted was to reach the Sea of Galilee alive. We had taken on more water and relieved ourselves. What little food we had left was consumed and we were about to ride when a cry went up, "Horses! It is Nur al-Din!"

"To arms!"

This time we did mount save the archers and crossbows. Those with spears readied them. It was a mighty host of horsemen. Although most were horse archers there were fifty horsemen. They each had a lance and a helmet with their faces enclosed in mail. Our archers and crossbows sent a flurry of missiles at their horse archers. It broke them up. The Master shouted, "Sir William, bring your men with me. Let us discourage these horsemen."

"Gladly! Follow me!"

We formed a line with twenty of the Hospitallers and we followed the Master as he charged. It was not reckless and it was not wild. He had brought enough men to make them fight us but not so many that they would decline. The enemy charged us. I saw that they wore no mail. Riding boot to boot we smashed into them. Louis and John of Chester were unhorsed but twelve of their number fell to our spears. I pulled my arm back for a second thrust. The Turk tried to block my strike with his lance. My spear had a steel head. I flicked aside the lance and gutted him. I saw a Hospitaller sergeant. His horse was brought down and he lay stunned. His shield and sword were thrown away in the fall. I saw a Seljuq warrior gallop towards him his spear ready to end his life. The sergeant was tough and he began to rise. I spurred Remus and charged the left side of the Turk. He saw me at the last moment. He jerked his horse's head around. The move saved the sergeant's life for the Turk's horse smashed down on his left arm and not his head. I stood in the stirrups and hacked through the helmet and skull of the Seljuq. Two Hospitallers ran from the shelter of the shield wall to rescue their brother.

The Master shouted, "We have done enough! Fall back!"

I saw that the horsemen had ridden off to join the horse archers who were riding west to chase easier targets. To my relief, Louis and John were on their feet. They grabbed the reins of their horses and mounted.

"Are you hurt?"

Louis shook his head, "The blow came from the side. It did not even break my mail but it was a powerful blow. It is nothing."

The only thing that was hurt was their pride. They would get over that.

Theobald said, "They call those warriors, Mamluks. They are good warriors. You did well."

"Why did the Master choose my men and not the men of Jerusalem or Nablus?"

"Simple. He wanted men who would obey orders instantly. You and your men have shown that you can do that. There are other knights who have a victory and have the smell of battle in their nostrils. The Seljuqs know this and draw our men away from the protection of shields."

We followed the Turks west. I saw as we crested the rise, that they had caught the men of Flanders. We were helpless to do anything. The horse archers galloped in and when the Flemish knights and sergeants pursued them the archers turned in the saddle to slay more of them and then the Mamluks picked off the survivors. It was sickening to watch. We kept moving down the slope. I saw that the men of Flanders were panicking. The horsemen galloped off to catch the French contingent. The ones left were on foot and they were slaughtered.

Over the next few hours, we found more bodies. They were all men who fought on foot. There were Germans as well as French, Norman, English and, of course, the Flemish. We walked again for part of the time. The rolling battle moved on ahead of us. The only evidence was the bodies we passed. Then we began to pass the bodies of the horses. They had not been slain. They had simply died. Some had legs broken and their riders had put them out of their misery. Others were in a pitiable state for they had been ridden to death.

As night fell we mounted again having had the last of our water. The next twenty miles would be hard but we knew that the Sea of Galilee and the River Jordan lay ahead. We would pass seasonal rivers but they would only be enough to give the horses water. Without them, we were dead men. We saw fires. The rest of the army had camped. They had not rested and their horses were exhausted. Of the horse archers and the Mamluks, there was no sign but we knew they were around. They too needed water and to rest their horses. The difference was that they knew where to find such things in this wasteland. We were aliens here and we did not.

Theobald said, “Ride ahead with your men and warn them we are not the enemy. They may try to attack us in the dark.”

“Aye lord.”

I led my men and we trotted towards the fires. By chance, the men I saw on guard were from Thiberville in Normandy. I recognised their device. Their lord, Geoffrey de Thiberville raised his arm. “I thought I saw you in Damascus. Do you wish to come into our camp?”

“No, I am here to tell you that the army of Jerusalem is passing. We do not wish you to attack us. You should join us.”

“Are you mad? Here is safer.”

“Have you food and water?”

He shook his head, “No but the river is ahead.”

“It is twenty miles.”

“I have sworn to stay here. Good luck.”

“And to you.”

I waited until the Master caught up with us and then we continued in our huge box as we headed west. We were now the vanguard but the enemy did not bother attacking us. We were ten miles closer to safety when we heard, in the distance, the sounds of battle. The Crusaders were being attacked. We reached the river before dawn. Water has never tasted so good. We buried the three men who had died in the night and, as dawn broke, headed for the castle of Tiberius. Riders were sent from the castle to warn the castles of Belvoir, Nablus and Jerusalem of the disaster which had overtaken us.

I was tired but I felt guilty about the men we had left. I think the Master and Theobald did too. We ascended the stairs to the tallest tower which faced east. It was hard to see against the sun but we saw a steady trickle of men heading towards the sea and the river. I knew that I wanted to mount my horse and go out to fight the archers who were slowly bleeding the army to death. The Master must have read my thoughts. "Sir William it would avail you little to try to help them. Your horse is weary, as are you. We have helped to save the army of Jerusalem. Now that we know we cannot trust de Waller we will need every knight that we can find to defend against Nur al-Din."

"Will he not be satisfied with Damascus?"

"When the County of Edessa is in his hands he will turn his gaze to the other counties and kingdoms. Jerusalem is the prize they all seek." He pointed. I saw the banner of Tripoli. The Count was heading north-west with his army. He was going home to protect his own border. "I have no doubt the Count of Antioch will join him. When the survivors from the Kings and Counts of Europe arrive they will take the northern road and take ship at Acre, Tyre, Sidon and Tripoli. There was not enough trust between the kings."

"And what will you do, Master?"

"We have a mighty fortress in the County of Tripoli. Krak des Chevaliers. It is on the border and when Nur al-Din takes Damascus we will be ready for him when he comes west."

"Damascus is not his?"

"Had we not left the siege it might have been for he would have defeated us and then demanded that the city surrendered. We did not hurt its walls and Mujir ad-Din Abaq does not share the same views as Nur al-Din. All is not lost but it is perilously close." He smiled at me. "By the way, Brother Peter thanks you, lord."

"Brother Peter?"

"When the Mamluks attacked, you saved his life. He was the sergeant who fell."

"I am pleased. He is a brave man."

"He has hurt his arm but we have good physicians at Krak. Perhaps he can be healed." A sergeant who had but one arm had no purpose in life. He would become a beggar.

All day we saw a constant stream of men heading north and west. Ships would be in great demand. I had no doubt that the kings would rattle their swords a little more but without unity, they could do nothing. The Crusade was over.

The next day the Master left us. I felt he was a good friend and he clasped my arm as he left. "You would have made a good warrior monk, Sir William, save that you could not be celibate. You yearn for a family. If ever you need me then send word. I know what you did for the king and I know that your heart is true."

We left in the afternoon. We would halt again at Nablus. The knights from Nablus, Baysan and Belvoir would have left us by the time we departed Nablus. The last part of the journey would be made by the twenty knights and eighty sergeants who remained. We had managed to keep over two hundred of the levy. That was a miracle. Had it not been for the Master and Theobald then we would have lost as many as the others had. Word had come to us that the carrion birds were feasting well on dead Christians and their horses. Many Christians ended their days as slaves. None were knights. They were the ones who had walked to fight the Turk. It was unfair.

Four days later, we left. We had just thirty miles to travel and we would be home before the king for we would join the Jaffa to Jerusalem road. I was looking forward to the safety and security of my home. We joined the road to Ramelah and it all looked familiar. My home was just ten miles up the road.

We should have had scouts out but all of us were exhausted. King Baldwin and Theobald had ridden in close conference all the way from Tiberius. They had much to discuss. My men were all now healed and we rode together. We knew not the other knights and sergeants. We rode at the rear with the levy.

Robert stroked his beard. He had grown it since we had come to the Holy Land. "It is strange is it not, lord, that all of those knights came from France, Flanders, England and many other places to defeat the Turk and yet it is we who run home with our tail between our legs. When we were in Normandy, I thought this would be a glorious venture and God would help us along the way."

"The trouble is, Robert, that is in the hearts of men. If all had the same honour and integrity as the Master or Theobald then it would have been both holy and noble. Thierry of Flanders and Conrad of Germany came here for glory, land and treasure."

"Yet we will go back richer."

"Perhaps that is our reward for having the right motives. At least I like to think it is."

Suddenly a mass of warriors began swarming from the scrubland at the side of the road. It was an ambush. I saw some of the sergeants fall to spears and axes before they even knew we were under attack.

"Garth, arrows! The rest of you, with me. Our war is not over!"

My helmet was hanging from my cantle. After pulling up my coif I drew my sword and spurred Remus I shouted to the levy, "Take shelter!" Theobald and King Baldwin had organised men to defend the horses. Even the King had his sword out. I saw that the ones who attacked us were Franks but I could see no device on their shields. They were plain white. That was not unusual. Many went to war against Damascus with white shields. They wore the brown cloak worn by many. They could have been any band of knights and sergeants.

We struck the ones at the rear of the line. Tom was ahead of me and I saw a sergeant smash his axe into the chest of Tom's horse. A good rider he rolled from the saddle but he hit the ground hard. As he lay there stunned the sergeant raised his axe to finish him. I leaned out and took the sergeant's head in one blow. I was angry and I urged Remus on. Theobald and the king were struggling to hold their own against what seemed like a sea of enemies. Then arrows began to fall and those who were trying to get to Theobald and Baldwin fell. My archers were doing what they did best, killing my foes. I took a spear to my shield and kicked the spearman in the face with my boot. I brought my sword down into the back of a sergeant who was about to take the head of a fallen knight of Jerusalem.

My wedge of horsemen had now driven a gap between the two halves of the enemy force. I saw that it was not as great a number as I had thought. Suddenly a knight turned to run at me with a spear. I say knight for I recognised him. It was Guy de Waller. He had two sergeants flanking him and they were coming for me. I spurred Remus and pulled up on the reins. He soared into the air. As I rose I brought my sword down and cracked open the skull of one of the sergeants. Remus hooves clipped de Waller's head but my horse landed badly. His fore hooves struck a dead body and he stumbled. I kicked my feet from the stirrups and rolled over his head. I let go of my shield but I held on to the sword. The wind was knocked from me as I landed. I looked up and saw the remaining sergeant triumphantly raise his sword to take my head. I blindly swung my sword at knee height and it hacked into the knee and tendons of the sergeant. He fell and I struggled to my feet. Using two hands I plunged the sword into his chest.

I heard Henry son of Will shout, "Lord, watch out!" Something struck my head and all went black. I saw no more.

Chapter 15

Part Three
Ascalon

I dreamed for a long time. I smelled Rebekah but I could not see her. My family's faces flashed before me. I smelled herbs. They made everything go black and when the blackness went I saw my dead mother. I tried to reach her but she shook her head and I fell. I smelled Rebekah and then it was gone. I saw Crusader and Turk in deadly combat. A snake etched knife plunged towards me and I was carried aloft by a mighty bird and then I fell. I fell for, what seemed like forever but I did not reach the ground. I heard a voice. It was Tom.

"John go and fetch my lady. He moved. It was just his finger but I saw it twitch. It is a sign."

"Should I ride for the doctor?"

I tried to speak but it came out as a croak. "He speaks! Go!"

I tried to open my eyes but they would not. Was I blind? The last thing I remembered was Henry's shout and then blackness. Had I lost my sight?

Tom's familiar voice was reassuring, "Drink, lord, it will help. The lady told me." He cupped my head in his hand and the goblet was placed against my lips. It was water and it was cool. I drank.

"See, he moves!" It was John's voice.

Then I smelled something from my dream. It was Rebekah. I tried to open my eyes and a sharp pain raced down the side of my face. Her voice, when she spoke, was soft and gentle. "Let me clean your eyes, lord."

I heard the sound of water and then something cool was pressed against my eyes. I felt her hand upon my rough cheek. I found myself smiling. I was not dead. This was not a dream. I felt her fingers dabbing at my eyes.

"Now try, lord."

I opened my eyes. A blinding light made me shut them again. Tom's voice barked out, "John, you fool! Move the light away!"

"Sorry master."

I opened them again and this time I was able to see. Rebekah's face looked down on me and behind her, I saw John and Tom. They were grinning. Tom came over and patted my hand, "We will go and tell the men, lord. They have been worried."

John nodded, "It is good to see your eyes open, lord."

They left. Rebekah gently cupped my head and poured water into my mouth. "Swallow. The doctor predicted this." I tried to speak but she put her finger on my lips. "One thing at a time. You can see and you can hear. We will wait a few moments to see if you can speak too."

I smiled. I was just overjoyed to be viewing Rebekah and I was alive.

"You have good men. Someone has watched over you since you were brought here." She dabbed my mouth with a cloth. She smiled and it was as though the sun had risen in my room. I was bathed in sunshine. "I am pleased that you live."

"How long?"

The smile widened, "You can speak! No more then. I do not wish to overtax you. It is ten days since you were brought to your home here at Aqua Bella and nine days since the Queen's physician, Michael of Constantinople, cut open your head."

"Cut open my skull? Why am I not dead?"

"It was no magic, lord. It was skill. I was here with him and I helped him. We had to shave your head for the doctor had to cut a flap of skin to bleed your skull. I thought him mad until the black blob of blood emerged. He sewed you up and said that you were in God's hands."

I smiled, "But whose God?"

"I think, lord, that we have different beliefs but there is but one God. All prayed for you. Those captives whom you rescued wept and prayed that you might live. I think God answered all of our prayers."

"When can I rise? I would like to thank my people for their prayers."

She put a hand upon my chest. "Lord you will stay here at least seven days. We have kept feeding you water and the doctor's draught only. You have no strength. We will feed you food and then you shall walk." I moved my right hand. I just wanted to see if I could. She looked down as I raised it. "The doctor said that if you regained consciousness you should heal."

I put my right hand on her left and gently squeezed her fingers, "You say my men have watched me every minute and that means that you have too. Why did you stay?"

She gave me a strange look, "You think I should have abandoned you? You did not abandon me when I needed you. I was repaying your kindness to me."

I put my hand up to stroke her cheek. She closed her eyes and smiled, "We both know that is not true." I slid my hand around to the back of her neck and pulled her face towards mine. She did not resist and when our lips met we kissed. I have kissed women before but I have never experienced what I did that morning, I wondered, for some time after, if it was the doctor's draught. It was not.

Suddenly she jerked her head back and I saw that she was upset. "You are healed. I must go!" She fled the room.

What had I done? I had offended her and I berated myself. I had been too forward and now I had lost her forever. I closed my eyes and felt the corners moisten. I had had happiness in my hand and I had squeezed too hard and it was destroyed. I heard voices. Opening my eyes, I saw Robert, Tom and Francis.

"It is true, lord. You live! God be praised."

Francis nodded, "The Lady Rebekah left strict instructions about your food, lord. I will go and get it organized! It is good to see you awake!" He left.

"The lady?"

Robert sat on the chair next to the bed, "She slept here since she arrived. The only time she left was to fetch food."

I tried to shake my head and it hurt, "No, I mean where is she now?"

"She said her work was done and she went back to her father's."

"Alone?"

"Of course not, lord. Has that blow made you forget that I know my duty? Garth and his men have escorted her. It was he who brought her here before the king sent his doctor. She helped the doctor. She cares for you, lord."

"Then why has she left?"

He smiled, "I know not, lord. Horses and men, I understand. Women?" He pointed at my head, "They are like the magic that the doctor did with your brains."

"What happened to the rest of our men? The ambush?"

"You were struck from behind by a war hammer. Had you not had such a good helmet the doctor thinks you would be dead. The helmet is ruined. We will need to get you a better one. When you slew young de Waller, the heart went from them and they fled. We lost few. The king knows he owes his life to you. I have sent word that you have recovered."

"And de Waller, the lord of Ramelah?"

"Is lord of Ramelah no longer. He fled with the rest of his men. None know where. The castle of Ramelah is now a Templar castle."

"Templar? I thought he would have given it to the Hospitallers if anyone."

"Politics, lord. The Templars wield more power than the Master of the Hospitallers. This way the pilgrims will be protected and the road from Jaffa to Jerusalem kept open. He would attack Ascalon one day and recover it. It is politics for he has the Templars to help him."

"Then our work is done here. We need no longer watch the road."

"It looks that way, lord."

"And Remus? Is he hurt?"

"He took a knock on his legs but he is resting too. He is recovered already." Just then Francis' wife Alice appeared with two slaves and some food. "We will heed the Lady Rebekah's words. I would not risk her wrath." He patted the back of my hand. "It is good you live, lord. The mood of the men will lighten. We feared we had lost our lord."

Over the next five days, I began to regain my strength. I had to force my nurses to allow me to stand and make water. They had wanted me to be as an old man and use a chamber. I was determined to recover in less than seven days. I had the servants shave me so that my beard did not look unruly and I made them fetch water so that I could bathe. Robert and Tom insisted upon helping me for they did not want me to slip and injure my head once more. Alice's food, which had been organized by Rebekah, worked and I began to feel stronger. After five days, I had my clothes brought and I stood and was dressed. I had walked for a short while for the last three days but I still had Garth close by when I descended to my hall.

My men had gathered as well as both Francis and Absalom's families. They cheered and clapped. Alice kissed my hands and said, "Lord, when time allows and you feel up to it then the workers on the estate wish to see you. They prayed for you."

"I know the lady Rebekah told me."

Alice nodded, "I think lord that she is a Christian at heart. I cannot believe that she is a Jew."

Alice was like most of the Christians who lived in the Holy Land. They thought to convert all they met. I did not mind any having different beliefs to me. The exception were the Muslims for they wished to change the world by their swords. My recovery began that day. I went to speak with the workers. Stepping out into the hot sun of late summer was a shock and almost made me have a relapse but my father and mother had bred strength in my bones and I fought it.

When I looked in the polished metal which acted as a mirror I saw, through the stubble on my head the scar where the doctor had gone into my head. I called Tom for the reflection was not clear, "Tom, what do you see when you see the scar?"

"I am sorry, lord, I do not understand the question."

"What is its shape?"

"It's shape I… oh now I see." He crossed himself, "Lord, it is a gryphon!"

"That is what I thought. Then it seems I was destined for this device. Today we will ride."

"Are you certain lord, the Lady Rebekah…?"

"Is not here and I am master. I say we shall ride. However, if it makes you feel better we shall ride and visit with the Lady Rebekah so that she may see I am recovered."

He grinned, "Aye lord. Remus will be eager to ride!"

Robert insisted upon a full escort. All of my men had recovered and with the Templars ensconced in Ramelah, Aqua Bella was secure. We had spoken often and Robert, like me was concerned about de Waller. A snake is less dangerous when you can see it. When it is hidden then it is more of a threat. As we headed to the home of David Ben Samuel I wondered about the Templars. They had managed to escape the disaster at Damascus with few losses. They had been amongst the first to leave once the exodus was underway. I could understand the King of Jerusalem wanting the castle at Ramelah in strong hands but was it a hostage to fortune? As we had discovered with de Waller, in the hands of the wrong man it could become a threat to all. The only saving grace was that the Templars were committed to helping pilgrims. Despite the fact that the king thought the road safe, we would continue to escort the caravans of those who did not enjoy the protection of the Templars.

"Do we have any word of where de Waller may have fled and were there any prisoners to question.?"

"The King's priest was on hand and Theobald used him to question Guy de Waller. He was dying and he needed absolution for his sins. He confessed to being ordered to kill the king. He had disgraced the family by failing to kill you, lord. He was given absolution and he died before we could discover where his uncle might have fled."

"It is unlikely that he would have known but I can see how de Waller might wriggle out of this. He would deny ordering his nephew to kill the king." This was the final proof as to the identity of the man who had hired three assassins. From what the Master had told me, their services were not cheap. He had warned me that I might become a target for one. I had spoiled their record of invincibility. Two assassins dead by my hand did not do their reputation any good at all. I wondered if he had gone back to Normandy or Anjou. I dismissed the idea instantly. There would be knights returning to those lands from the Holy Land and people would know what he had done. There might be some who would welcome him but most would shun him. Regicide was frowned upon, especially by the Pope. He would hide and I would watch for the day he resurfaced.

As we neared David Ben Samuel's estate, Robert added, "The Count of Provence is in Tripoli. It is said he has put a price on your head lord," he smiled, "and the rest of your brigands. His words, not mine. It seems he is desperate to have Alf returned to him."

"Perhaps not. He may just resent the fact that a lesser noble took Alf from him. He seemed an arrogant man. I will lose no sleep over it. The walls of Aqua Bella are secure."

"They are and the chapel was heavily used while you were ill. The Lord answered our prayers and you were healed. The doctor terrified me. Had not Lord Theobald assured us of his skill we would have halted his work. The Lady Rebekah was steadfast. I confess that when he opened the broken piece of skull in your head I thought he was trying to kill you."

"And he stitched back the skin?"

"Aye lord. He said that the bone would knit of its own accord but he recommended you drink goat's milk and eat cheese. It will speed the process." Robert turned to look at me. "He advised no campaigning for some time. You are not to wear a helmet for six months at least."

"I need a new one anyway. I do not think this peace will last but I am grateful for it gives me the chance to recover fully. I wish to live."

We entered the gates of the now-familiar estate. Servants came to take our horses. The men knew that there would be a welcome for them. They had friends amongst the guards. Robert, Tom and I took off our cloaks and put them over our horses. Before we entered the hall, we beat the sand from our clothes. Servants waited with water for us to wash. It was almost a ritual. It was as though we were entering a different world.

David Ben Samuel came to greet me. I saw him looking at my shaven head. "Rebekah told me of this doctor. You are a lucky man lord and I am sorry that I brought this upon you."

"You, David?"

"De Waller is my enemy and now he is yours."

"No, my friend. He was an enemy of my family too but this was an attempt to kill the king. He is not finished but he has no power any longer. However, until I have put him in the ground we had better watch closely."

"Of course. Come let us go into the courtyard."

"Before we do I would speak with you alone."

"Of course."

I looked pointedly at Tom and Robert. Tom looked confused until Robert pushed him in the back. "Come, squire and I will explain a few things to you!"

David Ben Samuel said, "This sounds ominous, lord. Come to my study. It is where I go to be alone and to recite passages from the Torah. It helps to give me peace." We entered the small chamber which had but two seats. "Sit and speak."

I hesitated. This was not as easy as I had expected. I almost stood and fled. Then I realised that I had been given a chance at a second life. I had seen death and God had granted me an extension. I would not waste it. I just came out with it. "I would marry your daughter, Rebekah."

He smiled, "This is the custom in your land, lord, to ask the father?"

"It is. Is it not so here?"

"Sometimes but often the father chooses the husband. You know she is not yet eighteen and … well, you know the rest."

"I do. I am but five and twenty years old myself. There is not much difference and I love her."

"Oh, that has been obvious to all of us for some time and she loves you too."

I smiled, "Then it is settled?"

"Would it were so. I told you once that her heart was hardened. Before…, well before de Waller, she was betrothed to the son of Judah Ben Joshua, Reuben. She said she would never marry any man. She could barely stand to see her brothers and me. It is why she spent over two years in Caesarea. You have wrought great changes in her lord but I fear it is too soon."

"You forbid me to ask her?"

"Of course not. You have my blessing. Others may be unhappy that you are a Gentile but I know that your heart is good and you will not hurt my daughter. Get her permission and she shall be yours."

"Then I have a new quest. I will ask your daughter to marry me."

"Come, let us go to the courtyard. They will be wondering of what we speak."

David's sons and his wife were there along with his other daughter, Mary, and Rebekah's mother, Ruth. David frowned, "Where is Rebekah? She is not here to greet our guest."

Mary said, "She was upset and said she was not ready to face the lord of Aqua Bella. She went to the fig tree."

I looked at David Ben Samuel. "The fig tree?"

"It is close to the south wall. She goes there when she is upset. She sits beneath its shade. It is surrounded by lemon trees. It is a pleasant place to sit. It is special to the whole family. There are birds which visit the tree and she takes comfort." He paused. "She spent long hours there…"

"Oh." I sat down.

David Ben Samuel shook his head, "You are not afraid to charge uphill into a horde of bandits and archers yet you baulk at speaking to a young girl. Lord, go. I will entertain your men."

I saw the confused looks from the others. He was right and I stood and strode through the arch of olive branches. It was like stepping into an oven. Here they had an orchard. I walked between the lines of peaches and nectarines. I saw in the distance a pale blue figure sitting beneath the branches of a huge fig tree which had smaller lemon trees flanking it. I forced myself to advance. She could only say no.

She saw my approach and I saw her eyes flickering from side to side as she sought an escape. There was none and, as I closed with her, her shoulders sagged in resignation.

"Rebekah." I sat next to her. I left her enough space so that she did not feel threatened.

"Did my sister not tell you that I wished to be alone?"

"She did but I am still here. That should tell you something." She looked up and I saw fear in her eyes. "Firstly, I wish to apologize for the kiss. It was not the act of a knight. I blame the medication but it is still no excuse. It upset you and you ran."

She shook her head, "No, lord, I wished to kiss you but it is wrong."

I was confused, "How is it wrong?"

She passed her hand down her dress, "Lord I wear blue. I should wear white for I am unmarried. I am soiled. I am damaged. Did my father not tell you that de Waller took me? I am not a virgin!"

"He did."

"It does not bother you?"

"It makes me angry but with him and not you."

"I had a child lord, it died!" She burst into tears and my heart broke with hers. I put my arm around her as she sobbed into my chest. Gradually her sobs subsided. "I am not certain I wished her to live but when they handed her to me I wanted to keep her. The babe opened her eyes and looked at me." She buried her head again. She said, into my chest, "And then she died. She lived but for a few heartbeats and she was gone. I did not get to tell her how I would love her. She died. …. She died and I wished to join her."

I lifted her chin with my hand and said, "Lady, I would marry you and keep you safe."

She shook her head and said passionately, "Were you not listening, lord? I cannot lie with a man. I wanted to kiss you but I could not bear it for de Waller was in my mind. If you marry me then you will never enjoy that which other husbands do. I love you too much to do that to you."

"You love me?"

"Of course, lord, Is that not obvious?"

"I am a knight. I thought I knew women but, as my father pointed out to me, I do not. I love you and I care not if you keep apart from me. I wish to care for you and be your protector. In time, I would hope that your heart would soften but if not then so be it. The past is past. I wish to spend the rest of my life with you."

"Truly? If I ask you to have a room apart for me you would do so?"

"Of course."

"And you would not go back to England as you wish to do?"

"If you want to stay here in the Holy Land then I will do so. I told you, I want to spend the rest of my life with you and I care not where I do that."

She stood, "Then you truly do love me and I am honoured."

"Then you say yes?"

She shook her head, "No lord, I say you will have to wait while I wrestle with my own demons. Return at the feast of the Passover and I will give you my decision. It is not long to wait, is it?"

"A heartbeat is too long to wait but I will give you the time. It will give me the chance to heal so that I can hunt down de Waller and end his miserable life."

She grasped my hand in hers, "That is not for me is it lord?"

"Not entirely, for he is my enemy and if I do not kill him then he will try to kill me again. I will not wait for a knife in the night. Come let us go back to the others."

"What will you tell them, lord?"

I smiled, "The truth of course. I am a true knight and I do not lie nor do I hide."

They were all watching us expectantly as we stepped beneath the olive arch. She still held my hand and I saw smiles on the faces of all those I saw. They misunderstood. "I have asked Rebekah to be my wife." Ruth's hands went to her face and her eyes filled with tears of joy. "She has turned me down and asked me to wait until the feast of the Passover when she will give me her decision. Until that time, she wishes me to stay apart. I agree to all those terms. She is my Grail and the quest is worth pursuing." I walked to David Ben Samuel and took his arm. "I will see you when we escort your caravans but I will not visit again here until the Passover."

"That is four months. It can be a long time."

"Your daughter is worth waiting for. If it is a lifetime then I shall wait. If she does not agree to be my wife then I shall become a warrior monk. There is no other woman I will wed."

Chapter 16

Life at Aqua Bella went on with or without my problems. We had the new wine and oil to deliver to Jerusalem and I was keen to speak with both Theobald and the King. I also needed a new helmet. This time Francis and Absalom came with me. The estate was safe and we had more slaves and servants to care for. This year we would have more profits but they needed to be ploughed back into the estate.

As we rode north Robert asked, "Are we to go to war again, lord?"

"I intend to ask the King for permission to hunt de Waller down. So, the answer is yes. I have naught else to occupy my mind until the Passover save the caravans. Why do you ask?"

"We need more men. In a perfect world, they would be archers but I knew we were lucky to get Robin Hawkeye. We have horses enough and we have weapons. We stripped the dead who ambushed us and we took their horses but men are not easily bought."

"They may be. There will be lords who perished in the retreat. There will be men who were abandoned and found safety. While I speak with the King I want you and our men to seek out any who might be suitable but a word of caution. We want none who might have served de Waller. We want no Lombards. English, Norman or Angevin warriors are all that I will lead. I will keep Tom with me. And if you can find a reliable smith I would have a helmet made. I remember that David Ben Samuel introduced us to one, Balion I think."

This time, when we entered the city, we were recognized. All of the soldiers who had served on the campaign waved and shouted as we rode through the gate. There were many of the levy: merchants, labourers, cooks and camel drivers who remembered my livery and my banner. There had been little good to speak of and we were, perhaps, something about which they were happy to talk. We halted close to the palace. My men took our horses and Tom and I entered the palace. It seemed a lifetime ago when I had come as a penitent and now I was admitted to the chambers of Theobald.

He actually embraced me. "It is good to see you up and about. I confess that Michael of Constantinople thought that you would not see Christmas. He did his best but he feared for your life."

"I was cared for. I am content."

"The King will be happy that you are now recovered. You are dear to him and I know that his mother, the Queen, wishes to thank you."

"She can thank me by telling me where de Waller is. I cannot rest until he is dead."

"Lord, you seem almost obsessed with him. He is finished!"

"He will be finished when he is dead. I have my own reasons, Lord Theobald. Do not ask but trust me. Where is he?"

"There are rumours. Some say he took a ship back to Normandy."

"But you do not believe that."

"Of course not. He will try again to gain power but he has run out of allies and, more importantly, funds. I fear he has become a renegade."

"How so?"

"My spies tell me that he has taken refuge with the Old Man of the Mountains. He is with the assassins. It will cost him all the money that remains to him but he and his people will be safe. From the lair in the mountains, they can raid and plunder."

My heart sank. I had hoped to spend the next months, before Rebekah's decision, in hunting down and killing him. That was impossible. I was not afraid but I would lose many men tracking him to his lair. I did not want my men to pay for my arrogance with their lives. I would have to wait until he returned. I knew he would do so. He would wait until he thought we had forgotten him and then he would come. He was a survivor and he would make himself richer and stronger.

"And the Crusade?"

"Over. It was not the glorious enterprise which captured Jerusalem. We have lost Edessa. Those castles which still hold out will soon fall and then we will be hemmed in once more. We must strengthen our castles."

"And that is why you gave the castle of Ramelah to the Templars."

"You do not approve?"

"Of course not. I know not what the Templars' strategy is but they seem able to avoid fighting and yet to reap rewards."

He gave me a knowing look, "You have a Byzantine mind. The king does not agree with you."

"But you do."

"Let us just say that Raymond de Puy Provence and I are old friends. I trust his views and they coincide with yours. He was much taken with you."

"Well, who knows. One day I may join his order."

"And you would be welcomed. Come I will take you to the Queen. The King is still receiving supplicants."

Queen Melisende looked no different to the last time I had seen here. She had a serene quality which I admired but her eyes were made of steel. "You may leave us, Theobald. I think I am safe with this young warrior."

I nodded to Tom. "Go and wait at the gate."

When we were alone she reached over to take my hand. "I owe you more than I can ever pay. You saved him from not one but two assassins. And then you saved him from the treachery of de Waller." She turned and took a chest from a small table. "This is a portion of the treasure we found when we took Ramelah. I have no doubt that de Waller took much more away with him but the King and I wish you to have this. It does not make up for the injury you suffered but it will be a start."

I did not look inside. That would have been rude. "Thank you, your majesty but I did not come here for rewards."

"But you will be staying in this land until we have retaken Ascalon?"

"I gave my words and I will keep it."

She seemed relieved, "My son will be happy. He regards you and your men as something of a lucky charm. He grew in the campaign. The venture might have been a disaster but Baldwin gained much from the experience. Do not be a stranger." She leaned back and waved to the wine, "Help yourself to the wine and then tell me what you have planned."

I poured a glass and asked, "Planned?"

"You are not the kind of man to sit idle. You came here today to sell your oil and wine but you also had other reasons."

"You are astute and you are right. We came here for men. If we are to take Ascalon then I need more men. With due respect, your majesty, some of those I fought alongside were less than reliable. They may have been knights but they did not compare with my sergeants. Your son will not attack Ascalon this year or even next. I have time to build up my retinue so that I can make a bigger difference on the field of battle."

She nodded and pointed to the chest. "When you need more money then come to me. Others beg for power and money. You ask for neither yet I know that you will use whatever I give you well."

I left. I now had time to prepare. I had time to win Rebekah. If she turned me down I would continue my quest.

John of Chester was waiting for me at the gate, "Lord, Captain Robert says he has found the smith. I am to take you to him."

"Good, then carry this."

I handed him the chest. "What is it, lord?"

I smiled, "A gift from the Queen. Open it and have a look."

He did so. Tom peered over his shoulder. Their eyes widened. "Lord, this is a king's ransom!"
"Then you had better take good care of it."

We went first to Simon where we deposited the chest. He asked, "Would you like any of it to use now lord?"
I shook my head, "My overseer is selling our olive oil now. There will be more money coming soon."
He smiled, "For a knight, you know the value of coins, lord and, if I might say so, you are less profligate than others. Many waste money on buying exotic items of which they soon tire or they purchase a large number of slaves all of whom need to be fed."
As we left I wondered if that might be a way to find de Waller. He had shown he had a rapacious appetite for young women and that would not alter. He would either have to take women or buy them. I would speak with those who knew of such markets. There was a buzz of conversation on the streets. The departure of the Crusading army and the sudden threat of Nur al-Din had everyone talking. John led us to a square which was filled with lively inns. This was the Christian quarter of the city. Jews and Muslims worked there but it was a place where pigs were cooked and ale and wine consumed in great quantities. Robert, Garth and Alf sat at a table waiting for us.
"I bought a pitcher of wine, lord. I thought we could celebrate."
"Celebrate?"
"Aye lord. We hired another six men, they are with the others being fitted out and Francis said to tell you that the profits have almost doubled. There is a great demand for oil and wine. The campaign drained many men who would have worked on estates producing grapes and olives. We have reaped the benefit."
"Very well but I still need a helmet."
"Do not fear, lord. I have found the smith, Balion. He is around the corner. Although from the words I have had with others there is little chance of war soon." I sipped the wine. It was rough but drinkable. "So many knights and sergeants were lost that the King cannot contemplate launching an attack on Ascalon. Some say it will take a year for the King to be in a position to do so. The losses at Damascus and de Waller's desertion mean we do not have enough knights here."
I nodded. I had thoughts on that. "And the men?"
"We managed to get two archers. Both are English. Their lord fell at Damascus. It took them twelve days to reach Nablus. They are pale shadows of the archers they once were."

Garth shook his head. "They were ill-served by their lord but they have the skills, lord. Even in their poor state, I can see that. Thomas and Jack will be useful additions to your retinue but they will need feeding up."

"Food is not a problem. We have the coin to buy plenty and I thought to buy some sheep and goats. The young boys we rescued, who live at Aqua Bella, could become their shepherds. It is time we produced more goats' cheese and milk." I remembered the doctor's advice. "And the other men?"

Robert drained the last of the wine, "Sound fellows. All were sergeants. They are all Norman or Angevin. Like the archers, they were abandoned after Damascus. Their lords did not die they just fled."

"Their names?"

"Roger of Hauteville, Pierre of Cherbourg, Christophe of Chinon and Alan Azay. Like the archers, they were the best we could hire. There were others but these four still had their weapons and shields. Many of the others had sold their weapons to buy food."

"Good. And you gave them coins to seal the bargain?"

"They did not need them but we did as you commanded."

"They know me not and it will do no harm to give them the dignity of coins in their purses." I smiled, "And that reminds me. I would suggest you do as Ralph of Bowness did. Buy a pigskin purse. It will deter those who would steal your money."

The camp at Damascus had been subject to much petty theft. Many sergeants had had their purses lifted in the dark of night. Our vigilance had meant we were not prey to such thefts but here in the busy streets of Jerusalem, there were many who made a living taking from those who toiled. Every city had such men.

"Come let us see this Balion. Where will we meet the men?"

"At the bazaar, lord. Francis and Absalom will be there waiting for us."

Balion was a huge Jew. He had a forge like Alf's in Stockton but here, the outside heat made it seem even hotter. I did not know how he could work in such conditions. Yet, as we approached sparks flew as he beat out a sword. He saw me and stopped. Lying down his hammer and sword he approached and gave a short bow, "Lord Aqua Bella, you honour my smithy."

He spoke in our language. That was not a surprise. Most of his work would come from the Gentiles. The Jews were not renowned for being warriors. Yet he knew my name. "You know me?"

"I know that the knight with the gryphon on his shield is a mighty warrior and a favourite of Queen Melisende and King Baldwin. The bazaars are full of the talk of you and your band of warriors. How may I be of service? Do you need a sword?"

"No, Balion." I turned my head to show the scar. Although my hair had grown it was still red and vivid. "I need a helmet. My last one saved my life and I need one as good."

He nodded. "You had an open helmet, lord, with a nasal?"

"I did."

"I am guessing that the smith made it in one piece with a reinforcing band around the bottom protecting the nasal?"

"You know your helmets."

"I would suggest one like this, lord."

He showed me a larger helmet than mine. This one had no nasal. The top was quartered by four reinforcing bands. They were not made of iron but another material. However, the front showed the biggest difference. It had a hinged mask. He modelled it on his own head. He struggled to put it on for his head was in proportion to his body.

"See I can lift the visor so that I am able to look with unimpaired vision and the visor affords shade. In this land that is useful. When it comes to battle, I can pull it down. The eye slits are wide but it would take a lucky strike from a bolt or an arrow to penetrate it. The front is also reinforced by strips and it is lighter than you might expect." He smiled, "The strips are made of a secret mixture of metals. It is my own invention."

"Which you will keep secret."

"Of course, lord."

"Then I will have one and make a second for Robert here."

Balion looked surprised, "Lord they are expensive. I have only made them for knights."

"The price you ask is a fair price?" He nodded. "Then make two. And I may need a third for Tom here."

"Me lord?"

"One day you will be a knight."

We were all carefully measured. It did not surprise me when Balion took longer to measure my head. He was particularly careful of the wound although, to speak the truth, it no longer irritated me. When the hair had first grown it had but not since then. We paid him half with the promise of the full payment on completion. He thought it would take him a month. That suited me. The doctor did not know my body. I would not need six months. I needed time to recover fully and from what Robert and Garth had said our new men did too. Until then I would leave the road patrols to my men and I would be the lord of the manor. It was a role I had rarely enjoyed.

We met Francis and the new men. I would have them swear an oath at Aqua Bella. I would still pay them but I liked oaths. It was a mutual binding of brothers in arms. So far I had not been let down.

For the next four weeks, I exercised each day. My new men and I practised with wooden swords for the archers had little experience with them. I liked archers who could fight as sergeants. The rest of my men rode the road. Although it was safer they were still needed for the bandits had returned. They had obviously found a different camp. We borrowed Masood and Robert and Garth sought out their new one. They had learned and we found them not. It was far away and well hidden. The bandits who were foolish enough to attack while my men patrolled paid with their lives. We lost not a man nor a camel driver. We knew the land and my men were at one with it. We had been novices when first we had come and now we were veterans.

We returned to Jerusalem for the helmets. I took just a few men. Leaving Robert to pay for and pick up our helmets, I went to speak with the King. He was not in the palace. He and his mother were at Nablus. Theobald, however, was at home. He saw me and I was taken to his quarters. They were as austere as a Hospitaller's and reflected the nature of this old warrior.

"What can I do for you, William?"

"I would knight Robert and, perhaps Tom, my squire."

He nodded, "Then do it."

"Do I not need the King's permission?"

"You are a courteous knight and your attitude is refreshing. There are many knights who think they are a mighty lord and can do aught that they wish. The King will grant you permission. But if you knight them then you should know that they will be as you and beholden to him. He will be their feudal lord. Aqua Bella has four outlying farms. They serve the estate. You can give those to the knights. It will give them an income although it will detract from yours."

"I do not mind that. Their duty will be little different from now."

"No, William. Now they follow your command. They will still follow your command for they are your knights but they will also have to obey the King."

"They are loyal."

"I know but I thought that you should know." He sipped his wine. "I hear that you may be married soon."

"Yes, to David Ben Samuel's daughter, Rebekah. If she will have me."

He nodded and folded his hands, "You should know, and I say this as a friend, that there are many in Jerusalem who frown on such alliances. Many lords have Jewish concubines but none have a wife who is a Jew."

"You are saying I cannot marry?"

"No, I am saying that the situation has not arisen before and there may be problems."

"Such as?"

"You may be shunned socially."

I burst out laughing. It was so loud that the guard on the door poked his head in to see why, "I can see that you do not know me. My father never cared for such conventions and I am his son." Even as I said it I felt like a hypocrite. He had tried to tell me, in Normandy, that I was just trying to be socially accepted and he had been right. Now I cared not. I have changed and I just wished my father could see the change. He had always been proud of me but he had had no reason to be. Now he had and he was many leagues hence in England. "If I am forbidden to marry her then I would leave the Kingdom, lord."

"You would not be forbidden but the King could never invite you and your wife to banquets and celebrations."

"Then that is good for I would not care to be anywhere which did not accept my choice of bride."

"And England? Has that changed so much that you could take a Jewess home and be accepted?"

That thought struck me like a blow. I had not thought of it. "I confess I do not know but I will cross that bridge when I come to it. It may be a moot point for the lady has not accepted my proposal yet."

"And she is... well, let us say she was badly used by de Waller."

"And for that, he will pay."

"There is a rumour that he was seen in Tripoli. I have not had it confirmed but I thought you should know."

"I thank you. And thank you for the advice and the warning. You have given me much to think on."

As I made my way back home my head was filled with new problems. I had given no thought to either Rebekah's race or her religion. Would she be persecuted if I took her to England? As I had said to Theobald, until I had an answer from Rebekah there was no problem. However, I knew that there could be one in the future. My father had taught me to plan for all eventualities.

When I reached Aqua Bella, I saw Alice. She was collecting eggs from the chickens. "Alice, I would like something special tonight. What can you come up with at short notice?"

"Your men went hunting yesterday. They slew an oryx. I could cook a haunch of that along with the sweetbreads and offal. We have figs and peaches which will enhance the taste and I could use some of the pepper and saffron." She hesitated. "It is an expense lord."

"I will buy more and make sure you cook enough for the families of you and Absalom."

Her face lit up. "Thank you, lord and I will serve honey peaches and rice for the pudding."

"Have we any goat's cheese yet from the new goats we purchased?"

"There is some, lord, but it is light and runny. It will be better in a month or two."

"Good. The doctor recommended more milk and cheese to help me recover."

She crossed herself, "We are all grateful, lord, that you were spared. My husband said that he has never known the land to be so fertile and the estate so prosperous."

That evening I dressed in my finest robe. I had much to say to my men. We used one of the larger rooms now for there were many of us. The room was not as luxuriously appointed but we were warriors. When and if Rebekah married me, we would eat in the room the old lord and his wife had used. It was more fitting for a lady. I made sure that Francis used the older wine. It had aged in the amphorae. The cool rooms carved out of the rock were perfect for keeping it in the best of conditions.

Word must have spread amongst my men that this was an important event for all took special care with their appearance. I smiled for Garth had actually washed and combed his unruly locks and tied his hair back. He looked almost human rather than the shaggy bear he usually resembled.

Before the food was served I stood with my goblet of wine in my hand. "Warriors of Aqua Bella. This is the first feast we have all enjoyed together. The warriors who followed me from Normandy and England have now been joined by new brothers. This is a new start for all of us. First, I should say that, as you know I have asked the Lady Rebekah to marry me." Garth led the men in banging on the table. I smiled. It was a tradition which went back to the Vikings and Saxons. I saw worried looks on the faces of those servants who were from the Holy Land. "Let us raise our goblets and toast the Lady Rebekah."

"Lady Rebekah!"

"Today I spoke with Theobald. He said that there may be some who oppose the marriage of a Christian to a Jewess." Their good humour disappeared. Like me, they had not thought that there would be a problem. "Know you that I will marry the lady and I care not what anyone says!"

This time the banging of the tables was deafening.

I smiled when it subsided, "I had thought to ask for your support but I can see that I have it."

Garth growled, "Aye lord, and I will cuff any who makes a disparaging remark."

"I hope it will not come to that. And I have more news. This concerns two of you." They all looked around, wondering what it might be. I had not spoken to either Tom or Robert on the way back from Jerusalem. I had meant to but my mind was still filled with the words of Theobald. "I intend to knight Captain Robert and Thomas, my squire."

It took them all by surprise especially as I had said Thomas and not Tom.

Tom looked up at me, "But I am the son of an archer, lord!"

"And the captain of your father was an archer made a knight by my father. I have spoken with Theobald. He approves but you should both know that you can refuse."

"Why should we do that, lord?"

I turned to Robert, "Because, my old friend, with the title, come responsibilities. You owe me duty and, so long as you live in the Holy Land, also to the King of Jerusalem. There are two farms which will become your manors. Both produce the sheep and goats we eat. The families there would be yours to command and to care for." I smiled as they took that in. "So, what say you?"

They looked at each other and nodded.

"Good and, Alf, until I can find another, you will take over as my squire."

For some reason that made him as happy as Tom. "Thank you. lord! That is an honour I had not expected although I have learned much from Garth."

Garth ruffled his hair, "Aye but you will never be an archer. You started too late. You will make a swordsman and, perhaps, you can learn to ride a horse properly now!"

"And speaking of horses: Robert I give you Leonidas as your warhorse and Thomas of Aqua Bella, you can have Strong-arm, the horse I brought from Normandy."

It was a fine feast and a fine evening. We all drank more than was good for us and poor Tom had to be carried to bed by Garth but as Francis said as he escorted me to my chambers, "That was well done, lord. The farmers, John and Matthew, will enjoy having someone to watch over them and the two young masters are both kind men. My wife wept with joy when she heard the news. They are like family."

"We are all like family, Francis, and I know how lucky I am."

Chapter 17

A month before Passover we had a visitor. The Master and a company of Hospitallers stayed with us. The Master was apologetic when they arrived. "I am sorry to have landed upon you, Sir William and feel free to say that there is no room but we are travelling to Jaffa and Jerusalem could not accommodate us. We are happy to sleep in the stables and to find our own food."

I shook my head, "You will eat with us. And this is serendipitous for I have need of your counsel."

He smiled, "Then we can both benefit from this."

Alice was delighted to be cooking for the Knights of St. John and it was a harmonious arrangement. I went, with the Master, to the roof while the food was prepared and the Hospitallers prayed in my chapel. We had rigged a canvas shade and the view was spectacular. The potted lemon and orange trees gave a pleasant smell. Francis had a servant bring up some chilled wine. Our rock-hewn cellars kept the wine at a perfect temperature.

"So, Sir William, what do you wish to ask me about?"

Having broached the subject with Theobald I found it easy to speak with the Master. I told him of my dilemma; the possibility of a marriage to a Jew.

He smiled, "I do not think there is a problem. The only one that I could see is that the ceremony would have to have two priests: one a Jew and one a Christian. Personally, I think that this is a good thing. It shows that not all of us come here as conquerors. But, as you have intimated, the lady may well refuse. I have no doubt that some of her own people might disapprove."

I nodded, "What you say is right and I have as yet no priest. I have my own chapel but no priest."

He suddenly laughed, "God works in mysterious ways does he not?"

I was confused, "I suppose so, what makes you speak thus?"

"We go to Jaffa not only to bring back new volunteers but also to take those brothers who return to England. The Empress Matilda gave us a priory there. It is small. Some of those who can no longer be warriors are going there. We suffered grievous losses in the Damascus debacle. One of them wishes to stay but we could find no purpose for him." He sipped his wine. "This is good wine. There is a connection to you for he is the sergeant you saved. Brother Peter lost the use of his left arm and he does not wish to leave this land yet. He has, like you, unfinished business. He could be your priest."

"Would that suit him? I would be happy but I would not like to force a man to stay here."

"We will ask him but I already know the answer for he wished to thank you in some way for saving his life. I will go and fetch him."

As he descended I went to look out over the valley. I had said I would go back to England to be with my father and yet this land suddenly looked more appealing. Here, I was rich and had a good life. I had people around me whom I could trust and, most importantly, Rebekah would probably not wish to leave her own family. If I solved one problem then I would create another.

"Lord."

Turning I saw the Master with Brother Peter. I had only seen him briefly and then in the heat of battle. He was a big man. With a mop of red hair and a red beard, he would stand out on a battlefield. He had a sword still but his left arm hung uselessly from his side. When he spoke, I knew him to be from the north of my country. There were many redheads there. They had come over with the Vikings and the Irish. "Sir William, the Master says you have need of a priest." I nodded. "If you would have me then I would serve under you. I do not wish to leave the Holy Land for I do not think my work here is done. I know I cannot serve the Knights of St. John but I can still fight and still be a priest."

"Then you are welcome, Brother Peter. By your voice you are English and from the north of my country. Whereabouts do you hail from?"

"I come from Cumberland. My father was a farmer at Coningestun by the Water in that shire. My family were slaughtered in a raid by the Scots. I was away serving with the Lord of Craven fighting Stephen the Usurper. I left England for it held nothing for me and joined the Knights of St. John."

I nodded, "My father has some of the men from Craven who serve him."

"I know, lord and that makes this seem right somehow."

"Welcome, Peter. I will show you the chapel."

He smiled, "Lord I found it already and I prayed there. My prayer has already been answered."

The meal was a lively affair. Our guests and my men had much in common. We had all emerged from the fiasco at Damascus with honour and shared experiences. When I told the Master that I was to knight

Robert and Thomas he was pleased. "They both fought well. We need honourable knights."

That led us, quite naturally, to speak of dishonourable knights. "Have you heard anything of the Count of Provence or de Waller?"

He nodded, "They both went to Tripoli. The Count of Provence and his men left for home but de Waller disappeared. When I was in Jerusalem we heard of rogue knights who were terrorising the land north of Galilee. From their activities both Theobald and I think it is de Waller. The knights from Nablus and Belvoir are now riding patrols in the area but it is believed that they are hiding in the land of the Assassins."

"But that is Seljuq land! Is it not dangerous for him?"

"He has the protection of the Old Man of the Mountains. However, one of his men was captured. He was tortured and, before he died, although he refused to give up the whereabouts of his former master, he did say that his master had sworn vengeance on you and… the family of Ben Samuel."

Although it was warm, I felt a cold chill flood over my body. "I must warn them!"

"They have been warned. The King sent a messenger two days since. I was asked to convey the news to you although neither the King nor Theobald feel you have anything to fear."

"Why not?"

He smiled, "For you are a better knight and the superior leader leading worthier men. And this might just be a house but it is stronger than many castles. David Ben Samuel might fear de Waller but not you."

They left the next day. I had slept little after hearing his news and so, after they had gone, I took half of my men on patrol. Sir Robert and Sir Thomas went into Jerusalem. They took with them John of Chester, for he had proved the best judge of men. I would have sent Henry son of Will but I knew he might get into trouble in the city. He had before. My two knights needed the best of men. They needed their own men at arms and squires and they needed to be reliable. In battle, it was their men who would watch their backs. As I had discovered that could be the difference between life and death. Their demesnes meant they could afford to have warriors of their own. It suited me for it increased the number of men I could call upon. I took my new helmet. It fitted well. Balion had had a leather, cushioned inner cap made. With holes for my ears, it would not impair my ability to hear and yet it protected my skull. I was still wary of damaging it further.

When we reached Ben Samuel's home, I saw that he and his sons were busy preparing their animals. They would have an impending caravan.

They stopped and walked over, "We did not expect you yet lord. It is still two weeks until Passover."

"I did not come here to speak with Rebekah. The spectre of her possible refusal still haunts me. I came because I heard of the threat from de Waller."

He nodded, "We were told but the land of the assassins lies far from here. However, I have taken precautions. Just Saul and David will go with this caravan. They only travel to Jaffa. I will be around with most of my men and we will keep a good watch. I have Masood watching for the trails of strangers. If we hear anything then I will send to you."

"Good. I am relieved. I will see you in fourteen nights."

He came closer to me, "I am sure, my lord, that the answer will be yes."

"And you are happy for her to marry a Christian?"

He shrugged, "Lord, if she does not marry you then she will marry no one. I wish to have more grandchildren. I am content!"

The road home joined the Jerusalem road and as we headed south I saw a rider hurtling towards us. It was John of Chester. He reined in. I could see that he was out of breath. "What is amiss, John?"

"Lord, we hired men and we were at the stables buying horses when I spied one of de Waller's men. He was there when I was whipped. I recognized him and he ran. By the time we had our horses, he had fled. He headed out of the north gate. Sir Robert and Sir Thomas are following him. I was sent to fetch you."

I whipped Remus' head around and led my column north to Jerusalem. I prayed that my two new knights would not be foolish. De Waller was a snake. He would ambush. They were both good men but they were not me. Instead of trying to negotiate the busy and crowded streets of the city we skirted and headed around the north side. As John told us that the man had fled through the north gate, we stood a good chance of meeting up with my men. Although I was anxious to catch the sergeant, I did not want to kill our horses in the process. We rode at a steady pace.

The road to the north led to rough ground. I wondered if the sergeant would turn to head either for Jericho to the northeast or the Dead Sea to the east. I dismissed both even as they came into my head. It would be too hard to remain hidden there. As we passed the last of the farms which lay close to the city a warrior awaited us. I did not recognize him and my hand went to my sword.

John of Chester shouted, "Hold, lord. It is one of the new men. I forget his name."

I reined in, "What did Sir Robert say?"

"He said the sergeant has left the road, lord, and he was heading east. I can show you the trail."

"Thank you. And what is your name?"

"Wilfred son of Tom."

"Then lead on, Wilfred son of Tom."

We left the road and took a cart trail. Up ahead I saw another figure. Wilfred, son of Tom, said, "That is Stephen of Tyre. He is one of our men."

When we reached him, he pointed to a huddle of rocks. "Lord, he disappeared into those rocks. My lord and the others are waiting at the base."

We went slowly for the ground was uneven and treacherous. We descended. This was an animal trail. The ibex and onyx used this but precious few men. I began to suspect that we were close to the hideout of de Waller. I wondered if we had enough men with us. I had left guards on my walls. Would I rue that decision?

Sir Robert had dismounted the men. He strode towards me, "We lost sight of him but I cannot see how a horse could get over those rocks."

"You have done well. He must be hiding here somewhere. Sir Robert take four men and head around the rocks over there." I pointed to the left. "Tom, take Garth and the new men and head around the rocks there. The rest of you spread out in a line. I want this man alive. He is no use to us dead."

I had my sword drawn. We had not taken our shields with us for it had been a social visit. I hoped that I would not regret that although we were just seeking one man. The secret of hunting a man who is hiding is not to look for the man, look for movement. He had to have a horse. He would be holding its nose and stroking it. I saw a sudden flurry of flies as they took to the air. That was a horse's tail. I waved to the right and John of Chester raised his hand. I liked John of Chester for he was a thoughtful warrior. Henry son of Will would run in and kill all who lay within the sweep of his sword. I saw John crouch. He had seen something. I rushed to his side and I saw a tail flick into the air. I held up my hand. This was my call. I counted to three and then leapt over the rock which hid the horse.

I found myself in the midst of three sergeants and their horses. I had caught them by surprise but I was outnumbered. I wanted them alive but I wished to live. I blocked the sword which came at my head and I dragged my dagger from my waist. As the second blow came in, I flicked it aside but there was no way I could avoid the sword which came towards my head. Even my new helmet could not save me. John of Chester swung his sword and the man's head flew from his body. The sergeant we had followed hacked at my neck. Instinct took over. I blocked it with my sword and my dagger plunged into his chest. I did not want him dead but I had given him a mortal wound. There was one left alive and I needed him to stay that way. I launched myself at him and I spread my arms to pinion him. As his head was pushed back it cracked against a rock and I saw the life leave his eyes.

"Nooooo!"

I turned to the man I had fatally wounded. I held his chin in my hands. "Where is your master?"

He grinned and a tendril of blood dripped from his mouth. "He is coming for you. Watch for the Jewess bitch! She pleased my lord. He would have her again! He is com…" His eyes glazed over and he was dead.

We had failed and it was my fault. My killer instincts had condemned my Rebekah. John of Chester put his hand on my shoulder, "Lord he is lying. These were scouts. The Lord of Ramelah has no intelligence. When these men fail to report, he will have to send more men. You have bought time!"

I nodded, "You are right, John of Chester, I thank you for my life. I was dead but for you."

He nodded, "You lord, have given more men life than I can count. We are not close to even."

We took the bodies and their horses with us when we left. There might be some clue on their person as to where de Waller was taking refuge. We were many miles from the land of the assassins. Was he closer now? We were being hunted and I did not like the feeling. None bothered me as we made our way home through the darkening gloom. They knew my mood. John was correct. De Waller was still in the dark and he was losing his men rapidly. How many more could he have at his disposal?

I waved Sir Robert forward. "As from tomorrow, I want three of our men to ride here and search for tracks. There is little point in hunting for them but I need to know when his men are close. Want another four men to patrol north of David Ben Samuel's home. De Waller will go there first. Aqua Bella is too big a nut for him to crack in one bite. He will try to draw us to Rebekah."

When we reached home, I was weary. Despite the training, I had endured this was the furthest I had ridden in a long time. I summoned Tom and Robert. "We need to keep a closer watch on our walls. Our enemy is close."

"We will watch lord. We were close today."

"Aye Robert but not close enough."

For the next few days, we were all on edge. Our patrols around Ben Samuel's home reported no enemies. The road patrol had no encounters with enemies and all seemed well. Yet I could not shake this fear which lay over me like a cloud. By the time it was the Passover, I was almost beside myself. I took all of my men when I went to David Ben Samuel's home. For the two days before the fateful day, I had had my men search the roads, trails and paths north of Ben Samuel's home. There was no sign of shod hooves and mailed warriors. I was still apprehensive as we headed towards Rebekah. My life lay in her hands.

The Passover was an important festival for the Jews. It compared with our Easter. Brother Peter rode with us and I could not help but smile when I saw him. He was the very antithesis of every priest I had known. He rode with a sword at his waist and a mace on his cantle. He was a warrior in a brown habit. I had made Alf train with him and my new squire had returned to me black and blue. This was a priest unlike any other. Each step closer to the merchant's estate made me more fearful. I had no idea what she would say to my offer. I had kept away from her and none had sent me word. Was that good or was that ill?

The house and the estate had been decked out for celebrations. I did not read anything into that. The Passover was an important festival for the Jews. It was a reminder of when they had escaped the oppression of the Pharaohs. I could not help but slow Alciades down as we walked through the gates. I knew that this could be the end of my hopes and dreams.

David Ben Samuel and his sons were waiting to greet us. He grasped my arm, "Lord we are honoured. This night we will feast." He leaned in to speak with me. "No matter what my daughter says this will not change us, lord. We are friends and we owe each other much."

I nodded, barely able to speak, "That may be so, David, but I fear my world will end if the answer is nay."

My voice pleaded but he shook his head, "She has kept apart from us this last four months. I know not what she will decide. I would that I did."

Our horses were taken to the stable. We left our cloaks with them and, after shaking off the dust entered the hall. The men of the family were there to greet us. I had impressed upon my men the need to make a good impression and none of them let me down. Sir Robert and Sir Thomas had left their new men on watch for they did not know the Ben Samuel family.

"We will gather in my lemon and olive grove. My sons have rigged shade. The air is from the west and it is cooling."

I greeted Ruth and Mary. Both grasped my hands firmly. Ruth said, "We have observed all the rituals before you came. Now is the time for celebration. My daughter awaits you by the fig tree. May God walk with you." As I left I saw her aunt from Caesarea and her daughters. She smiled at me too.

"Thank you. I will face my fate like a man." I strode towards the distant figure. I could see that her head was covered with a blue headdress which matched her dress. I felt like a man walking towards his execution as I moved closer to her. As I neared her she looked up and all I saw were her olive-shaped brown eyes. It was as I had first glimpsed her on the road from Caesarea. I could not tell if she was smiling or not. I stared at her eyes and I seemed to be drawn into them. I sat next to her not knowing what to do. She took the headdress from around her face and her headdress fell from her head. Around her hair, she wore a band of gold coins. She absentmindedly smoothed her hair.

"My mother wore this headdress when she married. It is said that every woman has worn this since the time of King David and each generation has added a coin. I know not if it is true but here," she held open her palm, "I have a coin to continue the tradition."

I stared at her, "You mean…?"

"My lord, outside of my father, you are the cleverest man I know. Surely you do not need this explaining to you."

I took her in my arms and squeezed her so hard that I thought I might break her. From the house, I heard a cheer which was like the one in Aqua Bella when I had announced that my men were to be knighted. The world was at peace and I was happy.

She looked up at me. "You are sure about this lord? I have told you all. I fear I can never be the wife you wish but …"

I put my finger on her lips. "I am content. Let us just see what each day brings. You will be my bride. You will come to live with me at Aqua Bella. For the present that is sufficient."

She smiled, "And who knows I may even get a bed this time? Although I can always use the chair again."

We walked back arm in arm. Ruth took my face in hers, leaned up to me and kissed me. David grasped my arm, "And now I have another son!"

Everyone seemed genuinely pleased and both Rebekah and I were touched. David took me to one side. "Can I make a request, lord?"

"Of course."

"Could my daughter be wed here?"

I nodded. "And I have a request to make too. I now have a priest. I know your rabbi will marry us but I would like her married before a priest." I shook my head, "It is not for me but for Rebekah. This way she will have rights. I am sorry."

"No, my son, it shows you are being a caring husband. It makes me even more joyous. When shall the day be?"

"As soon as it can be arranged."

"We will make it a small affair. All the family we need are here now. You are right, there are those who would try to stop this. I think it is good but there are others of my faith, and I have no doubt, yours, who will frown on such a union. The day after tomorrow?"

"That is perfect. Thank you, once again."

It was late when we left. I had not drunk at all but some of my men, Henry son of Will, in particular, had. We were noisy as we headed home. Had there been an ambush then we could have done little about it but God must have smiled on the union for we reached Aqua Bella safely. Brother Peter spoke to me on the way home. He was pleased that I had made the choices I had. He was a reluctant priest. He was a warrior first. When I had spoken to him he told me of his family and how they had all been warriors. They had driven the Saxons from their lands and defended it from all who would have taken it. He was proud of his Viking heritage. As he had told me, "Lord, a warrior's blood courses through my veins but I would be a priest also."

He had been delighted with the news. "It is good that you are to be wed again. A man should have sons."

When we were alone and I could speak in confidence I told him the secret I bore. He was my personal priest now. Whatever I said to him would have the protection of the confessional. "I fear that may not be possible for many reasons. My wife was taken, when a young girl, by de Waller. She had a child who died. There may be no children."

He was not surprised by my words and I wondered how much the Master had told him for the Master knew the story, "We cannot know what God intends. There was a brother who woke up one day and had no voice. He simply could not speak. The physicians in the order tried to find a cure but they could not. It was written off as an act of God but Brother James never gave up. He prayed each day for his voice to be returned to him. Then one day a stray dog came to our castle. It had a damaged leg and many wished to put the dog out of its misery but Brother James would not allow it. Over the next months, he brought the dog back to health. It walked again. It was never a good walker but it lived and then, one morning, Brother James regained his voice. None knows why or how. The first words he said were, *'Come, boy'*. He and the dog live yet and he has not lost his voice since."

"I am not certain what you mean by the telling of this tale."

"What I mean, lord, is that you should never say never. Brother James never gave up even when others did. Perhaps the dog was sent by God to save Brother James. It may be that God has sent you into Rebekah's life so that you may save her. You have a good heart and that means more than any hurt that Rebekah may have suffered. De Waller is evil but I cannot think that God would allow a young girl's life to be ruined by one such as he. Good will defeat evil in the end. The day that ceases to be true is the day this world ends."

The wedding was a joyous affair and all of my men, Francis and Absalom and their families attended. The day began early for we wished to travel back before it was dark. Saul and his brothers had all of Rebekah's belongings to bring. David tried to give me a chest of gold as a dowry. I refused. "I am taking that which is most precious. Gold and silver cannot compare with what you are giving me. You have given me enough."

This time when we returned home there were no high spirits. My men were escorting their new lady of the manor and they took that job very seriously. We rode with scouts out and my men around Rebekah and her servants. The three girls who came with her would augment my own servants. My household was growing. We made it back without incident and Rebekah's goods and chattels were stored in our room.

The carpenter on the estate had made a new bed for Rebekah. My quarters were large enough to accommodate both beds. I did not want to frighten my new wife. I hoped that one day, she would allow me to take her as my wife but I accepted that might not happen for some time.

Chapter 18

Before we could even get into a routine I was summoned, along with my two knights, to attend the King of Jerusalem. Neither of my knights had a squire, yet. They were unconcerned with the lack of, what amounted to a servant. Henri led the road patrol and I took just Garth and John of Chester as escorts. The rest were left for my new wife to command as she saw fit.

As we rode into Jerusalem my mind was preoccupied. I was thinking about my first nights with Rebekah. She had been more than shy of me. She had made me wait outside while she undressed. When I entered, she was beneath her sheets and our kiss had been as chaste as one might give a nun. However, we spoke long into the night and I was satisfied. We found out about each other. I discovered that her grandfather, Samuel, had been important in her life. He had been so affected by the attack of de Waller that he had died of shock. It was another reason why Rebekah felt the way she did about the Frank. She blamed herself for his death. I told her of my wife and my daughter. I told her why I needed to do penance. I thought it might have been a bar to us but she understood. Leaving her, even for a few hours, tore me apart and yet I knew that I would have to do so.

I left Garth, Alf and John with the horses and we entered the palace. The King was in his court along with Theobald. Other knights were there. I recognized some from the retreat from Damascus. I was now known also and greeted. With de Waller discredited and gone I was afforded smiles instead of scowls.

We chatted with some of the knights as more lords arrived. Then Paul, the steward, banged his staff, "Pray silence for King Baldwin of Jerusalem."

I looked around and saw that there were less than fifty knights now. De Waller's defection and Damascus had thinned our ranks.

The King began, "Welcome. It has been some time since we were gathered together. The treachery of some of our number has hurt us most grievously." He gestured to Paul who nodded to two servants. They brought out a piece of calfskin and on it was painted a map of the Holy Land. When he spoke, Paul pointed with a dagger at the salient points.

"Nablus and Belvoir are not represented here today. That is because they are improving their defences and patrolling the border. The Turkish warriors are growing bold. Last year I asked the Templars to see if they could take Ascalon. The Fatimids of Egypt repulsed them with great losses. That port remains a thorn in our side. My father built castles to contain the threat." The king pointed to a handful of knights who stood closest to the dais. "These warriors are the buffer against the attacks. They bring grave news. Work has begun on over fifty towers which are being built around the walls of Ascalon. Even worse they have become bold since the defeat of the Templars and they raid the lands to the north and the east."

One of the knights to whom he had referred, Geoffrey of Azdud, said somewhat plaintively, "Lord we can do naught with the knights we have here. It would be like trying to plug a breach in a dam with a finger. This needs hundreds of knights, not a handful."

"You are not gathered here so that we can begin to retake Ascalon. That day is some time off. The Master of the Templars is building up his army as is the Master of the Hospitallers. He and his men are rebuilding the castle at Gaza. William of Aqua Bella now has two more knights and I hope that, in a year or two, our numbers will have increased sufficiently for us to take Ascalon. Thanks to some of the knights in this chamber we now have an ally in the Emperor. He has promised men but not yet."

"Then why are we here, your Majesty?"

"That is simple Ralph of Gat, I wish you to contain the Egyptians. I wish you to harass their building work. In short, I want us to do to them what they do to us."

"And will the time we give to you come from our feudal duties or is this in addition?"

Geoffrey of Azdud shook his head, "Who can talk of days owed, Raymond of Acre? The Egyptians are even worse than the Turks. Many of our people have been taken as slaves. We came to this land to make it God's land once more. Our duty is to God and this land."

King Baldwin raised his hand for silence as the room buzzed with arguments, "I understand Raymond of Acre's words. Since the road is safer the bazaar in Jerusalem is more profitable. The merchants have agreed that they will contribute a tithe of the profits to support an army in the field."

I saw nods from some of the greedier knights.

Geoffrey of Azdud asked, "And who will command?"

"Theobald of Rheims will command. Does anyone object to my choice of commander or do you wish a council again!" I smiled. The King had learned and was more authoritative these days. It helped that he did not have Guillaume de Waller making waves. "Good. Then Theobald will speak with you all individually and give you his orders. Your tithe will come each quarter." He smiled, "When my general assures me that all is as it should be."

Others hurried to speak with Theobald. We waited. The King came over to speak with me, "I am pleased to see that you have knighted these two. They impressed me at Damascus. I appreciate that you asked permission first." He lowered his voice, "I would that you had asked our permission before marrying the daughter of Ben Samuel."

"Why your majesty? I thought a man's choice of wife was his own decision."

"It is but you have put me in a difficult position. There are many who will not accept such a marriage."

"Then that is their problem and not mine."

"You misunderstand me. I approve. She is a beautiful young woman and was treated monstrously but I cannot invite you and your lady to functions here at the palace. I would offend both Jew and Christian."

I nodded and smiled, "Oh I see then I have a simple solution, your majesty."

He brightened, "You do?"

"Of course. Do not invite us. We will not be offended."

"But…"

His mother had appeared from nowhere and she smiled as she put her hand on her son's shoulder. "Do not worry about the Lord of Aqua Bella, my son. He does not need to be feted and feasted to keep his loyalty. I have learned that our young Englishman is a man of his word. He needs no coin to do as you ask. He made a promise and he will keep it." She waved her hand and a servant appeared with a leather pouch. She opened it and took out a large ruby on a golden chain. "Here is a wedding present for your bride. My father gave it to me but I have no daughter. I would like your wife to have it."

"It is beautiful and will look even better around my wife's neck."

Queen Melisende laughed, "There is the difference Baldwin. Other knights would have said that it was worth a small fortune but William here sees it for its beauty only. You could learn much from him."

The two left us and I secured the present in my own purse. Most of the knights had already left and I was anxious to get home. Theobald said, "Sir William if the three of you would wait in my chambers. I can speak to you there."

As we went along the corridor to his chamber Robert said, "This sounds intriguing, lord. Why could we not be told when the others were here?"

"Firstly, we are more than forty miles from Ascalon. The other lords may be closer. Secondly, it might be that we are not to be used like the others are. We have archers and most of the other knights do not."

We had noticed since we had been in the Holy Land that the archers who were used were the peasant levy. Most just used a hunting bow. The Turkish archers could outrange them and the arrows they used did not penetrate mail as ours did. If we had Dick and Sir Phillip of Piercebridge with us then we could make the Turks fear us more than they did. Their archers could outrun our heavy horses. It was a dilemma.

We were admitted to Theobald's quarters by his servant. He poured us wine and then waited. I guessed he wanted to make sure that we were not too inquisitive. Theobald was not too long but he did look weary when he entered the chamber. He shook his head, "Some of those lords are little better than mercenaries. They want to be assured that losses in the campaign will be made good by the king."

"Campaign?"

"The other lords have castles which lie closer to the port. They are going to aggressively raid. We believe that if we can stop their local farms producing goods then they will have to bring more in by sea. The King has given Gaza City to the Templars and they are building a castle there. If we can take Ascalon then we can begin to take more of Egypt. The Emperor is sending some of his fleet to harry the Egyptian convoys. We wish to make this a war of attrition while we build up our forces."

I smiled to myself. This had Theobald's hand all over it. He had consulted the king but no more. "And us?"

"Ah, you and your men have some unique attributes. You showed that on the retreat and when we attacked. You suffered fewer losses than any other conroi. Quite remarkable. Even Raymond de Puy Provence remarked upon it. You are also the nearest that we have to assassins."

"Assassins?"

"You slew two and suffered no losses. You managed to spot and stop them. Do not be overly modest, William. You attacked and destroyed a bandit camp. No other knight has ever taken the war to the enemy quite so vigorously. We would have you do the same at the port. We want you to slow down the building of the towers. You cannot stop them but you could cause damage. If you could make them divert men to watch the walls at night then that would weaken them."

"I have just married, lord. I cannot leave my wife for months at a time."

"You misunderstand. That would be pointless. You would all be caught. We want you to do one raid and then return to Aqua Bella.

Return days later at a different place. We want you to vary the times, places and methods of attack."

"And what of the caravan patrols?"

"The Templars have promised that they will take on that role."

"Like de Waller!"

"No, lord. The Templars can be annoying at times but they keep their word. They have promised to protect all caravans: Christian and Jewish."

"I suppose we have no choice."

"Of course, you do. You can refuse. The King and the Queen both hold you in high regard. They would be disappointed but they would not force you to do anything you were not happy about."

"And you know that I will do as you bid."

He smiled, "Yes." He turned to Robert and Tom. "I believe that you two do not have squires."

"No, lord."

"We cannot have a knight without a squire. In the city here, we have eight orphans. They are the sons of knights who died in the battle for Edessa and were left without any to care for them. Two are English. They are both ten years old and the castellan has been training them in sword and horse. I believe they would serve you well."

Robert nodded, "That is kind lord but before we agree to take them on then we should meet with them and decide if they suit us. After all, they will be an expense. They will need mail and horses."

"Oh no, they won't, Sir Robert. They have them. Their fathers may have died in battle and they might have lost their land but that does not mean that they are penniless. The King paid for the clothes, mail, weapons and horses."

"That may be but we will still see them first."

In the end, both of my knights were more than happy with the two boys. Edward was the taller and he was keen to please. The other, Stephen, was shorter and stouter. I could see him becoming as broad as Garth when he became fully grown. He was affable and confident. My knights took them on and we headed back to Aqua Bella.

"Are you pleased or disappointed to be away from the palace, Stephen?"

"Oh, we are both happy, lord. We both wish to be like our fathers."

Edward nodded, "They fell together at Edessa. Another year and we would have been with them for we were due to be squires. My elder brother died with my father."

"And your mother?"

He looked down at his horse's mane. "The priest said we were never to talk of it."

Tom said, "Edward, there can be no secrets between a squire and his lord. Whatever you tell us will neither shock us nor make us think the less of you."

"It is nothing to do with me, lord."

He looked distressed. Stephen reached over and put his hand on his friend's arm. He said, quietly, "She threw herself from the top of Jerusalem's walls, lord."

Edward looked up with an anguished look on his face, "She will not be in heaven, lord! I will not see her again."

This was beyond me. "Edward, we have a warrior priest, Brother Peter. When we get to our home, I would like you to speak with him. I am a simple warrior and I do not understand such matters but I am certain Brother Peter can answer any questions you have, better than I."

"Thank you, lord."

I nodded to Alf, "Or speak to my squire. He lost his mother too."

Alf put his arm around Edward's shoulder. "Whenever you are ready Edward I can listen. I may not have answers but I have learned since I began to serve our lord that often, seeking answers is an answer in itself."

Garth laughed, "I can see my wisdom has rubbed off on you, young Alf!"

"Well something rubbed off, that is for certain!"

"You were less cheeky when you held my horse!"

"Then perhaps I got the sense from your horse, Garth the archer!"

We rode in silence for a while until Stephen could contain himself no longer. "Do we ride to war, lord? The other squires said that the King has ordered his knights to attack the Egyptians!"

So much for secrecy! "We have a task to perform but I fear Sir Robert will have his work cut out keeping his young squire silent while we carry it out!"

"Oh, I can be quiet, lord. Honestly!"

Sir Robert shook his head, "And if you are not then I shall cuff you about the head."

He nodded cheerfully, "That is what the castellan did!"

Both boys were impressed by my new home. They shared a chamber with Alf and that was more room than they had had in the palace where chambers were at a premium. I let Robert and Tom explain our task to our men. I went to speak to Rebekah. I was not certain how she would view my absence. We went to the roof. We both liked it there. The potted lemon trees and rosemary bushes provided both shade and a pleasant aroma.

After I had told her she nodded, "I expected nothing less but you should know that I will be here waiting for your return. I shall endeavour to make myself the lady of this manor. You have good people here. I feared they would look down upon me because I was a Jewess but they do not. And Brother Peter is the first priest I have seen who did not look as though he wished to spit on me."

"The Queen spoke of you."

"Queen Melisende?"

I nodded, "And she sent this as a wedding present for you." I took out the ruby. It looked even more beautiful in the dappled light beneath the lemon tree.

"It is a gift worthy of a queen." She held it for me. "Please, lord, put it on for me."

I went around her back and placed the ruby over her head. I had to lean to fasten it and I became heady with the smell of her oiled and perfumed skin. "I have told you, it is William or Will but you do not call me lord."

"I will try, Will." She giggled at her own words and whipped her head around. "It is beautiful!"

I put my hands on her waist, "As are you!"

She reached behind my neck and pulled my head down to kiss her. This was not the chaste kiss of our night times. It was the passionate kiss I had been desperate to give her.

"And I will try, Will, I promise I will try but I need time."

"Take all the time you like. I am content just to hold you in my arms"

Chapter 19

We took spare horses with us and as many arrows as we could carry. It would take the morning and some of the afternoon to be close to Ascalon. My aim was to spend one night scouting out the walls and then the second night attempt some sabotage. We would then return home. I had not brought all of my men. I brought Sir Robert, Henri, Garth of Sheffield, Walter of Derby, William of Lincoln, Ralph of Ely, Sir Thomas, Alf son of Morgan, John of Chester, Henry son of Will, Harold Longsword, Robin Hawkeye, Thomas, Jack, Stephen and Edward. It was mainly archers and those of my men who were good with knives. I also had a plan. I had brought with me the three assassin blades we had captured. I intended to have them worried that the assassins were their enemies.

We went to the castle of Azdud. It was a hilltop fort overlooking the port. It looked to have been built by the Muslims. Geoffrey of Azdud was more like me than many of the other knights. He was also devout. He was surprised to see me. “I wondered if you had refused to fight for the king.”

“No, Sir Geoffrey, I was given a different task. I will tell you but it is a secret and when I explain what it is then you will understand why.”

Afterwards, he said, “I am honoured by the confidence. What do you need from me?”

“We would leave our spare horses and supplies here. You are close enough for us to reach here should things go awry. Tonight, I go with two men to scout out the walls and then tomorrow we will see what mischief we can cause.”

“The towers are coming on, Sir William. Three are already built. From the foundations they are digging there will be fifty of them. I do not relish the thought of attacking them when the time comes.”

“And your work, how goes that?”

We made one joint raid yesterday. We caught them napping. We captured some animals and killed thirty or forty of their warriors. I do not think it will be as easy the next time we ride.”

“Then you will have to use a different approach. Can you see the walls from your castle?”

He nodded, "On a clear day you can. It is nine miles away but as it is along the coast there is naught to obstruct the view."

It was now summer and the land had a permanent heat haze but the cooler sea sometimes permitted a better view. It was strange to be inside a Muslim built castle. It was more of a fort than a castle. Stone had been faced with mud and the towers were not as high as a castle but, when we ascended the southwest tower I could see the walls of Ascalon. This did have towers already. They were not circular but looked, from a distance, to be almost half towers as though someone had cut a round one in two. I might not have been able to see it clearly but Geoffrey knew the castle and was able to direct my gaze.

"See, lord, there is scaffolding where they are working on the towers. My scouts report that they have dug foundations for all of them but they are working on the five which are on this side." He shook his head, "They are using Christians they captured. They work them to death and then throw their bodies in the sea. We have seen the sharks feasting. Someone told us that the ruler of the port has his men catch the sharks which he then has cooked."

"Barbaric."

"They are a barbaric people and they are fanatical. I do not envy you your task."

"We do not choose our tasks, lord. We will make the best of it."

I left most of my men at the fort and went, after dark, with Robert, Garth and John of Chester. We rode east first and then headed west. When we were half a mile from the fires of the men building the towers, we dismounted and we handed our horses to John. We wore no helmets and we carried no shields. We were not here to fight. We were here to see how to hurt them. Our dark cloaks hid us and we moved confidently through the huts and wrecked farms. Geoffrey of Azdud had told me that they had burned many farms. They would rebuild but so far, they had not. The burned-out buildings allowed us to get within three hundred paces of the walls. They had braziers for the days might be hot but the nights were cold. The wood smoke blew towards us. That was good for it meant our smell would not reach them. I saw that they had no sentries out. They were not expecting an attack. The builders were sat around fires cooking fish which I assumed they had caught. There was a great deal of noise from the camp. They were gambling and they were drinking. Both of those activities would cover our approach. The slaves who were Christian and laboured during the day would be inside Ascalon's walls. Any who were outside were Egyptian.

Having established that there were no guards we could look at their work and how we could disrupt it. The scaffolding was an obvious target.

It took time to build but we needed to damage the work on the towers too. I saw that they had more timber to build more scaffolding. We would use that. As much as I hated to do it I knew that by killing the builders we would slow down the work. We had two tasks we could complete. I looked around us and saw that the half-burned huts would make good cover for our horses. We could cover five hundred paces quickly especially if we were unencumbered by mail. My plan was almost complete. Then I saw the quick lime pit. I could feel the heat from it. They needed that for the mortar. If the aim of the raid was to slow down the building then we needed to sabotage the quicklime. I saw the answer by the side of the fire. Wine!

I tapped my companions on the shoulders and we headed back to the horses. We had done this before and none of us spoke until we saw Azdud looming up. Garth said, “We could eliminate the sentries lord.”

“We might do that another time. Let us keep it a secret that we have such fine archers. This is my plan. If you think of a way to improve it then tell me.”

“Aye, lord.”

“I want one group to slay the Egyptian workers. While they do so a second group pulls down the scaffolding and using the coals from their braziers they set fire to it. We throw their wine in the lime pits. It will render the quick lime ineffective. Then we flee.”

“That sounds remarkably simple, Sir William.”

“It is Robert but the purpose is to slow down the work. When next we come, we will have to be more imaginative. They will put guards and ditches around the work as a result of our attack. The King wants us to sap their will to fight. We may not attack for a year, perhaps even two. We cannot allow them to build fifty towers!”

Geoffrey of Azdud had told his sentries to watch for us and were admitted through the main gate. Everyone was in bed save for the sentries. Robert and Garth retired but I went to the tower to look at the port we were to attack. My mind was active and I suddenly realised that we could use the sea to attack them. What I needed was a small ship. If we made it a fireship and we managed to sail it close to the walls then the fire would weaken the walls. The problem would be escaping. With the idea in my head, I went to bed.

The next day the three of us told our men what we would need. “We do not need our bows, lord?”

“No William. We save that surprise for the next time. What we do need to do is to drive the workers inside the castle. I want them to think it is a major attack. That way they will look to their defences and not consider sallying. We need to light three fires in three towers. Once the towers are completed and the mortar and stones are set they will be impossible to destroy without great loss of life. I want us to weaken them so that they have to rebuild."

My men were all clever and they quickly sorted themselves into the teams we needed. All of us would attack the workers. That way they would think it was a major attack. Then we would work quickly. We made sure that we had all that we needed. My archers felt almost naked leaving without bows and without arrows but they had no need of them. This would be sword work.

We left at the same time and this time we walked our horses for the last two hundred paces. All of our mounts had been trained not to make unnecessary noise and that enabled us to reach the deserted huts without being seen. Stephen and Edward were charged with watching the horses. The rest of us drew our swords and daggers and headed towards the camps. We were in three groups. A knight led each one. The idea was to get as close as we could. When we were seen, we would charge but do so silently. That was always more terrifying. I wanted them to be afraid and exaggerate our numbers.

I had Harold Longsword, Alf and John of Chester with me. The workers were busy with what looked like a woman. The screams were loud and high pitched but that did not mean a woman. The noise distracted them and also meant that no one nearby was taking any notice of this camp. There were thirty men. If they stopped to count us they would realise we were outnumbered. I waved the other three to the sides so that we approached over a thirty-pace front. Garth nodded. He knew what he had to do.

The first Egyptian died silently without realising what was happening. Holding his head with my right hand I drew the dagger across his throat and then lowered his body to the ground. The next men were crowded around, waiting to take their turn with their victim. I slid my sword through the back of one man as I stabbed his neighbour with my dagger. John of Chester and Harold Longsword killed their men without pause but I saw Alf hesitate. Luckily for him, his target turned forcing Alf to slash him across the neck with his sword. He had made his first kill. That is always the hardest. As the Egyptians turned Alf had to slash and strike to move them back. It worked and with twelve of their number dead, they fled.

I saw that the victim was a white girl. She was a Christian. I had to change my plans. "Alf, take the girl back to the horses. Care for her.

"Aye Sir William!"

"John of Chester, coals."

He took the pot the men had been using for cooking and he poured the liquid into the quick lime. He tore the headdress from a dead worker and lined the bottom with it. I took the shovel the men had used and dug a spade full of glowing coals to drop them into the pot. John tied a piece of rope around the neck and picked it up.

I led the other two men to race towards the scaffolding. Harold Longsword had his axe. I glanced to my left and right. Robert and Tom had done as we had but now the Egyptians knew that there was trouble. I saw the survivors of our attack banging on the gate to demand entry. While Harold hacked at one side of the scaffolding John and I tied a piece of rope to the other. Together we pulled and heaved. Men on the walls pointed to us and threw things in the dark. We were shadows and the missiles missed but they only had to be lucky once. There was a crack and then a creak as Harold hacked through one of the supports. Suddenly the whole scaffolding gave way. We had to move quickly. The three of us picked up the biggest timbers and placed them at the base of the newly built tower. Harold and I put a couple more there as John emptied the coals on to the wood. It was dry wood. The summer heat had made it so. Flames flared up.

"Right, back to the horses."

As we ran I saw that the gates had been opened but the press of workers trying to get in impeded the warriors trying to get out. Garth was already back with the horses. "I poured the wine into the lime, lord. It was piss poor wine!" He chuckled. "Best use for it was to spoil the quick lime if you ask me."

I saw that Alf had the sobbing girl seated behind him. Her hands gripped my squire's waist. Robert and Tom led their men towards us. I saw that Henri was being supported by William and Ralph. Robert said, "A piece of scaffolding struck him. It is nothing." He looked at the girl behind Alf but refrained from speaking.

"Then let us ride. I think they are coming for us."

This time we did not ride the long route. We galloped directly north. There were worker's camps there too and we tore through them. The sound of our hooves brought men and women from their tents to see what it was. The result was that the horsemen who pursued us found their way blocked. Our horses had no mail to carry. They flew. Remus had never galloped as quickly. "Tom, where are they?"

"They will not catch us, Sir William."

We did not slow down. The sentry on the wall saw us and we were admitted. Geoffrey was summoned from his bed. As soon as he saw the girl he recognised her, "It is Isolde!" He put his arm around the girl. "We thought you were dead."

She buried her head in his shoulders, "I wish I were. My mother and sisters are with my father now."

Geoffrey was grim, "You shall stay with me as my ward and we will have vengeance. Raymond, take her to my wife." He turned to me as the girl was led gently away. "Come let us see your work." As we went up the stairs he explained that Isolde had been one of a brother knight's family. The Egyptians had taken their home.

We ascended the tower. It was dark but the three fires still burned at Ascalon. The dried wood and the coals had combined to burn despite the Egyptians attempts to extinguish them. The towers were on the opposite side to the seawater. "Well done, Sir William."

"We cannot repeat it but it will put their work back. They will place sentries around the perimeter."

"And my brother knights can join me to harass them. Our orders were to kill as many of the enemy as we could. You have done us a favour, Sir William. You have brought them out to us!"

"Then you could do me another. We will return in seven days' time. I will need a boat. It needs not to be a good one but it must float."

"I will do so, Sir William. What do you need it for?"

"I would make a fire ship. If we let the current take it then it will burn the towers by the sea."

When it was daylight I could see that the three towers had blackened marks on them and a sharp-eyed sentry told us that he could see that some of the stones had fallen. Perhaps we had damaged them more than we had expected. We rested during the heat of the day. It was growing closer to Midsummer Day and here in the Holy Land that did not mean garlands of flowers and celebrations on the village green. Here it meant you baked even more. We left for home when it was dark and it was cool.

Sometimes fate throws a bone to you when you least expect it. We were just a mile from home when Garth, who was leading held up his hand. We stopped and I nudged Remus next to him. We did not speak. He sniffed and pointed to a gully to our right. The wind was in the right direction and it blew the smell of the fire towards us. I saw a faint glow. There were men there. Using signs, I had the men dismount. I pointed to the horses and Alf, Edward and Stephen nodded. They grasped the reins. Drawing my sword, I stepped towards the higher piece of ground which hid the dell from us. I dropped to all fours as I neared the top.

We closed with the hidden camp. There should have been no one this close to our home. A friendly caravan knew they would have a welcome. I heard the sound of camels. They were unmistakable. I peered over and saw an encampment. That was not unusual. Many caravans camped for the night in such places when they travelled through remote areas but this was not a caravan. They were sergeants and they were led by a knight. I recognized Roderigo of Santiago. He lay asleep next to the fire. These were de Waller's men. As my eyes counted the men I saw a huddle of bodies. There had been a fight of some kind and men had been slain. Even as I planned our move I knew what had happened. Santiago and his men had ambushed a caravan. We were close to the Jaffa to Jerusalem road here. The merchant would have thought he was safe for he was close to my manor. Perhaps he was heading for it to seek shelter for the night. Theobald's plan had cost civilians their lives.

I waved Robert to the right and Tom to the left. Their men went with them. I had Garth with John and Harold. I rose and we moved through the scrub towards the camp. They must have had a sentry close to Robert for there was a shout of warning and then a cry as he was slain.

Roderigo of Santiago was on his feet in an instant with a sword in his hand, "To arms!" A groggy sergeant stood before me and I brought my sword across his middle. I felt the blade grate off bones as it tore into him. Harold Longsword ran directly towards the fire. Garth and John both stayed close to me to protect my sides. We had no shields. Two sergeants sprang up and ran at us with swords and shields. Blocking the sergeant's sword with my own I pulled the edge of his shield towards me and then flicked my sword over the top to rip across his neck.

I heard a clash of steel as Harold Longsword and Roderigo of Santiago brought their swords together. My new man at arms was overmatched. I pushed the dead sergeant to the side and raced towards the fire. All around me was the sound of battle. We had caught them unawares and the initial attack had slain enough of them to give us superiority of numbers. I saw that Harold had great strength. His blows were forcing the knight back but the knight had experience and cunning on his side. He feinted one way and when Harold's sword blocked fresh air the knight spun completely around to bring his sword through the spine of my warrior. It was a quick death.

Roderigo saw my approach and he grabbed Harold's sword. He held both weapons before him. He grinned at me in the dark, "At last a warrior who is worthy to fight me. You have annoyed de Waller you know? Why will you not die?"

"Because I have yet to kill de Waller."

"That will not be. You die this night. I can use my left hand as well as my right. You will die and any other who tries to fight me."

I put my left hand behind my back and pulled out the assassin dagger. It had been cleaned since the attack but Santiago was not to know that. I smiled when I saw the grin leave his face. "Recognise it? Your master wasted money did he not?"

It was not much but it was enough to dent his confidence. He hurled himself at me with whirling swords. I swept my sword in an arc to meet the two swords. There was a cascade of sparks as the blades met but the force of his attack meant I had to step back. Instead of stepping directly back I turned a little to the side and slashed my dagger at his exposed side. He was too far away for it to connect but he was so terrified of what he thought was a poisoned blade that he stepped back too so that there was a gap between us.

I was aware that there was silence around us. The rest of his men were dead. My men were standing in a circle. Garth growled, "Finish him, lord! His vipers are no more!"

It was my turn to smile. "It ends here Santiago. You could surrender and I will take you to Jerusalem. Who knows, the king may let you live."

He shook his head, "We all die, Sir William. It is the manner of our death which is the difference. Besides, when I kill you I will take your men one by one." He laughed, "I have been offered a prize. My lord will give me your whore when you are dead! She must be something to behold that you risked being ostracized and my master is so desperate to have her that he will take your home to do so!"

A chill spread through my body. Rebekah and my people were in danger. I would end this. I did not warn him. I lunged with my dagger and as he jumped out of the way I tucked my head down and did a forward roll. He had no idea what I intended and his blades sliced the air above my head as I rose beneath his flashing swords to plunge my sword up into his middle. As I stood I pushed and the sword's tip emerged through his shoulder. We were face to face, "Well done Sir William. A trick I would have been proud of." I pulled out my sword and, as he fell to the ground he said, "There was no poison was there?" As I shook my head, he closed his eyes and died.

I turned, Robert, have your men collect the weapons and animals. Who was the merchant?"

"Phillip of Jaffa lord."

"Bring their bodies with you. I am worried about Aqua Bella! De Waller has plans for it!"

We ran back to our horses. "Edward and Stephen, stay here and help Sir Robert. The rest, we ride like the wind."

I rode at the front expecting to see de Waller and his men. Later I realised how foolish that was. But Roderigo's words had shaken me. De Waller would only attack when he had all of his men. The sentries on my walls were surprised to see me but the gates were opened as soon as I hove into view.

Brother Peter came to greet me. “Is there trouble, Sir William?”

I nodded. “A caravan was ambushed less than a couple of miles from here.”

He shook his head, “I knew I should have ordered your men to investigate. Just after the sun had set we heard the clash of arms but it ended quickly and I thought no more about it. I am sorry.”

“You could have done nothing. It was a knight and sergeants. We only defeated them because we caught them napping. Henry Longsword is dead.”

My wife had appeared during my last words, “We have lost a warrior?”

I nodded, “And there is more. De Waller is hunting us.” I would not lie to my wife. I hoped she was strong enough to cope with the news.

She smiled, “I am safe here, husband.” She turned to Brother Peter, “Am I wrong to wish him dead?”

“Some men deserve to live and die. This de Waller deserves to die, lady and I believe that Sir William is the man who will end his worthless life and send him to hell.”

Dawn was already breaking and the house was coming to life. The smell of baking bread filled the air and that, combined with the sun rising to the east gave us hope. My men returned with the camels and their goods along with the bodies of the merchant and his people.

Francis made the sign of the cross when he saw the merchant. “He was a good man. He often spoke to us when he passed.”

“Has he family?”

“He has a wife and two sons. I think one of his sons lives in Jerusalem.”

“Then after we have eaten we will take their bodies and his animals. The king should know of this.” Francis nodded. “And for the foreseeable future, I will have guards in the fields with your workers. I do not trust this de Waller. He wants me and my wife but that will not stop him from hurting the innocent.”

Brother Peter said, “We will bury poor Harold before we do, lord. We owe him that.”

“You are right. He is the first of my men to die.”

“And let us hope he is the last. The graveyard where the former lord and lady lie is a fine place for his body to repose. It is shaded. There is no yew but the trees form an arch. It is good.”

The funeral meant that we did not leave for Jerusalem until noon. Normally I would not have travelled in the heat of the day but it was not far and I was anxious to tell the King my news. There were looks of surprise from the guards as we led the camels through the gates. The bodies of the merchant and his men were draped over the backs of my horses and were covered in hessian sacks.

"Do you know where the son of Phillip of Jaffa can be found?"

One of the guards said, "By the Christian bazaar lord."

I turned to Edward, "Do you know where that is?"

"Aye, Sir William."

"Then find him and bring him to the palace."

I left Garth, Alf and the rest of my men with the camels and our horses while I sought advice. Neither the King nor Theobald were present. They were at Ramelah speaking with the master of the Templars. Had the Templars done their job then Phillip of Jaffa might be alive.

Queen Melisende appeared. "You look troubled, lord," I told her my news. "That does not bode well." She frowned. "None mentioned de Waller's men."

"They do not wear his device now. They have adopted the brown mantles of Templar sergeants. If they were seen they would not be taken for enemies. It might explain how they were able to move so freely through this land."

She nodded, "You have the merchant's camels?"

"I have sent for his son. I brought the bodies of the merchant and his people. I did not wish to leave them in the desert."

"I will tell the King when he returns. Until de Waller is caught then you must stay close to your home. I overrule the King's commands."

"The three new towers they had built at Ascalon have been damaged but we could not destroy them. We have delayed their construction that is all."

"And you have done what was asked. The knights who live close by will take heart from your efforts. When you have ended de Waller's reign of terror you can resume your work."

When we reached the entrance Roger son of Phillip was waiting for us. "Thank you for doing this, Sir William. My father held you in great regard. This shows you to be a true knight and I thank you. I will continue my father's work."

"Then let me know when next you travel and I will provide an escort."

As we rode home Garth said, "So we do not return to Azdud?"

"No my friend, first we find de Waller and defeat him."

We began the next day. We returned to the ambush site. Already the carrion had begun to devour the bodies. The desert is a cruel place and before winter came there would be nothing to show where men died. The birds, foxes, rats and mountain lions had already made a mess of the area but we found the tracks of horses which showed that Santiago had come from the south-west. That was even more galling. They had passed along the road which was supposed to be patrolled by the Templars. We spent seven days searching the south and west for the enemy. We met travellers and Templars but none had seen any sign of them. It was as though they had disappeared.

I had begun to think that we had frightened them off. I was weary as I entered my gates eight days after the attack. Rebekah saw that I was weary. "Come, Will, I have a surprise for you." She led me to a chamber which had been used for storage. It was built into the rock at the far end of the floor in which we had our bedroom. I had never been inside.

Rebekah opened the door and revealed a bath. It was raised from the ground and had been made from blue and white tiles. There was a perfumed smell to the air. The bath had water in it and I saw steam rising. It was a hot bath. "How on earth?"

"As soon as I came here and found this I realised that this could be a room where we could bathe." She pointed to a channel. "I saw that water dripped from above but did not pool. It left through that channel. Absalom built it. Brother Peter advised us on how to make it watertight. We have lined it with clay. There is a plug which allows us to empty the water. The tiles we found in another room. Francis said that the lady of the manor had planned on using them for the floor of her closet. That would have been a waste. Come let me undress you and we will see if it is a success." She closed the door. The oil lamps made it look like a grotto. It was magical.

After she had undressed me I stepped into the water. Rebekah said, "If it is not hot enough, my husband, then I am sorry. I did not know when you would return."

"It is wonderful. Come and join me."

She blushed, "Will! I cannot but I will wash you." She looked like a young girl. Excitement was written all over her face. She must have been planning this since first she came. I was a lucky man.

She took a sponge and began to wash the dirt and dust from my body and hair. I lay in the water with my eyes closed. Her fingers were soft and delicate. As she washed my legs I found myself becoming aroused. There was a sudden splash and I opened my eyes. Rebekah had a strange look on her face. She was looking down at the water. I tried to cover myself. "I am sorry my love! I …"

She held her hand up, "Do not apologize, Will. It is natural but it just came as a surprise. I would have…."

I stood. "Hand me a towel and I will dry myself." I had to be careful with my frightened young wife. I had to treat her gently. I had frightened her.

That night, as I ate with Brother Peter, my knights, my squires and my wife I felt content. Robert smiled, "Considering we did not find de Waller again, lord you seem remarkably happy."

Tom chuckled, "And you look clean too!"

I put my hand on Rebekah's, "Let us just say that I have happiness here within these walls and nothing that de Waller can do will make that change. We have stout walls and even stouter men."

Brother Peter said, "Amen to that, Sir William. In the desert, they have oases which are a sanctuary for those in need. Here you have created an even better sanctuary for here you heal people."

"Heal people?"

"Have you not noticed that Edward is happier now? When first he came, there were nights when he tossed and turned and cried out. It is not just my counsel which has helped him. Sir Tom and Alf have done their part too. The women and children you rescued now blossom and bloom. They are happy. Why some of your men at arms have asked if I would approach you to ask if they could be married."

"They do not need my permission!"

"Of course they do, Sir William, you are the lord and the women and children are your property." He shook his head. "You are the most unlikely lord of the manor I have ever met. You take nothing and give all. Strange."

That evening I felt content. It was a peculiar feeling. Brother Peter's words had made me happy. I kissed Rebekah. Our kisses were no longer chaste and I lay in my bed. The sheets were newly washed and smelled fresh. Rebekah blew out the candle.

"Goodnight, my love."

Strangely there was no answer but I felt the movement of the sheets and Rebekah slid next to me. She slid her hand across my chest and kissing me on the ear said, "You will be gentle lord, will you not? And if I cry then…"

I rolled around and kissed her. "My love, I will be gentle and I promise that I will not hurt you."

"Then I am content."

Chapter 20

I was happy and my wife was happy. That should have warned me that all was not well with the world. My grandfather believed in three sorceresses who spun webs to entrap men. They lulled them with happiness and then snatched it away. Two days after we removed the second bed from our bedroom and as I was preparing to ride forth, Masood appeared at the gate. Normally taciturn he was distraught. I thought he would speak with me but he did not. He knelt at my wife's feet. I could now understand more words of Hebrew but he spoke too quickly for me to understand more than a couple. My wife's smile left her face to be replaced by stone. She put her hand on the back of Masood's head and stroked his hair. She said something and he nodded and rose.

"What is it, my love?"

"My father's house has been attacked. All have been slaughtered and my sister and mother abused."

Even as I asked the question I knew the answer, "Who was it?"

"From Masood's words, it was de Waller. He said there some bodies who were not my family. They were Gentiles. He said they were Franks and they wore brown mantles."

"That is de Waller. How did Masood escape?"

"He had been in the hills with his sheep. He said that, from the state of the bodies, the attack took place three or four days since."

That made sense. Few visitors frequented the lonely estate. "We will hunt them down. Fear not."

"First we must tend to the dead. I will come with you."

"I forbid it. It is too dangerous."

She smiled, "I will obey you in most things, husband, but not this one." She turned to Francis. "Have carts made ready."

I nodded, "As you wish. Garth, I want all but four men fully armed and ready to ride!"

"Aye lord."

I had my men in a protective circle around the carts which contained my wife, her women and the servants Francis had sent. When we came to the fork in the road I sent Alf to Jerusalem. I gave him the hastily written note. “Give this to Theobald, or the King or the Queen. Someone should know that de Waller is loose. He is a mad dog and must be put down.”

The vultures were circling and, as we rode through the gates the rats, wild dogs and foxes fled at our approach. Crows and vultures lazily flew into the air. Bodies littered the ground before the hall. They were mainly servants and slaves. My professional eye took in the scene. De Waller would have attacked at dawn, or just after. The guards at the gate would have been slain. Servants and slaves were always up early and they would have seen the intruders. That is why their bodies lay in untidy heaps.

“Ask Masood to find tracks.” Francis did as I asked. The hunter leapt onto his horse and galloped off. I turned to Rebekah, “Stay here. We will make sure that it is safe.” She nodded and with swords drawn, we entered. I did not expect to find de Waller but there were bandits who might seek to take advantage of the situation. David Ben Samuel and his sons had died bravely. I saw the six sergeants whose bodies lay before them. De Waller had not even bothered to give his own men the respect of a burial. He had abandoned them. It said much about the man we fought. Ruth was the next one we found. Before she had died she had been raped. I gently covered her lower body with her dress and laid a cloak over her. Mary was even more shocking. I found it hard to view. I picked up her body, “John, a sheet, a clean one.”

John of Chester had a stony expression as he carefully covered the body with the sheet. As I turned to carry her out I said, “Carry all the bodies of my lady’s family out. I do not want her to see this. The rest of you search the building and see if you can find any others.” There was blood, intestines and body parts lying all over the hall and the room where we had eaten so many pleasant meals.

Rebekah stood stoically watching as we came out. I said not a word but I laid her sister’s body as reverently as I could in the back of the cart. As I did so the sheet slipped and Judith, one of the younger servants cried out. Rebekah snapped, “Judith, compose yourself. They are dead! We cannot bring them to life but we can care for their remains.” She was showing me a harder side I had not seen before. I suspected it was an act for she was now the lady of the house. The last of the line.

By the time all of the bodies had been found Masood had returned. He spoke to Rebekah and pointed to the south and west. Rebekah nodded. “They have gone towards Ascalon. They have taken camels and all that they could carry.”

“Then when we have escorted them home we will follow.”

She shook her head. "First we need to do something. I want the house burning to the ground and then you and I must go and collect my father's fortune."

I shook my head, "De Waller will have it now."

She said, "No, he will not. My father was careful. Have your men bring two shovels. We will need them."

I followed my wife around the rear of the house. She headed purposefully towards the bench and the huge fig tree surrounded by the lemon trees beneath which I had first seen her seated. It was her special place and David Ben Samuel had said it was special for the whole family. Now I understood why.

"Move the bench and dig."

I saw that the soil underneath was not hard and compacted but had been turned over sometime in the last months. After a few shovelfuls of earth had been moved we heard a clunk.

"That is it." John and Henry struggled to lift the chest. Eventually, they wrestled it out of the hole. "That is my father's fortune. He has large amounts with Simon but he always kept half here. He feared that our home might be raided at some time."

"Let us get it back to Aqua Bella. The sooner we are on the trail of de Waller the better."

Rebekah wanted nothing more from her home. Her mother's jewels and those of her sister had been taken. The bodies of her family had been stripped of anything of value. She put the torch to her family home herself. As we headed home she did not look back. I did and I could not help feeling sadness as the pall of smoke rose higher into the sky. The whole family was gone in a heartbeat. At least I still had my father. She had nothing.

The first thing that Rebekah insisted upon doing was cleaning up the bodies of her family. It was a grim task but she and her women did it. Alice helped them and Brother Peter did what he could. We laid them in the ground close by Harold Longsword. Not long ago the cemetery had just contained the lord and lady of the manor. Now it was filling up. How many more of my men would end there?

The next day the hunt began. I left six men to guard my home. Theobald had sent a message to us with Alf. He said that he would have men guard my home. I did not fear that de Waller would try anything. He would get away as fast as he could. The fact that he was heading for Ascalon led me to believe that he might be trying to lose himself in the wild borderlands. There he could prey on the weak of both sides. Masood was like a hound. He had the scent of de Waller and he followed their tracks unerringly. It helped that de Waller had taken the camels. Masood was able to follow their spoor and the tracks of the Franks. Even when the camels crossed the tracks of other camels our prey was unmistakable. They had more than four days start on us but they would be moving more slowly. Camels, especially laden ones, did not move quickly.

We had a problem with our scout. None of us spoke Hebrew. We had to use sign language. That first night, as we camped forty miles from Aqua Bella I spoke of that to my men. “If we are to prosper out here then we need to speak the language. When we return, I will have my wife’s servants begin to teach us.”

Alf said, “Why cannot they learn our language, lord?”

I smiled. This was the old belligerent Alf raising his head again, “Because this is their land. You spoke Greek when you lived in Constantinople.”

“That was because my mother was Greek.”

I nodded, “And my wife is a Jew.”

Garth ruffled Alf’s head, “Think before you speak! I thought we had changed you. It seems we still have some way to go.”

Tom stood and stretched, “But are we to go back home eventually lord?”

“You tire of this land, Thomas?”

“Of course not, but I miss England and I miss Normandy. I would like to wake up and not be thirsty and know that I can drink any time I choose. I want to be in a land where I am not constantly covered in dust.”

Robert said, “If I remember England you will be covered in mud.”

Garth nodded, “Sir Robert is right but I still miss it.”

As I curled up in my cloak I realised that I had a decision to make but I could not make it on my own. I now had a wife and she would be involved in the decision I made. First, we had a mad dog to catch.

Masood left before any of us were up. He had his two horses and he rode them in relays so that he could cover great distances. He seemed to have a bond with the horses. He did not use a saddle, just a cloth held by a leather strap yet he had as much control as any of us. He needed no stirrups. Then again, he would not need to fight from the back of a horse. We would ride as hard as we dared and that would be faster than our prey was moving.

We rode hard all day. We began to see signs of the enemy. We saw discarded clothing and objects too heavy to carry. They had been taken from Ben Samuel’s without any thought to their use. We found the carcass of a butchered camel. They were either hungry or the animal had become injured. It was a hopeful sign. If de Waller could reach Egypt then we might have an impossible task to recapture him. So long as he was in the open, then we had a chance. Once he was behind walls we did not. When Masood returned, he was animated. By his gestures and his signs, we gathered that they were camped just ten miles away. Although we had travelled another forty miles which was our limit their camp was tantalizingly close.

I turned to Robert. "Do we push on or try to catch them on the morrow?"

"It is not like you, Sir William, to ask advice."

I pointed to Masood, "From our scout, we know that they have forty men. We need to plan our attack carefully. Nighttime gives us surprise but we have seven archers who cannot work as well in the dark."

Garth spoke for all of my archers, "Lord, we want vengeance for the slaughter at David Ben Samuel's home. We were friends with his men. We enjoyed their company. It matters not when we catch them just so we catch them. They are close to the land of Egypt. If we delay then we may lose them."

Robert said, "I agree. If we rest our horses for a couple of hours we can still catch them while they sleep. Garth and his archers can dismount and they can still kill many."

I looked at their faces. It was obvious they all agreed, "Then let us do this. Garth, you and the archers will leave first and go with Masood. You will conceal yourselves within bow range to the south of their camp. That way we can charge in without fear of hurting you and you and the archers can slay any who flee."

Garth grinned, "That, my lord, is a good plan!"

I took Edward and Stephen to one side. "I had hoped to give you more training before putting you into combat. I do not have that luxury. When we go into battle I want you to guard your lords' right side. Stay close by their horses' rump. Watch for danger. Do not leave them. These are vicious and dangerous men. If you have to fight then fight to kill."

"We will lord."

"Aye, lord, and we will not let you down!"

"I know Edward. What I fear is letting you down! You have a life to lead and I do not wish it to be ended here. De Waller is not worth it."

I fed and watered Remus myself. I had taken his saddle off and laid out his saddle cloth to let it cool. Our horses had ridden further than we ought to have ridden them. No matter what happened the next day we would have to take it easy on the return home. It would take four days, at least, to retrace our steps. I took out my whetstone and sharpened my sword and dagger. I put an edge on my spear. I hoped that we would catch them without mail but they could sleep in it. We could not afford to make assumptions. I knew that they would have sentries. They would hear us when we charged. That was why I was sending Garth and the archers to cut off their retreat. Garth would let none pass.

We mounted. Masood waved as he led Garth and my archers south. They would have further to ride and would be approaching the enemy camp from the south. Their horses were not carrying mailed riders. They would be able to make the journey. My archers would be fighting on foot. I had twelve men at arms, three knights and three squires. We were going up against forty ruthless killers. I had some untried boys and warriors who had been abandoned. This would not be easy.

We did not have Masood with us and so I had to rely on my own nose and my own estimation of time and distance. When I thought we were about a mile away, we halted and dismounted. I wanted us to lead our horses until we were within charging distance. It would rest the horses and we would be harder to see. My new helmet hung from the cantle of my saddle. My spear was still strapped to the saddle. Neither would take much time to reach.

I knew we were close. In the air, I could smell their fires. Even better I could smell their camels. As we drew closer to the hidden camp I could hear the camels and horses. De Waller's horses had not been trained with camels and they did not like each other. I smiled. They would not have had a good night's sleep since they had taken the beasts. When first we had escorted camels, we had had to spend time allowing our horses to walk close to the spitting camels.

I held up my hand for I saw a shadow standing on a rock some two hundred paces from us. I was patient and, eventually, the shadow moved confirming that it was a sentry. We would be able to walk no more. I signalled for my men to don helmets and to ready their weapons. Once I was seated on my horse with my spear in my hand I grabbed my shield. We would be fighting sergeants and knights. These were neither bandits nor Turks as Harold Longsword had discovered to his cost. We would be attacking in one long line. This time the warriors at the two ends were Pierre of Cherbourg and Christophe of Chinon. They were new men but I needed my better warriors in the middle. Tom and Robert flanked me. Alf rode behind me with my gonfanon and a spare spear. Henry son of Will and John of Chester rode next to Tom and Guy and Louis rode next to Stephen. We were not riding boot to boot. There was a gap between horses and men. We needed the enemy to think there were more of us than there actually was.

I waved my lance forward and we began to canter towards the camp. As I expected the noise of our hooves on the compacted desert alerted the sentry. I heard his voice in the night as he rousededed his comrades, "Stand to! Alarum!"

Suddenly he was pitched from his rock. My archers were close enough to use their bows but that strike had to be Garth. He had seen the shadow and heard the shout. I could not see their camp yet but I could picture what would be happening. Men would be grabbing weapons and donning helmets. Those without mail would have to forego it. Men who normally fought together would be locking shields for self-protection. The sound of our hooves would tell them they were about to be struck by mounted men.

We reached a rise and I saw, in the hollow, their fires and their animals. Some of the men were using the animals for protection. They were sheltering behind camels. The huge beasts were like mobile walls. I heard the voices of command as knights organised their sergeants. I lowered my spear. I saw three men sheltering behind a camel. I wheeled Remus to the left of the beast and thrust down with my spear. The sharpened head penetrated the mail and drove into the sergeant's shoulder. I twisted the head to the side gouging a hole as large as my fist. The other two men would be dealt with. From the far side of the camp, I heard cries as my archers began to rain arrows, blindly into the camp. Once they saw our horses they would move closer and choose their targets.

Forty feet from me a knight and four sergeants had made a wall with their shields. I saw that, behind them was a banner and another knot of warriors. That would be de Waller. As I might have expected he was making a barrier of men before him. I rode at the centre of the wall. I heard Robert yell, "Edward and Stephen join Alf!" He and Tom urged their horses next to mine.

I pulled back my arm. Robert and Tom had fought enough times with me to know what we needed to do. As we closed with the men we all wheeled left to allow us to strike at the same time. My spear found flesh as I thrust it over the top of the wall. A spear scored a line along my cantle. I heard a squeal of pain behind and, as we wheeled right to come behind the wall I saw Robert's mount stumble. It had been wounded. Edward bravely leapt from his horse and held the reins for Robert. Tom and I were behind the wall and as the two survivors turned to face us the integrity of their shield wall disintegrated I thrust my spear into the chest of the knight. It was an easy strike for his arms were open as he turned. As he fell the spear was torn from my hands. I saw that Robert had mounted and Edward rode behind Stephen.

All around us was the sound of confused fighting. It was dark of night and a body had fallen on the fire making it even darker. I could smell the burning flesh. However, even in the dark, I saw the standard of de Waller as it fluttered overhead. Remus was struggling. We had ridden hard. As I slowed up I saw that de Waller and the last of his men had formed a small shield wall. He stood within the circle. There were eighteen of them left.

I shouted, "Dismount!" Even as we dismounted de Waller's men were dying as Garth and my archers closed in. They were as deadly in the dark as assassins. They needed no poison nor hashish. I hefted my shield high and shouted, "Surrender and we will take you back to Jerusalem to stand trial before the king!"

De Waller snarled, "And be hanged? You think me a fool? We will take our chances here!"

"Is that why you cower behind your men? I offered you challenge twice before and you refused. Save your men's lives and fight me now!"

There was silence and I knew that we had won. How can a man fight for a lord who refuses a challenge? I raised my sword and we marched towards them. I did not look around for my men to see who followed me. Whoever it was I would trust with my life. We had swords and some of those we faced had spears. Mounted, I would choose a spear. On foot, it would be a sword every time. I deflected the first spear thrust with my shield. The shield was strapped to my arm but my left hand was free. I pulled the edge of the sergeant's shield towards me and, before he could react, I had thrust my sword into the gap and his throat. The shield wall was broken. Tom and Robert had despatched the knight and sergeant who had flanked the man I had killed and we were inside. One of the two sergeants who were in front of de Waller ran at me with an axe raised. He suddenly had a surprised expression on his face as an arrowhead blossomed from his chest. Tom and Robert advanced on the other man.

I saw that the knight next to de Waller had the same device on his surcoat as the Spaniard I had killed. When he spoke, it was confirmed, "You killed my brother and now I will kill you!" His brother had been skilled and I had no doubt that this younger version would be as skilled.

He feinted with his sword to make me fend off the blow with my own. I did not fall for it. I saw cunning in his eyes. He made the same move but this time it was not a feint. Instead of raising my sword I dropped to my knee so that the sweep went over my head. I hacked sideways into his knee. He was quick and he almost danced out of the way but I struck bone and my blade was bloody.

"Trickster!"

"Your brother would have called it skill." He was now weakened on his left side. His knee would give him pain but, more importantly, it would be leaking blood. I went on the offensive. I feinted with my sword and then punched with my shield as he raised his arm to deflect the strike. He had to step back quickly to avoid overbalancing. My shield connected with his sword hand. He held on to the blade but his hand would be numb. His eyes closed with the pain of putting weight on a weakened knee. I swung my sword at head height as he was off balance. His shield came up to block it but the blow had all my weight and power behind it. He reeled and as he did so I thrust at his middle. His numbed hand could not react fast enough and my sword slide through his mail and I angled it up into his heart. His body collapsed.

Behind me, the first rays of the new day were peering over the mountains to the east. They lit up de Waller. He was the last man standing. I saw Masood, Garth and my archers leading their horses towards us.

"So, after all, your refusals to fight me you are now forced to do so. Think how many men's lives might have been saved had you done so. And now there is nowhere to run. My regret is that I did not kill you before you attacked an innocent family."

"Innocent? They were Jews!" he laughed, "Why am I talking to you? You are a Jew lover! You would bed with the animals in the field!"

He was trying to anger me and that gave me even more confidence. I stepped forward and brought my sword over my head. I held my shield before me. De Waller tried to block the blow with his shield. The shield shivered and shook. I heard a crack. In this land, you oiled the wood of your shield else the heat desiccated it and made it fragile. He had not looked after his shield. As he reeled I swung again and hit exactly the same place. The shield split in two and my sword sliced and bit into his left arm. I raised my sword again and he lifted his sword to block the blow. I punched with my shield and hit his hand. This time he had to take three or four steps back. It was his standard which stopped him. I took three strides and swung my sword at waist height. I hacked through his side. My sword was stopped by his spine and his standard. There was a crack and the top half of the standard fell to cover his body with his device. De Waller was dead.

I looked around and counted the cost. Roger of Hauteville, Pierre of Cherbourg, Christophe of Chinon and Alan Azay lay dead. Gregor of Basle, Guy Gurth son of Garth had wounds but we had won. We buried our dead. I went to de Waller and, using the axe from the dead sergeant, I took his head. Putting it in a hessian sack it would be taken back to the king. The enemy dead were stripped of their mail and weapons. All of them had coins and treasure about them. I found the jewels from Ruth and Mary. I put them in my leather satchel. My wife would have them returned. It would not bring back her mother and sister but it would help her to remember them. We led the horses and camels and we headed back across the barren land. Only the wounded rode. Our horses were weak. It took us seven days to reach Aqua Bella although word reached my wife sooner than that. Masood left the day of our victory. She knew that we were safe.

Chapter 21

When we reached Aqua Bella the whole of the estate turned out to greet us. Rebekah threw her arms around me, "I am glad that you are safe." She saw the blackened hessian sack hanging from my saddle. "Is that…?"

I nodded, "I will take it with me to Jerusalem when I speak with the king." I pointed to the camels and the goods de Waller had taken from Rebekah's father. "What shall I do with those?"

"We will not need them. Sell them, my husband. I would say give the money to the families of those who worked for my father but all are now dead. Give some to Masood and some to the men who worked for him in Jerusalem."

"I will. We will leave in the morning."

"Is it over?"

"There are none left alive. He may have relatives in Normandy but I doubt that they will bother us. It is over."

"Then we can begin our life here."

We celebrated and, that night, I enjoyed my wife's company. She was as a different woman. She had been a fey and frightened girl. Since we had shared a bed she had become a woman. She laughed more and no longer shied away from my touch. I had seen this with nervous horses. With a woman, it was even more complicated.

All of my men were now richer. I had allowed them to plunder de Waller's dead and so they all wished to come with us to Jerusalem. I also took Masood. He had asked to serve me and he would need to buy goods for his home which he would build on the estate. All eyes were upon us as we entered the gates of Jerusalem. Our quest had been no secret. Other merchants knew what de Waller had done. Ben Samuel had been a popular man and a leader of the Jewish community.

We were applauded as we led the camels to the market. I saw Simeon Ben Levi there. He greeted me warmly, "I see that my friend has been avenged. They are all dead now?"

"His enemies' bodies lie where they fell." I pointed to the sack. "I will ask permission to put the head on the gate."

"That's is good. The people need to know that he is dead. And the camels and donkeys?"

"I am here to sell them. Some of the money will go to Masood, some to the men who worked for him here and the rest to his daughter."

"If you will trust me I shall sell them for you. It is the least I can do for my friend."

"Thank you. We will be in the city all day. My men have money to spend and I need to speak with the king." I knew that I could trust Garth to watch over my men and I went with Robert and Tom to speak with the king.

Theobald had heard our entry to the city and he was waiting for us at the palace gate. I held up the sack, "The head of de Waller."

He nodded and said to the Captain of the Guard, "Have it placed on a spike over the south gate. I wish all who enter to see the folly of defying the king."

"Aye lord."

"Come, the King is at home and we have much to say to you." We walked, "Where did you find him?"

"He was close to the border with Egypt. I think he was heading there to join our enemies."

The court was in session but, as we entered silence fell. King Baldwin began to clap and the others joined in, "William of the Gryphon has returned from a quest to destroy our enemies. Jerusalem is grateful to you, lord!"

I knew the game he played. He wished the other knights who were present to take heed of what I had done and now, what I would say. "I serve my king and it is an honour to defeat those who bring terror to this land."

That was the right response. Theobald said, "And we have displayed the traitor's head on the gate as a warning to others. The lord of Aqua Bella has a long reach. De Waller thought he could hide in the desert. Let all know that there is nowhere to hide from the gryphon's claws."

I looked at Theobald as the room burst into spontaneous applause. He shrugged and said, quietly, "You are a legend. The Queen thinks it is a good idea to build on that legend. Come we will go to see her. The King will join us soon."

The Queen put aside convention to embrace me. I knew that it was a signal honour. "I knew that the faith we had in you was not misplaced, lord." I nodded, "And how is your wife coping with the loss of her family?"

"She has a new one and she is strong, your majesty. She is happy at Aqua Bella although she mourns."

"And the death of her abuser will put her mind at rest too." The Queen was an astute woman.

King Baldwin arrived. He had now grown into his role. He had filled out a little and, with a neatly trimmed beard, he looked every inch a king. He grasped my arm. "The words I spoke in court were not empty rhetoric, William. I meant them." He grasped Robert's arm and then Tom, "And you are no less heroes in our eyes. Sit. We need to talk."

As we sat, he looked at Theobald, who nodded and then spoke, "Geoffrey of Azdud took your advice, Sir William. He used the boat you suggested he fire and he used it to burn one of the new towers on the seaward side."

"I did not expect him to do that. I would have returned. I made a promise."

Theobald shook his head, "But your promise to Ben Samuel was more important. What you have done has made the merchants of Jerusalem have more confidence in the king. You are seen as the protector of all. They talk of you as another El Cid but one who protects Jews as well as Gentiles."

King Baldwin said, "For that reason we wish you to continue to watch the Jaffa road. The confidence it inspires and the fear it instils in our enemies is worth more than your work at Ascalon. The Templars are busy building their defences at Gaza City. When that is complete we will have Ascalon encircled and we can assault the Egyptians."

"And how long will that take, your majesty?"

"It will not be quick and could take years. That gives us time to build up our own armies but they depend upon the finances of the Kingdom being in a healthy state. That is where you come in. By protecting the caravans, you make us stronger."

We were feted for some time and our role was discussed. The Templars new castle meant that they no longer had the forces at Ramelah to ensure that travellers were safe. I was happy about the arrangement for it meant I could be at home more and I could get to know Rebekah. After we had finished Robert and Tom went to make their own purchases while I went to visit Simon. I knew that he had David Ben Samuel's gold and I wished to ensure that Rebekah could have access to it, whenever she needed it.

"Of course, lord, and we are so indebted to you that my fellow bankers and I will not be charging you the interest we charge others. Whenever you need your money it will be there and you can have it anywhere you wish." He paused and gave me a meaningful look, "Even England."

"I am happy at Aqua Bella."

"That is good but things may change and you are now a rich man. The monies you have would rival the fortunes of some kings."

"I do not need money."

"Then you have found the true secret of life, lord. I envy you."

We hired another six men. Our success meant that there were many who wished to serve us. We chose the best. We had mail, horses and weapons for them. All that I had to do was have more surcoats made. The gryphon was now seen as a lucky omen. My men told me that others would ask just to touch the gryphon to see if they could benefit from the luck it brought.

We reached home before sunset and I was able to tell Rebekah all of my good news. It was a happy time. As winter began she gave me more good news. She was with child. My world was complete. I had lost a wife and I had a new one. I had lost my children and now I would have more. She had been worried that de Waller had robbed us of the chance to have any more children. I now prayed, with Brother Peter, that my child would be born and, this time, Rebekah's child would survive.

The road patrols were easier now for we had teams of riders we could send out. I did but one patrol a month. My knights were happy to bear the burden of riding. As Rebekah grew larger so I stayed at Aqua Bella more than I left. My world grew smaller and yet was more fulfilled.

My son, Samuel William, was born on midsummer day. It was an anxious time for us all. It was hot and Rebekah was in pain. We had women around her but, against all conventions, I stayed with her and held her hand. She wished it so. Even when he was born and the cord was cut she still had a terrified look upon her face. He was smaller than she would have liked and she did not smile until he sucked from her nipple. He was so small I could almost have held him in one hand. Even then she watched him closely for she feared she would lose another child. By the time the weather became a little cooler she was happier. Our son would live.

I made sure that this son would see his father. I had been missing more than I had been present with my first family. I had tried to emulate Geoffrey of Anjou. Now that I had a second chance I did not intend to waste it. Each day I revelled in the changes. It seemed that while he slept he both grew and changed. He became larger. His little fingers began to move and to grab. There was wonder in all that he did.

I had a perfect world until the raids began. It was after Christmas when a messenger arrived from Theobald, "Lord, there are Turks. They are attacking the settlements to the north of Jerusalem. Lord Theobald wishes you to bring your knights and sergeants to help bring order to the land."

It was a dilemma. Rebekah, however, showed her newfound strength, "You have to go, my love. This is our land and if the Turk gets a foothold then we will all suffer. We are safe behind our walls."

I left with half of my men. I would not risk my home. Over the last year, we had recruited more men and we had sufficient to leave a very healthy garrison at Aqua Bella. We could now talk with Masood and my scout rode with us as we headed to Jerusalem. Our orders were simple. We were to join the other knights and seek out the raiders. The horse archers made sudden attacks, destroyed farms, carried off captives and fled. We had to hurt them.

We were given the road north of Jericho to watch. The rest of the knights and sergeants appeared to want to react to an attack and then chase the raiders back over the border. I thought that was a waste of horses, men and, most important of all, time. I wanted to be at home with my wife and son. Samuel now recognized me. His eyes lit up and he giggled when his fingers touched my beard. I resented every minute I was away from the smiles, giggles and every strange noise and gurgle he made. I would send Masood to find the trails which the Turks used. They rode horses which were bred for the mountains. They did not bother with roads. The one weakness they had was that they had to come close to roads when they attacked farms.

We arrived after dark and I spoke with the leaders of the community of Jericho. The lord had died in the retreat from Damascus. His widow, Lady Sarah, and son, Henry, lived in their manor but they had just ten sergeants. They would not be able to do much. She was happy for us to stay in their fortified manor which lay at the north end of Jericho. It guarded the entrance. With just one tower it would not be able to hold off a determined attack but the walls of the town were strong.

We could now speak with Masood. Increasingly he used our language but there were some Hebrew words which could not be translated. We based ourselves in Jericho at the manor of Sir Richard. We did not show ourselves. The next morning, I sent Masood to find the trail while we found the farms which had not been attacked. John of Chester had become a leader amongst the men since he had joined us. "Lord, I would say that the farm we passed just south of Jericho last night would be a likely target."

I had learned not to dismiss his ideas. "How so?"

"When we passed through. I saw that the people there thought themselves safe. The wall they have could be jumped by a rider on a horse. They have a gate but it would not stop someone determined to get in. They think that because they are south of the town the Turks will not come." He pointed to the hills to the northeast. "See how this is a natural bowl. They can come down from there. They would not need to use the road."

"Perhaps. We will see when Masood returns." We spent our first day familiarizing ourselves with the terrain. We walked our horses through the streets of Jericho and then headed south. If anyone was watching they would think we were passing through.

That evening when he joined us he pointed to the north. "There are many tracks there, lord. That is the way they ride to attack."

"Is there anywhere we could wait for them? Could we ambush them?"

"Your big horses would struggle but there are rocks where archers could wait." He and Garth got on well for Masood was a skilled archer too.

"Then take Garth and his men and make a camp there."

Garth nodded, "Do we ambush them when they come south?"

"No, when they go north. We will wait here and keep a close watch on them. If John of Chester is right then they will attack the farm in the bowl. If not then they will attack the town."

"The walls are strong, lord."

"True, Sir Robert, but they may have grown bold. We have not stopped them. So far, they have sent bands of forty or fifty warriors only. Suppose they sent hundreds?" He nodded. "Sir Thomas, after dark, take your men and wait at the farm. Hide. Have a fire lit and if they attack then light it and we shall come."

Garth asked, "How long do we wait to ambush them, lord?"

"As long as it takes but they have not raided here for six days. They are due. We will wait at the manor." My two groups of warriors left after dark. They would not be seen. Masood and Garth were masters at hiding and Tom had learned skills from his father, Aelric the archer.

Lady Sarah was not old. She was younger than me and her son was just five. He had barely known his father before he had died. King Baldwin had not replaced the lord of the manor as Sir Richard had been one of the few knights to stay by the standard during the retreat. She was apologetic about the accommodation. "I am sorry, lord. My husband was not a wealthy knight as you can see from the furnishings. The Turks raid us too often for the people to prosper."

"Do not apologise, lady. Sir Robert and I have endured far worse, have we not, Sir Robert?"

"Indeed. If you like, Lady Sarah, we can use my men to improve the defences."

I shook my head. "Not yet Sir Robert. I wish to draw the enemy in. Let us keep hidden. If John is right then they may attack the farm in the bowl but if not then I think they may come here." I pointed to the nearest farm which lay deserted and forlorn. "They have been working their way down the valley. It may be that John is right. Sir Thomas and his men can give them some protection. We have the chance here to strike a mighty blow." I turned to Lady Sarah. Are the numbers of your men well known?"

She nodded, "Everyone is aware of how few men we have. The merchants of Jericho are kind. They often send over their camel guards when they are not needed for the caravans."

"Then the enemy will know. Sir Robert, have the horses kept in the stables with their saddles close by. Have someone with good eyes in the tower. It may be that no one attacks. But we are prepared."

Leaving Sir Robert with Lady Sarah I put on my cloak. I left my helmet in the house. If anyone was watching they would notice that. I would just look like a lone visitor. I walked the walls. I spoke to the sentries as I passed them. They were devoted to Lady Sarah. The Captain of them had come from England with Sir Richard. "Sir Richard was a fine knight sir. He left us ten here because we were the best of his men. His words, lord and not mine, and he took the younger ones with him. Twenty men he had and they were either killed or captured. A crying shame. She is young, lord. She needs a husband."

"There are many young knights who would woo her."

He shook his head, "Begging your pardon, lord, but they seek the manor and not the lady. That is not right, sir."

He was right of course. Just then a flash of light caught my eye. "Did you see that Wilfred?"

"See what, lord?"

"Slowly look around and scan the hills to the west." I leaned forward as though I was looking over to the north.

"Yes, Sir William. I saw a flash. Sunlight on metal."

I glanced up at the sun. It would be dark in a couple of hours. That would be enough time for whoever was there to reach the manor. I had divided my forces. Half of my men were either in the hills or at the farm. I would have to make do with what I had.

"I think they will attack and after dark too. Go around and warn the men."

"How do we fight them, lord?"

"We let them in, of course. We know they are coming. When we are certain that they will attack then I want the gates unbarring and you and your men to defend the south wall."

"You want to let them in, lord?"

"We have too few men to risk being slaughtered on the walls. They have horse archers. They can ride around and pick us off one by one. We let them in and then I will charge them with my horsemen. These horse archers are all well and good in the open. Here we can trap them so that they cannot run. As soon as we attack them you and your men race to the gate and use your javelins."

He smiled, "That might work, sir. Just so long as they take the bait. I hope they do not wonder why we leave a gate unbarred."

"That is the beauty of this if they do not then they do not attack and we lose no men."

Leaving him I went to tell Lady Sarah and Sir Robert what I had planned. I could tell that Sir Robert was not pleased but Lady Sarah seemed happy enough. "We will go to the top floor of the donjon. It is reached by a ladder. My people will be safe there Sir Robert but I thank you for your concern."

Once they were ensconced in the donjon we saddled our horses and my men waited. Carrying my helmet, I went back to the gate where Wilfred waited for me. "Where are the men?"

"They have taken shelter, lord. I made sure they were fed and knew what we are doing."

"Then let us watch, listen and smell."

"Smell lord?"

"The wind is blowing from the north and west. We will smell them. The Turks smell differently to us and we will smell their horses. If they are clever then they will muffle them."

"When do we unbar the gate, lord?"

I had thought about that. Sir Robert was right, an unbarred gate would make them suspicious. "Let them climb the walls and open it for themselves."

"I hope you know what you are doing, lord."

"So do I, Wilfred, so do I."

The sun had been set for some time when I heard the hoof slip on the stone. It was a small enough sound but it was enough. I sniffed the air and I could smell Turkish horses. I peered into the dark and saw shadows. "They come. To your places."

I hurried to the stables. I left the stable doors open. None could see us in the dark but the white walls outlined the gate. We would see them when they entered. Donning my helmet, I mounted Remus. We had our spears at the ready. I saw a shadow descend, like a spider, down the stairs of the gate wall. They had taken the bait. The dark gates loomed open and a flurry of archers galloped in. I could not see their faces but I knew that they were looking at the walls to see where our sentries were. I spurred Remus and we poured out through the stable door.

As I had discovered when I had first come to this land the Seljuq horse archer does not wear mail. He does not have a helmet. He has a bow and a fast horse. They would run away. However, we were so close that the sixteen of us were on them before they even knew. My spear struck an archer in the throat and threw him from his horse. I pulled my arm back and rammed it into the back of a second who was trying to turn his horse. I heard footsteps on the fighting platform. Wilfred and his men were doing as I had asked. We had them. It was too dark and they were too close for their bows to be of any use and they turned and headed for the gate. Wilfred and his guards threw javelins as fast as they could. Some archers escaped, just five of them. The rest were slain.

Even before we could celebrate I heard a cry from the walls.

"Sir William, there is a fire to the south and east of the town. I think it is a beacon!"

It was Tom. They were under attack. "Wilfred close the gates when we are gone and finish off any Turks. We ride to the aid of our men. Sir Robert, on me!"

My men just obeyed but, as we galloped Alf asked, "Lord, where do we go?"

"John of Chester was right; the Turks have attacked the farm. I pray we are not too late." My former squire had to hold on and defend the farm until we could cover the two miles to the farm. I thanked Wilfred's sharp eyes. If we could reach my men then Wilfred would have been the one responsible for saving them. The beacon seemed to draw us like moths to a flame. As we neared it I could hear the sounds of battle. Unlike us, Tom and his men would be defending a building. They would not be mounted. I still held my spear and for that I was grateful. A spear could break on mail but was less likely to be damaged fighting a horse archer.

The glow from the fire showed us the horse archers. They were not standing still to release their arrows. They were making themselves difficult targets by galloping around in circles. It helped us for they did not hear our thundering hooves. The gate of the farm had been torn down and we poured through. We took them completely by surprise. Once again, my spear took one archer in the back. As a second turned and levelled his bow at me I stood in my stirrups and rammed it into his neck. I threw his body from my spear and urged Remus to the next warrior. He must have been a leader for he shouted something. My spear struck him in the side.

Just then the doors of the farm opened and Tom led his men and the workers from the farm to fall upon the Turks. Horse archers are clever and wily. They knew they did not have the advantage. They fled. The difference was that they could just jump the wall. More of them would escape. The skilful archers leapt the small wall which surrounded the farm. We would have to flee through the gate. They would have a lead over us.

"Tom, mount your men. We must pursue."

"Aye, lord."

It took time for their horses to be saddled but at least it allowed our mounts to be rested. We knew where they were going and I just hoped that Masood and Garth were in position. We rode in a column of twos. The trail was marked for us by the body of one warrior who had succumbed to his wounds and, later, a lame horse. They were taking the trail. Soon we would have to go slowly for it became twisted and narrow. The last thing we needed was to lose a warrior over the side. We knew we were on the right trail when we found another lame horse. I was grateful when the sun began to rise and the trail gained definition.

Masood had told us where the ambush would be but we had no idea exactly where that was. My Hebrew was still rather basic and his English was even more rudimentary. The trail twisted and turned so much that it was hard to guess where our wily scout had chosen.

There were sudden cries ahead and the neighing of horses. It was the ambush. Garth and Masood had done as I asked. I did not want to leave them exposed. It was time to hurry. I led my men. I still had my spear but I was not certain how much of an edge it had. It had not had to pierce mail but bone blunted metal just as much as iron.

There was a sudden movement ahead. Two Seljuq archers fled towards me. I barely had time to pull up my shield and stab, almost blindly at the archer who tried to raise his bow. I struck one in the chest and Remus snapped his jaws at the other making the horse swerve. There was a rocky drop and horse and rider tumbled down the slope. I urged Remus to the sounds of combat. As we turned the corner of the trail I saw that Masood and Garth had created the perfect ambush. The trail rose and climbed over a col. The riders had to go in single file and I saw twelve bodies there and horses milling around. The men behind me effectively trapped the Seljuqs and this was a killing ground for my archers.

I hurled my spear into the back of an archer and, drawing my sword galloped into their midst. Once again, their numbers prevented them from using their bows properly. I charged into them swinging my sword widely knowing that any I struck would be hurt. There was no skill. My men fanned out behind me and even my new squires could not fail to kill. We took no prisoners. I wanted the slaughter to serve as a reminder to all Seljuqs of the price to be paid for such attacks. My sword was blunted when we had finished. We tended to our wounded and made sure that none remained alive. We took their weapons and led their horses down the trail. It was noon when we reached the manor.

Lady Sarah and Wilfred greeted me, "It is over?"

"It is over. We will head back to Jerusalem. I will leave one knight and his men here as a garrison for a month or so but the danger is gone. Sir Thomas…"

Sir Robert said, "Lord, let me and my men stay here. I have more experience than Tom."

Tom coloured but I saw the hint of a smile on Lady Sarah's lips. I turned to my younger knight, "Of course. Come, Tom. We will see which horses we wish to keep and which we will sell"

"Aye lord."

As we rode back to Jerusalem Tom said, "I have enough experience lord!"

Guy laughed. He knew Sir Robert and he had observed the same as I. "Do not worry Sir Thomas, the experience Sir Robert was speaking of was the experience of wooing."

Poor Thomas was still confused.

Chapter 22

We were able to resume our road patrols for the presence of Sir Robert and his men deterred the enemy around Jericho. We were not needed there. I was able to spend more time with my son. He was growing each day. It was a joy to be greeted by some new noise or action. Even the arrival of his two bottom teeth made me smile. When he gnawed on my finger then I knew he had a bite! Time flew by. Days turned into weeks and then months. It was measured in the growth of my son. And then my wife told me that she was with child again. I was delighted. I felt that God was smiling on me and that I had been forgiven. This time I was able to watch my wife grow. I was not needed on the road as much.

One day a rider came from Jerusalem telling me that the King wished to see me. The days of needing a large escort were long gone. The sign of the gryphon standard and surcoat kept the road safe. I just took Alf. He was no longer the awkward and sometimes truculent youth. He had been with us for more than four years and he had changed. He was now confident and skilled. He would be a knight soon.

When I reached the court, I found Sir Robert there. It had been many months since I had seen him. He gave me an awkward smile.

"My lord."

"It is good to see you, Robert. Francis and his family miss you."

"I was needed at Lady Sarah's lord."

"You have more raids?"

"No Sir William but that was because we have been aggressive in our patrols. We make them fear us."

"And Lady Sarah is well?"

"She is, lord, and, we are happy."

Before I could question his use of the word 'we', we were ushered into the King's presence. There was no court but I recognised Ralph of Bowness. I smiled, "I thought you were going home?"

"I was but the Emperor decided that, after my skill as a diplomat, he would use me elsewhere." Theobald coughed. "However, more of that later."

The King said, "Firstly, Sir William, we have asked you here to thank you for the work you have done on our behalf. Secondly, I have to ask you to release Sir Robert from your service."

"Release Sir Robert?"

"He wishes to marry the Lady Sarah and I have agreed. He will be the new lord of the manor. As you can understand he cannot owe you fealty."

I smiled and embraced my former captain, "I am delighted and do so without delay! We will be invited to the wedding?"

"Of course."

The King looked relieved. He obviously did not know me yet. "Good, that is settled. Thirdly, we begin our attack on Ascalon. Ralph of Bowness is here to bring us news that the Emperor is sending ships to help in the blockade. Gerard of Sidon will command our ships and the Byzantine ships ensure that we prevent the defenders from being resupplied. You and Sir Thomas will be needed."

I was disappointed but I said, "Of course, your majesty."

Theobald said, "And then, when Ascalon falls then you will be released from your oath and you will be able to return home to England."

I had forgotten that. I now had a dilemma. I had a fine home at Aqua Bella and my wife was happy. Yet I wanted to return to England. I would have to wrestle with those problems while I was at the siege.

"You have a week to prepare. I will be leading the army. The new Master of the Templars, Bernard de Tremelay and Raymond de Puy Provence will also be bringing their knights. It has taken longer than I hoped but we will finally take that port."

We spent some time going over the minor details and then we left. Sir Robert said, "The wedding will be in a month."

"Then I will not be there for I will be at the siege."

Sir Robert looked distraught. "Lord I owe you so much. I would have you at my wedding."

"And you know that I have to be with the King. I am sorry."

He clasped my arm, "I know. Then, when it is over, bring the Lady Rebekah and your son. Stay with me."

"That I will do."

Ralph said, "Could I impose on you and stay at Aqua Bella for a few days?"

"I would be disappointed if you did not."

Ralph had an escort this time. There were four cavalrymen with him. They had the distinctive fish scale armour and pointed helmet. Ralph gestured at them with his thumb and said, in English, "I said I wouldn't need an escort but the Emperor insisted."

"You have surprised me, Ralph. I was convinced that you would return to England."

"I was at the quayside negotiating my passage home when the Emperor sent for me. Between you and I, he was stuck for someone he could trust. The English Varangians may not be the cleverest of his guards but we are the most loyal and reliable." He laughed, "Of course the generous payment he gave me helped."

Rebekah was both delighted and irritated by the guests. The irritation was with me for I had not warned her of their arrival but she was a generous hostess. Ralph noticed that she was with child and he would not let her do anything. Most of our conversation was about Sir Robert and his change in circumstances. I teased Thomas. "Well you will be next, Thomas eh? Shall we find you a pretty young wife?"

He blushed and Rebekah reproached me, "Will, let him alone. He is young."

He nodded gratefully at my wife, "And besides I think I would like to marry an English girl."

Ralph smiled, "For that, you will need to be in England. Perhaps you will come with me?"

"I cannot. Like my lord here I swore that I would stay until Ascalon was taken. Neither of us can leave until then"

Rebekah looked surprised, "You would leave?"

I put my hand on hers, cursing Tom and his careless mouth. "That was before I met you. I am content to stay here now."

"Content?" There was something in her tone which made both Ralph and Thomas look down at their platters.

Ralph said, quickly, "Tom, would you and Alf show me the roof. I hear it has a fine view." The three of them gratefully left for there was a noticeably changed atmosphere.

Rebekah waved over Judith, "Take Samuel and prepare him for bed. I will be up in a while."

I knew that when with child she was sometimes more irritable. I cursed my choice of words. With men, it was easy. They did not react to a word's nuance. A woman could read much into one word! "I meant nothing, my love. Did I use the wrong word?"

"Content means you are putting up with it. I would not have you stay here just because you are married to me."

"My love this is your land and your home…"

"You have always been honest with me. It is one of the many things about you that I adore. Be honest now. If you were not married to me or we had never met then when you have helped take Ascalon would you go back to England?"

I made the mistake of hesitating. I should have answered quicker. As it was the damage was done. I saw her roll her eyes as I spoke. "I did meet you and we are married. Our paths are now as one."

"Answer me honestly."

Her fingers squeezed mine. She smiled at me and I had to answer. "Yes, I would."

"There that is better. Now tell me, where would we live in England?"

"My father is an earl. I have a castle which I call home."

"A big castle?" I nodded. She was silent for a moment. "England is cold?"

"Compared with here it is."

She nodded. "I will go to see Samuel." She kissed me. "I have much to think on."

I took the wine jug and ascended to the roof. Tom said, "I am sorry, my lord. I should have thought…"

"Do not worry. I also demonstrated that men are clumsy when speaking with women. It is for the best."

An uncomfortable silence settled on the four of us. Ralph slapped his forehead, "I am a fool. I knew I had some news for you. Geoffrey, Count of Anjou is dead."

"Killed in battle?"

"No, he died of … I know not what but it was not violent. His son Henry is now Duke of Normandy and I heard a rumour when I visited Sicily that King Stephen and he have met."

I said nothing for my mind was filled with all sorts of ideas and thoughts. The civil war might already be over. My father had been resolute and fought for Henry and his mother with unstinting loyalty. I wanted to be there at the end and yet I could not. We chatted about England and the impending voyage which Ralph would take. "If I write a letter would you deliver it to my father?"

"Of course."

I would explain why I was not leaving the Holy Land. I would tell him why I was not returning home. He would understand. He was that kind of man. I could hope that I would be as good a father to Samuel as he was to me. We chatted until the stars came out. In truth, I was avoiding going to bed before Rebekah was asleep. I envisaged an argument.

As I crept into our room the candle was still burning. "You are willing to face any number of enemies and yet afraid to risk the sharp tongue of your wife."

"You are with child and I did not wish to upset you."

"We women are far stronger than you men imagine! Come lie next to me so that I may nestle in your arms." I undressed and slipped next to her. "Here it is. Without you, I would be dead. If not on the road from Jaffa then when de Waller came to kill my family. I now have just my aunt in Jaffa. A good lady but she is not my husband. There is nothing for me in this land any longer. There will come a time when King Baldwin or his son will be defeated and the Muslim hordes will drive the Gentiles into the sea and then the Jews will be subjugated once more. We will go to England. I will ask my ladies if they wish to come with me. If not then I will use some of my father's money to give them a start. And I will buy lots of furs!"

I hugged, "You are a remarkable woman."

She laughed and kissed me, "Of course I am."

I was awake early and I wrote a letter to my father. It was not the letter I would have written the night before. I told Tom and Alf of my new plans and Tom wrote a letter to his father. Ralph was, of course, equally delighted. "Have you told your men yet?"

"No. I will gather them together before we go to Ascalon. If they wish to stay here I will send them to Sir Robert. He needs good men."

Ralph said, "If I am any judge of men then they will wish to stay with you."

He left and I went to tell Francis that we would be leaving for Ascalon when the King arrived. "The King is coming here?"

"He is."

"Then that is an unexpected and most wonderful honour."

My men were waiting for me at the armoury. I had told them of the impending campaign and we needed to choose what we would be taking. I stopped them all and gathered them around. I told them about my new plans. "You have a choice. You can all come with me to England and live in my castle in Stockton or you can serve Sir Robert. If any wish to leave both of our services then I will give them a horse, armour, coins and my good wishes. You have all served me well."

My words were greeted with silence and I did not know what to make of it. Then Garth said, "Well I don't know about the rest of you but I have had more than enough of this oven they call the Holy Land! I will be going back to England with his lordship."

Every single one of them chose to return with me. I would be heading back to England.

Chapter 23

Three months later I wondered if I would ever see Aqua Bella again let alone England. The siege was not going well. The Egyptians had sent a fleet north and they had managed to drive off Gerard of Sidon and his allied fleet. Moreover, the King's authority had been threatened by the new master of the Templars. If Robert de Craon was conceited then Bernard de Tremelay was both arrogant and fanatical. He wished to slaughter every Muslim that we encountered. He wanted us to charge the walls with horsemen as though that would bring down the mighty walls. The fifty-odd towers were not as high as they might have been but they had made the city much harder to take.

I was privy to the rows and arguments between the King and Raymond de Puy Provence on one side and Bernard de Tremelay on the other. The king usually prevailed but I could see that the arguments were wearing him down. We had finally built the wooden towers which would allow us to close with and assault the walls. The problem was the numbers within Ascalon's walls. They outnumbered us. We had no Crusader army. In fact, our army would have been pitiably small if a large number of pilgrims had not joined us.

The first months of the siege had been spent dealing with the Egyptian forces who were outside the walls. We had to chase their horse archers from the field. The aggressive Templars suffered for their Master was convinced that Christian might would easily defeat Muslim guile. He lost many brave but reckless knights that way. Then we had to gather the materials for the wooden towers. That was not an easy task either for there was perilously little timber to be had and we had to bring the wood from the north. All of that took time. The siege had begun in April but now it was July and the last month had seen some of the pilgrims, recently arrived from the cooler north die from the heat. My darker-skinned men would have been in the same position when we had arrived. We had learned to adapt and survive.

Things had become so desperate that the King had had to send for more men and Sir Robert of Jericho arrived with reinforcements. He did bring news, "Sir William, you now have a daughter, Ruth."

It had brightened an otherwise dark time. "She is hale? They are both well?"

"They are both well. Lady Rebekah sends you her love and prays for a swift end to this siege."

"I fear that may not be happening. You have come at a dangerous time. We are to begin to move the towers into position. First, we will have to clear their walls and then fill in the ditches so that the towers can be pushed close. But I am pleased that you are here with us. You will join my battle."

I had a large number of knights to command. Geoffrey of Azdud was my Captain. He was an able and level-headed warrior. We had two towers. The Templars had two and the Hospitallers two. The knights of Nablus had two towers: Ibelin, one, Tyre one and the rest of the army three. My knights and sergeants slept around our towers. It had taken us some time to build them. We would not let them be raided and destroyed. When the last piece had been finished on the last tower the King held a council of war.

"Tomorrow we begin the attack. The towers will be pushed to the edge of the ditch and we will rain death on their walls."

I was not so certain. The rest of the army relied on crossbows. They were slow to reload and awkward to handle in a tower. I was luckier. I now had twelve archers and our numbers had been swollen by another fifteen men who were with the pilgrims. We had attached them to our numbers. With six of my more experienced archers in each tower, we would have, with the pilgrims, thirteen or fourteen bows which could keep up a withering rate. The pilgrims did not have a war bow but from the elevated towers, they would have the range and power to cause more damage than crossbows.

"Have your men ready to fill the ditches with the stones and timbers when it is safe to do so."

The Master of the Templars said, "They can fill as soon as the attack begins. We need not wait!"

Theobald was the voice of reason, "We do not have the men to waste, Master. We are close to the end now. Let us not rush. You will soon have your fill of Egyptians to slaughter."

The Master nodded. He had made no secret of the fact that he wished to kill as many enemies of Christ as he could. Many of the enemy were fanatics. I had fought them. Bernard de Tremelay was just as fanatical. His fanaticism infected his knights and sergeants too. They were forever dropping to their knees to pray to God to destroy the walls and let them fill Ascalon's streets with blood.

When I returned to my men I gathered them around and explained what we would be doing. I pointed to the walls, "Let us be vigilant this night. I want one man in three on guard and watching. We have barrels of seawater close to hand. Those of you who thought me mad to bring them may thank me soon. When we attack, the enemy will use fire and that is the greatest danger for a wooden tower."

Sir Robert nodded, "Sir William is right. Many years since I served in Normandy. I was a young warrior then. I saw his father caught at the top of a burning tower. He managed to escape by leaping onto the walls but every man in the tower was consumed by fire. It took a long time to get the smell of burning flesh from my nostrils."

Giscard de Huberville asked, "But why keep watch?"

"Because if I was the Egyptians and saw the towers completed, I would try to destroy them with fire tonight. With our fleet scattered, until we can bring reinforcements, they can continue to keep the city supplied by sea. We will grow weaker and they will grow stronger."

I had good deputies and I did not need to keep watch but I did. I was with Sir Thomas and we had the shift which was in the middle of the night. To be fair I would not have slept well anyway. There might have been a time after my first wife died and before I met Rebekah when I might have been eager for battle. It was different now. I now had a son, a daughter and a wife. I had so much to live for that I now worried about losing my life. I wanted to see my son grown into a man. I wished to see my daughter married and I desperately wanted my father to meet Rebekah. Lately, I had wondered if I would ever see him again. He was not a young man any more. The death of Geoffrey of Anjou had shaken me. He had been just thirty-eight years old. My father was fourteen years his senior. Even if he did not die in battle there were many diseases which could take him. I wanted this siege over more than the Master of the Templars but I did not want to lose my life doing so.

Along the lines of towers, I could hear laughter and raised voices. Many of the other knights and sergeants were already celebrating. The completion of the towers signified victory in their minds. I had fought in sieges. It would not be easy. Tom was on the first level of the tower and he whistled down to me. In an instant I was alert. I looked up and he pointed. To the south of us, closer to the sea I saw shadows moving across the ground towards the tower of the nights of Tyre.

The enemy were attacking, "To arms! To arms!"

My men were awake in an instant. The men of Tyre were making much noise and they did not hear my words. Others did but it would be too late for many men. The Egyptians had launched a sortie. Garth and the archers raced up the tower.

"Knights and sergeants, a shield wall before the towers!"

Moving to twenty feet before the towers I stood with Sir Robert and Sir Thomas by my side. Behind me were Alf and the squires. Their spears were held over our shoulders. The Egyptians must have used their sally ports and then hidden in the ditch. Even as we braced ourselves for the charge I stored the information that the ditch around the walls had no traps and stakes within.

I saw flames arc towards the tower of Tyre. They were using fire arrows and bundles of oil-soaked faggots. I shouted up, "Garth, watch for fire!"

Suddenly arrows sprouted from our tower and I saw men pitched back. They had been carrying fire but it had been masked by cloaks. Garth and his men had seen them and now, as the flame bearers fell I saw the horde which advances towards us. They were a mix of warriors and ordinary men from within Ascalon. The vizier had seeded the large numbers of untrained men with his warriors to affect an attack along our line.

I heard the roar of fire but I kept my eyes before me for the Egyptians were advancing. Alf said, dully, "The tower of Tyre is burning."

Robert said, "At least there are no men within. A tower can be rebuilt. We cannot rebuild men as easily."

"Brace!"

The fanatical warriors hurled themselves at us. They had obviously never faced a shield wall. Many of these warriors were used to open plains fighting. With our shields locked and our spears before us, they perished. As the pile of bodies grew so their tactics became even more desperate. I saw young warriors, younger than Edward and Stephen run to jump on the piles of dead and dying men to try to jump over us. Our second line of squires and sergeants plucked them out of the air with their spears. There was the sound of screams as they were pierced and then the dull thud as their bodies hit the ground. A shout from the walls signalled the retreat. Garth and his archers continued to rain death on those before us so that they left a trail back to the ditch with their dead.

We had not suffered many casualties at all and my own men none. As I peered down the line of towers I saw, by the light of the burning tower of Tyre that some of the other towers had been damaged.

The next morning the devastation was clearly visible. The men of Tyre would have to rebuild their tower and three others would need repair. The King and Theobald rode along the lines. When he reached me, he stopped, "Thank you for the warning lord. Had you not done so then I fear this might have been a disaster rather than a setback."

"If I might suggest your majesty?"

"Of course."

"It will take time to rebuild the towers. We should take the enemy dead this night and put them in the ditch."

The king said, "In this heat, they will be stinking by dark."

I nodded, "And they will continue to stink and fester before their walls. If they take them within where will they bury them? It will be a reminder of the payment their warriors made."

"You killed the most warriors here."

"I know and the alternative is to burn them. I have smelled burning flesh and it is not pleasant."

"Then do so."

In the end, the other knights burned the enemies they had slain. We did not. I would use the enemy dead as a weapon against them. That night we put cloths around our faces and carried the bodies to the ditch. Garth and his archers followed us with drawn bows. I carried one body with Alf and we hurled it into the bottom of the ditch. The rest of my men followed. There was a cry from the walls as we were seen. It was a strangulated cry for an arrow took the sharp-eyed sentry. "Hurry!"

The thought of death or capture spurred our men on and soon the ditch had a layer of dead. "Back!" Before we ran back, I spied the sally port through which the Egyptians had sortied. It gave me an idea.

Theobald rode to see me the next day. A sea breeze brought the smell of the decaying bodies across to us. Theobald shook his head, "How much worse will it be for those within I wonder. They can see fathers, brothers and sons lying unburied before them. You are a clever warrior William. I shall miss you when you return to England."

"I cannot see that being any time soon, lord."

"It will take another week for the men of Tyre to rebuild their tower. We will keep a better watch on them this time."

After he had gone, I gathered Garth, John of Chester, Alf, Masood and Robin Hawkeye around me. "Tonight, I would enter the city and do some mischief." I took out one of the assassin's blades. I wish them to think we have hired killers in their midst."

My men were unsurprised but Garth said, reasonably, "How do we get in, lord?"

"When we were close to the walls last night, I saw that the mortar on some of the older stones was weak and had crumbled. There are handholds. Masood and Alf, do you think you could climb the wall?"

Masood peered at it and then he nodded, "Aye lord."

"Garth, you and Robin will keep watch with your bows. Alf and Masood will climb and then lower ropes. We ascend, using the ropes, and then kill as many guards as we can, silently of course. We will leave by the sally port which we would leave open. I will leave the assassin dagger in the hand of a likely looking Egyptian and sow seeds of suspicion."

Garth chuckled, "And they would not know how many enemies were within their city."

"We take no mail and we wear the garb of the Egyptians."

"How do we cross the ditch lord? It will be full of bodies."

"We take one of the timbers we will use to build a bridge when we attack.

When I told Robert and Thomas what we had planned they were less than happy. "But lord, you risk your life."

"I would have this siege ended so that I can go home. Besides, it is not as much of a risk as you might think. We have watched their sentries. There are two for every hundred paces on the wall. They meet, talk, walk apart until they meet the other sentries, speak and return. We have time."

We waited until the moon slipped behind a cloud and then headed, with our timber to the ditch. We had cloths over our faces for disguise but they also helped to mask the smell of rotting flesh. There were movements in the ditch as though the bodies were alive. It was rats. Robin and Garth stood with bows ready as we passed the timber across the corpse-filled moat. Once on the other side, I stood with my back to the wall. John of Chester did the same. Alf and Masood ran at us and, as they planted a foot in our cupped hands, we boosted them up the wall. The mortar had fallen away and the gaps were big enough for handholds. I felt Alf's feet on my head as he used me as a stepping stone. It meant he had but twelve feet to climb. I glanced up and saw that he and Masood were like spiders as they crawled up the stones. I heard the hiss of two arrows as Garth and Robin hit the two sentries. One pitched into the ditch and I heard a dull thud as the other fell to the fighting platform.

Within a few moments two ropes snaked down and John and I used the cracks in the stone to climb the wall like a ladder. Masood and Alf were facing the interior of the port next to the dead sentries. As we slid over the crenulations and began to coil the rope the two of them scurried along the shadows of the wall to slit the throats of the nearest sentries. John and I wrapped the ropes over our shoulders and headed for the stairs which led to the sally port. The town was quiet. Along the walls, I saw the moving shadows of other sentries but, as Alf and Masood joined us, I knew that there were none on this part of the wall.

I could hear the guards in the guardhouse next to the sally port. I had counted on there being men there. I could hear them talking quietly. I had no doubt that they were gambling. As soon as Alf and Masood joined us I opened the sally port so that it was ajar. Then we went to the guardhouse. I drew my dagger and the assassin dagger. I nodded to Alf.

He flung open the door and I ran in. There were eight men. I slashed the nearest across the throat with the assassin dagger while I lunged at a second with my own blade, my seax. My three men whirled behind me and began to slay the enemy. There was a cry and a shout.

Alf hissed, "Lord!"

I turned as a guard plunged his dagger towards my back. It snagged in the coiled rope and I tore my dagger across his middle. I could hear shouts. It was time to go for the Egyptians were all dead. I pressed the assassin's dagger into the palm of one of the men I had slain. He was the smallest and thinnest of the ones we had killed and then we left. Dressed in black and in the shadows, we were hard to see but I spied the men as they raced from the heart of the town. We hurried through the gate and over the makeshift bridge. While Garth and Robin watched the gate, we dragged the timber with us and hurried back to our lines. We did not have far to go and Robert and Thomas awaited us. Lights appeared on the battlements and we saw a glow through the open sally port. We had given them a mystery. In the scheme of things, it was not a major victory, but, like the crumbled mortar, it was a weakness in the resolve of the defenders.

Four days later and we were ready to begin the assault. This time we kept a better watch. We just had archers on the top of our towers and that made them easier to push into position. The defenders used their own archers but, while the towers were being pushed our own men took shelter. As we advanced my other men had bows and they sent their own arrows at the archers within Ascalon. None of them was as skilled as Garth and his men but it mattered not. So long as we sent arrows over, they could not do any damage to our men. Once in position Garth's skill and experience showed. He timed it so that half of our archers rose as one and killed the enemy archers on the walls. Then the other half rose and, as more Egyptians ran to replace the dead, they were slain. In such a fashion the walls closest to our towers were kept clear of defenders.

"Now!" I joined my men and ran to the ditch to hurl faggots of brushwood into it. The sally port opened and the crossbowmen I had placed around the base of our tower kept up a withering hail of bolts to make them bar it again. As soon as the brushwood was in place I ordered the huge timbers forward. We were far ahead of the other towers. We had our bridge ready while they were still filling the ditch with their faggots.

"To the tower!"

It was then time for us to prepare to push the tower over our bridge. We would then ascend and begin the actual attack. It took until almost noon for everyone to be ready. The order was given and we began to push. We had to hit the bridge we had made perfectly. There was little margin for error. Behind us I had pilgrims rolling the barrels of seawater I had collected. They would act as a brace behind the towers and then we would be able to use them should the enemy attempt to fire the wooden towers. Garth and my archers were incredibly effective. I had no idea how many men they slew but the cries, screams and sounds of falling bodies bespoke a large number. As soon as Garth shouted, "Ready lord!" we began to climb. The assault bridge was below the fighting platform which the archers used. I climbed up the ladders. The August heat was unbearable. How would we manage to fight?

I waited until all of my men were there and then nodded. Alf and Edward began to lower the bridge. I held my shield before me as did Sir Robert and Sir Thomas. The dark interior of the tower began to fill with light as the bridge was slowly lowered. As it did so I saw the town before us. In the distance, I saw men rushing to man the walls. We had taken a large number of defenders. As soon as it was down I ran across and leapt on to the fighting platform. My men were right behind me. Now they could use their own archers. Louis pitched from the fighting platform pierced by four arrows. He had been a little slow in raising his shield.

"Spread out!" We ran along the fighting platform and cowered behind our shields.

Then I saw that they had dragged war machines, the Romans called them onagers, into position and they had fiery balls ready to load. I shouted, "Fetch water and soak the tower!"

Garth and his archers used their bows to thin out those working the war machines but when the enemy brought up large shields then we could do nothing. I contemplated leading my men to destroy them but although they were tantalizingly close, I saw a mob of warriors it was too big a risk to take on. Then Alf shouted, "Lord, look!"

I saw where he pointed. Five of the other towers had been set alight. Men were fleeing from them. It was not the place to be caught. I heard the trumpet sound. It was the signal to fall back. "Back to the tower! Fall back!"

Even as we clambered back on board they began to lob flaming balls of oil-soaked earth and hay. One smashed against the side of the tower as we stepped through. The sparks and burning pieces of hay filled the air. The tower began to burn. Edward grabbed one of the wooden pails of water and threw it on the fire. It did not douse it but it stopped it spreading. As we pulled the drawbridge up a second ball hit the door. Stephen had another pail and he threw it against the inside of the bridge.

"The two of you keep throwing water there. If it gets out of hand then descend. The rest of you down. We will pull this out of range."

By the time we were down men were already pulling on the ropes to drag the two towers to safety. I joined them on the ropes and saw that there were just six of our towers which had been saved. The rest were burning out of control. Garth was almost the last one out of the tower and he said, "Lord, the wind is blowing towards the walls. Look!"

I saw that the flames had spread to the fighting platform. One of the drawbridges must have fallen on to it. I had seen for myself the poor state of the mortar. This could be our chance. Perhaps God smiled on our venture.

We did not have far to pull the tower for the men on the walls could do little to harm it and the onager was sending its missiles blindly. When we were a hundred paces from the walls, I ordered my men to stop pulling and the ones inside were able to descend. I saw the two blackened squires as they emerged. "Well done. That took courage."

A rider galloped up, "Lord, the king wishes to speak with you."

Alf said, "I will get your horse, lord."

"Geoffrey, take charge here. Do not let them destroy the bridges. Put the archers back in the towers. Have the men soak the tower with seawater and extinguish any flames."

"Aye lord. That was close. I thought we had gained entry."

"That may come about yet. It depends upon what happens down there." I pointed to the towers. They were an inferno. Black smoke billowed over Ascalon and the wall could not be seen. I mounted Remus and Alf leapt on his horse. We galloped towards the King's standard. As we passed the other towers, I saw many men lying beneath their cloaks. Others were blackened lumps. Some had leapt from the towers rather than suffer such a fiery death. There were many lords gathered outside the King's tent and a heated debate was going on.

Bernard de Tremelay was the most vociferous. "God has sent this as a sign. Let us attack now while the walls burn."

Theobald shook his head, "How would we ascend the walls lord? We have no towers."

De Tremelay pointed at me, "Sir William has towers! Have them manhandled here."

I shook my head, "You can have them and welcome, my lord, but I fear that it is too far to bring them. They would not reach here. The journey would shake them to splinters. If you wait until the fire has subsided then there may be a chance."

They all looked at me, "What do you mean?"

"My men and I scaled the walls. The mortar is crumbling and the fighting platform there is on fire. If you have stone-throwers ready then we could batter the wall down and make a breach. Then we could attack."

Raymond de Puy Provence nodded, "A good plan, lord." He turned to the Templar, "Wait, brother. The fire will die out soon and then we can see."

"We will wait until the fire is out but my knights will be readied." He sent one of his men to his knights. I wondered about the impetuosity of the Templar. We had a chance but the wall would not be repairable until the stones had cooled. By then the stone throwers could be in place. Baldwin sent for wine and we watched as the smoke thinned and the wood, burned towers became blackened charcoal and then crumbled. I saw a huge crack in the wall. King Baldwin pointed at it, "See, Master, Sir William is right. The stone-throwers will make that a breach."

Then, to our total amazement, we saw the crack widen as though a giant or a god had hit it. A huge section of wall between two of the recently built stone towers fell into the ditch. We could see the interior.

Bernard de Tremelay shouted, gleefully, "God has shown us the way. He has destroyed the heathen's defences! Let us attack now!"

"My lord, we have not enough knights ready. We can attack in the morning when we are prepared."

"No, King Baldwin, Templars wait for no man. God has shown us what we must do. We serve a higher power. The Templars will capture this castle! We will rid the land of these heathens!"

He ran to his horse and, to our horror, galloped at the head of fifty knights and sergeants towards the breach. There would be little opposition but the King was right, we did not have enough men who were ready. We watched as they rode over the rubble. They picked their way through the breach and disappeared into Ascalon. It was heroic but it was a mistake. They were all doomed.

The Master of the Hospitallers dropped to his knees and began to pray. King Baldwin said, "They may be victorious."

Theobald said, "Your majesty there are hundreds of men inside the walls. If the Templars were charging over an open field then they would stand a chance. We have lost more than forty brave knights, I fear."

We could hear the neighing of horses and the clash of arms. It seemed to go on forever and then there was a cheer and then silence. One solitary Templar horse galloped out and returned to our lines. The rest were never seen again.

A stunned silence fell over us. "God have mercy on their souls." The Master spoke for all of us. We were not to know that all of them had their heads removed and were taken to Cairo to be displayed on the gates there. That emerged much later, long after the battle which was to follow. We just knew that we had lost some of the finest knights we possessed.

We all looked to the King. For the first time in a long time, he looked as though he did not know what to do. The Lord of Ibelin shook his head, "This is sad, but it changes nothing. We can exploit the breach."

Theobald said. "But we must be cunning. Sir William, you have the only towers which made headway. Could you do so again?"

"I could, lord. If we attack with four towers there when you advance to the breach then I will lead my men to open the sally port."

"That is a difficult task you have set yourself."

"Not really. We have used the sally port once before. It opens easily and my archers can defend the walls."

The Master of the Hospitallers said, "Then we attack tomorrow. We need to use crossbows to harry their repairs. We will mass for an attack and when they bring their men to face us then the Lord of Aqua Bella can launch his attack. We will have two points of entry."

I rode back to my men to tell them. This time it would not just be the knights of Azdud and Ibelin I would be leading but a third of the army. It was a heavy responsibility.

After I had told the lords how we would fight I found a quiet place to pray, "Lord, help my right arm tomorrow and give my warriors the strength to overcome the heathen. If I am to fall in battle tomorrow I pray you to watch over my son, daughter and my wife. What we do is in your name. I thank you for sending the wind. Tomorrow we will reclaim your land for your son. Amen."

When I returned to my men, I saw Alf cradling the standard. "Lord, when we fight on the morrow can I carry the standard into battle?"

I looked at Garth who shrugged. "It will mean you cannot carry a shield."

"I know but I would have these heathens know whom we follow."

Garth put his arm around my squire's shoulders, "You are a good boy! Never fear, lord. When you step on to the walls tomorrow, we will watch out for Alf. Your standard will not fall. If it does then that means that we are all dead."

"Very well. One more thing. Tomorrow we fight together. The cry is Aqua Bella. I want no heroics." I looked at Henry son of Will, "That means you in particular, Henry."

"Me, lord? I know not what you mean."

"And when this siege and battle is over then we go back to Aqua Bella. There you can reconsider your decision to follow me home. I know you are rich men and the world is wide."

Garth looked at the others, "Lord, I speak for all. We are nothing without you. We follow you, even to the ends of the Earth."

Although we had far more men, I wished them hidden. I hid some of those who would be assaulting in the towers and others hid in the rocks and wrecked buildings. The larger numbers meant that we had more men to push the four towers. We had every archer with us while all of the crossbows were with the Master. We had emptied barrel after barrel of seawater on the wooden towers and hung sea-soaked blankets from it too. The Egyptians might set it afire but it would not burn quickly. Much depended upon the speed with which we could descend the stairs.

I heard shouts from the breach as the crossbows began a duel with the archers of Ascalon. It was the signal to begin our attack. I helped my men to push the tower. I had done so the previous day and I wanted them to see me. I had been told that they feared the knight of the gryphon. I would use that fear. Alf would carry my standard into battle. If this was to be my last battle in the Holy Land then I wanted to be remembered!

The Egyptians had more archers and crossbows on the walls and without crossbows to support us Garth and his archers did not manage to clear the walls as quickly as we had done. However, as the Master and Theobald began to draw the defenders to the breach, the arrows thinned a little. The onager was in place and, as soon as we reached the wall it hurled its flaming missiles at us. I entered the tower and began to climb. I heard the thump as the flaming objects hit the sea-soaked blankets and heard the hiss. The seawater would delay the inevitable and it spurred us on.

Edward and Stephen were already inside and they began to lower the bridge even as I ascended. As it lowered, I saw a flaming ball coming towards us. Henry son of Will gave a roar and he leapt towards it. I thought him mad but his timely action deflected the missile to the side although the force of it threw my man at arms to the ground. John of Chester reached down with his arm to help him up, "You will be in trouble for that! You know his lordship goes first!"

"Aqua Bella!"

I ran across the bridge and leapt down onto the four Turks who raced towards me. I am a big man and I was wearing mail. Two fell to the ground below, their bodies broken by the fall. One had his chest crushed and the last one I punched with my shield and he tumbled over the battlements to fall amidst the dead. I had no time to waste and I ran down the fighting platform. My shield was next to the wall but it meant I could swing my sword freely. I took the first spear on my shield. The impetus took the man closer to me and my sword hacked almost through his neck. I did not pause but ran towards the stairs. I knew where they were. Two men ran at me behind a large shield. They were trying to knock me from the wall. As they neared me I dropped to my knee and stabbed forward blindly. My sword struck one of the men in the knee and he screamed. I used my shield as a lever and they flew over my head. I heard my men's swords as they hacked their bodies.

I reached the stairs. Men were climbing up. Suddenly a flurry of arrows from the wall hit every single one of them and the stairs were clear. Garth and his men had left the tower. As I glanced back I saw flames licking around it. We had to find another way out if my plan failed. The three squires we had with us knew what to do. As I reached the bottom of the stairs I faced the interior of the castle. Already a mailed warrior was marshalling men to attack us. Thomas, John of Chester and Henry son of Will joined me. I saw that the gryphon on Henry's shield was burned black.

"Shield wall!"

We would be outnumbered until my squires could open the gate. We had to use an old-fashioned shield wall to hold them. Sir Robert and the rest of my men knew what to do. Spears bristled over our heads and we were covered by shields. It was not before time for the onager began to hurl flaming missiles at us. I was pleased they were not rocks. The first two were high but the third skidded along the top of the shields.

"Forward!"

We stepped on our right feet and began to move towards the mailed warrior who now ran at us with his men. That was good for it meant they could not use the onager against us while they did so. We came together in a mighty clash of wood and metal. They had more men but mine were all mailed. We were big men and we were locked together. Without even knowing it my sword was rammed through the middle of the mailed leader. He was alive as we pushed him back. He tried to speak but it was blood which poured from his mouth and not words. I was peering over the top of my shield and, through my new helmet's mask, I could see little. But I did see arrows striking men at the rear of the enemy formation. It was thinner than ours.

"Push! For England! Push for God! Push for Aqua Bella!"

I felt as though I was in an avalanche as the men behind pushed into my back. It was all that I could do to keep my feet. I almost fell over as the Egyptians before me fell. I heard skulls and chests crushed as my men stamped on the men who had fallen. And then there was no-one before us. Behind I heard a cheer as the rest of the army poured through the sally port. We had breached their defences. I felt cooler air wash over me as the shields above me were removed. Now we had to take the town.

"Aqua Bella! Forward!"

It was a grim and bloody business. I kept my knights and men close to me. Others did not and gangs of Christian soldiers rampaged through the streets. Had we all stayed together then the battle would have been over long before it was. We had losses and we had wounds. Henry son of Will had a badly gashed leg. We left Edward to watch him while we headed for the breach. Some Mamluks burst out of a stable. Gregor of Basle and Gaston of Lyons were slain in the furious battle. All eight Mamluks were butchered. The closer we came to the enemy citadel the more friendly soldiers we found. When I spied the cross of St. John and saw the Master wielding his sword then I knew that we had won. King Baldwin was sitting atop a horse. It was raw courage for he made a better target. We fought on with renewed vigour until finally there were no Egyptian warriors left. There were just civilians who were begging for mercy.

The King showed that he was a good king. He had the Master use his men to protect the innocent from rapacious sergeants and pilgrim peasants intent on revenge. This was a port of the Kingdom of Jerusalem and King Baldwin wanted all to feel safe.

He turned to me, "Well Sir William. We have won. Will you now stay? We could use a knight such as you. I will give you a great castle."

I shook my head, "No lord, I have done my penance. Now I will take my new wife, son and daughter back to England. I will go home."

"And here you will always have a home. We will not forget what you have done, William of Aqua Bella."

My penance was over. I could go back to my wife, my son and my daughter. We could pack our bags and sail home to my father. I could go back to England. I dropped to my knees, took out my sword and intoned, "Thank you Almighty God. You have delivered us from danger. I thank you and swear that I will be a good husband, a better father and knight in whom my father can be proud! Amen!"

Epilogue

Jaffa December 1153

I had hired four ships to take us home. I only took two horses back with me: Alciades and Remus. Strong-Arm had died. We would buy more in England. Aqua Bella was given, on my advice, to the Hospitallers. The King and the Master were both happy with that suggestion. Francis and his people would be cared for and I knew that the Master would put the funds to good use. It was a sad parting both from my people and the Master. I had had, in the Master and Theobald, the two grandfathers I had never known. It made me more determined than ever that my son should know his grandfather. Masood, Brother Peter and Rebekah's women all came with us as did all of my men. I was touched by their loyalty. My saddest parting was with Sir Robert and Edward. I doubted that I would ever see either of them again and Robert had been one of the first men to serve me.

"This is my home, lord. I have a family now. Sarah is with child. I am content save that I cannot serve you any longer."

"If things go awry here then there will always be a home for you in the north of England."

"I will not say no to that offer for I have no crystal ball but I believe that King Baldwin is a good king and I would fight for this land." Our embrace was silent for more words would have brought tears.

Rebekah had had a tearful parting with her aunt and cousins. Judith was a wise woman, "I can see why you go. If I was in your position then I would do so too but I will miss you and this Gentile who has made me review the way I view others such as you. When you came, I mistrusted you. I was wrong." She kissed me hard on the lips and hugged me hard. I was touched.

We boarded the ship. I had chests on both boats with money for the voyage and I had, from Simon, paper which could be converted to money anywhere in England. I trusted the old Jew but we had more than enough money anyway. It had been another successful crop and the Master had paid us for the horses, mail and arms we did not need.

My men also had many chests. That was why we needed so many ships. In addition, we all had goods to take home which could not be bought in England. There was olive oil and wine from Aqua Bella. There were spices and silks from the bazaars. There were crates of lemons and figs. There would be much that we would miss. All were going home as rich men. Some would leave my service but not until we sailed up the Tees to Stockton. The Captain would take us the safe route. We would travel to Cyprus then through the Greek islands to the two Kingdoms of Naples and Sicily. We would go around Corsica and down the Iberian Peninsula. The captain had told us that there were more pirates and we need to be cautious. The Second Crusade had not succeeded in the Holy Land but they had recaptured Portugal and the rats who had fled there now infested the southern seas.

As we waved goodbye to those who had come to see us off, I prayed that God would spare my father and, when we had finished this voyage, he would be alive and waiting to greet me in Stockton. My son, Samuel, was now able to talk as well as walk and he was a delight. When I had returned from the siege I had been amazed at the change. I wanted my father to witness how he grew. One day he would be like his father and his grandfather. One day my son would be an English knight. One day he would do as his father and grandfather had done. He would defend England and its king from all its enemies. I was content. I was going home and I had been forgiven by God. Would my father forgive me too?

The End

Glossary

Akolouthos – the leader of the Guard
Al-Andalus- Spain
Angevin- the people of Anjou, mainly the ruling family
Bachelor knight- an unattached knight
Banneret- a single knight
Battle- a formation in war (a modern battalion)
Butts- targets for archers
Cadge- the frame upon which hunting birds are carried (by a codger- hence the phrase old codger being the old man who carries the frame)
Captain- a leader of archers
Chausses - mail leggings. (They were separate- imagine lady's stockings!)
Coningestun- Coniston
Conroi- A group of knights fighting together. The smallest unit of the period
Demesne- estate
Destrier- war horse
Doxy- prostitute
Fess- a horizontal line in heraldry
Galloglass- Irish mercenaries
Gambeson- a padded tunic worn underneath mail. When worn by an archer they came to the waist. It was more of a quilted jacket but I have used the term freely
Gonfanon- A standard used in medieval times (Also known as a Gonfalon in Italy)
Lusitania- Portugal
Mansio- staging houses along Roman Roads
Mêlée- a medieval fight between knights
Mummer- an actor from a medieval tableau
Musselmen- Muslims
Nithing- A man without honour (Saxon)
Nomismata- a gold coin equivalent to an aureus
Outremer- the kingdoms of the Holy Land
Palfrey- a riding horse
Poitevin- the language of Aquitaine
Pyx- a box containing a holy relic (Shakespeare's Pax from Henry V)
Refuge- a safe area for squires and captives (tournaments)
Sauve qui peut – Every man for himself (French)
Sergeant-a leader of a company of men at arms

Surcoat- a tunic worn over mail or armour
Sumpter- packhorse
Theophany- the feast which is on the 6th of January
Ventail – a piece of mail which covered the neck and the lower face

Maps and Illustrations

The Holy Land 1146

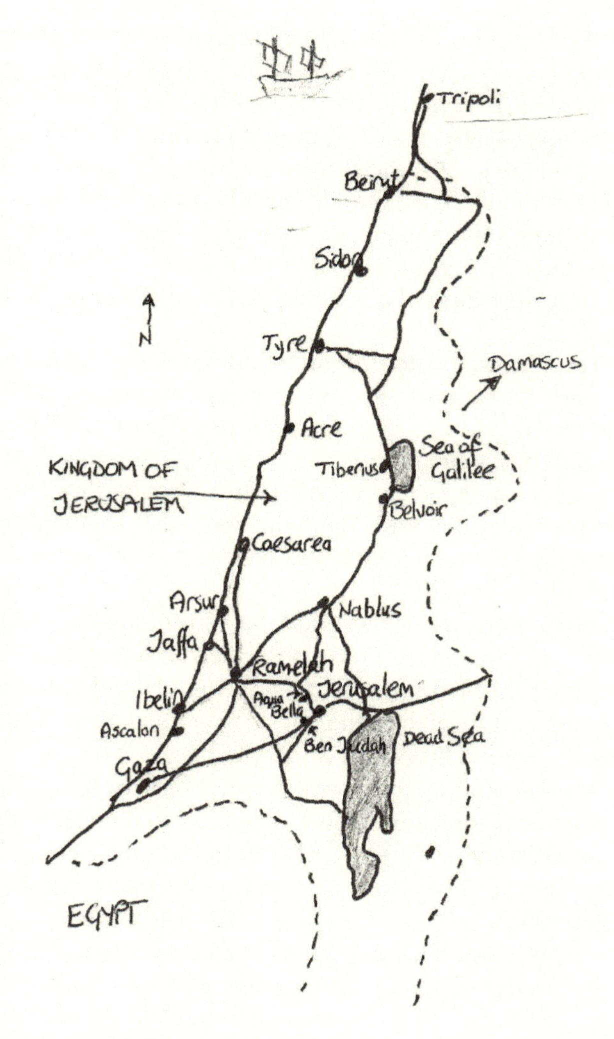

Source: File: Crac des chevaliers syria.jpeg - https://en.wikipedia.org

Historical Notes

Aqua Bella is a real place. The David Nicholle book, Crusader Castles in the Holy Land 1097-1192, shows how it would have looked in the time of the Crusades. It was most illuminating. When it was excavated, they found an olive press. It became a Hospitaller house in the second half of the twelfth century. The Byzantines did go to the aid of the principalities. Manuel was Emperor at the time. This may have been prompted by the loss of the fortress of Edessa. Certainly, that was the spark which ignited the Second Crusade. King Baldwin and his mother were both important characters. Melisende had been married off to Count Fulk. He had acted as a king rather than a consort. Melisende appeared to be able to handle him. She is a female like Eleanor of Aquitaine and Mathilda!

The Templars, Hospitallers and Teutonic knights held great power. The King of Jerusalem ruled only through the support of his knights and the holy orders. He owned but two castles. He did, however, have the right to award manors to those he favoured. This was more common than might have been expected. Whole families might die. The Seljuq Turks and bandits roamed at will. Baldwin's use of William is just one example of the political acumen which was needed to rule such a land.

Assassins

Assassins (Persian: حشاشين Hashshashin) is a name used to refer to the medieval Nizari Ismailis. Often described as a secret order led by a mysterious "Old Man of the Mountain", the Nizari Ismailis were a Persian sect that formed in the late 11th century from a split within Ismailism – itself a branch of Shia Islam.

The Nizaris posed a military threat to Sunni Seljuq authority within their territories by capturing and inhabiting many unconnected mountain fortresses throughout Persia, and later Syria, under the leadership of Hassan-i Sabbah. They were responsible for many murders and attempted murders over a three-hundred-year period.

The combination of heavy horse and archers working together became uniquely English. The 12th century saw its genesis and it culminated in the army of Henry V which defeated a much larger army. To work properly the two arms had to work together. When the Scottish light horse managed to get at the English archers at Bannockburn the English lost the battle. Even Henry V's brother the Duke of Clarence made mistakes. When he left the safety of his archers he and his knights were easily defeated. The archers relied upon the huge number of arrows they could release. Even when fighting at Agincourt where the plate armour could deflect most of the arrows the sheer number they used still managed to find cracks in the armour. They often used a flat trajectory to try to penetrate the tiny gaps in the helmet through which the men at arms peered. Most importantly the English archer was unique in that he was a master light infantryman. He could use a sword and a buckler and he knew how to kill.

Squires were not always the sons of nobles. Often, they were lowly born and would never aspire to knighthood. It was not only the king who could make knights. Lords had that power too. Normally a man would become a knight at the age of 21. Young landless knights would often leave home to find a master to serve in the hope of treasure or loot. The idea of chivalry was some way away. The Norman knight wanted land, riches and power. Knights would have a palfrey or ordinary riding horse and a destrier or warhorse. Squires would ride either a palfrey if they had a thoughtful knight or a rouncy (packhorse). The squires carried all of the knight's war gear on the pack horses. Sometimes a knight would have a number of squires serving him. One of the squire's tasks was to have a spare horse in case the knight's destrier fell in battle. Another way for a knight to make money was to capture an enemy and ransom him. This even happened to Richard 1st of England who was captured in Austria and held to ransom.

At this time a penny was a valuable coin and often payment would be taken by 'nicking' pieces off it. Totally round copper and silver coins were not the norm in 12th Century Europe. Each local ruler would make his own small coins. The whole country was run like a pyramid with the king at the top. He took from those below him in the form of taxes and service and it cascaded down. There was a great deal of corruption as well as anarchy. The idea of a central army did not exist. King Henry had his household knights and would call upon his nobles to supply knights and men at arms when he needed to go to war. The expense for that army would be borne by the noble.

The plague and pestilence were two terms used for contagious diseases which usually killed. The Black Death was a specific plague which could be attributed to one cause. Influenza, smallpox, chickenpox even measles could wipe out vast numbers. The survivors normally had anti-bodies within their bloodstream. Medicine was of little use.

The ram and the stone thrower were the main siege engines used at this time. Later weapons such as the trebuchet would render the stone thrower redundant. The skills of the Romans had been forgotten but Crusaders returning from the East brought back plans and ideas which were still used in the Byzantine Empire.

Sieges at this time relied on starving to death the occupants. Wooden castles, the early motte and bailey, could be fired but a stone one with a good ditch could defeat most enemies. The ditches they used were copied from the Roman ones. Once an enemy was in a ditch it was almost impossible to retreat. The trebuchet was in its early stages of development and the onagers and other stone-throwers had to be used close enough for them to be subject to archers. Rams were useful but they were not particularly robust and could be set on fire. They also needed a smooth surface. That was not common in the twelfth century. Wooden towers were used at the siege of Ascalon and they were burned. The resulting inferno caused a breach and the Templars disobeyed the king to attack immediately. Their heads were displayed on Cairo's walls. Sometimes the onager was called a mangonel. I have used the Roman name here.

Books used in the research:

- The Varangian Guard- 988-1453 Raffael D'Amato
- Saxon Viking and Norman- Terence Wise
- The Walls of Constantinople AD 324-1453-Stephen Turnbull
- Byzantine Armies- 886-1118- Ian Heath
- The Age of Charlemagne-David Nicolle
- The Normans- David Nicolle
- Norman Knight AD 950-1204- Christopher Gravett
- The Norman Conquest of the North- William A Kappelle
- The Knight in History- Francis Gies
- The Norman Achievement- Richard F Cassady
- Knights- Constance Brittain Bouchard
- Knight Templar 1120-1312 -Helen Nicholson
- Feudal England: Historical Studies on the Eleventh and Twelfth Centuries- J. H. Round
- Armies of the Crusades- Helen Nicholson
- Knight of Outremer 1187- 1344 - David Nicholle
- Crusader Castles in the Holy Land- David Nicholle
- The Crusades- David Nicholle
- The Times Atlas of World History

Griff Hosker
April 2017

Other books by Griff Hosker

If you enjoyed reading this book, then why not read another one by the author?

Ancient History

The Sword of Cartimandua Series
(Germania and Britannia 50 A.D. – 128 A.D.)
Ulpius Felix- Roman Warrior (prequel)
The Sword of Cartimandua
The Horse Warriors
Invasion Caledonia
Roman Retreat
Revolt of the Red Witch
Druid's Gold
Trajan's Hunters
The Last Frontier
Hero of Rome
Roman Hawk
Roman Treachery
Roman Wall
Roman Courage

The Wolf Warrior series
(Britain in the late 6th Century)
Saxon Dawn
Saxon Revenge
Saxon England
Saxon Blood
Saxon Slayer
Saxon Slaughter
Saxon Bane
Saxon Fall: Rise of the Warlord
Saxon Throne
Saxon Sword

Medieval History

The Dragon Heart Series

Crusader

Viking Slave
Viking Warrior
Viking Jarl
Viking Kingdom
Viking Wolf
Viking War
Viking Sword
Viking Wrath
Viking Raid
Viking Legend
Viking Vengeance
Viking Dragon
Viking Treasure
Viking Enemy
Viking Witch
Viking Blood
Viking Weregeld
Viking Storm
Viking Warband
Viking Shadow
Viking Legacy
Viking Clan
Viking Bravery

The Norman Genesis Series
Hrolf the Viking
Horseman
The Battle for a Home
Revenge of the Franks
The Land of the Northmen
Ragnvald Hrolfsson
Brothers in Blood
Lord of Rouen
Drekar in the Seine
Duke of Normandy
The Duke and the King

New World Series
Blood on the Blade
Across the Seas
The Savage Wilderness

Crusader

The Reconquista Chronicles
Castilian Knight

The Aelfraed Series
(Britain and Byzantium 1050 A.D. - 1085 A.D.)
Housecarl
Outlaw
Varangian

The Anarchy Series England 1120-1180
English Knight
Knight of the Empress
Northern Knight
Baron of the North
Earl
King Henry's Champion
The King is Dead
Warlord of the North
Enemy at the Gate
The Fallen Crown
Warlord's War
Kingmaker
Henry II
Crusader
The Welsh Marches
Irish War
Poisonous Plots
The Princes' Revolt
Earl Marshal

Border Knight 1182-1300
Sword for Hire
Return of the Knight
Baron's War
Magna Carta
Welsh Wars
Henry III
The Bloody Border

Crusader

Baron's Crusade
Sentinel of the North

Lord Edward's Archer
Lord Edward's Archer
King in Waiting

Struggle for a Crown
1360- 1485
Blood on the Crown
To Murder A King
The Throne
King Henry IV
The Road to Agincourt

Modern History

The Napoleonic Horseman Series
Chasseur a Cheval
Napoleon's Guard
British Light Dragoon
Soldier Spy
1808: The Road to Coruña
Talavera
The Lines of Torres Vedras

The Lucky Jack American Civil War series
Rebel Raiders
Confederate Rangers
The Road to Gettysburg

The British Ace Series
1914
1915 Fokker Scourge
1916 Angels over the Somme
1917 Eagles Fall
1918 We will remember them
From Arctic Snow to Desert Sand
Wings over Persia

Combined Operations series

Crusader

1940-1945

Commando
Raider
Behind Enemy Lines
Dieppe
Toehold in Europe
Sword Beach
Breakout
The Battle for Antwerp
King Tiger
Beyond the Rhine
Korea
Korean Winter

Other Books

Great Granny's Ghost (Aimed at 9-14-year-old young people)

For more information on all of the books then please visit the author's web site at www.griffhosker.com where there is a link to contact him.

Made in the USA
Las Vegas, NV
13 February 2021

17781831R00152